PRUE PHILLIPSON was born in Newcastle
London University. During her working life s
journalist and supervisor for offenders on com
Prue has lived for the last forty-six years i
Her husband, Alan, has been her mainstay in ... ... w......g ycais. Jne nas
five children, twelve grandchildren and four great-grandchildren.

She has written fiction for many years, winning prizes for short stories
and even having one read on the BBC. Prue spent fourteen years caring for
her elderly in-laws and finally her mother. She wrote *Lesson of Love* drawing
on her experience of her mother's dementia in the light of her Christian faith.
Since then, Prue has had seven novels and a short story collection published
on line by E-bshop and historical novels in hard and paperback published
by Quaester 2000 and Knox Robinson publishing. These last two have
ceased trading but information about all her books can be obtained from
her website Prue Phillipson Books and orders placed via her email address:
pru.phillipson@btopenworld.com

Her latest novel *The Unloved Wife* is published by SilverWood Books
and is the sequel to *The Unloved Child*.

8/6/23

PRUE PHILLIPSON

The
Unloved
Wife

SilverWood

Published in 2021 by SilverWood Books

SilverWood Books Ltd
14 Small Street, Bristol, BS1 1DE, United Kingdom
www.silverwoodbooks.co.uk

ISBN 978-1-80042-073-1 (paperback)

British Library Cataloguing in Publication Data
A CIP catalogue record for this book is available from the British Library

Page design and typesetting by SilverWood Books

To my friend Jen Black for suggesting the titles for
The Unloved Child *and* The Unloved Wife

Chapter 1

Ovingham on Tyne, December 1831

Dee

The dictatorial tinkling of the bell checked the sharp knife in Dee Heron's hand as she chopped leeks for Mrs Hammond's broth. Jack, coming in from feeding the carriage horse, beamed in sympathy. His smile swept away her irritation. She was his life and joy, and she must keep it that way for both their sakes.

She laid down the knife and left the kitchen at a scamper. What sort of person would I be without his smile? she asked herself, as she set her foot on the steep back stairs. I can never hurt him. He has submitted to the last seven years of our lives here with unswerving grace and kindliness.

She emerged through the door onto the wide upper landing, panting a little. This was what I longed for, she reminded herself. Space, passages, stairs, carpets, a real house like the one I was born in. Jack was happy in our one-room home. Sweet Mrs Hammond offered paid work, two bedrooms, a small sitting room and the run of her large kitchen. What luxury! I never thought of dependency and servitude – or that the post of housekeeper would become 'maid-of-all-work'. If I grumbled to Jack, it would reawaken his guilt at losing his job. Bless him! He *wanted* to stay in that one room. He was upset at leaving his childhood home, the river and the waggonway and the safety of familiarity. Beloved Jack! I will not let this woman make me cross.

Running along to the drawing room, she wondered if the summons was about the still unironed laundry. She tapped at the door.

Her mistress was standing in the centre of the Wilton carpet, ready with one of her pronouncements.

"Dee, Francis's wedding must be postponed. That is incontrovertible." She gave to the six syllables the full exercise of her mobile lips.

Dee was taken aback. Their son's wedding was only two weeks away. "Oh no, ma'am. Why?"

"I will not venture eastward until this epidemic is over. We are safe here in the country air. I have read that cholera is spread by bad smells." The last two words were drawn out and accompanied by a crinkling of the nose.

"But ma'am, they say the disease came in a ship from the Baltic that docked at Sunderland. The Batey family live in North Shields, where the wedding is to be."

"And I would have to pass through Newcastle to reach North Shields, and that I will not do. Did you not read in the newspaper that Newcastle has closed its theatres and no assemblies are to be held at Christmas?" Her voice rose to a crescendo.

"But I'm sure Jenny Batey will *not* postpone her daughter's wedding." Dee clasped her hands fiercely behind her back, twining her fingers in the bow of her apron. "And Jack and I *must* be there. The young people have waited long enough, and now that Mr Trace has taken Francis into a junior partnership they have the means…"

Mrs Hammond pressed her lips together, and her eyes took on the warning glare that dried up Dee's speech. It said plainly: 'You and I were social equals once when you were a young lady at Sheradon Grange. Then you lost everything and married a labourer. Still, I was pleased to help you when Jack lost his farm job. But from that moment, you and he became my *servants.*'

Mrs Hammond moved to her high-backed armchair and settled in it with an air of finality, folding her arms across her solid bosom.

"It's good for young people to wait. That's what my dear Godfrey always said. He was happy to become Francis's godfather, but he always said to me, 'I do not want the boy to be coddled, but to learn the rough and smooth of life.' I grant that Francis had the rough when he was all but hanged for a crime he didn't commit, but he has had it smooth since, and a delay till this scourge has passed should not trouble him."

Dee bit her lip. She wanted to say 'It would not trouble *me* if *you* did not attend', but rudeness was no more in her nature than servitude, as she had discovered in the last seven years. Gradually a cook, a scullery maid and two outside men had disappeared, and she and Jack did everything between them. Mrs Hammond's years of doctors' bills for Godfrey and her need to keep up appearances had reduced her savings and simultaneously increased her pride.

Mrs Hammond was smiling at her.

"Just pen a letter to Jenny Batey pointing out the unsuitability of holding any sort of gathering at a time of pestilence, and I'm sure she'll agree."

Jack's diffident tap at the door made Dee start. The handle was within her reach, but she had to look at Mrs Hammond for permission to let him in.

"You may enter, Jack, for this concerns you as father of the bridegroom."

His round, rosy face appeared, and his outstretched hand held two letters.

"If you please, ma'am, the post-boy brought these."

One was written, Dee could see, in the childlike hand of Jenny Batey and addressed to herself, and the other was to Mrs Hammond from her man of business. Dee dreaded seeing his writing, as it usually left her employer in an irritable temper.

So she said quickly, "May I just glance at this, ma'am, as it may concern the very thing we were speaking of."

She broke the seal as she spoke, and drew Jack into the room. He stood against the door in the humble posture she hated to see – a big man, broad-shouldered, trying to hunch himself into a small space.

Mrs Hammond laid aside her own letter and snapped, "Well, has Jenny Batey anything important to say?"

Dee was too shocked by Jenny's news to answer at once, but a few seconds' working of her vigorous imagination gave her the right words. "Well, ma'am, you will be pleased. The wedding is to be postponed till the spring."

Mrs Hammond frowned, and at another time Dee would have felt a giggle rising. Her mistress was so predictable. But it behoved her to explain. "Yes, ma'am. Lily Batey, Francis's betrothed, is very upset. The lady she served as a companion for many years has died suddenly, and as her symptoms were very like the cholera, Lily won't wed till she knows herself to be out of danger."

She felt Jack shudder at the words.

"Lily – danger. Oh Dee, what's happened?"

She soothed him with a smile and muttered, "*Sarah* has died. She rebuffed all my advances of friendship for the last seven years, and now she has died."

"Sarah? You mean my brother Joe's wife?"

"Yes, your sister-in-law."

Mrs Hammond cut in. "If you two wish to discuss your letter, you may leave the room. I am pleased the wedding is to be postponed, but I will say a prayer for poor Lily. I invited Francis to bring her once, and she seemed a nicely spoken demure little thing to have come from Batey's pie shop. Of course, I hoped Godfrey's godson would choose someone with more social standing, but who can tell the future?"

Dee hustled Jack out and they scurried down to the kitchen. He stood and looked at her, his face crumpled with anxiety.

"Sarah has died, you say, angel? We haven't seen her for a long time, and my brother Joe for even longer. Did not a bad thing happen to Joe? Was he not murdered? I don't like it when people die. And dear little Lily in danger?"

There were times, Dee knew, when she had to stop what she was doing, sit Jack down and make him look into her eyes and listen. This was such a moment. Mrs Hammond's leek broth could wait.

"Jack." She took his hands across the kitchen table. "Your brother Joe was *not* murdered, and you must never repeat such a tale. He had a seizure and fell in the river. It was my evil son Billy who tried to make it look as if Francis had killed Joe. Those were bad days, but they are all in the past."

"Ay," he said, his eyes still on hers, "all past. But Sarah? Was she not way back in the past too?"

"No, she lived on, but we never saw her. We heard about her from time to time because Sarah took Lily on again after Joe died. Lily was the only person she could endure to have about her when Billy disappeared. She wanted Billy to live there, but he was off – God knows where. Lily became more a companion than a maid, so 'twill be a sorrow to her gentle little soul."

Jack's fair brows were creased in a frown. "But you spoke of danger?"

Dee saw she had been too quick for him. She locked eyes again. "I didn't tell madam all Jenny wrote." She took the letter out of her pocket. "Listen to this. Jenny says, '*I don't believe Sarah had the cholera though she was terrible sick. She tried so many medicines she must have poisoned herself. So now Lily's stopping in that horrid tall house till she's clear. She hides when lawyers come for papers and such but works like a slave cleaning and turning out cupboards, poor little lamb.*'" Dee refrained from reading Jenny's speculations about Sarah's

10

will. Jack had enough to take in. "So you see, Lily won't catch the cholera, so we needn't worry any more."

She jumped up. "Get some coal, or madam's broth won't be ready in time."

"I'll do that, and I shan't worry about Lily if you say I mustn't. But there was a mass of things to understand in Jenny's letter. Fancy her writing all them words!"

Jack, who had never managed to read or write, was in awe of anyone from his own walk of life who could. He lumbered out to the coal bunker with the bucket. Dee looked after him and longed for Francis. There were so many subtleties in her life that she could share only with her son.

Jack brought the coal and made up the fire. He straightened his big frame and looked down at her. "Sarah will have to be buried, and we're all the folk she had left. I don't like funerals."

So he had been *thinking* out there in the yard. She reached up and pulled his face down and kissed him. His eyes shone with delighted astonishment.

She said, "I don't either. But we can't go, because the funeral will be in Newcastle and madam wouldn't hear of it. The lawyers will see to it. You remember 'that horrid tall house' she lived in. You saw it when we went to *Joe's* funeral."

Jack scratched his head. "I mind seeing them put poor Joe's coffin in the ground. I'll never forget that, for I wanted him with Da and Ma in Ovingham churchyard, but it wasn't. It was a strange place in the big town."

Dee was buttering a slice of bread cut as thinly as she could. "That's where Sarah will be put now. It's right for husband and wife to be together. But she didn't let us in her house that day. Do you not recall standing in the street outside? It was raining, and you were worried I'd catch cold."

"Ay, I mind that all right. The houses was like a great cliff going up into the sky, and didn't Sarah say they was all hers now Joe had gone? She pushed her face up close to mine and then went in sudden-like and shut the door."

Dee clapped her hands. "You *do* remember. Yes, she and Joe had four tall terraced houses in a row, grandly called Heron Mansions, all let out to tenants except the one they lived in, where poor little Lily has her attic room."

"But she and Francis will be man and wife soon. Will they live there then?"

She set the broth and plate of bread and butter on a silver tray. "Francis has a home to take her to – two rooms in Mrs Trace's boarding house." Jack looked puzzled. "She's the wife of Mr Trace, the engineer. Francis has been seven years apprenticed to him, and lived there all the time." But Jack had never seen it, so he had no picture in his head. Maybe they *would* have Heron Mansions to live in, if Jenny had guessed correctly that Lily was the heir.

When she carried the tray up to Mrs Hammond, she found her in a benign mood. Perhaps her lawyer's letter had been cheerful this time.

"My dear, you will be troubled about Lily, but I am sure it will all be for the best. Now, let me give you a piece of news which will interest you very much."

She unfolded the *Newcastle Courant*, which she still had delivered despite the cholera. "Sheradon Grange," she announced with a flourish of her arms, "is sold!"

"Oh." Dee was unimpressed. Her childhood home had been let to the army as a refuge for war veterans, to help pay her father's creditors. Then no one would buy it, because of her parents' suicide. Although they had not died in the house, there were fears of hauntings. So now someone made of tougher mettle had bought it and would, perhaps, restore it to the grandeur that had eaten away the Sheradon fortune. Whatever they did, she had no wish to see it again.

"Would you not like to pay it a visit?" Mrs Hammond said. "This report says the new owner is abroad, and possibly a foreigner. I'm sure there will be workmen in who would let you look round."

"No, ma'am. My only happy memories of the place are from my first five years, while my grandfather was alive. He hoped future generations of Sheradons would be noble figures in the community. He welcomed the poor to garden parties and Christmas feasts, but after his death my father and mother ornamented the whole house with the most lavish furnishings. I expect it would be well knocked about when the army had it, and to be truthful I care not."

It was a long speech, not interspersed with 'ma'am', and Dee saw a frown beginning to form; but Mrs Hammond was not prepared to leave so interesting a subject. Dee dreaded what might come next.

"I know it has painful memories for you of your handsome lover. I recall him at your birthday party – seventeenth, was it?"

"Sixteenth." Dee stood stiff and straight. This was an endurance test.

"Your parents had invited him as a potential suitor" – Mrs Hammond was chuckling – "because he wrote 'Sir' before his name. A penniless baronet! Could they not guess he was after the Sheradon fortune?"

It was agony to recall how in love she had been, but Dee was too proud to beg her to stop. She could hear now Ralph's words of passion and feel the joy of her young self when the wedding date was set. She would be Lady Dione Barnet and have this fine officer in his regimentals at her side as they walked back down the aisle. Then it was wiped out at her father's bankruptcy by his lawyer's letter. 'The inability of Mr Sheradon to honour the marriage settlement...'

Mrs Hammond was gleeful in the recollection. "Eh, my dear, how you were punished for letting him into your bed too soon. You were very lucky to get Jack to be a husband to you in the nick of time, but that son Billy was a scourge for you all, and nearly had his brother hanged. What a time that was!"

She shed gracious smiles over Dee's rigid body.

"You've had your good fortune too since then. Not everyone would have taken you in and given you a place as I have."

If she thinks I am going to grovel in thankfulness, Dee thought, she is wildly mistaken. I had been respectably married twenty-five years when she needed a reliable housekeeper and carriage driver, and she has had impeccable service from us both for seven long years.

Mrs Hammond seemed to expect a reply, but when none came she waved her hand in dismissal and arranged her lips in imperious fashion. "Off you go. Bring cake and fruit in five minutes."

Dee left the room in a fury. My tragedy – a laughing matter for her! 'Let him into my bed', indeed. He beguiled me into the empty gamekeeper's cottage and used the most loving caresses to tempt me. He already knew my father's perilous state, and thought to enjoy his lovely bride before her fortune turned to dust.

She couldn't enter the kitchen and let Jack sense her distress. Taking several deep breaths and settling in her mind that Mrs Hammond was not worth a second's anger, she trotted in and met his happy smile with one of her own.

The next letter to come was from Francis, '*wretchedly disappointed*' and '*frantically worried*' for Lily, but as the days lengthened his letters grew impatient. It became obvious that cholera had never struck in Heron Mansions. But now Jenny Batey wanted to wait for the reading of Sarah's will. Francis wrote:

Lily's mother won't hold the wedding till we know if Lily is to inherit a fortune. She would like to buy new dresses and make no end of a fuss. I've persuaded

Lily to go home from Heron Mansions. She can't do any more in that bleak place and the lawyers have let her go without a word. I'm sure she can't be Aunt's heir or they would have told her.

Money, money, Dee thought. Jenny was happy-go-lucky when I first knew her as a girl, but now that a fortune hovers on the horizon for her daughter, it is corrupting her nature.

She wrote back to Francis that he must be bold and insist they marry without more delay. She and his father would come whatever Mrs Hammond said.

It seemed that her words were effective, as his next letter, at the end of February, announced a date for the wedding in the middle of March.

He wrote:

There have been fewer cases of cholera since ships from infected places are not allowed to discharge cargo or passengers. Aunt Sarah's lawyers are not proving the will till someone lands who is on board a ship held up in quarantine. Why this person is important I don't know but Lily's mother is beginning to have doubts and "won't wait any longer for these snails of lawyers" she says.'

In the next paragraph Francis wrote, 'If Lily is not Aunt Sarah's heir it might be me. You know that when Uncle Joe died I was to be his heir. Only he had promised Billy he would put him in the will instead. That was why Billy thought he had a good case to prove that I murdered Uncle.'

Dee shivered. She had no wish to recall that dreadful time; but she was compelled to go on reading.

After my acquittal Aunt Sarah seemed sorry for Billy and wanted to give him a home but we know he went to sea or some such adventure so she might have kept Uncle's will as it was, leaving everything to me after her death. She always petted me as a child. I can't mention my thoughts to Lily who keeps saying she doesn't want a fortune – we must make our own way. Well, I don't mind a fortune if it helps my work. With money I could try out ideas and become a great engineer. Mother, you'd better burn this letter but I just had to unburden myself to you. I've missed you so much, but I didn't want to upset that old dragon by bringing "cholera to Ovingham" which she feared so much. But you will brave her wrath and come, won't you? You and Father can have the room in Mrs Trace's boarding house next to what will be our living room. Will Mrs Hammond let you have her carriage if she's not coming herself?

Oh Mother, I love Lily so much and can even feel sorry for Billy who wanted her too. No wonder he hated me, but before he left I did believe he had some good feelings for us all.'

Dee's eyes filled with tears. She had thought the same, and her yearning for a repentant Billy had persisted for a while, till the years with no news swallowed it up. But, as for Francis's speculation about the will, she thought, if I had him here, I'd shake him by the ears. Forget the money, I'd say. That fortune Joe built up was a curse on you and Billy. I hope Sarah *hasn't* left it to Lily or to you. Jenny will badger Lily to set up all her family in luxury, and it'll be a bone of contention between all of you.

When Jack came in from the stables, she told him only that Francis had written and the wedding day was fixed.

He chortled aloud, skipping around the kitchen. "I can wear my best coat." Then he stopped suddenly, his brow creased with worry. "Angel, you'll keep close to me all the day and put me right if I do anything wrong. It's a terrible big thing to be the father of the bridegroom amongst all the people that'll be there."

She laughed joyously and hugged him tight.

Chapter 2

North Shields, March 1832

Dee

Dee gazed through the open porch of Christ Church, North Shields, bright and newly refurbished – unlike the sombre Saxon gloom of Ovingham Church, where they drove Mrs Hammond every Sunday.

She, Jack and Francis were enjoying the wind off the sea before venturing inside. Life with Mrs Hammond, she was thinking, is cramped and unchanging. Today I feel exhilarated. Last night Jack was worried about driving the unfamiliar road from Newcastle to North Shields. But now he has safely stowed Mrs Hammond's precious carriage at the inn down the road, he is chuckling with relief and teasing Francis. "Eh, fancy our wee boy a married man shortly!"

But the moment they were inside the church nervousness seized him again, and Dee could tell Francis had caught it too. She giggled at the stiff backs and arms of father and son as they teetered at the back of the church like puppet figures on strings. Francis was a slender version of Jack, tall and fair, his young face more oval than round and his shoulders not so broad, but, dressed in their best, they were obviously father and son. Dee, half-listening to the vicar greeting her volubly, turned her giggle into a smile of joy and pride.

A lanky young man bounded up to them, bowed low to her and Jack and accosted the vicar. "Where do we sit, Reverend? I'm the bridesman. I've never been a bridesman before, but I'm supposed to look after this fellow." He grabbed Francis's arm.

The vicar assessed his height and his fair hair. "Ah, you must be his brother, of course. Who else should support a man in his hour of need?"

Francis reddened with distress, and Dee felt the chill blast that used to strike her when Billy came from the pit and walked in their door – a brother who had all but contrived her darling's death.

"He's a friend. George Clayton," Francis managed to tell the vicar.

Dee fought the dark memories of her firstborn, the son of her hated early love. She must not think of him on Francis's wedding day. Yet all the old questions clamoured for answers. Where *was* Billy? Did he exist somewhere? Would he ever know Francis was marrying Lily, whom he had coveted? It's best for us all if he was killed on some wild adventure, she thought.

People were arriving, and Jack clung to her side as Francis was whisked away to the front pew by George Clayton.

Jenny Batey, her yellow hair topped by an absurd hat, bore down on them.

"Don't look so petrified, Jack Heron. It's my Tom has to make a speech."

Mr Hurst, Francis's schoolmaster, and Mr Trace, the engineer, entered the church at the same moment, their wives greeting them as old friends, which Dee presumed they were. She produced smiles for them all.

A small man and his large cushiony wife approached her with outstretched hands. Dee hadn't seen her little printer, Septimus Brandling, since she had written to tell him she wasn't writing any more *Moral Tales for Children*. It was Sarah who had told her, when her sin with Ralph Barnet had become public knowledge, "Well, Dee, that's the end of all those *Moral Tales*!" Dee had thought of writing a novel using the drama of her own life, but every attempt had gone on the fire back in their old home, and Mrs Hammond's service left no time for creativity.

Mrs Brandling embraced her. "Ah, the great authoress – Dione Sharon! But I need a new *Moral Tale*. I have read every one a dozen times to my granddaughter."

Dee felt her face flushing, but Mr Brandling frowned up at his wife. "My dear, do you not recall my telling you that Mrs Heron is writing a full novel now? Mr Francis informed me many years ago that it would be a wonderful tale with a happy ending." He looked up at Dee, who was a little taller than himself. "I fear that by this time it will be too great a work for a little printer like myself, and sadly you have lost your sister-in-law, Mrs Sarah Heron, who acted as your publisher under the name of *House of Heron*. Pray allow us to offer our sympathy."

Dee murmured her thanks, but dared not say the novel remained unwritten.

The vicar was waving people to their seats, so she tucked her arm through Jack's, and they made their way to the pew behind Francis and his bridesman.

Francis turned round, and Dee could see he had banished the painful mention of Billy. "George is staying on with Mr Trace too."

Clayton held out his hand, saying, "I'm right glad to know you, Mrs Heron, and you, sir, on Frank's wedding day."

Dee saw Jack look round to see who he was speaking to but, finding his hand shaken heartily and a pleasant young man grinning at him, he beamed.

"Ay, my boy's getting wed too."

Francis blushed. "He means me, Father. My friends here all call me Frank."

Dee said quickly, "We'll call you Frank too. So you are also an engineer, George?"

"I am, Mrs Heron. But Frank is Mr Trace's favourite, 'cos he's the cleverest. You've got a mighty clever son, Mr Heron, but I wager you know that already."

Dee saw that Jack was on safe ground now. "Ay, he's clever, is our Francis."

Then he whispered to Dee. "When do we eat? I'm hungry."

"Why, there is to be the wedding feast on the beach. Batey's pie shop has been baking all night. And you will see the sea, my man, for the first time in your life."

His mouth opened to exclaim, but at that moment the vicar came scuttling down the aisle. "She's here! The bride is here. I must tell the organist."

Jenny Batey, who was chatting in the front pew on the other side of the aisle, leapt up and said, nodding her head at Dee, "Lily must have dragged her da here early. She's so particular about time. I don't trust Susy and Daisy to put her veil right." And she hurried to the back.

Francis peeped round, but Lily was evidently not in sight yet. He caught Dee's eye. "Oh Ma, it's really going to happen, isn't it?"

He looked like a little boy again, and her stomach contracted and tears came into her eyes. She gripped Jack's hand. "Lily's arrived."

"Oh ay, Lily. She's a canny wee thing." He peered round as the organ began playing, and the whole congregation peered round too. "There's a mass o' people here," he whispered. "An' I really don't have to make a speech, do I?"

"Not a word," she repeated, loving him intensely as she said it. Losing her son, she still had her baby.

Francis's eyes lit with delight, so Dee looked round too. The sight of Lily and her father, Tom Batey, made her think of a small delicate flower clinging to a stout tree trunk. Through the veil she could see that Lily's colour, usually pale, was high and her light blue eyes were shining with excitement. As she passed their pew, Dee noted her neat, perfectly formed features aquiver with joy that the day had finally come. They love each other with a passion, she reflected, and I am so happy for them.

The vicar, flustered before, was a new man with the prayer book in his hand. The words rolled off his tongue, and Dee felt the solemnity of it all. The frustrations of her own life fell away. Jack was at one with her in this, she knew, for contentment was his nature. When Francis and Lily made their responses, he nodded with a big smile on his face. She knew he was recalling their own wedding.

It was not till the two families were in the vestry for the signing of the register that Billy again flashed into her mind. The novel she had thought of writing was to have the bad brother return for his brother's wedding. Thank God he didn't, she thought. And then, remembering her new heavenly peace, she prayed, "Nay, Lord, be with my poor Billy, whether he is dead or living."

Jenny Batey, the absurd hat pushed awry as she kissed and hugged everyone, nudged her elbow. "Take that solemn look off your face, Dee. It's all fun and feasting from now on. And we're not to go on the beach. The east wind is bitter and the waves like mountains. A gentleman who has just bought the New Inn has sent word we are all to walk there, and it's but a step away."

Emerging from the vestry, they found the congregation chattering about the new arrangements. Though March had been balmy till now, this day would have been a disaster. Who the benefactor was roused much speculation, but the boys recruited to wheel barrows of Batey's pies were already heading to the New Inn.

The vicar was trying to arrange the bridal procession to leave the church in some sort of order. Dee found herself grabbed by Tom Batey.

"Jenny says it's you and me, Dee. And her and Jack to do it proper-like."

Dee nodded, and looked ahead down the aisle as Francis and Lily were being manoeuvred into the front place. As she looked, a small boy on his own came running towards them. Where had he come from?

As he drew near, she turned icy cold. It was Billy – three-year-old Billy. She clutched Tom Batey's arm, or she would have sunk to the ground. I have conjured him up, she thought. I was so happy for Francis – for escaping his brother's plot and living to see this day. I am punished. The unloved Billy is haunting me.

She shut her eyes on the apparition. Please God, calm me, she prayed. I have been too excited. I slept ill.

She opened her eyes again and the boy was still there. He was standing looking up at her with that enquiring stare that Billy had, the dark eyes asking 'Are you going to love me now?'

Tom said, "Well, wee laddie, what are *you* wanting?"

Tom can see him, she thought, but he *is* Billy. She was shaking.

Tom said again, "What d'you want, then? You're holding up the procession."

The child cocked his head, looking at Dee. "Want my Grandmamma."

The shock of the word rocked Dee on her feet. She gripped Tom more tightly as he tried to push the boy away, saying, "You got the wrong lady."

"Papa said blue lady." He began to cry.

Dee's heart was thumping so hard she thought she would faint, but a burning instinct made her hold out her hand to the boy. He gripped it, and a happy smile broke over his face. When had her Billy ever held up his arms to her with such a smile? The memory of not loving him tore her heart. Crouching down, she took this child in her arms. Tears flooded from her. But there must be a presence somewhere near. The boy had not dropped from the sky.

Fear and hope warred within her. She looked desperately over the child's head. Yes! A tall, bearded figure was pushing his way through the curious crowd that had spilled into the aisle. He was indeed a presence – bold, advancing, taking them all in, emotions hidden, wary, as he had always been.

Dear Lord, save and protect us all, she prayed. He is here in our lives again.

She turned to Jack and pulled him forward. "Look, look."

She heard a strangled gasp from Francis of "God in heaven! No!" and from Lily a frightened whisper. "Who? Oh, can it be…?"

Dee, still quivering, saw Jack look at the approaching man. They were of a height and both broad in the shoulders, but as unlike as day and night. Jack smooth, fair and baby-faced, the other dark, swarthy, spare and harsh of feature: a face that had seen hardship, and looking so much older than – she reckoned quickly – his twenty-eight years. Her fast-moving mind now had hold of the reality. Billy was back, and had produced a son. How he had heard this was his brother's wedding day and resolved to be here she couldn't imagine, but she met his gaze, the tears still on her face, and her hand still clasping his child's.

"What's going on, Dee?" Jack said. "Who is this? What's happening?"

Billy stroked his beard, and a twinkle of a smile lit his eyes.

"Don't you know me, Jack? Mother does, and I see Francis and his bride are delighted to welcome me on their wedding day."

"That voice!" Jack's expression went through all the shades of anxiety he displayed when he had something momentous to take in. He looked at Dee. She nodded.

"What? Our Billy?"

Others in the party were now shouting out his name. Jenny Batey and her eldest married daughter, Ally, yelled out, "Saints alive, it's Billy Heron!"

The vicar, flummoxed by this interruption to proper proceedings, stepped forward and tapped Billy's arm.

"Excuse me, sir, but the bridal procession should be leaving the church in seemly order. As you appear to be known to the family but have sadly come too late for the ceremony, I am sure you will be welcome at the wedding breakfast. I understand it is to be held at the New Inn. Perhaps you and the child will follow us."

Billy looked down at him and smiled again.

"It is to escort you all there that I have come, sir. I only heard about the wedding late last evening. This morning I found I could provide a more comfortable location for the feast than the beach on a blustery day. Come, Mateo. Mamma is waiting at the inn."

He reached for the boy's hand, but he clung to Dee. "Grandmamma coming."

Dee, choking with fresh sobs, said, "I am." She looked up at Billy. "You are the owner of the New Inn?"

"Ay. I've done all right in seven years. I told you I would have money before I married, and now I have even more. Aunt Sarah bought the New Inn as an investment, and now it's mine."

Dee heard another gasp from Francis and a murmur from Lily: "Oh dearest, I'm glad." Looking round, Dee caught a hurt, angry frown on Francis's brow, and Lily tearful at the sight. This was not how their day was to be.

Dee turned, straightened her back and looked Billy in the eye. "Then I hope wealth will be a blessing to you, not a curse."

He bowed. "Wise words. I told Mateo his grandmamma was one in a million." He stepped aside and motioned Francis and Lily to head the family group.

"What did he call the boy?" Jack asked, his face still bewildered.

"Mateo. It's Spanish," Billy said, "as is my wife."

Jenny Batey said, "He'll get Mat from me. My Ally's got a Liz and a Meg. I likes things simple."

They were moving off, and Billy did not reply.

Dee was still linked with Tom Batey, but she was conscious only of the child's hand in hers and the words Billy had just spoken. They started a great rush of thoughts about Billy's seven blank years. He had made money on his own or with Sarah's help. He had been abroad and found a Spanish wife, who had borne him a child in his image and – miracle of miracles – he had told the child about his English grandmother. She realised her heart was still pounding. Before Billy had left, she had asked him what he would want of a wife, and he had said, "To be like you." It had been a shock then. Despite the terrible emptiness of her mothering, he had seen in her something to admire. She was quaking now at the thought of meeting his wife.

As they moved up the aisle, the congregation was cheering and clapping, and voices were saying, "It's Frank's long-lost brother!" "Is he the man from the New Inn?" "The wee laddie must be Dee's grandbairn." "What a story!"

A crowd had gathered on the pavement outside. A wedding was an attraction whatever the weather. As Dee and the family emerged, she heard an old man yell out, "They're to feast at the New Inn. Let's join in. This wind's killing me."

Billy had heard too. He strode over to him. "Old man, you'll start a stampede. There is room only for invited guests." Dee saw him pick out a flunkey in a livery. "Mason, I told you to keep a way open for the bridal procession."

"I'm trying, Sir Ralph, but they jostle so."

Dee stopped in her tracks, pulling back on Tom and the boy.

"What's up, Dee?" said Tom. "It's that way. See the fellow in fancy dress."

"Come on, Grandmamma," squeaked the little boy. "I'm hungry."

Dee swallowed. Her throat was dried-up. She looked down at the little face peering up at her. Billy. Accepting her. Already at one with her.

She asked him, "*What* did that man call your father?"

"Sir Ralph. Sir Ralph Barnet. I'm Mateo Alonso Barnet, and I'm nearly four."

Dee made herself step forward with the others. Francis and Lily hadn't heard. This was shock upon shock. Billy had taken the name *and* title of his real father. Billy Heron, the bane of her life, was no more. But this reincarnation was worse. I never hated anyone, she thought, as I hated Sir Ralph Barnet. He cast my young love back in my face. What could be more cruel? I shall never speak that name. I cannot endure what is happening now. This was to be so wonderful a day. All for my sweet Francis and his Lily. Now this man has broken into it, is taking charge of it and flaunting his wealth. He knows what will hurt me.

On the short walk down to the New Inn she saw him stride ahead to be on the steps to welcome his guests. Her imagination was churning like one of the new steam engines. I want to break free. He must not suck us in. We must live our own lives. This is too much to bear.

No; her thoughts must slow down. There was this day to live out – the next few moments, indeed. How was she to greet a Spanish Lady Barnet? How could she extricate herself from this wee boy without hurt to them both?

She looked down at him, and he was at once aware and responding with a happy grin as if they were in a conspiracy together. He was all that Billy might have been to her if she had only been able to embrace his baby form with loving arms.

I am punished, she said with every step. And this is his father's deliberate doing. He has devised this exquisite pain.

"Here we are," Tom said. "You seem a bit put out, Dee, with your son popping up like this."

She forced a smile. "Just a shock. Not a word in seven years."

Ahead of her, Francis and Lily were mounting the inn steps. She sensed from their backs that they were nervous and apprehensive.

Billy, standing there, was all charm. Where had he learned that?

He shook hands with Francis and congratulated him. Then he took Lily's hand, raised it to his lips and kissed it. He said something in a low voice and they looked at each other in surprise, but nodded, and he waved them through to the inner foyer, where more uniformed servants were waiting to attend to their needs.

Jack was now pressing up behind, and Jenny tapped Dee on the arm.

"Here, you'd better have him back. He's not comfortable without you. Give me Tom and we'll meet this great lord o' the manor."

She grabbed Tom's arm and mounted the steps ahead of Dee and Jack.

"Ee, Billy, I hardly knew you under all that hair. You were after my lassies once, but I wager you've gone a bit higher, though I won't say you could do better."

Billy bowed and kissed her hand. Then Dee heard him say plainly, "I would be grateful, Mrs Batey, if you drop the name 'Billy'. I am now Sir Ralph Barnet."

"What? Given yourself a title! Well, I'm the Queen o' Sheba then."

Tom said, "Haway inside, Jenny. I'm starving for a couple of me own pies."

"You will find much else to enjoy with them, Mr Batey," Billy said, and Dee, looking for anger in those dark deep-set eyes, saw only composure.

He did add quietly to Jenny as they passed him, "My mother will explain the name to you, Mrs Batey."

And now it was her turn and Jack's, with little Mateo in tow. She lifted her eyes and saw not Ralph but a transformed Billy. The wariness of the first encounter had vanished. Either he had resumed a planned role or his warm smile was genuine.

She felt a desperate urge to embrace him and find out, but the bridesman and Lily's sisters were clustering them closely, and Mateo still clutched her hand.

Billy said, "When the company is settled at the tables, Mother, I will take you to meet with my wife in our private room. We will not come down to the dining room. Today is Francis's day, not mine."

It was a statement that brooked no argument. Dee was astonished at the sensitivity that prompted it. Or was it a decision on the spur of the moment after the encounter with the Bateys? Whatever it was, her own emotions were swinging this way and that, out of her control. She just nodded and began to edge Jack past him.

As she did so he added, "Pray tell everyone my true name."

She gave him a pleading frown but Jack was now pulling her along, his big boots stumbling over the thick carpet that filled the grand entrance. He came to a halt when they were well inside, and stared up at the intricately plastered ceiling. Then he shook his head at her.

"Oh Dee, what are we doing here? That wasn't our Billy after all, was it?"

"Oh yes it was." She found an upholstered seat against the wall and sat him down. Across the lobby double doors stood open, showing tables with white cloths and with dishes set out, and now the people were flooding in and making for the signs of food. She sat down, and Mateo climbed up beside her and then crawled along the red velvet seat, stroking the soft pile but looking back to make sure she was still there.

"Jack," she said, "Look at me. This is the wedding feast for Francis and Lily. Not on the beach, because the wind is too strong."

He nodded. "Wind strong."

"Our Billy is there welcoming the people in because he owns this place."

"Billy owns this? It's a palace."

"Nay, it's a mansion, built in the last century, I'd say, by a coal owner. Sarah bought it for a hotel to make money and has left it to Billy."

"Ay, I saw he had a fine coat on his back like a gentleman."

"That's what he is now, so he doesn't want to be Billy Heron any more. He's taken a different name." She wondered if she could bring herself to say it.

"What's that, then?"

"Ralph. It was his father's name. Sir Ralph Barnet." There, it was out; but she saw Jack's fair brows knitted. "You haven't forgotten you are not Billy's father?"

"Nay, I was glad I wasn't. He was a bad lad, and his da wronged my angel."

She inclined her head, still holding her eyes on his. "But, God willing, Billy is to be a good Sir Ralph Barnet. Here he comes."

The outer doors had been closed, and a liveried man stood by them.

Billy approached. Yet he was not Billy. The name still stuck in her head, but this was someone else, moulded by strange experiences, a being she didn't yet know. She would be happy to give him a new name, but not Ralph.

He said, "Jack, pray join the company. There are two places reserved for you and Mother at the bridal table." He pointed to the open doors. Chatting and laughter were already breaking out.

Jack leapt up and tucked Dee's arm into his. "Ay, I'm mighty hungry."

"I will just take Mother to meet my wife first." Billy took hold of Mateo, who had jumped down ready to go with them. "Grandmamma is coming to meet Mamma," he told him.

But Jack would not be abandoned in this wide carpeted space. He clung to Dee's arm as she tried to draw away.

She looked up at Billy. "This is all strange to him," she murmured. "He has never been inside a place like this. I will take him to his seat first."

Billy inclined his head, but she saw a mocking flash in his eyes that took her back to his first discovery, as a child, that 'his father' could neither read nor write. The old Billy is still there, she thought. I must keep my head clear.

They walked into the dining hall and were greeted with cheers. It seemed there could be no eating till they were in their places.

A separate, shorter table had been placed at the end of a long one, making a 'T' shape, and Francis and Lily were at the centre of it.

"There," Dee said, propelling Jack to the space beside Lily, "you have the honour of sitting next to the bride. I'll be back in a moment. Pray start feasting."

She saw Francis was trying to signal to her. It was a pleasure to look at his eager, open face and know that she knew him through and through.

"You won't get caught up with them, Mother, will you? He's cunning as hell to have worked on Aunt Sarah all these years without anyone knowing."

Lily glanced up. "I knew someone corresponded with her from abroad, but I had no idea…" Her small features were creased in a regretful frown.

Dee said, "Time for talk later. I won't be long, Jack," and she turned to find Mateo standing between the double doors, stamping one foot with impatience. She scurried over and took his hand.

Billy was waiting at the foot of a staircase with carved newel posts, and Mateo made her almost run towards him. As they ascended the stair, her thoughts swung from Francis and Lily and the fortune they were not to inherit to this utterly unexpected acquisition of a Spanish daughter-in-law and grandson.

Billy said nothing till they were outside a door on the landing above. Then he looked hard at Dee. "She knows nothing of my background, and believes that you and my father were married. He was killed, and you remarried – a farmer – and had another son, whose wedding happens to be today."

She lifted her eyes in shock. "I cannot endorse lies!"

"She will not question you. Just speak in your best voice."

He tapped on the door and opened it.

Dee had an impression of a hastily-arranged sitting room with a big fire roaring up in the hearth. A flamboyantly beautiful young woman was settling herself in the one high-backed chair and turning towards them with a gracious smile. She didn't rise, but held out her arms.

Mateo ran into them, exclaiming, "Mamma, I bring a new grandmamma."

Over his head she looked at Dee. "Señora Heron, pray excuse. I so tired. What a journey, and then wait wait wait on ship – no comforts. When we find his house in horrid street in that so dirty Newcastle, what is it but we must come to fishing place for his brother to be wed here today. And he say will meet his mother there! Your dear boy make so quick deciding. I happy to meet you but he – how you say – he take away my breath."

Dee felt Billy gently propelling her towards the chair so she could take the proffered hand. It was pale and smooth and heavily ringed. Her own fingers itched with their thickness and roughness.

She said, "I am sorry you are tired, but I am most happy to make your acquaintance. Bi…believe me, I knew nothing of my elder son's marriage or his child." This conversation was beset with pitfalls. She felt herself breaking into a sweat.

"Ah, he is bad boy. I told him to write in letters, but he say must be face to face. He have so much to tell you. Of course, he is also very humble and not wish to boast how we met. He save my life. I tell you great sad story with happy end."

Dee heard a tut of exasperation from Billy and saw a sharp frown crease his brow – a flash of the old Billy – before he composed an indulgent smile.

"Not now, Sophia. My mother must go back to the wedding party. I will stay with you and Mateo until they are ready to depart, and then I will go down and wish them Godspeed." He turned to Dee, all graciousness. "But for you, Mother, and my stepfather I have had a room prepared here for tonight, or indeed as long as you wish, so we can become better acquainted and discuss future plans."

Dee had withdrawn her hand and was only too eager to go, but at this she had to stop and stare into his face. His expression was complacent, which infuriated her deep inside. She said, "We have our arrangements for tonight, thank you, and will be expected home tomorrow."

Now she saw hurt come into his eyes, and was sorry; but that he should think he could walk back into their lives and start reordering them was outrageous.

Then Mateo slithered down from his mother's lap and came and held her hand. "I go with Grandmamma to the feast."

Billy looked at him, and now Dee sensed something she had never seen in her elder son: adoration. It flooded his eyes, and though his lips said, "No,

Mateo," the joy and pride in his son was palpable. He added, "I have ordered a meal to be sent here to our room."

Dee saw a tantrum about to explode, but Billy held up a firm hand. "A special treat in it for you."

Mateo bit his lip. "Very special?"

"Very very special."

Mateo grinned. "I see you later, Grandmamma."

Dee nodded. "Of course." She gave Sophia a tentative smile. "Pray rest, and I will call upon you later when you are more refreshed, if that is agreeable."

She received a wafting of the hand in reply, and slipped out of the room without another glance at Billy.

Going down the stairs with her right hand on the polished banister, she was smitten with regret at how she had answered him. She told herself, He loves his son. There was no posing in that look. But his plan with me? Is he trying to make up for past wrongs, or is he showing me that wealth is power? I felt love stirring when I saw how I disappointed him in my answer. Can I relate to him now after these empty years? And Sophia? She is as unlike me as she could be.

She was down the stairs and heading into the dining hall. That upstairs room and its occupants must be put from her mind. She looked about. The faces at the table were almost all known to her and, as coarse as some of the speech was, there was nothing hidden behind it.

She fended the questions about the mysterious Billy's wife with, "She's lovely but she was tired from travelling, so I didn't stay above a minute or two."

Francis whispered behind Jenny Batey's back, "Why did *he* come to spoil our wedding day?"

"He didn't," Dee said. "He must have had word from lawyers that Sarah had died. He had to come. *They* told him about your wedding when he arrived." She looked about at the elegantly laid table. "Nothing is spoilt. Would you rather be on the beach with that howling gale?"

Jenny sat back and chuckled at them both. "Ay, your Billy turning up was a godsend, I'd say, whatever fancy name he calls himself now."

"It was his father's name," Dee said softly. "Now let's say no more about it. Is Tom prepared to give a speech?"

"Oh ay, he's writ down a pack o' words, but reading 'em'll be another matter."

Dee settled into her chair. This was the world she had lived with, from her marriage to Jack to the colourless propriety of their life at Mrs Hammond's. She would enjoy its boisterous goodwill for a few more hours.

Chapter 3

Ralph

"So that is your mother," Sophia said. "She very plain dressed for your brother's wedding. Why she not grateful for all you done? You give all those orders last night when the lawyer told you the wedding today. You drag me here to meet her and is no joy. Your mother not seen you seven years? Why she not happy?"

Ralph Barnet knew that in his mother's presence he had been Billy again. Was it a terrible mistake to have come back? Yet the scene when he parted from his mother seven years before was vivid in his mind the moment he saw her. Had she not begged him to stay then? Was there not a hint of reconciliation even with his brother Francis? Had he not struggled since then to forgive her for her lack of love?

No, he had never succeeded in doing that; and when his own son had been born, his heart was hardened even more against any mother who failed to love her child. Sending his beloved Mateo to her first was a test. He himself had had love from Jack's father, and that had been precious. Now that his own son was here, he wanted him to meet his only grandparent. Sophia's father and mother had died at sea on the calamitous day when he had saved her life. Could his mother, who had had such a capacity to love Jack and Francis, produce the same for little Mateo? He had watched her face when the child appeared, and had seen the shock and horror. It had never occurred to him that she might see a reincarnation of himself. But then she had passed the test. The warmth of her embrace had won Mateo in an instant.

Did I presume on that, he asked himself, by expecting her to fall in with my plans? It has been a shock. She was absorbed in Francis's wedding and then...

"It was a shock," he answered Sophia.

It had been a shock to him to be called Billy again. Taking his father's name was the first thing he had done when he left home. He had traced his history and found that when his father was killed in a duel the baronetcy had died with him, but there was no one to object to its resurrection. Indeed, he had run to ground his father's retired commanding officer, who had declared he was the spitting image of Lieutenant Sir Ralph Barnet. The date of that officer's intended wedding to the heiress Dione Sheradon fitted with his own date of birth, and the account in the *Courant* of the bankruptcy of the Sheradon business and his mother's speedy marriage to Jack Heron of Wylam coincided perfectly. From that day he had created for himself a character in his mind: a worthy Sir Ralph Barnet, confident, brave, courteous, gallant, a leader of men.

Seeing the family members and many other known faces had shaken him to the core, but he had held himself together for the encounter and he was proud of how he had struggled back into the character of Sir Ralph Barnet. As benefactor of the feast, he had played the gracious host. These people respond to wealth, he thought, and will forget Billy Heron in a jiffy, but for Mother and Francis and Lily I see it was too sudden. I will do it, though. Wealth opens all doors, and that I have.

There was a tap on the door and two waiters appeared with trays of food.

Mateo, who had been dozing in Sophia's lap, jumped up. "What is my treat?"

Ralph smiled. "A cup of chocolate just like the grown-ups'."

He clapped his hands.

Sophia said, "But it too rich for a child so young. Will it not make him sick?"

The boy had his hands round the mug. "Ooh, hot. I sip it slowly, Mamma."

Ralph shook his head at Sophia and watched Mateo with aching love. He was seeing him as the magnet that would draw him at last into his mother's heart.

Dee

Below in the dining hall, Dee was listening to Tom Batey's speech.

"We've had four lasses, and two of 'em wed now, and Ally's give us two more, so, Lily, I wants a grandson to carry on Batey's pies. Franky lad, mind you get busy tonight." There was a roar from Francis's mates, and he and Lily blushed scarlet.

"Nay, divn't be coarse, Tom," Jenny said. "That wasn't in what you had writ down."

"I ken that, woman, but I cannot read me own writing."

There was delighted laughter. Dee saw the stiff waiters lined up at the table of drinks, trying to suppress smiles. They are just local Tyneside lads, she decided, embarrassed at being dressed up in colourful tight-fitting uniforms.

"Anyhow," Tom said, "I know fine well I have to end up with the health of the bride and groom, so you fellows yonder fill us up with some good ale, not your fancy wines, and we'll drink to Frank and Lily."

Francis, quite shaking with nervousness, stood up and spoke some fumbling but heartfelt words of thanks. Dee was pleased to see that the shy innocent little boy was still there inside him. She prayed, Please God, let him not shrivel up with envy that Billy has Sarah's wealth and *he* must work at his profession to earn a living.

As the company became more inebriated and noisy, her thoughts flew upstairs. Could *they* hear the sounds of revelry?

I must learn to put names to them, she thought. Will I ever think of them as Ralph and Sophia? She, I am sure, will resent that her husband has gone to all this trouble and expense for a family who have not yet said a word of thanks. Do I *want* to be under an obligation to the Billy we used to know? Francis cannot stomach it, I'm certain, but that may change if they meet together alone and put the past to rest. She gave a long drawn-out sigh.

Francis said, "Oh Mother, was I so very bad?"

She met his eyes and laughed. "You were your dear honest self." She sighed again. "I was asking myself if the past can ever be put to rest."

His face changed, and she wished she could snatch back her words. "You mean Billy, Mother? It *was* at rest. I rarely gave him a thought. But he's back, today of all days. I've tried to forget he's in this very building. And we have to call him Ralph Barnet. *Sir* Ralph Barnet if you please."

"Oh pray don't say the words."

"I'm sorry. Does the name still upset you?"

"Two weeks before our wedding, the first Ralph Barnet ordered a lawyer to write to my father and call it off and sent not a word to me. Would not Lily hate you if you had done such a thing?"

"Is that how it happened to you? You never speak of it."

"And I believed in his love and returned it wholeheartedly. Then his child came, with his same deep, dark eyes."

Francis's eyes were moist. "No wonder you couldn't love Billy. Do you think we have to give him a chance?"

"Oh yes," Lily said. She turned her head towards them. "I'm sorry, I couldn't help listening. Don't you see? I too hurt Billy." She turned a furrowed frown on Dee. "He thought I loved him, and I just blurted out that it was Francis."

"And he took a terrible revenge on me." Dee saw a hard look come into Francis's eyes. She thought, He is remembering the prison cell and the dread of execution. Looking at Lily, she knew she had seen it too. But there was that in Lily which made Dee rejoice that she could now call her 'daughter'. Lily truly wanted love and peace with all about her. She took her hand and squeezed it.

"You are right, my sweet. We must give Billy a chance."

Then she looked beyond her at Jack, whose head was on his chest, his arms flopped in his lap, and Susy and Daisy Batey giggling at him.

Beyond him, and beyond the whole raucous gathering, she saw a tall, dark figure appear at the open doors.

She tapped Francis's arm. "And here he is," she whispered, "to try us out."

As he advanced, heads turned and the table fell silent. Yet he is not a sinister presence, Dee thought, but he *is* a presence. I recall the day he became overman at the pit. He quelled the miners with his authority even then. He is more of a man than his father was.

"Good people," he said, spreading out his arms, "I have been delighted to offer you some small hospitality, but I fear it must come to an end. I am not yet familiar with the customs here, but I understand this inn is expected to open the doors of its drinking parlour round the corner in the evening for passing trade. Then we close the hotel door to residents only, so they can have peace and quiet."

"Ay, we've made a terrible din," shouted Tom, whose voice had been one of the loudest.

Sir Ralph made a gracious deprecatory gesture.

"I should explain that we have only a few rooms available for residents, and my wife and I and our son are occupying one suite. I can put another at the disposal of the bride and groom if they would like that, and the last for my mother and Jack. For the rest, I trust you will make your own way to wherever you planned to go, or, if you wish to head round the corner to our other door, you are welcome as customers."

"Ay, at a price," Tom cried. "The likes of us don't drink at the New Inn. But, by heaven, ye've give us a roof over our heads from that gale, and carpets under our feet for cold sand, and I say we should give a cheer to – what's he call hisself now?" he hissed at his wife. "Oh ay, Randy Barton. Hip hip…"

Dee jumped up. "He is Sir Ralph Barnet, and should rightfully have been named so or ever he was Billy Heron. Now you can give your cheer."

There was an uncertain noise, but Tom got them going again with "Three cheers for Sir Ralph Barnet. Hip, hip…" And this time, for the sheer pleasure of making a noise, there was a loud "Hurrah!" Some rolled off their chairs in their exuberance.

As Sir Ralph was making a small speech of thanks and waving to his servants to fetch coats and shawls, Francis looked at his mother with reproach in his eyes.

"Have you accepted his offer of a room?"

"No, I declined it, but perhaps for your father's sake…" Jack was sitting up gazing round with blurred eyes. "He is not used to so much drink."

"But Lily and me? I couldn't – in his house." His cheeks flushed.

Mr Trace had come up behind him, and he spoke suddenly in his gruff manner.

"There's an offer you can't refuse, lad, for your first night. You'll be a damn sight warmer here than in my boarding house, where there'll have been no fires lit in your two rooms, for Molly falls asleep over the kitchen fire whenever Mrs Trace and I are out. We'll be driving home now, and can send all your bags back here by our man. What do *you* say, Mrs Heron?" Lily looked round at Dee. "Nay, I meant you." He pointed at her, and there was a rare twinkle under his bushy grey eyebrows.

Lily blushed. "I'll do what Frank wants."

"Nay, you mustn't get off on that foot, not four hours married!"

Dee intervened. "If that is not too much trouble for Mr Trace, let us all accept Ralph's kind offer, just for tonight."

Everyone was moving about now, and she hadn't noticed Ralph approaching.

"That would be very gracious, Mother."

Francis looked round, startled and angry, Dee could see. She laid a hand on his arm. Lily was nodding and smiling at him. He subsided with an effort of will as they all waited for his reply. There was a long appraising look between the brothers. Then he stood up abruptly and took Ralph's hand.

"I'll stay if we can start again as Ralph and Frank."

Dee gave a huge sigh of relief. She looked from one to the other. Surely those were not tears in Ralph's eyes? Perhaps it was the brightness of the chandelier above them. There was still Billy inside that bearded man-of-the-world exterior.

"Nothing would please me more." There was a catch in his throat as he gripped his brother's hand. He seemed to shake himself, and the confident poise was restored. "My wife will be delighted. Pray come up now. We can pass some time together before Mateo has to go to bed."

A noisy ten minutes followed. Jenny said, "Have I to say goodbye to my girl *now*?"

Lily gave her mother a hug. "We'll come round to the shop in the morning, Ma, before we go."

Jenny insisted on hugging Francis then. "I lost a wee fair baby years ago. I wager he'd have grown into a right bonny lad just like you. Now, you'll keep visiting, won't you? I sees Ally and the bairns all the time, with them just being in Cullercoats, but I don't want to lose my Lily."

Francis pecked her cheek and teased her. "I'll keep coming just for Batey's pies."

Soon all the company had gone, except Francis's young friends, led by George Clayton, who said it was their duty to escort Francis and Lily to the bridal chamber; but something in Sir Ralph's expression stopped them at the foot of the stairs in a giggling group. They had to be content with a cheer as Francis and Lily mounted to the unknown upper regions of the hotel. The liveried servant ushered them off the premises and closed the doors.

Dee saw Francis and Lily glance round at that with a shiver of unease which echoed in her own heart. Have we surrendered, she asked herself, to a controlling power? Billy showed emotion for a second, but as Sir Ralph he has wealth. Wealth can dispense with emotion. Wealth is power. I desire harmony, but I must be on my guard.

She saw, ahead on the landing, the doorway to Ralph and Sophia's suite of rooms. Her two sons, with their wives, were about to meet together. She was tense with excitement and apprehension.

But at the top of the stairs Jack, who had stumbled up clutching her arm, muttered, "Where are we going, angel? I think I'm not very well."

"I will show you your rooms," Ralph said quickly, and stepping past his own door he opened the next one a few yards on. Dee saw into an inner bedroom, with a basin and ewer on a stand, and steered Jack towards it.

"Excuse us tonight," she said to Ralph.

"Nay, I beg you to come when you have made Jack comfortable. Frank and Lily will be with us. The evening is young. There is the bell pull if you need a servant."

He backed out and closed the door as Dee grabbed the ewer out of the basin so Jack could lean over it and vomit.

When he had done, he straightened up and said, "Eh, that's better. I'm right sorry, but I had to be rid of that."

She dipped her clean kerchief in the ewer and mopped his face. "You told me once you had been drunk with some lads when you were young and you fell over and banged your head, so you would never do that again."

"Ay, I mind that, but I was thirsty today and they kept filling my glass and I was still thirsty."

"If I'd been beside you I'd have allowed you only water." She was now looking round the room. The bed was a four-poster. A memory of her bedroom at Sheradon Grange leapt into her mind. She had begged Betty, her nurse, to sleep with her because the bed frightened her.

She turned back into the sitting room to escape the smell of vomit. "We must get rid of that." And she walked over to the door where the tasselled bell pull hung, and tugged it.

Jack stared. "We can't answer that. We're not in the kitchen."

Dee laughed, but she had shocked herself. The action had come to her so easily.

A chambermaid appeared and removed the basin without a word being spoken. Jack stood rigid till she had gone. "Oh Dee, where are we? What's happening to us? Who was that?"

"Just a maid. We're still in the hotel. We can spend the night here."

"When can we go home?"

"Tomorrow. Mrs Hammond expects us."

He nodded slowly. "That'll put things to rights. It's our job to answer the bell, isn't it?"

And what will tomorrow bring, Dee asked herself, and many tomorrows after that? We may be at the brink of something very new, and this dear man of mine will be utterly bewildered.

She hugged him. "I must go back to the others. You rest on the bed."

"Nay, I'm coming with you. I'm well now. You can't leave me here."

"Come, then." She took his hand. If only, she thought, my fears were as simple as his.

Chapter 4

Ralph

In the presence of his brother and, particularly, Lily, Ralph found himself struggling in the role of benevolent host he had assumed for the evening.

Frank had not changed much from the Francis of seven years ago, but at twenty-five he was firmer in face and manner. His hand grip was a man's. He's wary of me, Ralph thought, but I must win him round. That 'starting again' was a good word. I know he is honest and will strive to do just that.

He looked at Lily. She was still the girl in whose face he had first seen perfect symmetry, and he had resolved to have her, because he must have the best. She still had, in repose, those twin arcs of eyebrows, the neat nose and shapely lips, and even the three honey-coloured curls on her forehead. Above all, her open, honest eyes would suddenly lift up with the hopeful look that said 'Shy as I am, I want to know and like you'. She was doing it now to Sophia, who beamed amused tolerance. Ralph could see her appraising the tradesman's little girl in her now rather crumpled bridal gown. The creamy lace at her neck did not enhance her pale colouring, and hung asymmetrically. His fingers itched to straighten it.

He felt again the rising anger of the moment Lily had told him, all surprised innocence, that it was Francis she loved. And here they were before him on their wedding day, trying very hard to behave as if the past had never happened and he was in fact a totally new acquaintance.

Fortunately, his nurse brought Mateo in from the inner room to greet his new uncle and aunt. When she had retreated back into the bedroom, Mateo looked the visitors up and down and pouted. "Where's Grandmamma?"

"She'll come presently," Ralph said. "This is your Uncle Frank and your Aunt Lily." Lily held out her hand in the most natural way.

"I am so happy to have a nephew. I have only two nieces."

Ally's children, thought Ralph. God forbid that Sophia should ever meet my brother's new relations. Again he wondered if coming 'home' had been wise; but he had been summoned on Sarah's death and could hardly have avoided it.

"What are their names?" Mateo demanded.

"Elizabeth and Margaret." She gave a little giggle. "But they get 'Liz' and 'Meg' all the time." A pity she added that, he thought.

Sophia waved Frank to an upright chair on her right when she saw that Lily was happy to play with Mateo. Frank had politely asked about their voyage from Spain, and Ralph saw that Sophia was happy to lay her hand on his arm and tell this fair, handsome young Englishman all the heightened horrors of the Bay of Biscay, followed by their confinement at the port of Hull for two whole weeks.

I must think of Frank as a fresh face, the Billy inside Ralph reminded himself. At this moment he is just another of the good-looking gentlemen with whom my wife cannot help flirting.

A tap at the door heralded his mother's return, which would give him the opportunity for his next move. But when he opened it to usher her in, there was Jack lurking behind her. She raised her eyebrows, and a slight lifting of her shoulders showed him she couldn't stop him coming. He gave a nod of understanding. Jack would not be left alone in unfamiliar surroundings.

The communication between them took a fraction of a second but showed him plainly what he had missed as a child. This was a quick-witted woman with whom he could have had a delightful bond if only she had loved him. Well, surely she would love him now when she learned what he could offer her.

He invited her to the sofa, and Jack sat down beside her when he had been presented to Sophia. He had said, "I'm honoured to meet you, my lady," and retreated backwards to Dee's side like a child who has said his piece.

If he says nothing more, Ralph thought, no harm is done. Sophia does not recognise the coarseness of his accent.

Mateo had run to grasp Dee's skirt the moment she appeared, but Ralph said, "Your grandmamma and I have much to speak of. Show your Aunt Lily the ship the old sailor made for you." The child looked at Dee as much as to say 'Don't you go away' and ran into the bedroom, to produce a small pirate ship with its little black flag at the masthead. Lily got down off her stool by the fire and sat on the hearthrug to admire it.

"That flag," cried Sophia. "You know it frighten me," and she leaned close to Frank and said in a loud whisper, "Five years ago, on the voyage home from Puerto Rico, pirates attack us. My poor parents die in the first shooting."

"But how dreadful!"

Ralph could see that Frank was genuinely shocked. He thought, This is still the youthful Francis I loathed all my childhood for his innocence and Mother's care of him. I want to forget all that. And I don't want Sophia to unfold this story. I want to talk with Mother. It is the future that matters now.

He made negative gestures to Sophia, but there was no stopping her.

"Oh, it is worse. They grapple us and come on deck to seize our cargo. Spices. They sell at high price. I hide under sail but they see and try to haul me out. They are brutes. Not seen woman maybe four months. I think death better, so I wriggle to the side"– she made twisty movements with her hands – "and before they stop me I leap overboard."

Ralph could see she was revelling in Frank's astonishment.

She finished in triumph, "Then come your brother and he save my life." She patted Frank's arm again. "Now you know and your mother and your new wife – if she has been listening – how we met."

Lily blushed. "I couldn't help listening."

Mateo piped up. "I know it hundreds of times. Go on, Aunt Lily, make more waves in the rug." She had been creasing it up to make his little boat bounce. She blushed again as if she might have done wrong. Ralph's heart lurched towards her.

Frank asked, "But how did he save you? Where did he come from?" and Sophia was launched again.

"Ah, you see, there was great fog. The pirate come upon us out of fog, but the privateer chase the pirate and he come out of fog too and see the pirate's evil work, and the captain" – she pointed at Ralph – "he jump in and save me. Take me on board. His men kill the pirates and mend our poor ship and we all sail for Spain. And Mateo, you can be quiet. It is necessary your father's family know these things. Your father is great hero. He not tell. He too modest."

Ralph could sense his mother's intense interest and knew questions were coming, so he broke in with, "I only let her tell you this now, Mother, so you will understand how I have made a fortune and can do what I am about to propose."

Sophia burst out, "Ah, Señora Heron, this is his moment he wait for. How he excited when he receive letter of lawyer! I give it her, he cry. We go to England soon so I do it."

Ralph glared at her. "Sophia! Pray be silent. I wish to explain my plans in my own way so we can discuss the changes that may come in a quiet, civilised manner."

He turned to his mother and saw a pallor in her face and fear in her eyes.

Beside her, Jack leaned forward with that half-eager, half-puzzled look he remembered from his childhood whenever anything fresh was afoot. It had angered him then, but now it might be a blessing. She would have to unfold it to him slowly, and that might soften the unexpectedness of it all.

Sophia smiled at Frank and laid her finger on her lips.

Ralph ventured to take hold of his mother's hand and look full into her eyes.

"Mother, it is of Sheradon Grange that I wish to speak. You enjoyed its comforts for about eighteen years, I believe, and were then forced to leave. I have to tell you that I am the new owner and wish to give it back to you."

A greyish look superseded her pallor, and her eyes were wide with shock. She pulled back her hand and leaned away from him. "Not – not the grange! I thought for a moment -" she looked at Sophia – "your wife was hinting at one of the Heron Mansions."

"Oh, them!" cried Sophia. "He not need to *buy* them. They come to him from old aunt. He not house a dog in them."

Ralph shook his head. "I will keep them as an investment, Mother. But the grange! One of my lawyers went to look at it and says it is set in the country with its own woodland, and though the house has been knocked about by the army it can be restored to its former splendour. Workmen are in it now. I gave orders at once. But you shall see it yourself and make your own choice of improvements."

He stopped and searched her face for signs of relief. She must have heard from gossip in the Tyne Valley that it was standing empty in a derelict state. "You are living in Ovingham, I understand, as *companion* to a widowed lady. You would be happy to have the freedom of your own home, I am sure."

He beamed round at Frank and Lily. "Of course, there would be room for the bridal pair. A good address for a rising engineer to place at the head of his letters."

He saw excitement in Frank's eyes and a questioning look at their mother, but it was her reaction he wanted.

Jack suddenly said, "My angel, you're upset. What are they talking about?"

"Nothing important." Her voice was cold. "We'll go to bed presently, and home tomorrow." She tried to rise but it was a low couch, and with a man each side of her she couldn't do it.

Ralph held her down by turning her towards him and seizing both her hands again.

"Mother, what is the matter? You must answer me." He struggled to keep the hurt and anger out of his voice.

Sophia was screeching, "Why she not happy?"

Mateo was looking up, eyes and mouth wide. Lily had sat back on her heels, her face distressed.

His mother said softly, "I'd rather you and I were alone."

Sophia exclaimed, "No, no, *I* must understand you, Señora Heron. You are mother for me now. You were not happy before to stay here but you stay. Now you not glad for beautiful home. You change mind soon?"

Ralph watched his mother's face. She seemed to come to a decision, pulling her hands away and sitting back on the cushions and folding her arms. She looked round at all their faces, ending with Jack, to whom she gave her most loving smile of reassurance. He settled back too, and his eyes were serene again.

What is coming? Ralph wondered. I had forgotten that she could always take command of a situation. What have I done?

First she turned to his wife. "Sophia – for I may call my daughter by her name, as I call Lily. I have two sons, and now I have two daughters."

Sophia inclined her head – warily, he could see.

"One son I have neither seen nor heard of for seven years. Then without warning he is here, a very rich man. Plainly our lives must be rearranged to fit his new status." Ralph drew in his breath, but noises of protest came from the others too. She held up her hand. "But he has not told you, his wife, the truth about us. I *did* live in Sheradon Grange, but since that time—"

"Mother, think what you are saying!" The words burst from him. "Sophia is a condesa in her own right—"

"And she was Lady Barnet," Sophia cried. "I care not she is now Señora Heron. What is this? We not mind rank any more. Ralph want you live in own house for rest of life. That is good, no?"

"*I* think it's good," Frank blurted out.

Lily, her arms wrapped round Mateo, murmured, "It would be *comfortable* for you, would it not, dear mother-in-law?"

Ralph exulted. He had done right not to broach this to her alone.

He began quickly, to forestall more speech from her. "I know I've been hasty, Mother, for which I humbly apologise. I never thought what a shock it must be to my family that I made money myself long before inheriting my aunt's wealth. I was glad because I could do good with it. Finding that I could meet you all speedily if I bestirred myself today was a delightful surprise. I never saw my hopes for you all as *interference*. You shall have all the time you need. Confer and deliberate together. But now I think it would be wise to break off. Mateo, you must say goodnight to everyone."

"So you have your say and I am not to have mine?" his mother murmured at him as Mateo got up and began to circle the room.

"Of course you shall, when you have had time to think about it."

He gave his attention to Mateo, who had said, "Goodnight, Uncle Frank," and then stopped in front of Jack.

"What do I call him, Papa?"

"'Step-grandfather', or 'Mr Heron' if it's easier."

Jack chuckled. "Nay, I never been a 'mister' in me life. You can call me Jack, laddie."

Mateo nodded. "Goodnight, Jack. Goodnight, Grandmamma."

Ralph saw her hesitate and then suddenly clasp the boy to her knees and give him a prolonged hug. She set him down, and there were tears in her eyes.

He said, "I see you tomorrow, Grandmamma," and trotted on to Lily.

"Goodnight, Aunt Lily. Thank you for playing with me." He picked up the boat. "Mamma, you read to me in Castilian?"

"I think Papa has English book for you."

43

Ralph jumped up. "Of course. I had forgotten. Did you pack them, Sophia?"

"I pack two – one of horse and one of sparrow."

"Mother, we found a little pile at Sarah's. Your *Moral Tales*."

Sophia laughed aloud. "He leap in air shouting *Sandy Horse* and stood there still in travelling cloak and read it all through."

He looked down at his mother. "My happiest memory."

She looked up with a wry smile. "And you tore up *Susie Sparrow*." Then her lip trembled and she stood up quickly, Jack moving with her. "We must go. Pray excuse us. Come, Francis, come, Lily."

They scrambled to their feet. Ralph sensed a torrent of weeping rising up in his mother's eyes and was glad. She has a hard shell, he reminded himself, but there is a fire of emotion in there.

"Frank," he said, "yours is the room beyond Mother's. I think your travelling bags will have been delivered there by now."

Sophia called out, "Sweet dreams. Is that you say? Sweet dreams."

They were gone, and the nurse had come for Mateo.

Ralph sank back onto the sofa and clasped his hands behind his head.

She is like me, he was thinking, proud. Too proud to take from me.

Sophia said, "So odd. Your mother. I not like her."

He shook his head, smiling. "What an amazing day!" In his heart he was saying, I did well to buy that place. I have them all in the palm of my hand.

Sophia was assessing him with a crooked smile and admiration in her eyes.

"You manage people like you manage privateer. But your mother tough woman, I think."

He shook his head again. "No, I have her now."

Dee

Dee, with Jack's arm round her, struggled to their door. Francis – but he must be Frank now – made as if to move on, but she shot out an arm and pulled him in. Lily followed. She will weep too, Dee thought, without understanding why.

Flopping onto the sofa, she let the tears come in heaving gasps. All Billy's childhood had risen up to curse her through the memory of *Sandy the Horse*. It was her first book, and the first time Billy had loved something she had

44

done for him. He had lain absorbing it and demanded it again and again. Now he was a great man with a beard and a wife and he had never forgotten that. He even wanted to read it again.

Jack was utterly distressed till she could lean towards him and murmur between gulps, "*Sandy the Horse*. Billy loved it."

"Oh ay. So did I. It was my Sandy what pulled the wagon for years."

Lily knelt down before her. "Dear Mother, you have him again and now he only wants to do good, but it's all been such a shock it's hard to think about it all."

Dee sat up and brushed the tears from her eyes. "Yes, it's been a shock. I am tied in knots and *he* has done the tying. Lily, my sweet girl, you say Bi… Ralph only wants to do good. In your eyes all the world has good intentions. But he is also grasping power and control. I dread to give him that. He cannot *make* me live in that house. After my grandfather's death I was not happy there."

"I didn't know that," Lily murmured. "I'm sorry."

"And I don't want money from him. My son captain of a privateer! Surely such men were little more than pirates themselves."

"Ah no, Ma," Frank said. "They received Letters of Marque from their governments to protect their own country's ships and destroy pirates if they had the chance. I've heard they could make fortunes because most of the booty that came to them from enemy ships or pirates remained in their hands. If that strange tale of a Spanish ship attacked by pirates was true, Ralph would be rewarded, I'm sure."

Dee put an edge of sarcasm in her voice. "He was evidently rewarded with the hand in marriage of an orphaned condesa. You saw how desperate he was to stop the revelation of our humble lives? I am Mrs Hammond's '*companion*', indeed!"

"It's the way of the world," Frank said. "Well, *I* will not object to some of his fortune. Uncle Joseph wanted his wealth to come to *me* till Billy got round Aunt Sarah by some clever trick. It's only right, and I'm pleased Billy sees it that way after all this time."

"Ralph," Lily said in a small voice.

Dee turned her head to Jack. How much had he followed the conversation? He met her gaze with a hopeful expectant smile.

"You're not upset any more, angel? Is the new Billy giving away his money? But those were not happy tears just now. I knows happy tears when I see them."

Dee shook her head and saw her serious look instantly reflected in his eyes.

"His money will not bring happiness. It is already awakening greed and longing in our Frank—"

"Nay, Ma, that's not fair. Billy… Ralph is *offering* it. I still want to work at my profession, but surely, Da, you would want Ma to have her own grand house in a lovely wood and never have to work for that Hammond woman any more?"

Jack's eyes opened wide. "Is that what…? Course I would." Then he put his hand over his mouth. "You don't mean Dee would leave me, sudden, like she came?"

Dee's heart almost burst with pity at the fear and horror in his face. Her arms flew round him. "Never, never, never. We are one, my darling, from our marriage day. We can never be parted."

He sank into her embrace with a great sigh.

Frank got up. "Come, Lily, that's our cue. Let this all wait. Nothing can be decided in a moment."

Lily jumped up. "Oh, you're right, Frank. My ma always says 'if there's trouble sleep on it, and like as not it'll be gone in the morning.' Goodnight, dear new parents-in-law."

She gave a small curtsy, looking so appealing in her tousled bridal gown that Dee disentangled herself from Jack and stood up to embrace her.

"My lovely new daughter!"

Jack scrambled up. "Ay, mine too." He virtually lifted her off her feet to give her a hearty kiss on her forehead. "They're still in their wedding clothes!"

Frank smiled ruefully. "Ay, it's been a mighty long day." He grasped his father's hand and then bent towards Dee. "You're not cross with me, Ma. I'd just love to see you have an easy life for your—"

"Old age?" She laughed. "Go on with you. And God bless your marriage."

She watched them sidle out, blushing hotly.

I'll not sleep, she thought, with a son in the room each side, and both crowding my mind with hopes and doubts.

Jack had his arms about her. "Let us to bed too, my lovely. And what a bed it is! I never been in one that wide – and a roof on top!"

She kissed him. Perhaps I will sleep if he comes to me first, she was thinking. I am tired to death, but I need that love of his that never tires.

They locked the door to the passage and went hand in hand into the inner room.

Chapter 5

Ovingham
(next day)

Dee

Mrs Hammond reared up in her high-backed chair. "What are you saying, woman?"

Dee, just as rigid to hide her inner trembling, repeated, "I would like to give a month's notice, ma'am." She was not in the least afraid of Mrs Hammond, but she was afraid of what she herself was doing.

Jack, who always woke early after a sound sleep, had stood that morning at the hotel window and asked when they were going home.

"Now."

She had risen, rung for a maid to bring warm water and a light breakfast, and asked her to rouse Mr and Mrs Heron next door and do the same for them, asking them to be ready to depart by half past eight. The carriage, which had been left at the hotel's livery stables, was to be brought round, and they would wait for it in the hotel lobby.

The maid ventured to say, "Sir Ralph and Lady Barnet are not up yet. The little boy's nurse has taken him down to have a breakfast in the kitchen and see the hens out at the back."

"Very good." Dee pointed to the writing desk. "There is a note there for Sir Ralph. Please see he gets it after we have left."

Jack had watched all this giving of orders with amazement, but was happy that they were leaving. Little was said till Frank and Lily joined them in the lobby.

"What's all this creeping away, Ma?" Frank demanded.

"I'm sorry to have had to rouse you, but if I hadn't you'd have had to hire transport as far as Newcastle. We are taking Mrs Hammond's carriage back to her – and having passed the night further away, we have further to go."

"Is that all? You're not running away from Billy?"

"Ralph," murmured Lily.

"I'm running away from more talk. I left Mrs Hammond's address for Ralph. I've told him my decision, and I'll tell you on the way."

There had been a little squeal as the carriage drew up outside. Mateo, dragging his nurse by the hand, had come running across the entrance hall.

"Grandmamma going away!"

Dee turned and took him in her arms. "Only for a very little while. This carriage is not ours. We have to take it back."

"You come again soon? And Aunt Lily?"

"Very soon."

The ostler got down and handed Jack the reins. The bill for the overnight stabling had been paid, he said, on orders given last night by Sir Ralph Barnet.

Mateo's crestfallen face stayed in Dee's mind long after he was out of sight, and no one spoke at first as Jack drove to Batey's pie shop so Lily could take leave of her family, and then they headed in the direction of Newcastle and Dee told them her decision.

Now the moment she had dreaded in the night was here. The decision had to be put into irretrievable words to her employer.

"Notice!" cried Mrs Hammond. "We have no such agreement. You and Jack live here till I no longer require you."

"If you recall, ma'am, about two years back when Jack was repairing the kitchen window frame he dropped a hammer on a plate and cracked it. The next day I broke one of the two matching Greek vases, and you said, 'If I can find a couple more careful than you two I'll dismiss you forthwith.'"

Mrs Hammond's face reddened. "I was angry."

"I know, and I was sorry, but it made plain our status as hired servants. Servants can also give notice when their circumstances change – and ours have changed."

"Changed! How is that possible? You have been away two nights for your son's wedding. I presume he and his little Lily are safely married and no one has died of the cholera."

Dee, still standing before her like a servant under reprimand, with her hands behind her back, said straight out, "At the wedding I met the gentleman who has bought Sheradon Grange, and he has offered it to me."

Mrs Hammond flopped back in her chair. "*Offered* it! Offered you a country mansion! Good heavens, woman, under what conditions? That you leave Jack and become – his *mistress*?"

Dee stamped her foot. "How can you think that of me? Jack and I will live there. The property will be mine."

There; she had brought out the words that had filled her sleepless hours with doubts and fears. 'Jack and I will live at Sheradon Grange.' It was impossible to picture such a life.

Mrs Hammond now reared out of her chair altogether and, advancing a step, gripped Dee by the shoulders and shook her.

"You are driving me mad. Who is this man and why should he favour you so?"

She is ferociously jealous now, Dee thought. Sheradon Grange is grander than this house. I must be tender with her.

She helped Mrs Hammond back into her chair and knelt down beside her so that their eyes were on a level.

"Pray, dear madam, do not be upset. The situation is unexpected, but not as extraordinary as it may seem. You will recall that Jack's brother Joseph, a miner, married a wife whose parents owned some property in Newcastle. Leaving the pit, he, with Sarah's help, developed the property, through letting, till it became four houses called Heron Mansions."

Mrs Hammond flapped her arms about.

"I recall all that, for there was a great fuss over which of your boys would be the heir. Was it not that very thing that made your wicked older boy accuse his brother of murder when poor Joseph fell in the river? There was talk of a woman in the case too. That must have been Lily, who, God be praised, is safely married to our good boy, Francis. But what has any of that to do with Sheradon Grange and this mystery benefactor?"

"The mystery benefactor inherited Heron Mansions *and* Sheradon Grange."

"And has given it to *you*? Why? Why?"

"Because he is my wicked son, as you call him – but perhaps now a good son."

"What? Billy Heron? He appeared at his brother's wedding?"

"Just after it. He and his wife and son had only arrived in Newcastle the day before and learned what was to take place in North Shields."

"His wife! His son! Where has he been?"

"He has been in Spain after time on the high seas where he has made a fortune. His wife is a Spanish condesa."

"Condesa! A countess! My, he *will* be proud of himself! And are you saying Joseph's widow made *him* her heir, not Francis?"

"So it seems."

Mrs Hammond sat staring ahead of her, her arms loose in her lap.

She is taking in that this is all true, Dee thought. Jack and I are leaving her, and her future is suddenly a vast empty space. For me it is crowded with questions I cannot answer. How do we upkeep a place too big for us? Will I always be beholden to Ralph? Can Frank and Lily live as his murderous brother's guests? Has there been true reconciliation? Does Ralph want Mateo to grow up with me? Will Sophia long to go back to Spain? What will be Jack's daily life? He has always had orders to obey. Why have I chosen this path? Is it the lure of wealth and ease? I am ashamed, and dread the consequences.

At last Mrs Hammond turned her eyes on her. "And will you forget all we have done for you, Dee Heron? Godfrey in his life and I since his death. How would you have travelled to the wedding if I had not let you take the carriage? Where would Jack have found work seven years ago when the pit farm dismissed him, if I had not offered you work and a *home*?"

This was just what Dee had been dreading. The only answer was that they had served her faithfully for their bed and board and a wage that just covered replacement clothing and small luxuries like pens and paper. There were no days off. It was the relentlessness of the daily Hammond routine that had finally, in the small hours, swayed Dee's mind to accept Sheradon Grange. Would she gain her freedom? The answer was behind a closed door. What she had said over and over to herself, and to Jack, Frank and Lily on the way, was that she would keep control in her own hands. How she could do that was the great uncertainty pounding her brain.

"You can't trust Billy," Mrs Hammond rushed on. "He and his family will live in Sheradon Grange and you will be a skivvy to them, as you never were to me – and *no wage*. Think again, Dee."

Dee shook her head, but her doubts reared up. When Ralph sees my note, will he tell Mateo they are all going to live with Grandmamma in a fine country house? Sophia spoke very ill of Heron Mansions. Have I set us on a path which already sprouts thorns and brambles?

Later, back in the kitchen with Jack, who had been cleaning the carriage, she told him the interview with Mrs Hammond had ended in tears.

"I never thought she could weep, Jack, but weep she did."

"Eh, that's bad. Maybe we can't desert the poor old lady. What do you think, angel?"

"I think she will soon find a couple in the village eager to change a hovel for rooms in a comfortable house like this."

Jack nodded slowly. "My angel always has the answer."

In the morning Mrs Hammond had a surprise for her.

"Get Jack to bring the carriage round. I have a fancy to go and look at Sheradon Grange. A month is a very short time for all the refurbishment it will need. You will be staying here as my housekeeper for *much* longer."

Dee, brimming with excitement, asked, "Am I to come with you, ma'am?"

"Of course. You were indifferent before, but now it has dropped in your lap!"

Dee thought, She is gripped by curiosity as well as jealousy. If I am ever installed there, she will want an invitation. She will want to be the first lady in Ovingham to visit Sheradon Grange, and perhaps meet a Spanish countess.

They were ready to set off at eleven o'clock when Jack, wearing his worried look, said, "Which way do I go, Dee?"

"Westwards on the Hexham road, and I will point out the turning."

She kept her voice level, though her heart was fluttering now the moment had come. She was reliving her wretched wandering through the fields on the day she left home. The intervening years vanished like the snapping shut of a telescope. Could she endure to be there again? She held herself together as Mrs Hammond chatted brightly about the calm after "that horrid wind" and admired the early primroses on the south-facing bank. She hopes to see a wreck of a house, Dee thought, and that I will change my mind.

They came to the right-hand turn that climbed the hill. The last time Dee had been driven along it was on the Sunday before Sheradon's crash. They had been to Corbridge Church, which they attended because Grandfather had been born there, and there had been a long sermon. She was hungry for the roast beef that awaited them, but her father was very tetchy. He must have known what else was coming.

"Right at the top road and right again down the drive, Jack. You will see the gates. I'll get down and open them for you."

There was indeed an opening, but no gates or gateposts. Was she mistaken? There was a rutted drive, and it curved where she expected it to curve, round a wooded bankside. But that was all. She felt a weird sense of relief that perhaps there *was* no Sheradon Grange. Maybe there never had been. No lost son had returned and bought it. The whole thing was a chimera.

Jack said, "Do we turn in here, Dee?"

Bemused, she had to nod, and Mrs Hammond snapped, "If the gates are gone, the house, too, must be in a dreadful state. Uninhabitable for a year or more."

They rounded the bend and Sheradon Grange was revealed, snug under the hillside as it had always looked, proud of its classic pediment over a pillared porch.

Dee drew in her breath. In front of the house there stood a carriage, with a man holding the horse's head.

"Someone is here. We mustn't—"

"Nonsense," cried Mrs Hammond. "You say you are the owner now."

The sound of the hooves brought voices from within, and a small figure came running out and, looking towards them, shouted, "Grandmamma has come!"

Dee put her hands to her mouth. "Mateo!"

Suddenly the present and the imminent future overwhelmed the past. Her head buzzed with doubts and wonder.

Out from the porch came Ralph and Sophia.

"My son and his wife," she breathed to Mrs Hammond.

"That is *Billy*?"

"Hush, ma'am! They are now Sir Ralph and Lady Barnet." She was thinking, Madam was right. I am to be *their* housekeeper.

Jack had reined in the horse behind the other carriage. "Why, it's the family we saw yesterday. Or was it the day before?" He got down and reached up to help Dee. Mateo was jumping up and down as Ralph hurried forward, all smiles.

Dee introduced Mrs Hammond, who descended with dignity and gave no more than an inclination of the head to Ralph. To Sophia she gave her sweetest smile.

Sophia exclaimed, "I see why Ralph so quick, quick, quick. Señora Heron want his big present after all and now must come take it. Ralph too drag us from Heron Mansions – how you say – crack of dawn. Come, come, he say, I see the work – how it is doing."

Mrs Hammond replied in her most clipped voice, "Ah, but it was I, madam, who particularly wished to see the house. I saw it in its glory days before the war."

Ralph bowed and gestured for her to come in. "And you are most welcome to see all over it."

"I hear no sound of workmen." Her sharp eyes darted everywhere. "I understood great improvements were taking place."

Ralph smiled. "They are indeed, but I sent word yesterday that the men were to bring the gates today from the ironworks where they have been repaired, and also the new gateposts, for the old had rotted away."

Mateo said, "I'll pull some grass for your horse, Grandmamma."

He ran to the edge of the drive and wrenched up a bunch of dry stalks. Dee smiled. How my grandfather loved to see the lawns all neatly trimmed! I know not whether to weep or rejoice that I am here. Sophia's words suggest they spent last night in Heron Mansions. She will not endure that for long.

Curiosity drove her to follow Ralph and Mrs Hammond up the staircase that swept before them from the wide hall. Mateo, having fed the horses, came and slipped his hand into hers.

"Papa says this is *your* house, Grandmamma. Papa unlocked the door and I ran all round downstairs – and it is big."

"Had you just arrived before we came?"

"Yes, yes. I've not been up here yet."

Dee saw new wood here and there among the banisters and fresh plaster on the walls. She thought, There is painting or wallpapering to do. Will *I* choose the colours? She began to feel hot excitement as the upper landing opened before them, with her old bedroom door to the left and the nursery where Bessie had slept. But when they looked into the rooms, they were all empty and vast and characterless. That was eerie. They had been so choked with furniture and hangings and ornaments. Mateo ran to the door at the end of the passage.

"More stairs here, Grandmamma."

"Just a moment. Wait for me."

She went to the window of her old room and looked out. Even the view was a little different. Of course; the trees had grown. She could make out the gleam of the Tyne because the leaves were not open yet, and the colliery wheel at Hedley was just visible on the hill across the river. Sophia didn't know that her Ralph was the boy Billy, who had worn with pride the night-darkness he dragged up from the depths of the earth and flaunted at his pale clean brother when he came back each day.

Ralph joined her at the window. "This was your room? Would you wish to have it again?" She looked up at him: a tall, manly figure, bearded, handsome, smiling. She spoke without thinking.

"Tell me, Billy, did you really enjoy hacking coal, as you always claimed?"

The colour drained from his face, and he grasped the window frame as if he would have fallen. She was shocked at the change.

"I am sorry – I shouldn't..."

He drew a painful breath. "No, Mother, I will answer – but never, ever take me back to that again." His eyes turned to the window. "You saw the winding gear." She nodded. "Well, I'll tell you. I was angry all the time down the pit. I fought the trapdoors, then I fought pushing the corf. I was glad when I was made hewer like Grandfather, but there was still anger in every stroke of the pickaxe. When he was crushed I dedicated every blow to him, fighting the coal to tear it from the rock." He was breathing heavily as he spoke, and had to pause.

She had a moment of inspiration. "And when you found William Heron was *not* your grandfather...?"

He nodded. "The passion died. I was proud they made me an overman. I felt it was my destiny, but you know I had to go away – I can't speak of that – I went for the wideness of the sea, and now the thought of those small spaces..." He shook his head. "Passing through Wylam today I averted my eyes."

The grey look of shock was fading. She ventured another question, "So why, Ralph, did you decide to come back to the Tyne Valley?"

He straightened up and smiled. "That's easy. I wanted Mateo to have a grandmother."

"Oh." She felt a great flood of warmth towards him. "Truly? Was that all?"

"I was curious about you all. I kept in touch with Sarah. She liked me writing to her and sending exotic presents from the Indies, and she kept track of what you were all doing through Lily living there. My lawyers were her lawyers and they told me this place was for sale."

"You were in Spain when you heard of this?"

"Yes. I sent word at once."

"You wanted it for me?"

"I wanted it for you because I should have grown up here with you. If your father, my grandfather, had not ruined himself, you would have married my father and I would have been born here, since he had only a title to offer you. I might have had a different childhood here."

She stood staring at him. "You mean I would have loved you." She seized his hands. "If *he* had loved me I would. I know I would. You came trailing the hatred I felt for *him*. So you must have this house and live in it. That's what you intend. Of course."

"No, I want *you* to live here, and we will visit you often. You are to have your proper sphere of life as you would have had if our fathers had been wise, honourable men."

Sophia called out: "Mateo gone up to attic. Is it safe?"

Ralph sprang away from the window and rushed out. "No, it is not safe. That door was supposed to be kept locked."

He brushed past Mrs Hammond as she stood at the landing window. At the end of the passage he went pounding up the narrow stair, shouting "Mateo!"

Dee followed him as far as the landing. Sophia was at the foot of the stair.

There were giggles and shrieks of "I'm hiding!" and Ralph's voice was stern.

"Come out of there. The floorboards are rotten."

Mrs Hammond tapped Dee's arm. "You see, the roof must be leaking if the boards are rotten. I shall go down and inspect the kitchen."

Dee saw Ralph descend the attic stairs, with Mateo struggling in his arms.

"Wanted Grandmamma to find me."

She was pondering what Ralph had said – this would have been his home. She gave Mateo a little wave and followed Mrs Hammond.

She could hear Ralph scolding Mateo. "I heard Grandmamma say 'Wait for me' – but you didn't wait. That is bad. You must learn to obey orders."

Sophia shouted back, "He only little, you great bully."

"And that is when he must learn."

Dee was distressed. They should not argue in front of the child. In the kitchen she could still hear their voices. Without much heart for it, she looked about her. The empty fireplace and oven were of the newest design, but she could picture sitting with Bessie as a child before a good fire. The old scrubbed table had gone, replaced by marbled surfaces and new shelves and cupboards. A scullery area had a sink with a pump and mangle. A new way to the back door was through a boot room. She tried to picture Jack trudging in from the stables. That would make him happy. We will eat in here, she thought. A table and chairs before that new dresser. This room is twice the size of Mrs Hammond's kitchen, and that was larger than our whole home in Wylam. But how do we live without an income? I must not depend on my son's pocket.

Mrs Hammond said, "It's all very fine, but you have nothing to put in all the drawers and cupboards. This whole business is ridiculous. Come back with me, my dear, and we will go on happily as before."

The others came and joined them. Mateo was whimpering. His hand crept into Dee's. "I wanted to play hide and seek."

"We will, but not today." She tried her paradise smile on him. His face lit up and he gave a little skip.

Ralph said, "Have you looked in the drawing room, Mother?"

She let him lead her there, the large room with the handsome windows to the right of the front door.

"Your grandfather was a practical man," he said. "He didn't put the drawing room upstairs, as most grand houses did. He was thinking of servants carrying drinks and tea kettles. It opens to the dining room, and the dining room to the passage to the kitchen. Very sensible. Now tell me what colours you wish in here."

Dee looked round to see who was listening. Mrs Hammond had strolled through to the dining room and was doing the round tour back via the kitchen. Mateo, happy again, had gone out to feed the horses and talk to patient Jack. She couldn't see Sophia.

"Son," she said, "I must understand this." They were facing the window, and beyond the two carriages she could see a prospect of a wilderness of grass and shrubs that had once been a lawn and a tangle of woodland beyond. "There is endless work here for Jack to do, and he will love it. *I* could love the designing and furnishing of this house. Empty now, it has a different air from the grange in which I was often unhappy."

"And that is precisely what I want you to enjoy." He looked down at her with upraised eyebrows.

She gave him a steady look. "And how will we earn our bread?"

"'Earn'! Oh, your pride! Your pride! I will pay for it all and make you an allowance."

"Jack has earned a wage all his life."

"I will send him a separate package."

"We cannot live like that."

"You don't trust me?"

"Do you trust yourself to go on making money? This house will absorb hundreds of pounds, and no return at all."

A sharp voice said, "Just what I tell him." Sophia had appeared in the doorway.

Ralph turned on her. "I am doing this for my mother. It is expiation, reparation. You wouldn't understand. And she accepted it in her note at the hotel." He looked back at Dee. "You are not revoking that? The house is now legally in your name."

Dee thought quickly. "I *have* accepted it, but," she hurried on, "I wish your family to have rooms here to come and go as you please, and Jack and I will keep to ours, and I also wish to be free to earn money any way I can."

Sophia clapped her hands. "Good, good, good."

Mrs Hammond strolled into the room. "Pray follow our carriage back to Ovingham and take tea with us." Dee guessed she would tell her friends that she had invited Sir Ralph and Lady Barnet to tea, and *she* was a Spanish countess!

Sophia clapped her hands again. "Good. There is nowhere here to sit down. Señora Heron tell all her wishes there!"

Ralph said, "Can you remember the rooms, Mother, to give your choices if we leave here?"

"I will only express an opinion for *our* rooms. We would like the room on the left of the front door – the parlour where my mother entertained friends – and my bedroom and my nurse's. The kitchen can be shared when you are here, I suppose." But who will do the work? she was wondering. "And there is my father's office looking on the herb garden. It can be my writing room."

Ralph beamed. "You are going to write! Excellent. But you have taken barely a quarter of the house."

"It's my house." She gave him a coy smile. "I can divide it up as I please."

"What about Frank and Lily?"

"There are the two rooms at the back on the first floor above the kitchen. But I think Frank must work with Mr Trace, and he cannot travel from here."

Dee told herself she had rushed into the very situation Mrs Hammond had sarcastically predicted. But *I* have chosen our part of the house and suggested I can earn money myself. I *will* be in control. I want to see Mateo grow up. Only I will not like to hear husband and wife quarrelling. What am I doing?

Ralph said, "Sophia has an estate in Galicia. I haven't seen it yet, for we stayed in Madrid. It is Mateo's inheritance." She saw the tender gleam in his eye. He shook himself and added, "To visit here will be a great joy – but it is *your* house."

Aware of Sophia, Dee didn't give way to an urge to hug him. Those moments at her bedroom window had shown her the depths of hurt and passion lurking beneath the hard-headed businessman. If she could fully trust and love him, they could become mother and son as they should have been from the beginning. She looked up, met his eye for a moment and murmured, "Thank you."

The carriages set off, and as they rounded the bankside they saw two very large carts bearing the iron gates and posts. Ralph gave orders to the men and the carts were manoeuvred so the carriages could drive out.

When they reached the house in Ovingham, Mrs Hammond said, without a flicker of an eye, "I gave the servants the day off, but dear Mrs Heron will prepare a tray of tea for us, I know."

While Jack and the groom attended to the horses watched by Mateo, Dee, having produced the tray of tea, sat down next to Ralph, while Mrs Hammond invited Sophia to sit by her and tell her about the Spanish court.

"Ah, so sad," Sophia wailed. "King Ferdinand strive to keep brother Carlos from the throne. He make woman succeed. Princess Isabella – a baby. We have civil war. Ralph say England safe place. So we come. Go back when Spain quiet."

Dee noted this. Was Spain their real home? She saw Mrs Hammond was startled by the flow of words, but Ralph was waiting with a pencil poised over his pocketbook. She drew her eyes away.

"A wallpaper of pale green for the parlour, with a delicate pattern of leaves."

"I will bring samples from the town."

"Nothing else expensive. The kitchen – whitewashed. Our bedroom – sunshine there, and the dressing room – primrose yellow. Paint – yes." She was thinking, Ralph will complete his business here, and if Spain settles down they may go back. But oh, little Mateo, I want to love him. "My office, as I will call it, could be a cool sand colour, very pale, workmanlike."

"I am glad you are to take up your pen again," Ralph said. "Now furniture. I think your tastes are not for the flamboyant?"

When Ralph finally put away his pocketbook and stood up, Mrs Hammond threw up her arms. "What, is all settled? It will take a year or two, I wager."

"Mrs Heron's rooms can be ready in a month – if you don't mind workmen in the attic and elsewhere, Mother, for a little longer."

"I will see they are kept at it."

Mrs Hammond rose too. "What about the leaking roof?" she demanded.

Ralph smiled. "That was attended to *first*."

As they went down the stairs, Ralph said, "Now I know where you are, Mother, how do I find Frank and Lily? I'd like to give them a wedding present."

"Oh, that's kind. There is a terrace next to Trace's engineering works in Heaton. Mr and Mrs Trace run a boarding house at number six. Frank and Lily have two rooms on the second floor."

He nodded. "That is satisfactory. Frank has his profession to follow."

Mrs Hammond, seeing a neighbour in her garden, said loudly to Sophia, "Pray call again, my lady."

Dee smiled, but as they drove away she was torn with doubts. Should I have told him Frank's whereabouts? Is Ralph a transformed Billy? Do I trust him? A new life lies before us, but I have to face it: everything depends on his money.

She turned back into the house and fetched the tray of tea things to wash up.

Mrs Hammond glared at her. "You saw I did not reveal your servant status. Billy won't want *her* to know your past history. *I* won't speak but others may, and *that* will cause trouble. I expect you'll end up back in the gutter where I found you."

Dee, carrying the tray into the kitchen, couldn't ward off a stab of fear. Have I plunged Jack and myself through a suddenly open door, as I did seven years ago? With all my imagination, I never foresaw how that would turn out, and now I march blindly forward again, designing rooms, if you please, that I may hate to live in.

Jack, making up the fire, turned round and came to her.

"Well, angel, what's to happen now? I don't rightly understand anything."

She beckoned him to sit down opposite her and look into her eyes.

"Jack, there will be a big change in our lives, but nothing to be afraid of. We will always be together, and we will be working for ourselves."

His brow crinkled. "But *I* cannot pay us what her upstairs pays us."

He had put in a nutshell one of Dee's fears. But, for Jack, she must sound sure of herself. "Ralph is happy to pay us to look after the big house you saw today."

"Wasn't that the unhappy place you ran away from and found me?"

There was a deep sorrow in his eyes which she understood at once. If she could be happy there again, was he no longer important to her? That day had been a turning point for him. No one had needed his love or any of his small abilities until that moment. He was the clumsy one with his days of shame.

She took his hands. "Jack, that day was the best day of my life. You gave me your love. Without it I couldn't be happy anywhere. There will be good work for us to do in the grounds of that big house now spring is coming. I will work with you out of doors when it's fine, and no one else shall tell us what to do."

"Eh, that sounds like a wonderful life." He squeezed her hands, and tears of joy ran down his cheeks.

Chapter 6

Sheradon Grange, June 1836
(four years later)

Dee

"I ought to tell you, Frank," Dee called to him as he put his foot in the stirrup, "Lily has gone into labour."

"Oh!" He withdrew his foot and looked round at his mother. "Doesn't it sometimes take a long time?"

Dee couldn't help smiling. This moment had been long awaited, through three sad miscarriages. Now at last Lily had gone full term. But today a great celebration of the railway linking the Tyne and the Solway was taking place, and Frank was eager to ride to Prudhoe, their nearest station, to see the train go through.

"Yes, it may take a long time," she said, "perhaps not till tomorrow morning, and Lily begged me not to tell you, but I thought you would be angry if I didn't."

"If I go, I'll only worry." He still held the reins. "But I did want to see it. You know I did a study of gradients and the effect on engine power while I was still with Mr Trace, and my paper on it was sent to the company that built the line."

"I know. You told me all about it. Go. I won't leave her side."

He hesitated. "I don't like it that Ralph and Sophia and the children are here. They may be noisy."

"Ralph will be giving Mateo his lessons, and Nurse is good with the little girls. They will all keep to their east wing, and I will bring Lily to what I still call Bessie's room to give birth. Then if it's slow I will be at hand in the night."

Frank nodded. "You've thought it all out, Mother, as usual. Well, I won't be long." He leapt into the saddle and was gone.

Dee turned back into the house, her own fears surfacing the moment he was out of sight. Lily was such a little thing, and her baby bulge had given her back pain for weeks. She never complained, saying every day, "Baby's still here. All is well."

Now that the time was ripe, Dee knew Lily was fearful, though she reminded herself that her sister Ally had produced her four little girls with very little trouble.

Dee went back to the parlour, where Lily was reclining on the sofa with her hands across her stomach. "You told him, Mother Dee," she said. "He hasn't come back."

"Oh, my pet, he was torn in two, but I said it would be slow, and he'll be back in two hours. How are you feeling?"

"It's an hour since the waters broke, and no pains yet. Is the midwife come?"

"Jack rode to Ovingham and he'll bring her back with him."

"Do the others know?" Dee knew she meant Ralph and Sophia.

"No. Now they have shut off their own wing of the house I often don't see them till the afternoon. Mateo comes running through sometimes."

"Do you mind them living here all the time now, Mother Dee? *We've* not been with you a year yet, and I sometimes feel you and Papa Jack are crowded into a little space in your own house. It wasn't how Ralph meant it to be at first, was it?"

"No, it wasn't. They went back to Spain when Jack and I settled here. Sophia was pregnant and wanted the child born there."

"And she had *twin* girls. Why was she so blessed and I lost three?" Then she scolded herself. "That was a wicked thought. Women lose babies all the time – but I shan't lose this one. I'm determined."

Dee bit her lip and prayed hard.

"But why did they come back if Sophia loves Spain so much?"

"Well, fighting broke out when King Ferdinand died. His brother led troops against the supporters of the infant queen. Ralph persuaded Sophia that England was a more peaceful place. He needed to be back to see to his business interests. She agreed if they came to this house, not Heron Mansions."

Lily nodded. "She told me once this house is really Ralph's but 'he so kind he give to his mother'." She giggled a little. "She never bothers to learn proper English." Then she drew in her breath and pressed her hands on her bulge. "Ah – that was the first real pain, I think."

"Good, my pet. And here's Maisie Potts at the right moment."

Maisie was all bustling cheerfulness. "Come up to the bed where you're to lie in." With muscular arms, sleeves already rolled up, she helped Lily to her feet.

They had reached the gallery from which the bedrooms opened up when Mateo came through the connecting door downstairs and called out. "I've come to see you make the stotty cakes, Grandmamma."

Dee looked round. "Not today, Matty. Aunt Lily's going to have her baby."

He came halfway up the stairs. "But it's my birthday tomorrow."

"There'll be time to do them for tea tomorrow."

Maisie looked round. "I can manage, Mrs Heron. You've all the time in the world to make stotty cakes."

"No, he's not to be demanding. Matty, if you've done your lessons go and help Jack to rub down Sandy."

Mateo mumbled, "You promised stotty cakes," but he went out and turned right towards the stables.

Dee felt redundant as the pains progressed slowly, and Maisie chatted constantly with funny tales of her sister, who had been 'companion' to Mrs Hammond for four years but had been, in fact, maid-of-all-work. Then she was curious about how the grange was divided up, and was the stuck-up Spanish lady really Lily's sister-in-law? The village had also taken a dislike to the Spanish nurse who never replied when Jack took her and the twins out in the carriage and people stopped to admire them.

"She doesn't speak English," Lily said.

"She could at least smile. Ah, there's another, isn't it? Let's hope they come more quickly. You've not fallen downstairs with *this* bairn, have you?"

"No, that was why we moved here. The stairs back there were steep and awkward."

Dee went down to the kitchen to fetch bowls of broth, and while she was setting them on a tray Frank burst in at the back door.

"How is she? Is the baby come?"

"You've not been gone an hour."

"I know. I couldn't stay. The crowd is in holiday mood and my dear girl—"

"You may carry this up to Bessie's room and see her in Maisie Potts's care but then you should stay away, for Maisie will need to see how far she's coming on."

"Oh Ma, she *will* be all right, won't she?"

"Yes, yes. Did you see Matty in the stables?"

"Yes, he and Father are playing a game. Matty tells him what to do."

He carried the tray and Dee followed slowly.

She heard Lily asking if the train had gone through.

"I couldn't wait. I had to come back."

Maisie laughed, "And you can just go away again, Mr Heron. Fathers are not allowed till there's a wee bairn to look at."

Frank, wincing when he saw Lily wince, crept away.

The day wore wearily on as the baby seemed reluctant to negotiate Lily's narrow hips. Maisie stopped gossiping and began to look worried.

"I'd be happier if Dr Gorst came and had a look at her."

Jack was despatched to fetch him from Ovingham, Frank being too distraught to remember where he lived.

It was growing dark on the long June night when at last Lily had the urge to push. Dr Gorst was looking worried too.

"It's a big baby."

Lily had been very controlled, not wanting, Dee knew, to disturb anyone, but at last she let out a scream. Dee thought of the day Billy was born, when she had begged Emmie Charlton and Jack's mother to let her die.

Ralph came through the connecting door with a bottle containing whisky and laudanum, which he said Sophia had had when her twin girls were born, but Dr Gorst was reluctant to use it because "the mother stops work then and baby grows sleepy."

Ralph confided to Dee that Mateo had been upset that Aunt Lily's baby had taken the attention from his eighth birthday, but now, hearing her scream, he was hiding his head and sobbing. "He's a sensitive child – too much so, I often fear."

Dee said, "Frank should be out of earshot too. He is afraid he will lose Lily."

"And you, Mother?"

"Yes, I am afraid. Dr Gorst has told me the baby is vigorous and could be saved, but at great risk to the mother."

"Oh God, not our little Lily."

Dee, looking up by the light of the brazier in the hall, saw tears in his eyes.

"You loved her once."

"I loved an idea of her when I didn't know her. Now that I know her as Frank's wife, I love her as a sister." He brushed the drops from his cheeks.

All she could do, back in the sick room, was let Lily clutch her arm while she murmured prayers and encouragement to her. Somehow – miraculously, Dee felt – there was an almighty heave and tearing of flesh, and the baby's head was through. Blood flowed, and Dr Gorst grasped the head to turn the mouth from the onrush. Lily gave one more convulsive movement and the rest of the body slithered out.

"Oh my darling, you have a fine boy to live for," Dee cried. But Lily had sunk back, unconscious.

Maisie cleaned up the baby while Dr Gorst called for more linen to stem the blood. Lily was soon trussed up like a chicken, her face deathly pale.

"Will she live?" Dee asked him when Jack had brought up a pail of fresh water for him to wash his hands.

He could only purse his lips and lift his eyebrows.

"She must drink to replace the fluid she has lost."

It was only then that Dee looked at the clock on the mantelpiece. "It's gone midnight by a quarter hour. He is born on my other grandson's birthday."

As she said it, she heard Frank's voice below. "Oh what does the quiet mean?"

Dee ran onto the landing. "Oh my boy, you have a son."

He came pounding up the stairs, Mateo scampering after him. "But Lily – how is Lily?" He went into the room, and Dee just managed to grab Mateo and stop him following. She could hear Frank gasp and break into sobs at the sight of Lily, but Maisie was proud that there was a live baby to show him.

"Here, Mr Heron, see what a lusty lad you have."

Dee turned to Mateo, who was gazing up at her.

"Is Aunt Lily going to die?"

"No, she has a baby son to live for."

"I hate the baby. It hurt Aunt Lily. I hate it for coming on my birthday. I won't share my birthday with a horrid baby."

"You must go to bed and sleep, and then it will be your birthday."

"No, for I heard the grandfather clock chime twelve times."

Dee led him firmly downstairs as Sophia emerged from the connecting door.

"How is Lily?" she asked Dee.

"The baby is born, but Lily is very weak."

She shook her head. "Poor Lily! I have lit candle for her."

"It's a boy and it's come on my birthday," Mateo said. "No one has given me birthday greetings but it's after midnight."

Sophia clasped him in her arms. "See! He knows it is new day, clever boy!" She kissed his ruffled dark hair and led him back inside.

Dee said, "I must go back to Lily. The doctor is still there."

Ralph stepped up to her and took her hand. "I am happy you have another grandson. He will be loved as you have loved Mateo. You have so much love within you to give."

Dee felt sobs welling up. This tall, bearded man was the very one she had not loved when he most needed it. She gave him a tearful smile and knew that he understood her great well of regret.

Maisie now appeared at the top of the stairs, with the baby squirming in her arms and uttering plaintive cries.

"Mr Heron says his father will take me back to the village in your carriage. I know a woman who will wet-nurse him."

Dee ran to the kitchen to find Jack, who was making up the fire again as the only thing he knew he could do to help.

He bustled out to the carriage house, and Dee returned to Dr Gorst.

"Will you sit by her, Mrs Heron, and send word if there is any change. Her pulse is weak but steady. I will return in the morning."

After a quarter of an hour the house was deathly quiet. Frank and Dee sat watching Lily. The one candle in the room burned low, and Frank got up to light another. He had been stroking Lily's hand, which lay inert on the bedcover. She opened her eyes. "Frank?"

The sound was so weak he didn't hear it.

"Oh Lily!" Dee said, and he looked round and came back to the bed, his face alight with hope.

"My darling!"

"Where's my baby? Did it die?"

Tears streamed down his face. "He is well. We have a fine boy. He had to be fed, and there is a young woman in the village who can nurse him till you are well."

"*I* will nurse him. Bring him back, Frank." She accepted the drink Dee put to her lips, and then closed her eyes and drifted into sleep.

After that, everyone, including Dr Gorst, was astonished at the speed of her recovery. In days her determined spirit fought her physical weakness, and she demanded her baby be brought so she could feed him herself.

She was thrilled by his likeness to Frank, though the dents and bumps on his head had not yet smoothed out. "He has his fair hair and blue eyes. But no name." She asked Dee, "What was your grandfather's name who built this house? You loved him. Baby may not be here always, but he was born here."

"His name was John."

Lily looked at the baby and up at Frank. "Let him be John. A good name."

It was settled at once, to Dee's delight.

Sophia insisted on coming up to see Lily.

"John good plain name," she said, "and he plain baby now, but he better soon." She clasped Lily's hand. "How I pray that night, with my candle to blessed Virgin! I know she save you. She save me when I drowning, you know. She send Ralph." And she told Lily again of their welcome when they reached Spain. "Of course, I famous at the royal court. My father emissary of the king. The king grieve for him and my mother. When he know I love Ralph, he order we marry in Madrid so he come to wedding. Did I tell you that?" Dee saw Lily nod wearily. "He was good king but now dead, poor soul, and country torn to bits with fighting. But good news today. I have letter from my cousin Juan." She chuckled in an aside which Dee was meant to hear. "Poor Juan wish marry me, but my hero too quick. Still he send family news. And hear this, Lily dear. Mateo is true heir to all de Villena land in Galicia province. Lawyers at last prove it. Conde Mateo Alonso de Villena!" She looked at the baby. "And here tiny cousin, John Heron."

Lily began to murmur congratulations, but Dee got up. "Lily must rest now."

Sophia lifted her eyebrows, gave Lily a smile and a shrug and went out. Lily said, "Oh, I hope she's not hurt."

"Not her. She has had her little triumph. But I fear for Mateo. She may want to take him back to Spain. Ralph will oppose it but…" She turned her eyes on John. "This one has a straight road of love and peace ahead of him." Lily looked up with shining eyes. "And tomorrow your parents are coming. They hope to travel on the new train, and Jack will meet them with the carriage at Prudhoe station."

"Oh yes, I long to see them."

Jack told Dee afterwards, "Eh, what a great clanging noise the train made, and the passengers sit on benches in wooden boxes on long wagons. Terrible hard."

But Jenny and Tom, splashed with rain and smuts, burst in on Lily, full of excitement about the train as well as the baby.

Tom shook Frank's hand. "By the Lord, you did it, lad. You got me a boy."

"And he'll be a fine one," Jenny said, "when he's got over the birth. Eh, pet," she said, kissing Lily, "Dee says you had a rough time of it. And there's Ally drops hers as easy as a cow. Now what time is the train going back? Jack'll take us. Eh, what exciting times we live in!"

Lily was exhausted when they had gone, and Dee said, "No more visitors while you are still confined to bed."

"Let Ralph bring Mateo to see his little cousin. I want them to be friends."

Dee beamed at her. "You speak my hopes. In a week, then."

When they came, Mateo was very subdued. He looked at Lily's radiant smile of welcome as if he could never reconcile that with the screams he had heard. Then he looked at the baby in his cradle. He was asleep, the lumpy brow now smoothed out. He looked utterly serene.

"But he howls at night," Mateo said. "I can't believe it."

"You'll love him when he doesn't howl at night and can toddle on the grass with you," Dee said.

"Well, I'll try, but I can't imagine that ever happening."

And that was as much as they could get out of him.

Chapter 7

(three weeks later)

Dee

On a warm day in July Lily took her first walk outside on the front lawn, long since restored to an expanse of green sward. Dee wheeled the baby in a carriage engineered by Frank. He had taken over the old gamekeeper's cottage as a workshop and made a frame with wheels and handles on which to rest a large basket. "John is a big baby," he said, "and Lily mustn't carry him as he grows heavier."

Ralph came out and admired the contraption. "We should have had a thing like this for our twins. Frank should patent it and make a fortune. I claim my right to try it out as the baby's only uncle," and he took the handles from Dee and pranced along. Lily burst out laughing, but Sophia, at their drawing room window, looked horrified. She came running.

"My caballero, my capitano, my English baronet! To push baby basket on wheels! What for are there nursemaids? I pray Rosie not see and tell all village." Rosie was her maid-of-all-work.

Ralph was unabashed. "I will gain a reputation for eccentricity among the populace."

"But we are to meet gentry. Señora Hammond has sent invitation to Sir Ralph and Lady Barnet of Sheradon Grange. We are nobility. Eccentric? No!" Then she turned to Lily. "I have place for you – sunshine and no wind. Come and see."

She took her arm and walked her round to the east side of the house. Dee followed, irritated. She had not examined their new porch after the workmen had left, feeling that this side was all foreign territory. Now she saw that not only was the entrance as grand as the main doorway but a bower of trelliswork had been constructed on the edge of the trees, facing south and fitted with a bench. Flower beds with freshly planted geraniums graced it on both sides.

"See," cried Sophia, "the perfect shelter." There were already two cushions on the bench, and Sophia sat down, saying, "Not custom of Spanish ladies sit in sun, but I make Lily company."

Dee raised her eyebrows at Lily with a smile and slipped away. On the front lawn she saw that Ralph had brought out two of her kitchen chairs and set them next to the baby carriage. He motioned her to sit.

"I like the breeze, Mother, if you do."

"I do, but I was interested in how you have transformed that side of the house. It was a wilderness before."

"Do you mind? Sophia rather took over and gave orders I hadn't authorised."

Dee was glad to speak openly of the work. "No, Ralph, I chose our rooms, and your home is the east part of the house partitioned off, and the attic floor, which we don't need, is perfect for the twins and their nurse."

"And cook has a room there, and Sophia wishes to send for a Spanish manservant from Galicia. Can you bear so many in your house?"

She laughed. "At least Rosie goes home to the village in the evening. No, if you can afford it and Sophia needs a larger household, that is right and proper." She thought, *I* am spared the drudgery Mrs Hammond predicted. If only we can all live in harmony...

He sighed. "Mother, I know you do not care for my choice of wife." She was startled and began to protest. He pressed on, "I once said I wanted a wife like you." She felt her face flush and covered her cheeks with her hands. He smiled. "I did. All my life I observed your character from the outside: your capability, quick-thinking, capacity for love – yes, I saw that – your dislike of idleness and your indifference to rank." Overwhelmed, Dee held up her hands, but his words were pent up and must be spoken. "Mother, I want you to understand. I didn't *choose* Sophia. I might say she thrust herself upon me. I was young, she was beautiful, an orphan, and she all but worshipped me. I responded with passion, but I didn't *know* her. You think she looks down on you all, but I will say this for her. In Spain she knew her place in society. She was at ease. North East England is a strange, hurrying, thrusting place of new wealth from coal mines, iron and steel, steam engines, railways. I gather that Galicia, with its fine old town of Santiago de Compostela, is very peaceful and beautiful."

She broke in to ask, "Did you not go there the time the twins were born?"

"No, we stayed in Madrid. Sophia wouldn't take me till the lawyers had settled her ownership. Some of her family tried to claim that by marrying an Englishman and living here she forfeited her right to the place, but she has now heard from a cousin that Mateo *will* inherit his grandfather's title."

"The cousin who thought to marry her?"

He gave a snort of a laugh. "An arrangement between their people. He's older. He wanted to get his hands on the estate. He resented me, of course, but he put an apartment he owned at our disposal. We were the couple in favour with the king."

Dee leaned forward, moved by his frankness, and dared to ask the question uppermost in her mind. "Does Sophia want to go back now and live on the estate?"

His brows drew together, and she guessed it was his hidden worry too. "Not yet, I trust. Spain is unsettled. She sees Sheradon Grange as an oasis in this vale of industry. But it troubles me that I gave you this house and have now snatched back more than half of it to fulfil her vision of me."

"But I was happy to see you with your new babies and have Mateo back. The house is big enough."

"And you thought we could live as one family, including Frank and Lily when they were ready to join us."

"I was wrong. I see a condesa shouldn't have to live with Jack from the local pit, or Lily the daughter of a pie-shopkeeper."

He spread his hands. "You see, you *do* think of her as a snob."

She shook her head vigorously. "No, I am at last trying to put myself in her shoes. There is only one thing I would like to change in our household." He looked at her with wary eyes. "The connecting door from your drawing room to our front hall. I never lock it from our side. Indeed, there is no bolt—"

"And she asked Jack to put one our side. I'll see it removed."

"Nay, be not so hasty." The subject was delicate. "Sophia feels more comfortable with it, and I am happy that when she wants to walk through she can at any time." He was looking at her with a puzzled frown, so she finished quickly, "I just don't want you two to quarrel about it."

He bit his lip. "You and Jack never quarrel."

"No one can quarrel with Jack." She thought, We are being very honest with each other and I will press home another point. "I can tell you, though, that it irritates me when he says 'Lady Sophia wants the carriage tomorrow so I'll just give it a good clean'. I want to tell him he is not the general handyman, but he is so happy that I swallow my words and love him all the more for his humility."

Ralph bowed his head into his hands. "I am guilty too. I let him rub down my horse, Zephyr, when I ride back from Newcastle. That must change."

"No, he loves horses. He has a relationship with them which is precious and which he cannot have with a human being."

She turned John's basket. A sunbeam had lit his closed eyes, and he squirmed in his sleep.

Ralph was squirming too, she was sure. He looked up. "Guido will come to be our handyman, but you must have your own maid. When do you have time to write? Sophia admires your diligence but is puzzled too. You were not in the kitchen when you grew up here."

"Ah, but I have been longer as a North Country housewife than I was as the pampered daughter of the mansion. And, thank God, dear Grandfather encouraged Bessie to teach me all her housewifely skills and always said that happiness lay in purposeful work. I can plan a big novel while I work. I am happy, but do not want you running off to Spain for Mateo to be a count."

He shook his head. "We may make the occasional visit to Galicia, but now that Sophia is satisfied about Mateo's inheritance, she is more settled. I never wanted her to lock the door on you all, but I will try to show her we are one family. She finds it so hard to understand how we all fit together." He laughed uneasily.

She looked him straight in the eye. "Is that not because you never told her the whole truth about yourself and your family? There are lies between us."

He clasped his hands and pressed his thumbs against his lips. "But, Mother, you must see that the tale I told Sophia was the only one possible at the time."

"No, I don't see it. I have learned, bitterly, that the truth is the only right course. For over twenty years I lived a lie, and the consequences were horrible."

72

"You think if you had told Jack you were with child that he would still have married you?"

"I'm sure he would. I needed his love, and nothing like that had ever happened to him before. It would have been hard with his family, but they were good-hearted and would have been sorry for me."

"And do you think you might have loved *me* then?"

"With their support and no lie looming when I looked at you, I am sure I would."

He gave a great sigh. "Well, let me tell you how it was for me when Sophia came into my life. I was wearying of the sea and fighting on that day when I dived in to save a drowning woman. I had satisfied my hunger to be a leader of men. I wanted more in life. I suppose it was love." She saw he was red and perspiring. "On the voyage back, Sophia showered me with her love and gratitude. It was when we reached Madrid that I realised she had been the belle of the Spanish court, and they were overjoyed to make a hero of me. Poets made ballads about us. She saw me as the wild son of a baronet with an ancestral home back in England. How could I admit I had once been a miner? Indeed, I had shut it from my mind."

She had to ask, "But you kept in touch with Aunt Sarah?"

"Yes, she meant secure wealth one day, but I had made a small fortune already and that made Sophia's family willing for me to have her. They had land but not ready money."

"When did you start thinking about home?"

"Not home. You. And not till Mateo was born. I held this child and it was like an earthquake inside me." He broke off, struggling with tears. She laid a hand on his arm.

"And you wanted *me* to love him. That is my great joy. It is all clear to me now. I know that Sarah's lawyers wrote to you of her death, and that you were her heir and this house was for sale. Sophia believes your father and I lived here and when he died I inexplicably married Jack. So it is your ancestral home restored to you. But I still say good does not come of lies. You know it from your sufferings as a child." She swallowed and put the question she had long wanted to ask him. "Can you ever forgive me for my lack of love? Be honest."

"Oh." She could see the question disturbed him further. "I see the love Mateo needs. I am strict, but he knows it is out of love. Sophia pets him like a baby."

"I have seen that and wondered why, now that she has twin girls."

"Nurse has them while they are still toddling and wetting themselves. Sophia will enjoy them when they become young madams to dress up and teach to be ladies. I love them at a distance, but not as I love Mateo."

"So you will never be able to forgive me for the love I failed to give you?"

He leaned towards her, his eyes very bright. "Mother, we are building a new love with our new selves. Before I went away all those years ago, I had a moment when I thought it was possible *then*, but I had to make something of myself in the world's eyes. Coming back here – to you – has shaken me up. I need your love and wisdom."

She thought, He has lost the bravado we saw at first and I ache with love for him now. I could sit here with him for ever. There is so much to say.

"I have a well of love to give you now, Ralph, but no wisdom in business. I was too young to understand why my father failed. Mother was extravagant, but he was reckless. You have spent lavishly in a spirit of generosity, and must be careful now. Frank pays for the west wing expenses, so I need no more rent from you."

He moved his hands in a negative gesture. "It's your house. I wish only to be here with my family. When Frank said we could start again as Frank and Ralph, I rejoiced. I have put away for ever the Francis I loathed all my childhood." He looked up into the trees behind the house and went on with an effort. "If we are speaking of forgiveness, I need to be sure that he has forgiven me." He drew his eyes back to hers.

She said quickly, "Frank never thinks of it, and I forgave you years ago. It has been harder to forgive myself for being the original cause."

"What about the daughter you should have had when I knocked you down and caused you to miscarry? I find it hard to forgive myself for that."

She smiled wistfully. "You didn't know I was with child. But now I have a daughter in Lily – and in Sophia, if I can draw close to her."

Hearing voices, she turned and saw Sophia, with her arm tucked under Lily's elbow, coming round the corner of the house.

"So much more to say, Mother," he murmured, standing up.

Sophia said, "Lily worried John too hot."

Dee had paid scant attention to the baby since they had sat down. He had kicked off his blanket and his arms were flung wide, but he looked serene.

Lily said, "All is well. It is not so hot here with that breeze." She looked at him with adoration. "He is so peaceful. It is at night that he is wakeful."

Sophia gave a little laugh. "So Mateo tell us. Crying keep him awake. He asleep now daytime. Not good."

"I'm so sorry," Lily said.

Ralph turned abruptly on his heel. "I'll fetch him out."

He went round to their own entrance and Dee heard him pounding up the new flight of stairs, which were polished, not carpeted. When they didn't appear, she supposed they had gone out the back door. Perhaps Ralph was avoiding Sophia.

Sophia said, "Lily and I have so sweet talk. She wish advice from experienced mother. Now he want feeding. He toss and turn. Eyes open and then mouth. Mamma, I hungry." She laughed as the pathetic wailing began, then waved a hand and retuned to her own door.

Lily said as they wheeled John inside, "I didn't *ask* for advice, Mother Dee. She leaves *her* babies to the nurse. Still, she meant it kindly."

Dee thought, I must learn patience from this dear girl, for I was quite incensed at the break-up of my time with Ralph.

He came again later that afternoon. She was at the tub, washing some of John's little gowns while Lily was resting.

He looked round to make sure they were alone. "Mother, come and sit down. I must tell you what happened with Mateo."

She was eager to hear but said, "Stand there and I will go on working."

"Oh, very well." He leaned his elbows on the mangle and peered at her face. "Mateo was *not* asleep. He was lying on the floor reading *Gulliver's Travels*. I hauled him out and said we'd go in the woods and split logs for the fire. I dread him being a weakling, and told him so. We found Jack in the tool shed and his smile restored Mateo's good humour, and he told him he was going to chop hundreds of logs. Of course, Jack pointed out we don't need so many in hot weather, but Mateo said he had to get big and strong like me. Then what do you think Jack did?"

"Gave you the saw and the axe, I suppose." She filled up the tub with fresh water from the jug.

"Yes, he did, but first he playfully squeezed Mateo's arm and said, 'I mind a day that I felt your da's arm, same age as you, when he come up from the pit and his muscle was that hard.' Those were his words."

"Oh Ralph." She faced him. "Did Mateo question him?"

"Of course he did. 'What pit? They call coal mines pits round here.' I hustled him out and we climbed up into the wood. But he wanted an answer and I longed to be honest after all you said. Then I thought if he told Sophia she would hate you for letting me go down a mine – even though I seemed desperate to do it."

"Oh let her hate me. Was that the only reason for a lie?"

He shook his head. "You know it wasn't. She would feel she had married an imposter, and perhaps I had never been the son of a baronet and she had dragged her family's name through the dust. Oh Mother, I just said it *was* a coal mine and in those days boys were allowed down to see what it was like."

"How did he take that?"

"He said *he'd* be too frightened, so I said it wasn't permitted now, so we cut firewood and had a splendid afternoon. I pray he's forgotten all about it."

"Have you never feared that village gossip might reach your new family?"

He stroked his beard. "I hoped this was my disguise. I did fear what Mateo might pick up if he went to school here. That's why I'm teaching him myself. When he is older I hope to send him to the ancient Grammar School in Newcastle, where he will meet no one who knew us. Had you asked Jack to be careful what he said?"

"I told him on Frank's wedding day that we don't speak of the past, but it would just slip out. You see how lies ensnare us."

He gulped. "Maybe I should never have come back here."

She moved his elbows from the mangle and pushed a bunch of the clothes through it with one hand while turning the handle.

He watched her. "You are disappointed in me now. *You* survived the truth, though living where you were known. Could I survive it? Would my marriage fail?"

Concentrating on the mangle, she said, "Do you not hold the purse strings?"

He thought for a moment. "You're right, Mother. She still needs me."

She squeezed out the clothes and laid them on the bench.

"I survived because the local people learned the truth through my very public revelation at Francis's trial. They judged me – some favourably, others not, but time passed. Your return at Frank's wedding revived memories, but you had made a fortune and are putting it to good use. You have nothing to fear from those who *know* the truth. It is when your family mingle in the community that they may hear of a story which may shock and surprise them. To save yourself from *that* fear, tell *them* the truth."

"But Sophia will despise me and never trust me again."

"If there is love between you, she will be glad to be entrusted with the truth."

He stroked his chin. *Does* he love her, she wondered, now that he *knows* her?

"Would *you* tell her?" he asked.

She considered this. "I wish to seek a new intimacy with her, but it would have to come from you first. Tell her that I would like her to know more of my life."

He chewed his thumbnail. "It must be done quickly. This evening. Will you come and dine tonight? On your own. Can you manage that? After the children are in bed. Will Jack think it odd?"

"I will tell him the truth. That his word to Mateo excited curiosity and I want to explain it all to Sophia. He has Frank for company when Lily is feeding John."

He bent to embrace her. "I'll do it, but I am jeopardising everything – the life I have built up here, my status with my son and my marriage."

Evidently Sophia agreed, because he came back quickly. "She says 'yes, but not Jack'. She will try to talk to you about Spain, but we will turn the talk around. She would like to present you with a Spanish dish, but cook is making leek and mutton pie tonight." He mopped his brow. The late afternoon was quite cool, but Dee saw he was in a sweat of fear over what the evening might bring.

In the event, Dee felt it was a wasted effort.

She tried to comment in the most natural way on her memories of the dining room. "I can see Ralph's father sitting opposite me at my sixteenth birthday party. He was so handsome. I was to marry him at eighteen."

Sophia sighed. "Ah, I presented at court at sixteen. Many suitors! But the king send my papa to Puerto Rico and we go too. Many suitors there but I no like."

Ralph said, "I'd like you to hear *Mother's* memories. Some of what I told you was inaccurate."

Sophia spread out her hands towards her. "I guess picture not so pretty, my dear Dee, but it is all over and you happy now. You have your house."

"Yes, and I lost it through my father's foolish investments. I never thought to regain it through my elder son's wealth. But it was the loss that made his father desert me *before* our wedding."

"Oh, Ralph so clever. He make money grow like oranges on our trees in Spain." And she blew him a kiss.

Ralph said, "Mother is saying that my father never actually *married* her."

She brushed it aside. "It is all past. Why you want to tell me these things? You not eating cook's pie. Ah, Dee, you no idea how I miss Spanish food."

Ralph persisted. "I'd like to tell you I once worked in a coal mine."

She put her hands over her ears. "Why you spoil dinner party with this talk? Poverty so horrid. Ralph is come back to you, Dee. There is wealth for all of us. You happy grandmother. Two grandsons, two granddaughters."

Ralph gave his mother a despairing look. Dee suspected Sophia had taken several glasses of wine already to prime herself for this encounter.

She began to speak of Mateo. "He will be Spanish count and English baronet and *rich!*" She clapped her hands. "Oh, he will be great man. And news from Spain better. I have another letter from Juan. Carlos rebellion doomed. General Espartero have bigger army. We go back when no more fighting."

"My work is here," Ralph snapped. "I need to watch my new investments."

"What for are there lawyers? You pay them. They watch." She forked up a piece of leek and mutton pie. "Food for pigs!"

Ralph made no more attempts to bring up the past. They moved into the drawing room and Rosie brought in a tray of tea. Dee drank one cup and rose to take her leave. She kissed Sophia, who arched her brows.

"Goodnight, my dear, and thank you for inviting me."

Ralph drew the curtain that hung over the connecting door and ushered her through. He whispered, "I'm so sorry. I despair of her. She cares only for money and status."

Dee mouthed back, "Don't give up. She is homesick and needs the comfort of wealth. Between us all we will show her a better way. Love."

She heard Ralph sigh and close the door behind her, and Sophia called out, "Shoot the bolt."

Dee stopped to listen to Ralph's reply. "We are one family, woman!"

She hurried back to Jack in the kitchen.

Chapter 8

Newcastle upon Tyne, June 1840
(four years later)

Frank

Frank clicked open the gate and walked up to a green door that had once been very familiar to him: the home of his old headmaster, Edmund Hurst. The school was next door – two Georgian houses knocked together. He looked up at it, recalling his first day there, when he had been both excited and terrified.

Mr Hurst opened the door before Frank reached it.

"Saw you from the parlour window. How are you, Frank? Come in."

Mr Hurst still wore his hair onto his shoulders, which was odd for a man in his sixties, but he carried his height well, with a straight back and flamboyant air.

They went into the parlour and Mrs Hurst blew in with a tray of cups and a coffee jug. Frank hadn't seen her since his wedding, and she didn't look a day older.

"Welcome, Frank. I won't stay. I'm making pastries for my sewing class."

"Pastries for a sewing class?"

Mr Hurst laughed. "They're hungry. Daughters of the very poor. Isobel is giving them a skill so they can earn extra pennies. Were you in town last summer when we had the riots? Many men lost their jobs, and the families were starving."

"No, I've been working down the Tyne Valley railway line on bridges and culverts, but Ralph was in Newcastle and saw some of the demonstrations."

"Ralph? That was the erstwhile Billy? Brotherly harmony now?"

"Yes, sir, there is. More so than our sons, I'm afraid. I need some advice about them. If you could come to their birthday celebrations...? And Mrs Hurst, of course. Mateo is twelve and John four."

"Not ages where you would expect much harmony."

"That's true, but I hoped Mateo might be an older brother to John. The doctor said Lily can't have more children, and I was glad to have a family with us. There are twin girls, nearly six, but Mateo shields them from John, who is too rough."

"You intrigue me. I shall come, but isn't Mateo at school most of the time?"

"No, sir. Ralph has taught him at home, but now thinks he needs school to get him away from Sophia. She comes of Spanish nobility and might tolerate tutors but she pets Mateo and keeps him close."

"As your mother did to you, if I remember correctly. You were the most shy and nervous child I ever had when she sent you to my little school in the village. She took you away again because I frightened you, but she let you come as a youth of – how old? – when I opened up next door with senior pupils."

"I was fourteen, sir, and just as nervous, but you won me over the first day and I never looked back. That's what Ralph knows Mateo needs – a new world opened up to him, away from the nursery of his little sisters."

"And will John also benefit from schooling?"

"I think so. Lily tries to control him, but he's too strong-willed for her. He behaves well with my mother."

"Ah, the formidable Dee Heron. I will never forget her outburst at your trial. Does she run the whole household at Sheradon Grange? No, don't answer that. Drink your coffee. I will come to the birthday party and judge for myself."

"Will you travel by train, sir?"

Mr Hurst held up his hands in mock horror. "I will ride, Frank, in God's good air. No choking smoke or hard seats and rattling noise."

"Will Mrs Hurst come?"

She declined when she knew the day. "My sewing girls." She looked Frank up and down. "You have a four-year-old son and still seem a mere youth yourself!"

Frank ran his hands through his fair curls, not sure if this was a compliment or not. She laughed and scuttled back to her pastries.

Mr Hurst remarked, "Well, *Billy* had certainly changed when I saw him on your wedding day. I must remember to address him as Sir Ralph. I am curious to see this large family together."

"We do live in separate parts of the house, but the plan is for a picnic outside if the weather is fine."

Mr Hurst agreed to assess the two boys, and they chatted for a while about the depression and the state of the Reform Bill. Then Mr Hurst rose.

"I must go next door to take a senior science class. Isobel wants me to retire from the school, but, damn it all, I built it up from nothing and love the work."

Frank walked round to the livery stable where he had left his horse. He thought how pleasant the Hursts were. At Sheradon Grange the atmosphere could prickle with animosity between Ralph and Sophia.

The birthday dawned hazy, with the prospect of a hot day to come. Frank was setting chairs on the front lawn when Ralph sauntered round from the east door.

"Sophia would like us all to picnic in her arbour, as she calls it. She has ordered a new contraption, an iron frame with a swinging seat on which three people can sit, and she expects it to be brought and set up today."

Ralph's tone of voice, Frank noticed, was carefully neutral, so he refrained from any comment, except to say, "It gets mighty hot round there. Ha! This may be your contraption." The sound of hooves and creaking wheels came from the drive.

Ralph abandoned neutrality. "God, it's not *my* contraption."

Two horses drawing a heavy cart appeared where the drive swept round the bank side. An old sailcloth covered the burden on top and three workmen sat round it, keeping it from shifting on the bend. Ralph directed them to pass the front of the house to the paved area at the east side, where the thing was to go.

Frank heard the excited voices of Sophia and her children as they emerged from their front door. Ralph was engaged with the men, so Frank went back into their kitchen, where John was watching his mother and grandmother make stotty cakes.

"Has somebody come?" Lily asked. "We heard wheels."

"Something Sophia has ordered for our picnic."

His mother looked round. "Not more food, I hope."

"No, to sit on. Or perhaps swing on."

"A swing!" John leapt up and rushed to the door. Frank checked him there.

"Men are setting it up. Don't get in their way."

John moved like lightning, his blonde hair catching a sunbeam as he emerged into the bright hallway and out by the open door. Frank followed and found him held by Ralph's arms, with Mateo and the little girls in a line behind Sophia's seat.

Frank approached with a little bow. "Good morning, Sophia. Do you mind us watching? John heard the word 'swing'. And I am curious about all artefacts."

Sophia gave a gracious gesture and Frank took up a position next to his brother. Ralph released John to him, but in that second of freedom John rushed over to the cart as the men were lifting off the tall V-shaped support for the iron structure. Frank leapt after him, but one of the men, startled, let go of his end and dropped it on his own foot. He hopped around clutching it as the other man lowered his end and John looked up at his father, half ashamed, half giggling.

Frank dragged him back. "Now see what you've done."

"You get a beating," cried Sophia. "Wicked boy."

The man had sat down and was pulling his boot off.

"Me toe's broke. I'll swear me toe's broke."

Ralph went over to look at his foot as he warily drew off his knitted stockings and exposed grubby toes. The big one was already swelling. Ralph felt it.

"It's not broken, but you'll have a great bruise soon. If you can hobble into the kitchen, we have an ice box and I'll put some on it quickly."

Sophia looked round at the children. "See, your papa can turn his hand to anything. He learned to treat wounds when he was at sea. But now," glaring at John, "we shan't have our swing for the party."

Frank said, "*I'll* help set it up. John, you stand next to Mateo and don't move an inch. Your punishment will come later."

John, a little subdued, looked up at Mateo. "I won't get beaten. My father doesn't beat me."

Mateo said nothing. One of the twins – Frank could never tell them apart – said, "Matty's hardly ever naughty. Not like you."

Frank, fearing this day was doomed from the start, rolled up his sleeves and joined the other men, who had been lifting more parts from the cart.

The man who had muscles like tree trunks looked at Frank's slender form with some dismay. "Are you sure, sir?"

Frank bent down and lifted one end of the piece that had fallen. "Come on, man." They set to work.

Frank enjoyed the next two hours, oblivious of the comings and goings of the family. The limping man came back when he could put his boot on again.

"That ice was a wonder. I reckon I can help now, sir." But Frank told him to lie on the grass and rest the foot.

When the work was complete, he and the two workmen sat on the seat and swung gently to test it. It was then that he noticed John had disappeared.

"Where's John?"

One of the little girls said, "He went to see if the stotty cakes were baked."

Mateo said, "I've just been there, and he wasn't."

"He'll be in the stables with Jack," Ralph said. "Is it safe for the children to try the swing now?"

Frank nodded, but Sophia rose, fanning herself. "I first. My idea. My swing."

She swept the seat with a clean duster and lowered herself onto it, lifting her feet off the ground and propelling herself gently backwards.

"Ah, so good! Ralph, this soothe my nerves." She rocked forwards, pointing her feet up. "The children may try it, but it for me, their mother."

Ralph sent the men to the kitchen for mugs of ale.

Frank left the family to it and went to wash himself, ready for the luncheon party and Mr Hurst's arrival, expected at noon. His father would be on the way to the station to fetch Tom and Jenny, coming by train.

In the kitchen he asked his mother, "Did John go with Da to the station?"

Lily looked up from a display of fruit she was preparing.

"No. Wasn't he watching the work all the time? Your mother and I have been too busy to go and look."

"He'll be hiding somewhere." Frank, with some apprehension, went over their house and then ran round to the east side, where Ralph was lifting the girls onto the swing, one each side of Mateo.

"Has John been round here again?"

Sophia shook her head. "He bad boy. Ralph give man five shillings for his wounded toe. Five shillings!"

Ralph joined Frank. "I'm sorry. She's just trying to make you feel ashamed of John. I'll help you look for him. I'll go east, you go west."

Frank headed across the lawn to the belt of trees and shrubbery that lined the western wall. John was a compulsive climber. From babyhood, as soon as he could crawl, he could climb stairs. Throughout his four years, Frank had felt the inner force of the child and a fear that he and Lily would never be able to contain him.

He met Ralph back in the kitchen, where everything was laid out on trays ready for the party. They shook their heads at each other.

"You haven't found him?" Lily was in tears.

Frank saw his mother take off her apron and adjust the lace collar of her dress. She pointed to the clock, which said quarter to twelve.

"Your parents will be here any minute, Lily, and Mr Hurst at noon."

"But where's John? Sophia scolded him and he's run away."

"He's tougher than that. He'll be back. Let's go outside to welcome our guests."

"He's only four," Lily sobbed, but they all went to the front door and heard the sound of hooves and carriage wheels.

"It's Da and Ma," Lily cried, and round the bend they came, waving. Frank saw them looking all about as Sophia and the children appeared from her arbour.

"John's not come to greet us!" Jenny cried as Jack helped her down.

"Oh Ma!" Lily hugged her, sniffling. "We can't find him anywhere."

Tom jumped down. "Nonsense! A little tot like that can hide in a maze of a place like this. He'll not miss his birthday. He'll get hungry. And I'm gasping for a mug of ale." He picked out Mateo. "Your birthday too, eh, lad? Twelve, is it? You've got a fair bit of growing to do. Greetings, your ladyship, and Sir Ralph." He shook his hand and gave a mock bow to the twins. "Lead me to the drinks, Frank, and Dee, I can smell your stotty cakes from here."

Jenny was already at the front door yelling, "John, come on, show yourself. Granda and Gramma are here. We're going to eat all the food."

A few minutes later they heard another horse approaching down the drive.

This'll be Mr Hurst, thought Frank, and I'm with Lily in sick apprehension about John. Where the hell can he be?

Everyone, including the Bateys, gathered to see the new arrival. Mr Hurst's hat was first seen above the bushes on the corner, and then he was in view and trotting towards them.

There was a concerted gasp and cries of joy. Perched in front of him, and grinning from ear to ear, sat John.

Their instinctive surge forward was checked by Mr Hurst's raised arm.

"The mare is nervous." He patted her neck. "Greetings to you all. Frank, step forward slowly if you want something I found on the way. I believe it's yours."

Frank, breathing great gulps of relief, approached cautiously. Mr Hurst lowered John into his arms, where he instantly wriggled to be set on the ground.

"I've come back for the party. It's exactly twelve o'clock, isn't it?"

Outraged noises came from Sophia, but they were lost in the cries of Lily as she took John in her arms and buried her face in his curls.

Tom Batey already had a mug of ale in his hand. "I said he'd come back."

Mr Hurst dismounted, and Frank saw his father, in his role of ostler, hurrying back to take charge of the mare. Mr Hurst shook his hand.

"Good day, Mr Heron. I thank you. She'll drink your well dry, I'm afraid."

"Ay, and you'll be gasping yourself, sir. May I ask where you found the wee lad? They've been all over seeking him."

John pulled from Lily's arms. "I was coming back from the village," he announced to the company. "He" – pointing to Mr Hurst – "stopped, so I asked him the time and told him I had to be home for my birthday party at twelve. Then he said was I John Heron, so he gave me a ride."

"You're a pickle," cried Jenny. "Your Granda and Gramma came in a great puffing train to see you and you weren't here!"

"Well, I am now!"

"And where's your 'thank you' to Mr Hurst?" Frank heard his mother say in her sternest voice.

John looked up, "Thank you very much, sir."

"Or an apology to the rest of us for the worry you caused."

That was not so readily forthcoming. "I only went for a walk. Da was going to be busy for a long time. Is the swing up yet?"

"You not get on it ever, wicked boy," Sophia declared.

"Enterprising, not wicked, ma'am," Mr Hurst suggested, and Frank thought, She'll hate him for that.

"What? You a schoolmaster and approve bad behaviour of boy?"

Frank, hot with embarrassment, said, "Mr Hurst, may I present you to my sister-in-law, Lady Barnet?"

Mr Hurst bowed and kissed the hand she grudgingly offered. She beckoned her children forward. "My son, Mateo, and my daughters, Maria and Lucia."

"Delighted," he said, "and my congratulations on your twelfth birthday, young man." Mateo blushed and mumbled something.

Mr Hurst then answered her question. "John knew where he was going and when he should return, which is quite remarkable." He turned to Frank. "We have had a good conversation on the way, and I say he is indeed ready for school."

Lily put protective arms round John. "Do you think so? But oh, Mr Hurst, we cannot thank you enough for bringing him safe home to us."

Ralph shook Mr Hurst's hand. "Ralph Barnet, sir."

Yes, thought Frank, you are blotting out the existence of Billy Heron.

His mother, with an older lady's privilege, embraced Mr Hurst. "God bless you, sir. We feared John had left the grounds, but to walk three miles! What a blessing you saw him. Come in and refresh yourself from your ride."

Sophia drew herself to her full height. "And when you all ready, you find good repast laid in my rose garden." She stalked off to give orders to her servants.

Frank took Mr Hurst up to his own room, where a basin and water jug and fresh towels were ready. Mr Hurst talked of John all the way up the stairs.

"He's remarkable, Frank. Unusually articulate for just four. He knows his numbers and says he can read words in his grandmother's little books."

"Will he not be too advanced for the village school?"

"Ah, but he needs to be among boys his age and learn discipline. I gather he goes into the twins' nursery and throws things, and they go crying to their brother. He wants more than Sheradon Grange, big as it is. That's why he walked out today. He said when you go to church you come straight back. The Spanish family have been across the sea. He'd like that. You should take him further afield this summer."

"I dare say, but I have my work, and if Lily takes him alone she can't hold him. Sophia just snaps at him when he's naughty."

"A somewhat overbearing character."

"And patronising to my mother."

Mr Hurst washed his face and emerged from the towel. "No one could patronise Dee Heron. I wager she laughs to herself and carries on her own way."

"True enough. I think you have the measure of us all."

"Not Mateo yet. He's shy, of course. I will try and hold talk with him, and your brother too. Shall we go down? I smell something very appetising."

"Mother's stotty cakes warming up again."

They went down and found her carrying the tray to the rose garden, John keeping very close to her and bearing a mound of butter on a dish.

Sophia was waiting to show her guests their places. She beckoned Lily to the swing. "I'll join you there, my dear, under the canopy."

Frank grumbled to his mother, "I wish Sophia wouldn't make a fuss of her. Lily doesn't like it." He saw that the rest of his family had a bench down the other side of the table while Mateo and the twins had the seat in the bower of roses.

His mother whispered, "Her kindliness to Lily is one of her *good* qualities."

His father, with his fair mop of hair wet from standing under the pump, said, "Am I supposed to be here, angel?"

His mother nodded, her eyes brimming with loving smiles.

Jenny sat down facing Sophia. "Ee, what a big hat! That'll keep the sun off."

"Mr Hurst, you sit there." Sophia ignored Jenny and directed him to a chair at the top of the table next to Ralph. "My maid Rosie and manservant Guido serve what you ask. It not possible make all Spanish dishes I love." She spread her hands. "Not grow, not sell in north England."

"Ah, but we have stotty cakes, my lady. I'll start with them."

She smiled grimly. "Local peasant food."

Jenny said, "Your young 'uns grabbed 'em first of all."

With ham and cheese and chopped onion, and the butter swiftly melting, they were soon all gone. Jenny exclaimed, "First empty tray, your highness."

Frank nearly burst out laughing at Sophia's face, but he saw Lily shrinking smaller than ever and hardly able to nibble at anything.

The heat in this corner was intense. Conversation flagged. Frank longed for his mother's idea of the picnic spread on a cloth on the open lawn, where there might be a breeze. Mr Hurst made an effort, asking Sophia about the situation in Spain.

"Is it true that the regent, Maria Christina, is taking power into her hands from the municipalities and the more liberal element is dissatisfied with her rule?"

Frank saw her very expressive eyebrows shoot up. An English schoolmaster knowing anything of her country! But she only replied, "Liberals are always angry."

Ralph remarked, "Victoria was only eighteen when she became queen, but Isabella was an infant, younger than John, so her mother *had* to act for her. She's doing her best, but it's an unstable situation."

John said, "I'm old enough to be a king."

Laughter eased some of the awkwardness but there was general relief when, after only half an hour of the 'picnic', Ralph announced that, if anyone wanted to eat any more, they should take their plates round to the lawn.

His mother said, "Jellies and sweetmeats are on the marble bench in our kitchen. I let the fire go out and it will be cool in there."

Mr Hurst drew Mateo aside. "Can you show me a walk in the wood behind the house? It will be cool, and we may gain more appetite."

Mateo said, "Yes, sir," before his mother could forbid it, and off they went.

Sophia helped Lily down and then, fanning herself vigorously, took her girls indoors, and Frank had to check John from instantly trying to climb onto the swing.

"That's your punishment for vanishing this morning. No swing."

John flew into a rage. "It's my birthday. I didn't vanish. I went for a walk."

Lily said, "Let him have one little swing, Frank. He's been good since."

"Very small swing, then."

One of the twins came running out to pick up her doll from under the bench. Hearing the swing, she looked up.

"He wasn't allowed. Mamma said." She ran back inside calling "Mamma!"

Frank gave John two pushes and then grabbed him off and set him running to the kitchen for some jelly. Only then did he notice a dark figure in the shade of the porch. Ralph was trimming a cigar and smiling sardonically.

Frank joined him in the shade. "I know, I know, damn it. You would have been firm. Matty is afraid of you."

Ralph frowned. "Not afraid! I have to be strict. He's twelve and Sophia still coddles him. You'll have to watch Lily with John." He held out the cigar box, but Frank shook his head. Ralph looked up towards the wood. "Has Hurst taken Matty to test him like he did John?"

Frank shrugged. "Yes, it comes naturally to him. He would be at your twins but Sophia wouldn't let him near."

"Well, they're girls. She thinks too much knowledge is bad for them. That's why she's in awe of Mother and keeps her distance if the talk gets serious."

"Ah, Mr Hurst said she couldn't patronise Mother however hard she tried."

"You think he's a wise fellow? Matty must have schooling and I rather favour *his* school. I've heard talk in Newcastle that the Royal Grammar has lost reputation and pupils. Sophy likes the sound of 'Royal' but doesn't want her baby to go to school at all." He grinned at Frank. "Like Lily with John. Wives, eh?"

Frank didn't smile. Lily in the same category as Sophia! Ralph speaks of his wife with active dislike, he was thinking. Lily may be too lenient with John, but I love her for that very sweetness.

"John will start in September. Lily knows he should."

"And I must get Matty away from Sophy or she'll ruin him. God knows I don't want to lose him but he's too nervous and diffident. His true character has no chance to develop."

They walked round the house to the lawn, where the others were sprawled with bowls of jelly and little tarts, enjoying the breeze. Lily had joined her mother and was laughing at news of her sisters' families. Frank thought how animated she looked. On the swing she had been tense and silent.

When Mr Hurst and Mateo came back, Sophia brought her girls out again, and Mr Hurst found a ball and put Mateo in charge of organising a game. John took over at once. "Stand in a square and throw it, and the first one who drops it is out."

One of the twins snapped at him, "*Matty* has to say."

The other said, "Let's try it, Lu. Come on."

Ah, thought Frank, that's Maria. Can I distinguish them at last? Lucia is the one who wanted to tell tales. He was amused to see that Maria was the best catcher and therefore the last one out.

"Hey," John said, "you're good. Show me how you do it."

Frank whispered to Lily, "A pleasing sign." She nodded.

When they were all tired, his mother offered to read *Edward the Elephant* to the three young ones.

Mateo walked over to sit down behind his sisters. "May I hear it too?"

"My darling boy, of course, but it has no exciting adventures."

"I don't mind that. I like the way you show the moral at the end."

"Well, that's the best compliment I've ever had." She gave him her special smile and began to read.

Frank saw Sophia wave airily to the guests. "I retire now – quite overcome."

Mr Hurst bowed to her and strolled away across the lawn with Ralph.

He's reporting on Mateo, Frank thought. I hope he'll have him in his school but there'll be battles ahead.

When they came back and the story was finished, Jenny suddenly screamed, "Ee, we mustn't miss our train. Jack, bring the carriage round!"

Mr Hurst said he must take his leave too, and Frank fetched his horse.

Tom said, "Now, Lil, this has been fun with the grand folk, but you must bring John to us while the weather's fine. He scarce knows his cousins on our side."

John jumped up and down. "In the train, yes!"

Lily looked at Frank, who thought, If John is engrossed in a new experience he won't give Lily any trouble, so he nodded.

When the last hoof sound had faded, Ralph came over to Frank.

"You said Mateo was afraid of me. Hurst thinks it's his *idea* of me. Sophia so exaggerates my prowess he can never live up to my standards, which is rubbish. I like Hurst. He's honest and perceptive. He'll have Mateo in September to board during the week – for a fee, of course. I'll miss him, but I'm devilishly busy just now. Sophia can say what she likes. And will Lily dare to go on a train alone with John?"

"She'll have to. *I* have work, too."

Ralph smiled as they walked back while the women began the clearing up.

Chapter 9

June–September 1840

Dee

It was a wearing summer. Ralph refused to listen to Sophia's arguments and Dee could hear her sometimes pleading, sometimes screaming at him. He kept a bed in his office in Heron Mansions and began to spend the night there when he had board meetings. Mateo took refuge with Dee.

"I know I should go to school, Grandmamma. I'd never see you if we lived in Spain. But I'm frightened. Mr Hurst said new pupils give a talk to the school about themselves the first day. How can I do that?"

She laughed and hugged him. "Five nervous minutes and it'll be over. You will blossom there. Your Uncle Frank did. And your Papa has met Mrs Hurst, who is a very easy, friendly lady. Truly, he just wants you to grow up. He loves you deeply and it's hard to let you go."

He nodded solemnly. "I love him very much, only I'd like more time alone with him." And less time with your mother, she thought.

He was near to tears, and slipped away to hide them.

"Take Matty with you," she said to Lily, "when you go to North Shields. It'll be a distraction for him, and he can help you manage John on the train."

Lily reported that John bought the tickets and looked after the return halves. "Mateo was very polite to Da and Ma and carried things, but he was just quiet the whole time. John, of course, never stopped talking. He told Pa and Ma that his Aunt Sophia called his Grandpa Jack a 'litrat pheasant' and he wondered what that was. Did she mean 'illiterate peasant'? I've explained to him that his grandfather sees letters jumbled up so he's stopped trying to teach him himself."

They had a little chuckle about John, but Mateo was never far from Dee's anxious mind.

Not feeling much sympathy for Sophia, Dee was not pleased when she came to her study on the day she was at last planning her novel.

Without preliminaries she complained, "Ralph neglect me. He think I only want him make money."

Dee looked up at her flushed face. "But, my dear, if you want his love, don't oppose him about school for Matty."

Sophia threw up her hands. "Ah, you don't understand. I – how you say – homesick."

And she went, leaving the door open. Dee soon heard the squeaking sound as she soothed herself on the swing.

It was a rare wet day when she came again without knocking and drew up a chair beside her. Ralph was to be another night in Newcastle. Dee was sure she had been weeping, though much cream and powder had been applied.

"No one here love my country," she began. "You and Frank and Lily not. Why should you? But Ralph not, yet he marry me. And now Mateo to have English school, and twins forget Spain. Santiago de Compostela fine city. Newcastle – pah! Cousin Juan tell me our family estate wait for us now. The Castillo de Villena." She hugged herself and repeated the words in a voice full of emotion.

Dee sat back and closed her notebook. "I am sorry if you are unhappy, Sophia, but I am glad you have agreed about school for Mateo."

Sophia waved that aside. "Unhappy. That is word. I am flower in wrong place."

"You have your Spanish household with Nurse and your manservant Guido. You hear Spanish spoken?"

"Ralph say Nurse and Guido to learn English. They no like."

"Well, you are settled here. You have an English husband who loves you, and English friends."

Dee was probing for the denial, which came at once.

"He love me? And what friends?"

"You are on visiting terms with Mrs Hammond's circle and the Catholic families from your church."

"They are nobodies. They not know who I am. None of them know Spain. Nothing beyond Tyne Valley."

Dee looked down at her notebook. She said, "Sophia, it is a wet and gloomy day, and you are in low spirits. Why not play a game with your children and cheer yourself up?"

"Mateo read, read all the time. Nurse is with twins."

"They are six and do not need a nurse. They want *your* attention. Maria came to me lately and asked how to make stotty cakes so I showed her, but she said your cook wouldn't let her try in *your* kitchen."

"No indeed, we have servant do cooking." She got up abruptly. "You and I, Mistress Heron, are in different worlds. We not think same at all. I sorry I came."

"Oh please, Sophia, call me Mother Dee, as Lily does. We have led different lives but are both mothers of families."

Sophia looked down at her and then out of the window, where Jack was scraping up weeds round the foot of the stable wall. She shook her head. "I not understand your marriage." Still shaking her head, she walked out.

Dee was cross with herself. I should have found a way to talk with her. Has Ralph ceased to love her? She is still handsome when she is smiling and gracious.

All too quickly the days drew in towards September, when the boys were to start school. Sophia came no more to seek Dee.

One morning Dee was delighted to find Ralph staying at home and setting off for a walk with Mateo. She was tending her vegetable patch when they returned, and Ralph came straight to her while Mateo ran round to the swing, where he could hear his mother rocking herself. Jack had driven Lily and John to the station and Frank was out at work, so Dee welcomed time with Ralph. She stood up with the garden fork in her hand and faced him. He looked flushed and agitated.

"I've done what you wanted, Mother. I've told Mateo the truth – that I worked down a mine and was born out of wedlock."

She dropped the fork and clasped him by the arms. "My brave boy! How did he take it? He has run straight to Sophia."

"Oh, he knows I told her all that years ago and she wouldn't listen. If he tells her again she'll brush it away. She is happy as long as I am rich Sir Ralph Barnet."

"Do you think so?" A shiver of apprehension chilled her. He has noted none of the signs of hurt love that I have seen. She is raw and all too alert now. But it has upset him, the telling. I have never seen him so shaken.

"But Matty…" He choked on the name.

There was a bench by the stable wall. She drew him to it and sat him down.

"Tell me."

"Have I destroyed myself in his eyes? I love him so much. Have I crashed from the pedestal his wretched mother built up? He was tense, excited."

"Excited that his father was confiding in him, man to man. Honoured."

His eyes searched hers for reassurance. He drew a long breath. "You think that's what it was?"

She pressed his clasped hands. "I am sure of it. He has longed to be closer to you. He told me."

"Did he?" He brightened. "He did thank me."

"There you are." She was curious, though. "But how was it, speaking of the pit again?"

He shook his head with a lopsided smile. "Hacking coal happened to another person. I now *own* a mining company. Indeed, that distant time belonged to two other people, for *you* are a different person to me now. You are my rock."

He put his arm round her with a little squeeze.

She felt tears rising. "But what will my precious Matty think of *me* now? I let you be a pit boy. And I had an illegitimate child."

"I don't believe he grasped 'illegitimate', but I told him I *wanted* to go down the pit like other boys, and when I hated some of it I was too proud to admit it."

"He'll admire you more than ever."

"Really? Do I want that? *She* distanced me from him by her silly praise. Mr Hurst noticed that. I wanted to get closer to him through the truth – as you said."

"And you have. He may still feel awe, but with love, not fear. Did you put courage in him for school?"

"I told him to work hard and never fear the unexpected but use it to strengthen himself, body and soul."

She returned his hug. It was easy to hug the man Ralph coming to her open-hearted, when it had been impossible to hug the surly boy Billy.

A thought struck her, and she drew back to look into his eyes. "Did you tell the tale of you and your brother?"

Was there shame in his eyes as he shook his head? He answered defensively.

"We were not brothers then in any sense of the word. The petted Francis has gone. Matty knows only jolly Uncle Frank and gentle Aunt Lily. They are part of the world of Sheradon Grange, his world. No, it wouldn't do."

"You may be right." But there was a niggle of fear in her mind that it was *that* story that folk still remembered.

He got up. "Thank you, Mother. You have banished my fears." He took out his pocket watch. "The day is still young. I must go into Newcastle. A tenant owes a month's rent. I may have to evict her."

She saw a hard set to his jaw. Then he smiled down at her. "I've interrupted your weeding. Sophy is an idle creature. It's work that keeps you and Jack happy."

Not long after he had gone, she was perturbed to find Mateo waiting at the end of her row of cabbages.

"Grandmamma," he said, "were you and the father of Papa not married?"

She gulped, straightened up and sought a moment of grace. "Good morning, Mateo. Yes, that is correct."

"I'm sorry. Good morning, Grandma. I don't mean I'm sorry you weren't married. I'm sorry I didn't greet you properly." He stood on one leg and fidgeted. "Well, I *am* sorry you weren't married, because Mamma seems to think it matters."

Her heart began to thump. What has my urging of the truth let loose after all? She smiled at him. "*I'm* not sorry, because your grandfather was not a good man, and Jack, whom I *did* marry, is a very good man."

He nodded. "But Mamma wonders if Papa is really a baronet after all."

"His father certainly was, but do *you* mind, Mateo, whether he is or isn't? Come and sit down. I've finished weeding the cabbages."

They sat where she had sat with Ralph.

Mateo perched on the edge of the bench, very tense. "Perhaps I shouldn't have spoken to Mamma. She didn't remember Papa saying anything about being a miner. Why did he tell me?"

"Because you are growing to manhood. Your father wants you to learn from life as he has. Work hard and do good in the world. That is more important than titles. You are taking a new step, so your father wanted to take a new step with you."

She was watching his face and saw his lip tremble. "I love him so much for confiding in me, but school is not a step I want to take."

She squeezed him close. "You're not cutting ties with home. I will always be here to listen to you."

He jumped up. "I know. Thank you, Grandmamma." He was struggling not to cry, and she didn't stop him running off.

She went inside to her office and hung on the door her cloth embroidered with the word 'Working'. But that won't deter Sophia, she thought, if she comes for me in a great passion. She put her head in her hands and prayed.

Sophia did not come, and she heard no shouting behind the partition later that day. Next day John started school, so she gave all her outward attention to him, with Mateo never out of her mind.

When John came home he announced, "I was put in a higher group after the morning because I know my letters and numbers. And Farmer Robson collects boys from the farms in his wagon and comes past our gates, so he'll pick me up too."

John, at four, already had his life arranged, but Dee was concerned at the silence from the east wing.

Ten days later, on the morning before Mateo's term started, she saw Ralph heading for the stables. She ran out to him. "Ralph, she is keeping the children away. Am I a fallen woman in her eyes?"

He laughed. "No, I had a windfall and gave her some money to keep her sweet. She's said nothing about the revelation. She's been quite bright, getting Matty's things ready. I'm off now for a board meeting and won't be back tonight, but the girls want to see the school, so if Jack can take them all to the station for the early train tomorrow, I'll meet them at Heron Mansions and we can all go together. Matty's nervous but I had to do this. She would cosset him for ever. Hurst and his wife will be a breath of fresh air for him."

It was good to see him go off smiling, but Dee went back into the house, uneasy. Sophia is keeping Matty away from me even on his last day.

To her surprise, Maria came round just before bedtime when they were all sitting at the kitchen table and John was in his nightgown drinking his warm milk.

A bright little figure, she stood in the doorway on the step from the passage.

"I come to say goodbye."

John looked up, "*You're* not going anywhere – just Matty."

She was giggling. "But we *are* going in a train to Newcastle to see his school. Papa is staying in his office tonight, so he'll join us there. I'm excited."

"*I've* been on the train lots of times." John said, "*and* on to North Shields and the seaside in Granda's pie cart."

"Well, we might see the sea too." She put her hand over her mouth, giggled some more, added, "Well, goodbye," and ran off.

John said, "Their nurse will have to go too. They're really babies."

Jack scratched his head. "Which of the twins was that?"

Frank said, "Maria. She has a sweeter temperament, I think."

"Eh well, I can never tell them apart."

The morning was wet. In good time for the train, Jack drove the carriage to their front door. Dee put her shawl over her head and ran round to find them all gathered in their porch. Guido was loading Mateo's box into the luggage space. Jack, already wet, was lowering the carriage step. Sophia bundled the children in when she saw Dee. Nurse followed.

Dee called out, "Matty, God bless you. Enjoy the week."

He peeped out with a half-smile and mouthed, "I'll try, Grandmamma."

Guido jumped on the back step of the carriage as Jack clicked at the horses. Only Rosie was left in the porch, waving. Dee was surprised.

Rosie said, "They need Guido in Newcastle, ma'am, for a hired carriage to the school. They said I could go home."

Dee nodded and ran back to the kitchen, where she found Lily washing the breakfast dishes. On an impulse she told her what had passed lately with Ralph and Mateo.

"Oh Mother Dee, I thought her ladyship had been keeping her distance."

"She has, but I will greet her kindly when they come home. Love is the theme of my novel."

Lily clapped her hands. "So go and write it while the house is quiet."

Chapter 10

Mateo

Mateo looked out at the rain streaming down the windows of the first-class compartment, which had cushions on the wooden benches and was the only covered part of the train. His sisters, opposite him, were swaying with the motion of the train, exchanging glances and giggling at him. He was disappointed in Maria. She was his favourite, and it hurt that she seemed to be amused by his discomfiture.

His mother, her colour high and an air of excitement about her, kept squeezing his arm and murmuring in Spanish, "Nothing to be afraid of. Everything will turn out for the best."

Lucia said, "Not if we have an accident on the way, Mamma. Uncle Frank told me the bridge they built to get the railway over the Tyne into Newcastle is just a temporary one. He said there are plans for a railway bridge with a road underneath, but that won't happen for a long time. He'd like to build it himself, but he doesn't think he's clever enough."

She giggled at Maria and their mother said, "I'm sure he isn't, and he shouldn't try to frighten you. When did he say such things to you?"

"Oh, long ago. At the birthday party. He said we should use the train because carriages will soon be history."

Maria nodded. "That's what he said. And *I* think he *is* clever."

Lucia giggled. "Well, it doesn't matter now, does it?"

Mateo ignored her words because his mind was marvelling at how easily Spanish came to them when they were together without Papa, but he must soon stand up and tell a mass of boys something about himself in clear English. He would stumble and stutter and they would think he couldn't speak it properly.

His mouth dry, he peered out of the small window. Heavy late summer trees gave way to glimpses of the river and, on the far bank, a colliery. In the passing second, he saw the winding gear moving and thought of his mother's face when she had repeated: "A miner, and I marry him!" He didn't know if she'd spoken to Papa about it. Papa had ridden off cheerfully to Newcastle yesterday and told her what time to come to Heron Mansions this morning so they could all go to the school together. She had answered him with a smile that they would be there.

Mateo shifted his gaze to Nurse's stolid face and remembered Guido in an open wagon getting soaked, and then he pictured arriving at the school with two servants and all his family. How the boys will stare! I will never live it down.

By the time the train had safely crossed the temporary bridge over the Tyne and halted at a platform in Newcastle, Mateo's stomach felt like jelly. In the street a hired closed carriage was waiting for them. Had Papa sent it? Mateo wondered. Guido transferred his box into it, and Mateo imagined it sitting in a strange room in Mr Hurst's house, where he would sleep alone tonight. He broke into a sweat.

They all climbed in, and Mateo closed his eyes to the streets of Newcastle. Shortly they would reach Heron Mansions, and Papa would join them and say stirring words which would fail to reassure him. Papa, who had dared as a small boy to go down into the bowels of the earth, couldn't possibly understand how he could be terrified of anything as tame as going to school.

Maria snuggled up to him and murmured, "It's a long way to Papa's office, isn't it?"

Lucia, on the opposite seat, kicked her.

"Is it?" Mateo said. "I didn't notice. I don't know how far it is. Newcastle's a big town. Last time I went with Papa, it was on horseback."

"Open your eyes, Matty. We are by the river."

Lucia said, "Stop babbling."

"Heron Mansions is not far from the river," their mother said. "You remember the first day we came and had to stay there, Mateo?"

He nodded. He had been bewildered by all the travelling. The next day he had met Grandmother for the first time, and somehow he had known at once that he loved her. Yet even she hadn't grasped how much he dreaded today.

The carriage stopped. He opened his eyes. They were right beside the water, and a steamship lay alongside.

"Out we get." His mother led the way. At once his ears were assailed by the screeching of seagulls. The rain had stopped, but there were puddles everywhere and porters with barrows splashing through them.

"What's happening?" he cried out. "This isn't right."

It was a quayside. He knew Heron Mansions was on a steep road that led down to the river. Were they to meet Papa here because there was level space for the carriage? No, there was too much coming and going from buildings marked with the names of shipping companies. There were people everywhere. And the gulls, noisiest of all, swooped overhead and perched, chuckling, on every post and railing.

His head ached with the battering of his senses. "What's happening, Mamma? This isn't right."

Guido set down his box and summoned a porter in uniform, who came running with a barrow. Mateo saw his box placed on it and carried towards the ship.

He said again, "Mamma, what's happening?"

Then Guido was running with some papers to an office, and the ship was emitting strange eruptions of steam.

His mother took him in her arms. "It's very right. It's my lovely surprise for you. You don't have to go to school to that horrid Mr Hurst. We are going home."

"Home?" Her words were lifting a great cloud, but he was shaking with bewilderment. "Home?"

"To Spain!" the twins squeaked in chorus and jumped up and down, giggling into his face.

"Spain? And Papa is joining us?" He thought of his father's words: "Do not fear the unexpected." Was this what he was hinting at? No, it had all been arranged with Mr Hurst. Plans could not have been changed so suddenly. If they had, why had he been kept in the dark? Why had the twins known all along? "Mamma. I don't understand. Where's Papa?"

100

There was another toot from the ship, and people were moving on board. A voice shouted through a loudhailer and his mother ushered them forward, her face radiant. He hadn't seen such a blaze of joy in her eyes for years. He had to move with the crowd, but she hadn't answered his question. He tried to brace his knees to halt the momentum but people behind were pushing. He grabbed his mother's arm.

"We can't go without Papa."

"It's all right, darling boy. Let's just get on board. I want Guido to check that the portmanteau I sent ahead earlier is safely stowed."

Earlier? A few days ago, she had ordered a carrier to take some clothing to the destitute of Newcastle. Mateo had heard her say to Papa, "You are always telling me our chests and tallboys are overflowing. There are outgrown things of the children's and some of my older clothes for the poor." Papa had seemed pleased, but he had said, "Make sure the portmanteau is brought back." She had told him it was safely stowed back in the attic. She had lied.

His feet were shuffling across a plank with rails each side. Water swished below. His mother had his arm in a tight grip. Nurse was behind, holding the girls' hands. They were squeaking with excitement.

There was an entry port ahead which led inside to a row of ten cabins at the stern of the ship marked 'First Class'. Panic seized him as a porter held open a door and his mother hustled him inside. Guido appeared and blocked the doorway when Mateo scrambled to get out.

"The portmanteau is in your private cabin next door, milady," Guido said, not meeting his eye. "I share a space below with four other menservants."

"Nurse, go in and start unpacking what I need. You will sleep in here with the children." Guido moved to let her through. Then he bowed as if departing, but kept standing in the narrow doorway with his hands on the sides.

Mateo pushed at his chest. "Let me out. I'm not going anywhere without Papa." Guido stood his ground.

His mother laid her hands on his shoulders and turned him to face her. "You have no Papa now. I am the Condesa de Villena and you are my son, Mateo de Villena. We are going home."

"No, I am Mateo Barnet." He stamped his foot.

Above them there was shouting of orders and the crashing and clanking of chains and shrill emissions of steam. He flung himself round and beat at Guido with his fists. Guido suddenly smiled at him and gave him his own personal bow. "The gangway has been hauled away, my young lord. Feel it! We are getting underway. Let us pray for a safe voyage." He crossed himself and stepped back into the passage, closing the door.

Mateo hit his fists on it in a passion of angry tears. He could dash out and jump into the water and swim to shore – but he dared not. His father had sprung into the sea to save his mother. *He* had the courage of a lion. The ship was vibrating. He was caught, trapped. He rounded on his mother. "What have you done? Have you *left* Papa?"

She nodded, smiling.

A thought went through him like a knife wound. He screamed, "It was what *I* told you. He was a miner. I wish I'd died rather than spoken that word. You couldn't bear that, could you?"

She shook her head. "No, that only confirmed the rightness of my decision."

"Rightness! You've lied. You've cheated Papa. He believed you were taking me to school. He *believed* you."

She held out her arms in a gesture of surprise. "But you didn't *want* to go to school. I did it for your sake. Now that's enough. You're upsetting your sisters."

Maria, at least, was in tears. She came and drew him away from the door.

"You'll love it in Spain, Matty darling. Mamma has told us all about the great estate she has. The mansion is twice the size of Sheradon Grange."

The words brought a howl of anguish from Mateo. Sheradon Grange was Grandmother who loved him. It was Jack, the kindest man on earth. It was Uncle Frank and Aunt Lily, and even infuriating John. It was home.

Lucia was saying, "Stop it, Mateo. Come choose your bed. Maria and I want the top ones. Nurse will have one of the lower ones 'cos she couldn't climb up."

He flung himself upon the nearest, his whole body racked with sobs. He was just aware of Maria patting his shoulder and crying.

"Maybe Papa will come later," she gulped. "*I* didn't want to say goodbye to him either, but Mamma doesn't want him talked about."

Mateo turned to look up at his mother.

She shook her head. "He will *not* come later." She was divesting herself of her cloak. "I have left him a note. He is not to follow us or write to us." She shook out the cloak as if she were shaking Papa out of her life.

He stared at her, fury momentarily stifling his tears. "What are you saying? All my life you've told me how wonderful he is. How he saved your life! You made me feel I could never match him, and now—!"

She flapped her hands. "Of course I wanted you to admire him – but as for jumping in the sea, what man who was anything would not have done the same if they saw a woman drowning?" She paced up and down the cramped cabin with angry steps. "You'll be saying next that I loved him. Of course I did. But when we went to England – when you were not quite four – he grew back into his old haunts. His family. I made him come back to Spain for my dear girls' birth, but there was civil war and I feared for you all, and he wanted to go back for his business and his precious mother—"

Mateo sprang to his feet and thrust himself into her path. "Don't you dare say a word against Grandmamma."

She halted and put her hand before her face. "I say nothing about Dee – absurd name – she is in a different world since marrying Jack Heron. Though she was never in *our* world. Her family owned Sheradon Grange by trading in such things as coal and iron. But we are an ancient Spanish family, nobility. Oh Mateo, I am taking you home to your rightful place." She tried to clasp him in her arms, but he dodged out of reach and braced his back against the cabin door.

"You lied to me. You deceived everyone. How could you do that? You told Papa a huge lie that we would meet him at Heron Mansions. He will be looking for us in vain. When we do not appear they will *all* be looking, all of them."

The awfulness of that struck him for the first time. His back slithered down the door and he slumped to the ground, overwhelmed by the sense of their desolation. All of them. He clutched his head in his hands, a ball of wretchedness. Oh, he had escaped school, but what was that when Papa and Grandmamma had been so full of love, so eager for him to do well, to fight his fears? And now to be torn away from them! Would they think he had known about this all along? That he had put on an act of dreading school and was laughing secretly at their concern?

His mother was trying to raise him, speaking in the soothing voice he had known all his childhood whenever he was hurt or sad or Papa had scolded him. He hated it now, and pushed roughly up, actually shoving her so hard that she sat down on the bunk beside her and banged her head on Maria's bunk above.

He was aghast when he saw tears come into her eyes.

"I'm sorry but you did a terrible thing. You lied to me."

She flared up. "You keep saying that. But didn't your father lie to *me*? He pretended to be of a noble family, a baronetcy given by James the First. I was innocent of English history but I have found out lately. Many landowners paid money to the king for their titles and a baronetcy was no great thing – and then I find he is a bastard son! Do you not call that deceit? And when did he ever tell me he had been down the pit hacking coal? When did that Dee ever tell me about his childhood? They are all deceivers. I only desire good for you. I wanted to save you from rough boys and lead you to your true destiny, the scion of a great Spanish family. You will be feted and admired and have servants to perform your every wish."

"He *did* tell you it all. He told me he had but you wouldn't listen."

Lucia said, "*You're* not listening to Mamma. She's telling you how wonderful it's all going to be."

He subsided down on his bed, glum and silent.

Maria came and sat by him and peered into his face. "No more tears, Matty. I did run round last night and said goodbye to them all, though they didn't guess then, but they'll understand now."

He shook his head and muttered, "*I* wasn't given a chance to say goodbye." Then he lifted his head and yelled at his mother. "Why did you have to do it like this? I don't see how I can ever love you or trust you again."

Her eyes were watery. It was not the bump. He had hurt her. She was truly moved. He began to shake his head back and forth to banish all the emotion that was clogging the reality of what had happened. There was one clear fact. He was on a steamship passing down the Tyne to the open sea, away from England. He thought back to their voyage home from Spain last time. They had gone to a port in France and thence to London and another ship to the Tyne. Papa had held one of the twins himself, he remembered, and had tried to soothe her crying. Mamma had laughed to see a big, tall man with a baby, but he had sensed that her laughter was tinged with dismay that Papa should do anything so unconventional. Yes, he had often felt since then that Papa didn't please her in England as he did in Spain, where he was constrained by the manners of society. There were strands of truth among her lies.

He stood up. "I'll go on deck."

His mother looked alarmed. "Go with him, girls. I will send Nurse up."

104

Lucia and Maria were excited, because they didn't remember sea travel, and Mateo felt suddenly proud of his superior knowledge. He shepherded them along the passage and up the steps. "This is called a companionway," he told them.

On deck it was refreshing to feel the breeze and smell the sea and watch the riverbanks moving past. The river was wide here. He went to the edge of the rail and leaned over. A seaman shouted at him. He stepped back.

He asked himself, Could I jump into that swirling water? No, not if a dozen women were drowning. She knows that, and that's why she has always boasted of Papa's bravery till now. Now she doesn't want me to be a man like him. If I cling to her, Papa will not be around to reproach me. She will make everything smooth and easy as she says. No school, no goals to aim at. No expectations from Grandmamma.

He gulped. He could put his hands on the rail and spring over. The river looked dirty, but he would take mouthfuls of it quickly, holding his arms straight up so he would go down at once. He supposed there would be some horrible moments of choking pain, and then oblivion.

He heard the same seaman telling Lucia and Maria to stop skipping about and getting in the way. He walked away from the rail and took charge of them.

"You see these ropes. You could trip over them."

One or two adult passengers were standing quietly looking ahead as the prow of the ship rode the water. One of them pointed to a great patch of black rocks jutting out from the land on the north side. Their ship was keeping well clear of that. He saw that sails were set on the two masts, one at the front and one at the rear of the vessel. The wind was behind them, so they were using sail to reduce the pressure on the engine. He would like to ask Uncle Frank about it. That was denied him. All the life he'd had up to Mamma hustling him into the carriage this morning was gone at a stroke. It was like an execution. Tears were coming again. Where could he go to hide them? He bit his lip and turned to face the wind. That could excuse watering eyes.

Nurse had joined Lucia and Maria and they were watching the shore go by. Their glossy black hair hung in identical thick plaits from their straw hats tied with primrose-yellow ribbons. Their dresses and cloaks and shoes were identical, but he knew which was which. Lucia was inward-looking and it showed in her pose, clutching the rail for self-protection. Maria, with her hands on it lightly, was looking everywhere with eager curiosity. He would love to be an elder brother they could respect; but it would never be like that now. They had seen him in tears.

Surely Papa would come for them all? He would enquire. He would find them. But that would mean a tug of war between Spain and England, between Mamma and Papa. If he kept with Mamma, she would always be tender with him as if he were still a child. Papa could be a stern father, a believer in work, discipline and achievement, but that other day he had spoken man to man: a revelation, a new beginning. He looked down at himself. A new shirt, trousers and shoes for school. But he was here on a ship sailing for Spain. It was like a division down his body. He was cut in two.

They were approaching the open sea. By now he would have been in the classroom at Mr Hurst's school. Perhaps he would have been on his feet, shaking and sweating, trying to produce coherent words. He drew a deep breath of the sea air. Surely this was better. He walked over to his sisters, going between them and putting an arm round each.

"We're out at sea," he said.

Lucia looked back at the Northumberland coast. "Goodbye, England."

Nurse turned and met his eyes, and a small smile twisted her mouth.

Maria looked up into his face as a shiver went through him. "All right now, Matty?"

He compressed his lips tightly and nodded.

"I'm glad," she said. "Now we can all be happy."

Chapter 11

Dee

By their usual dinner hour of noon, Dee began to feel uneasy. Lily agreed.

"It's the silence next door. It's uncanny. But her ladyship will be showing the girls the sights of Newcastle after they've said goodbye to Mateo."

"But she loathes Newcastle."

Dee heard thumps as Jack shed his boots at the back kitchen door. He always knew when the dinner was ready. The rain had eased off an hour ago but the ground was spongy. He walked in in his stockings and said, as he invariably did, "Something smells good." There was mutton broth, cheese, eggs from their own hens and lettuce and radishes from the vegetable patch, with hunks of Dee's homemade bread.

"They'll have to wait for their train back," Lily suggested.

Jack picked up on the words. "Oh ay, the family. I'm to meet the afternoon train. 'Half after two,' she said. Them's was her words. 'Half after two.' You'll keep me right, angel. I can eat my dinner first."

Relieved, Dee gave him her paradise smile, and they sat down at the table.

Lily had just started to say, "I hope I gave John enough for *his* dinner. He gets so hungry—" when Jack laid down his spoon and jumped up.

"Hooves!"

Lily held up her hand. "Nay, Papa Jack, sit down. If it's Frank, he can see to his own horse. He said he might be home for dinner."

Jack was halfway to the back door with his hand up to his ear. "That's Zephyr's whinny. It's Ralph. He's galloped round to their door. I ought to go and stable the horse for him. He'll just tether him at the door, and the horse'll be in a sweat."

"No, you'll eat your dinner. Zephyr is Ralph's responsibility." Dee beckoned him back and he came, but shaking his head.

"The air's chill after the rain. It's not good for a horse when he's in a lather."

Dee's heart was chill. She had heard the speed of the hooves. Ralph was upset or angry, or he would have gone to the stables first.

There was a sound of knocking on the east door, a brief pause and then they saw Ralph's head as he passed their window.

With the briefest rap on the outer door, he was through the back kitchen and in among them. His face was flushed, his eyes wild, but he checked at the sight of the three of them at the dinner table.

"Oh, excuse me." He was panting. "Where are they? The place is locked up."

Dee took down another bowl from the dresser behind her. "They're coming on the afternoon train. Did they not tell you?"

"Ay." Jack put his word in. "Half after two. That was what she said."

Ralph seemed bewildered. He took off his hat and sat down as Dee pointed to a chair and spooned broth into the bowl. He looked at them one after the other.

"They never went to the school."

"What?" cried Dee, and now her mouth seemed to dry up.

He repeated angrily, "They never took Mateo to the school. Mr Hurst sent a boy to me with a message. I thought – I feared – God knows what I feared. They've locked up the outer door. Can I try our connecting door?" He half-rose.

Dee shook her head. "It's bolted the other side. I tried it myself when I expected them back sooner. Have you not got a key to your front door?"

"There's just one big heavy thing. I don't carry it around with me. God, what can they be doing?"

"Eat something," Dee said.

He shook his head and stood up again. "I must see to Zephyr. No, sit down, Jack. He's *my* beast. I can't eat, Mother. I must be doing." He passed his hand across his damp forehead. "She never wanted him to go to Hurst's. I thought I'd persuaded her. She was to make it a great ceremony. She wanted to see the bedroom he would have. Would it be good enough for a future Spanish count? All that nonsense."

Dee grabbed at his hand. "Be patient till the train comes."

He pulled away. "It was so wretchedly annoying. This morning I was held in talk by a tenant, lately widowed, and didn't notice how much time had passed. Then I thought Sophia had gone to the school without me, deliberately – till I had the message from Hurst. So I supposed they had never left home. I was so angry. But I couldn't leave Heron Mansions at once. The woman came at me again, pleading. I had to give her a week's grace to get rid of her, and then I fetched Zephyr from the livery stables and rode like hell – and they're not here. But why the blazes doesn't Guido answer my knock, or Nurse, or Rosie?"

Dee laid a hand on his arm and made him look at her. She dreaded passing him her worst fears. "My dear, Rosie told me she'd been given the rest of the day off. Guido and Nurse went with them."

She saw the angry red drain from his cheeks. He clutched at the edge of the table, and Lily looked up into his face with alarm.

"Then they're not coming back." He gasped out the words. "Damn her to hell!"

Jack was edging towards the door. Dee knew it would be to attend to Zephyr and to escape the released emotions he didn't understand.

"One moment, Jack," she called out. "Tell Ralph exactly what Sophia said when you went to the station this morning."

He paused, and Ralph turned and fixed him with a desperate eye. "Ay, everything you can remember." He emphasised it with a clenched fist.

Jack gulped. "Half after two. I was to come back. Half after two. I got it fixed in my head." He sent Dee a pleading look.

She walked over to him and put an arm round his broad back. There was so much man here and so little confidence, except about that one thing.

Ralph demanded, "More must have been said, here or at the station."

"It was raining mighty hard. They didn't linger."

Dee said, "Think, my love. Weren't you surprised to find Guido there?"

His face split with a grin of delight and relief. "Oh ay. I said, 'What are you doing here?' I can't talk his lingo, so milady answered for him. She said, 'He's to drive the hired carriage in Newcastle up to the school.' I remember, for it made me pleased they were taking the train and not asking *me* to drive all that way, not knowing where the school was."

Lily had been leaning off her stool, following it all intently, Dee could see.

Now she exclaimed, "So Sophia *meant* to go to the school. Maybe *Mateo* took fright. He was ever so nervous. Then he'd be afraid to face you, Ralph, and would put it off and they'd drive around – but they'll come back for the train…"

She tailed off. Ralph was shaking his head. Dee thought the idea just possible. Jack slipped out while the talk was going on.

Ralph looked from Lily to Dee. "Mateo wouldn't do that. I *talked* to him. He *couldn't*. Surely he couldn't." There was a break in his voice. "Oh Mother, my first fear was that she'd taken him away from me. And when you said Nurse *and* Guido – Where's Jack gone?"

"He had compassion on Zephyr."

He smote his hand against his brow. "And none of you has eaten any dinner." He looked at the clock on the mantelpiece. "It is an age till half past two. I can't wait. I must get into the house. There may be clues there. But Jack – he mustn't—"

"Let him," she said. "He loves the horses, and upsets distress him."

She could see in his eyes that he accepted that and immediately dismissed Jack and Zephyr from his thoughts. His mind was probing the access problem.

"The attic." He clapped his hands together. "The partition in your corridor that used to let you get up there. It's a flimsy thing. I can break it down in a minute."

He made for the door to the hallway, then turned abruptly and stared wide-eyed at Dee.

"What is it?" she cried.

"The portmanteau! My God, if *that* is not there – oh pray God it is!" He dashed into the hallway and they heard him pounding up the stairs.

Dee had an overwhelming sense of impending disaster. She sank down on her stool and clasped her face in her hands.

Lily said, "Oh Mother Dee, that business with the portmanteau and clothes for the poor! Sophia said it had been put back in the attic. She surely couldn't have planned *then* to – to *leave* him?"

They could hear ripping and tearing noises. "He took no tools," Dee said. "He's kicking that panel in." There was crashing and then footsteps above as he rampaged through the rooms up there. She was holding her breath. And then the howl of anguish came and her heart plummeted. "Oh no, no, no."

Lily's face crumpled. She was biting her thumb as they heard Ralph trampling all through his house down to the drawing room, when there was a brief silence, and then he shot the bolts on the connecting door and burst through into their hallway. Dee rose and met him as he came stumbling down the steps into the kitchen and into her arms. He was clutching a piece of paper.

Dee drew him towards the table, where the bowls still stood, unsteaming, and sat him in a chair. "She's gone, has she?"

He looked up with tears streaming down his face. "She's taken Mateo to Spain." He choked the words out. "She says I'll never see him again. My boy!"

His whole body shook.

Dee's mind was at its usual gallop whenever something momentous occurred. She saw that he cared nothing for Sophia's going, and little perhaps for losing the girls, but Mateo was everything. The scene with Sophia and her homesickness flashed before her, with Mateo poised at the end of the cabbage row. A pang of guilt cut through her. She had urged truth, and this was the result. She held Ralph in her arms and was just aware of Lily weeping and hesitating about withdrawing from the scene.

"I can hear Frank at the stable. I'll go…" and she slipped out by the back door.

Dee was already framing plans. Ralph would go to Spain and confront Sophia. He was a man of decisions and action as soon as he had recovered from the first shock. I can go to Newcastle and find an agent to look after Heron Mansions in his absence, or Jack and I could stay there for a little while.

She tried to raise him. "We'll go into my study, where we can be alone and see what is to be done. Lily will tell Jack he is not to go to the station."

He looked at her, his chest still heaving. He struggled to bring out words.

"The lies," he gasped. "Everything was a lie. If I had her here I would kill her."

She said again, "Come into my study." He became aware of her urging and stood up. "Frank has arrived," she added. "Lily will tell him what's happened. You need see no one but me." He moved his limbs with an effort, and she propelled him along the passage to her little room, which looked out to the vegetable patch, and beyond it to the stable wall. She let him sink into the armchair, and turned her own chair from the desk to face him.

"You'll go to Spain," she said, "but not till your anger has subsided. I know you'll want to go at once but—"

"I shan't go." He stared at the floor. There were tears on his cheeks, but suddenly the life had gone out of him.

"Not go?" She was appalled. "You want Mateo back."

"He won't come. She's poisoned him."

"Poisoned?"

"Don't echo me. Poisoned his soul." He looked up then, and she saw the anger in the depths of his dark eyes, as she had seen it in his boyhood – and feared it. "You and your damned truth. It kept coming at me on the hellish ride from Newcastle. Has the truth killed whatever love she had left for me? Has she taken him away body and soul to punish me?"

"But you expected to find them here."

"Oh, you can't kill hope. They'll be at home, I convinced myself, and she'll grin and say, 'Mateo never wanted to go.' But all the time it was there – the dread. And when the portmanteau had gone" – he glared at her – "and I found her note, God, I knew it had really happened. And it has. It's real. They've gone." He leapt up and she shrank back in her chair. "Why the hell did I ever listen to you?"

"No," she cried, "no." She held her hands before her face and spoke fast. "She was homesick long before you spoke to Matty – early August. She came to me. She was unhappy. She'd had letters from that cousin. I couldn't help her. We had no meeting point, and she walked out. This has been festering."

His rigid, fierce presence above her subsided a little. "You never told me that."

She began to speak again, but he turned on his heel. "Talking won't change things." He pulled Sophia's letter from his pocket. "She says Guido will put the front door key behind a geranium pot. Ha!" He marched out, and she watched him out of the front door and saw him take huge strides round to the east porch. She stood trembling with a hand on the door frame, and when she heard Frank's voice behind her – "Mother, this is terrible news" – she turned to him and let tears flow.

He put his arms round her. "Don't cry for Sophia. Ralph's well rid of her."

"Mateo," she sobbed. "He loved his son with a passion."

"He'll go after them. They must have booked passage on a merchant vessel to London. Nothing goes direct to Spain from the Tyne. He could make inquiries. He could get a berth on a steam packet… Why are you shaking your head?"

"He believes Mateo is corrupted and wouldn't come back. *I* don't believe that. I wonder if Mateo even knew what she was planning."

"Maria did, now I think of it. Her manner when she came to say goodbye – I swear she knew. Should I go to Ralph? How is he taking it?"

"Listen." He was in his part of the house now, and smashing and banging sounds came from upstairs.

"It's your house, Ma. I must stop him."

"He'll be destroying her things." She looked up into his kindly, open face. "Oh Frank, will we see Billy come back again? His pride will be deeply wounded. All that confidence from wealth and having his own family—"

"I'll go to him. Let him see that he still has family." He was edging towards the now open door to the drawing room.

"Oh, be wary of him. He was angry with me."

Lily came from the kitchen to say she had reheated the broth and Jack was hungry but wouldn't start without them.

"He still thinks he's to go to the station at half after two. I tried to tell him they'd gone to Spain, but he said they might still catch that train."

Dee hurried back to the kitchen. Jack would need her word to countermand the order. Frank came too, wanting his dinner.

The sounds upstairs had stopped by the time they'd eaten a few mouthfuls. Dee could only force down a little to please Jack. Then she took a bowl and filled it.

"I'll take it to Ralph," she said. "I'd like to see Sophia's letter. I fear he might tear it up."

"Let me come with you," Frank said.

"Leave it a little longer. You have your wife and son. The old jealousies can rise up. He will be all right with me now. And Jack, you are *not* needed at the station. Finish your dinner and then I'd like you to clean and polish all the gardening tools this afternoon." She gave him her paradise smile and he beamed back.

"Polish tools. Ay, good work, that." He took another hunk of bread and cheese.

Dee walked into her old drawing room, where she had first seen the other Ralph Barnet. What a lifetime since that disastrous moment! It was hard to believe that so many dramas had passed and gone – and now this one! It must be lived through somehow. I am getting old, she thought.

Here there was the strange new stairway replacing the old servants' stair to the attics. Carrying the bowl, she began to mount. There was silence above. The first Ralph's son was up there somewhere.

She called his name softly but there was no reply. She paused in the truncated passage. That partition could go if Sophia was never coming back. She peeped in the front room, which she knew had been their bedroom, and saw a mass of debris on the floor. He had smashed up the chair she used when she sat at her toilet, but there were not many of her broken possessions – a hand mirror, some bottles of scent, a few torn garments. Everything else had gone into that portmanteau. She crept out, and then she heard a moan from the back bedroom, where Mateo had slept.

She called again, "Ralph, you must take nourishment." She pushed the door gently. He was sitting on the bed amongst Mateo's clothes and books. In his hands was *Gulliver's Travels*, open at the front leaf. He held it up to her and she read, 'Mateo Alonso Barnet. His book', and then underneath in a more mature hand, 'My favourite book'. Ralph's eyes were red and shiny with tears.

"I made him stop reading it and go outside and chop wood. Sophia gave him a scolding. Galician nobles, she told him, never work with their hands. But she didn't let him take this, his favourite book. Oh Ma, she is evil through and through."

"Put the book down and take this." He did so, seeming unaware of what he was doing, but automatically lifting the spoon to his lips.

"You see what this means?" She pointed to the things on the bed. "These were in drawers and cupboards?" He nodded. "She couldn't pack them because she hadn't told him her plan. She knew he would rebel. His sisters were in the secret. Have you looked in their room?" He nodded again. "Cleared out?"

"Ay, pretty well. I know. I understand what it means."

"Is that not some comfort?"

He continued eating till the bowl was empty, and handed it back to her.

"She'll get at him to be a Spanish count. He's only twelve. There is this cousin who will make much of him. She will never speak of me, and we will all fade from his memory. New sights, new places, hearing no English."

She laid the bowl on the washstand and sat down in the bedside chair. "But, my dear boy, that is a good reason for you to go to Spain. Surely she cannot in law remove your family from you."

He fished in his pocket and handed her Sophia's letter. "You'd better read that. It's in English – her English – a scrawl, written in haste."

Dee took the paper as if it might explode in her hands. It was indeed a scrawl.

There was no preamble, just his name, *Ralph*, and, underneath, a few broken phrases.

Dead to me – not man I married. I free. I go home. Widow. You come after me I say imposter, not know you. I have large land – I and children – live well. Cousin good – help. Mateo great man. Vizconde de Villena. Lovely twins – great marriages. I happy woman. Tell your mother. Sophia de Villena.

At the bottom she had written about Guido and the key.

Dee shook her head and handed the paper back to him. "Poor, wretched woman. She will *not* be happy on a bed of lies."

He frowned. "She has the wits of a devil. How can I go back there now? You see how she will twist Mateo to her ideas." He looked at the boy's clothes scattered about him. "Oh God, I want my son." And he broke down into sobs that tore at Dee's heart. "I could have borne it if they had all been killed. This is hell!"

"No, listen to me. Mateo is twelve, as you say. He has known us since he was not quite four. She can't blot out those years. We all love him and he knows it. And that talk you had with him. It made a great impression. He thought deeply. He knows her values are not ours—"

"Ah, but he loved her petting and comforting him if he so much as bruised a finger. I was stern. Now he only has her. He will become the pampered darling I dreaded she would make him. How can he resist that? You see what it has done – this damned truth business. A miner! She feels disgraced, so I am to be dead to her. She'll tell everyone I am dead."

"People there will remember you. There will be a record of your marriage. Even in Spain there are laws. You are legally the father. She cannot do this."

"But she has. They are on board ship. The girls will be so excited, because they were babies when we came. I can see it now. Their excitement will infect Matty and he'll be glad not to be going to school. What use was my talk with him? To him I am now a villain who deceived his dear mother, and they are well rid of me." She could see the anger mounting in his face again. "So much for the truth. If I'd known she was pining for Spain we could have paid a visit, stayed on this estate of hers. Now it's all too late." He leapt up and hurled the soup bowl at her head. "I'll never see my son again." He flung himself onto the bed and clutching up the clothes he buried his face into them, shouting, "Go away. Leave me alone."

Dee had dodged the bowl, which had flown through the open door and smashed on the floor of the landing. She was quivering in every limb as she backed out and closed the door on him. Instinctively she bent to pick up the pieces, and then heard Frank's worried voice as he came bounding up the stairs.

"Ma, are you all right?" He saw the breakage. "What? Did he throw it? I heard him shout."

She stood up with the pieces in her apron and motioned him downstairs again.

"We'll leave him. He's right. I am guilty."

"You, Ma? Why, you're shaking. I'll give him a piece of my mind."

He took a step without much conviction towards the closed door.

She gestured again, more imperiously, that he should go ahead, and he went, but looking back with a hand out to help her. He was muttering, "How dare he?" She clutched her apron and followed. When they passed through the door to the hallway he said, "I'll put a bolt on our side."

She gave a hysterical laugh. "He's broken through to the attics already."

"Well, we're not safe from him. He's turned into a wild beast."

She shook her head. "He'll think. We must give him time."

"But to blame you! What could any of us have done? We all saw she was restless, and he was busier than ever with his houses and businesses. I think he'd fallen out of love with her. This is her revenge. What is one supposed to say? If you are not careful your wife will leave you?"

She restrained him as he was striding to the kitchen to join Lily.

"Frank, I *am* guilty. I had urged him to tell her his true background. I feared someone would talk – now that they were going about more and Mateo was to go to school. He spoke to Mateo, man to man, and Mateo told his mother. He was so innocent but so interested. I told him his father believed in hard honest work, which is better than titles and grandeur. I have been a fool. I suffered a lifetime from my own deception and now Ralph, our old Billy, is reaping the consequences. I too, for I love Mateo so much and fear how she may change him."

They heard running footsteps and John flung open the front door. "Old Bunny-Hop let the school off for the harvesting."

Dee wanted to silence his boisterous presence at once. His voice would be a sharp pain for Ralph now. Noticing everything he pointed to the open door to the drawing room. "They left the bolt off."

She told him Aunt Sophia had taken the children to Spain.

"Hurrah!" he yelled. "Now I can go on the swing as often as I like," and he raced off.

Dee looked at Frank. "You and Lily must keep him quiet as best you can." She went into her study and shut the door. Dear God, she thought, how wonderful to be four years old.

Chapter 12

Ralph

Ralph did not know himself. He was in hell within his own body. Not enduring to see himself, he smashed the mirror in the bedroom. He was a failed man. At every turn in his life he had gone wrong. He cursed himself. He cursed his mother. Seized with frenzy, he went out and fetched the axe from the shed and slashed at trees. He was just aware of Jack and Lily rushing John out of his sight.

Back in Mateo's room, he locked the door. When his mother called to him to open up and eat something, he shouted, "Go away." He curled on Mateo's bed when he was exhausted, and fell into a nightmarish sleep.

Next morning, he heard someone across the landing clearing up in the bedroom he had shared with Sophia. He opened the door a crack and saw it was Rosie. Of course – she would come back to work as normal, so she must have been told what had happened. That was shaming. He closed and bolted the door. Of course, his mother would say he was ill, so Rosie would have to minister to him. He had used the chamber pot under Mateo's bed, so very quietly he reopened the door and put it on the landing. Rosie was wiping the window and didn't look round as he slipped back inside. I am safe here, he thought. Mother will tell her to knock and leave a breakfast tray outside. I don't have to eat and I don't have to see anyone.

That evening he did creep out when Rosie had gone home and he had heard John being put to bed. He peered into every corner of the room he had shared with Sophia, to eliminate any sign that she had ever been there. Yet all the time his body was remembering their intercourse, which until lately had given them both pleasure, though love had gone. Around the marble washstand, the aroma of her scent faintly lingered despite Rosie's cleaning. He went to the window and pushed open the casement and breathed the night air. Then, hearing footsteps on the main stair, he slipped back to bed. He heard his mother call "Goodnight" but made no answer.

He became unaware of time passing. Had two days passed or three? He woke to the breeze coming from the open window at the front and bringing a chilly September morning under the door of his room. He got up and peeped out. A breakfast tray was there, and he could hear Rosie down in the kitchen. He ran softly across the landing to close the casement.

Even as he did so, he heard a horse's hooves and shrank back. With one eye peering round the curtain, he saw a man ride round the curve of the drive and draw rein at the front door. Jack came running from the stables. The man dismounted and, raising his hat, shook Jack's hand. There was the sound of their voices. He recognised that long full head of grey hair: it was the schoolmaster.

He realised he could hear the words.

"Took them to Spain! Was that not very sudden?"

"Oh ay, sir. Been a shock to all of us."

"He could have sent word, saved me a journey."

"I reckon it's sent him out of his mind."

"Should I speak with him?"

Then he heard his mother's voice, apologising and asking Mr Hurst in, and they disappeared and the front door clicked shut. That meant they were in the house. He scurried back into Mateo's room, took in the tray and bolted the door. Why was there a bolt on that door? He didn't know; but he felt safe behind it. Only…he was with Mateo again, and all his possessions were more agony than comfort. Mateo was far away, living another life, talking to others at this very moment, looking at other sights, waves perhaps. He could see the waves in his mind's eye, but not his boy.

A sharp rap at the door made him gasp. The handle was tried.

"Open up, man, and let me have speech with you. You know me. Mateo's disappointed schoolmaster."

No, he thought, no, and, creeping round Mateo's bed, he lay down behind it and covered his head with the pillow. Infuriatingly, he could still hear Hurst's voice.

"I know you're there. Your mother is worried that you are neither eating nor drinking enough. That's not a manly way to take a setback in life."

Manly? A man who cannot keep his wife is no man. A man whose wife robs him of his children is no man.

"You are still young," the voice went on, with an edge of impatience. "Good heavens, I can give you twenty years. I took little Billy Heron into my Wylam school out of pity for your mother. You were three years old then. And I'm not too old for a fifteen-mile ride to find out what went wrong on Monday."

The man is entitled to an apology, he thought, but he is not getting one when he brings up my childhood. I, a trouble to my mother? Does not my whole life come from then? She failed me as a mother. I have failed as a father. Oh Mateo, he moaned inwardly, pulling the pillow round and burrowing into it as if he could draw from it his son's face and peer into his deep dark eyes that hid so much. If I had him here and could *ask* him, do you hate me? Why did you go with her? If—

"I took you for a man of action. Mateo was in awe of you. Did you not know that? He desperately wanted to please you, but feared he could never be good enough."

He leapt up and yelled, "Don't you speak of my boy. You hardly knew him."

"That's better, Ralph. Now we can talk. Come out and tell me more about him. I'd like to know more."

Ralph sank onto the bed, shaking his head violently. He couldn't do that. What the man had said already had torn painfully at the wound.

He beat his clenched fists against his head. Mateo in awe of me! Ah, but what I told him shocked him, and he ran to his mother and she finished the demolition. He *wanted* to escape me. That morning when she revealed where they were going – when? When they passed Heron Mansions? – Matty was thankful not to go to school, thankful that I wasn't the man he'd imagined, and he could go to Spain and be what *she* said he was, a Spanish count who would be admired whatever he did.

He heard his mother's voice as if she were coming up the stairs. "Did he not answer you just now? That's more than *I* got from him."

"He didn't want me to speak of the boy." Hurst spoke it softly, but Ralph now had his ear to the door. The knock came again and he withdrew with a start.

Hurst said, "You should come out and talk to your mother. She needs to know what arrangements to make about your Newcastle houses. She says she's willing to go and reside there, she and her husband, when you go to Spain."

Oh no, this was madness. He walked away from the door and round the bed, and found himself looking out of the window at the woods rising behind the house. He'd been out there with an axe. When was that? How had he managed to go out? He couldn't do it again. Meet people? No, he was safe here. He mustn't be seen. He shouldn't have spoken. Better to say nothing. They must go away.

Shuffling and whispering was going on. He couldn't bear that. One last time would do it. He went to the door and beat on it with his fists.

"Leave me alone!" He could hear the crack in his own voice. If they didn't go away he would start screaming.

His mother said, loudly and clearly, "We are going, Ralph. We will give you time to be quiet and think. Think who you are and what the good Lord expects of you."

Their footsteps retreated down the stairs. He lay down on Mateo's bed, and tears welled up and flowed uncontrollably.

Mateo

"There's land over there," Lucia cried.

"That is still England. We are to disembark at Calais, but not for another day or two. Then we take ship for Spain. A different vessel."

"Oh, it's not Spain yet?"

Mateo heard the conversation as he had for most of the voyage, words flowing round him, a part of him always in Sheradon Grange, with the ache of not knowing what they were thinking and doing. Then the import of these words struck him. They would be briefly on land with access to postal services. He slipped below to their cabin and found writing paper, pens, nibs and an ink bottle in his schoolbag. He set these on the shelf between the beds; it was just wide enough to serve as a desk. Kneeling down to it, he began, *Dear Papa,* and then wondered if that was right. He had never written a letter to his father. Tears began to drop onto the page and smudge it. He screwed it up and dropped it on the floor.

After several false starts he ended up with: '*Dear honoured Papa, I think of you all the time and wonder what you must be thinking. I never knew what Mamma was planning and it made me very unhappy. We are on a ship which is docking in Calais and I hope I can send this to you. Mamma wishes us to end contact with you but I cannot obey her. This makes me unhappy too but I know it is wrong what she has done. Will you come to Spain and try to make it all come right? I had no notion she would take it like this when I told her about your life which made me admire you more than ever. I want to be like you and not be fussed over. Your loving son, Mateo.*'

When the ink had dried, he enclosed the letter in another sheet and wrote '*Sir Ralph Barnet, Sheradon Grange near Ovingham in the County of Northumberland, England.*' But how to seal it? Perhaps one of the stewards could provide wax. He opened the door and found Lucia and Maria coming along to find him.

"Mamma wondered where you were," Lucia said. "What's that you've got there?" He had put the letter behind his back.

Maria said, "If you've written to Papa we won't tell."

He produced the letter. "I need wax to seal it."

"That's easy," Maria said. "There's a man at a desk sealing passengers' letters with the ship's seal. You give him a coin and he'll see it's sent off when we dock. He's asking half crowns for letters to England. I'll show you where he is."

Mateo thought half a crown was a huge charge, but he was so relieved that he fetched his purse from under his pillow, followed Maria up the companionway and found the man under an awning at the far end of the deck. A few passengers were waiting, so he joined them. Then he noticed Lucia hadn't come with them. That made him uneasy. When his turn came and the man said, "Now, young sir," he heard a footstep behind, and his mother's hand shot out and grabbed the letter.

"That one's *not* going. A mistake." She gave a little laugh, and the man shrugged and turned to the next person waiting.

Maria squealed, "Oh Mamma, please," as she hurried them out of hearing.

Mateo dug in his heels and came to a halt. He was grinding his teeth as he spat out the words, "Lucia told you. I hate her and I hate you. Give me back my letter."

Maria was crying. "Mamma, that was cruel."

Their mother stood still and cocked her head at them with an oddly comical look. "What are you saying? The letter will still go. I know this trick. The man takes your money but doesn't send the letters. I will send Guido to the *bureau de poste*, or whatever the French call it, as soon as we dock. I have letters to go too to cousin Juan." She bent down and peered into Mateo's face. "Now you take back those words 'I hate you'. That is not a thing to say to your kind mother."

Mateo frowned at the sudden change. "You said no contact with Papa."

"I allow it once because it can make for a full stop – you understand."

He looked at the letter in her hand. Of course, she would read it. "But I ask him to come to Spain. I want him to come."

"And I will add a few sentences to show him that would be unwise. Now go to your cabin and be ready to disembark. Do not worry. I will alter nothing you have said, and it will be properly sealed. I see you have written the directions in a neat hand. Well done, Mateo."

She had triumphed. Maria came with him to their cabin, saying, "It *will* go to Papa. He'll know you love him. Mamma is *not* cruel, is she?"

That was Maria. There was something of Aunt Lily in her, wanting everyone to be happy and good. But she was a fighter too. A fighter for justice and at the same time still young and trusting. He wished he could be like her.

In the cabin they found Lucia folding her dresses and petticoats neatly in her bag. He poured out his fury and frustration on her head. "The meanest hatefullest telltale that ever lived."

She let him finish. "*I* never said I wouldn't tell. We have to obey Mamma and she asked us to tell her what you were up to 'cos she worries about you."

That started a fierce argument between his sisters, which Mateo ignored as he wondered what his mother would add to his letter if she really sent it, and what Papa would think if he ever got it. The uncertainty was horrible.

Chapter 13

Sheradon Grange
(two weeks later)

Dee

No letter came to Sheradon Grange.

Ralph stayed in Mateo's room, eating little but taking tea. Dee told Rosie not to give him alcohol. They sent for a doctor, but Ralph wouldn't admit him.

"Don't feed him at all," the doctor suggested, but this Dee couldn't agree to.

Jack struggled to understand. "He's sad, of course, but we could comfort him if he wouldn't shut himself away."

She said, "He is not the man he was, and he can't bear to meet anyone. It is like nakedness. He is ashamed."

Jack scratched his head. "Surely Sophia should be ashamed. *She* took his children away from him. Why hasn't he gone to this place Spain to fetch 'em back?"

Dee gave the only answer he might understand. "He fears they won't come."

A voice piped up. "I never thought Uncle Ralph was afraid of anything."

They hadn't realised John was hiding behind the settle in the kitchen. He came out and stood there, a small, pugnacious figure, with his wild mop of fair curls which he wouldn't have cut.

"I don't really want them back, but I don't like Uncle Ralph to be miserable."

"None of us do, but I'm afraid he's ill." She studied him. "You would look more of a boy if I trimmed your hair."

He screwed up his lips in his thinking mood. Then he jumped onto a kitchen stool and said, "All right, Gran. Do it now."

"I was just going to pick a lettuce for tea."

"I'll pick you a lettuce. Cut it off."

"I ought to ask your ma and da."

"They want it cut, but I wouldn't 'cos I hate sitting still. Do it now, quick." He reached for the drawer with the scissors.

Dee laughed and took them. She could see herself in John, with her childhood impulses and imperious demands which amused her father and annoyed her mother and often earned a gentle rebuke from her grandfather.

In a few minutes there was a pile of fair curls on the floor and a head of stubble like mown hay.

"Lift me up to the mirror."

"Nay, you're too heavy for me."

"Granda, then." He lifted his arms to Jack.

Jack said, "Ay, you're a tall lad. You could pass for a six-year-old now."

John looked at himself and grinned happily. Then he ran out to the vegetable plot to pick a lettuce. Lily was out there, weeding.

Dee, following, heard her cry, "My baby's gone!" but she seemed pleased.

They thought no more of this till an afternoon a week later, when Farmer Robson knocked at the back door and said, "Is John sick? Do I call in the morning?"

Dee had her hands in the mixing bowl, so Lily went out to the big, florid man and looked up at him, puzzled. "You took him to school this morning?"

"Nay, he wasna waiting where he always stands, and I was a wee bit late, so I supposed you was keeping him at home for summat."

Ice-cold at her stomach, Dee wiped her hands and went to the door.

She kept her voice steady. "Jake Robson, listen. John went to wait for you at the usual time this morning. Are you saying he hasn't been to school today at all?"

"Ay, teacher said would I find out if he was sick." His face looked grey as he said the words.

Lily let out a screech. Dee clutched at her as she began to tremble all over.

"Oh Mother Dee, he's been seized by gypsies. We'll never find him."

Farmer Robson was shaking his head. "Ay, that's bad. I heard there was gypsies at the Hexham Mart yesterday buying horses."

Lily shrieked again. Dee hustled her into the kitchen and she collapsed into the armchair. Jack came running from the wood, where he had been gathering kindling.

"What's to do now?"

"John has been missing all day," Dee told him. "I will ride into the village and tell Constable Naughton."

"Nay, *I* should…"

She wished he could, but without a grasp of the facts he would not convey the urgency of it all. She turned to the farmer. "Jake, take the other boys home, but see they spread the word around. You know what he looks like now? Not a halo of curls."

"Ay, you cropped him good and proper. Don't you worry, Missus. We'll find him." He ran back to his cart. Dee thought, Yes, John wanted to be cropped. Was it for some plan – to look older for someone or something?

"Saddle me Zephyr," she told Jack. "That horse needs exercise."

"Zephyr, angel!" Jack was flapping his hands to ward off the crisis. "John came back hisself last time he went off." He laid a hesitant hand on Lily's shoulder. "Don't take on so, Lil. He'll turn up soon."

A deep, husky voice called from upstairs, "No one is to ride Zephyr."

Jack's eyes widened in fright. Dee ran to the open door to the hallway.

"Come down, Ralph, and help us. John is missing."

Footsteps retreated. His reply came from over his shoulder. "He was always out of control." And then another shout aimed downstairs. "Mateo obeyed *me*." Dee was trying to scamper up the stairs to stop him disappearing again, but she stumbled, and as she recovered she heard him sob out, "Now he obeys his mother, God help him." The door was slammed, and she heard the bolt shot into place.

Distress and anger warred in her heart. Forget him, forget him, she told herself. John is in peril. We must act quickly.

In the kitchen Lily was shouting, "How dare he say that! I'll never forgive him." She turned to Dee. "Oh, why isn't Frank here? What are we to do?"

Jack could only shake his head and look at Dee. Bewilderment numbed him. She spoke gently. "Will you go to the stable and saddle Rusty, the carriage horse. I am going to ride to the village and tell Constable Naughton and

Mr Bunson, the schoolteacher, and everyone I can that John has been missing since early morning. I'll put on my riding skirt now, so be ready with Rusty."

He went out, muttering, "Saddle Rusty, not Zephyr."

Lily said, "I should go, but I am a coward. I never learned to ride." She broke down again. "Will the gypsies harm him? Where will they take him? Oh my baby!"

As she ran upstairs Dee remembered it was John who had named the new carriage horse. "Is he all right?" he had said. "He looks rusty."

John was such a vibrant presence in the house the moment he came in from school – never still, never silent, always inventive, with an opinion about everything. His absence now was palpable. As she changed, Dee was praying frantically.

When Jack led Rusty out, his eyes were deeply troubled. He knew she loved riding as she had when young, but he always begged her to keep within their walls.

"Pray God you come back soon, angel," he managed to choke out.

The day ended with no John. Constable Naughton promised to send messages to every constable in the Tyne Valley to start a search. A special troop of militia would be raised to trace the gypsies. A description would be given to the newspapers and street vendors. Posters would be printed if he didn't turn up soon. Villagers would come to help search Sheradon Grange and the surrounding woods.

Dee wondered if John had heard talk of the gypsies and had run off to join them. Was school too constraining for him?

The first villagers bringing lanterns followed her home, eager for the excitement of a midnight hunt. Riding ahead on Rusty, Dee was greeted by a white-faced Frank, who said he would organise the people into groups as they arrived.

Dee said she would tell Ralph what was going on.

"Tell him nothing," Lily cried. "I'll never forgive him for what he said!"

Dee just shook her head and went upstairs. "We are all in grief down here for John," she called at Mateo's door. There was silence. "Be thankful you know your son is alive." Her tone was sharp. There was still no reply. She came down, and Lily looked at her with reproachful eyes.

The search groups scoured the estate and surrounding woodlands to no avail. The search was called off. The family gathered in the kitchen, and Dee made mugs of chocolate.

She tried to bolster Lily by telling her Mr Bunson had said, "No one will keep John Heron down. He's far ahead of his own age group and wants to sit at the table with six-year-olds. He'll survive."

Jack said, "I telt the wee lad just lately he looked like a six-year-old." It was his only contribution.

Frank said, "He gets sudden ideas, like walking to the village on his birthday. I'll ride to the station in the morning and make inquiries."

And how they were to endure the rest of the night Dee couldn't imagine.

Next day Frank came back with no news from the station.

Some villagers straggled up to search in daylight, eager to see more of the mysterious Sheradon Grange. Constable Naughton came, a plump, bald man, and sat down in the kitchen with a glass of ale.

"Children run away from home all the time," he said, "especially boys. Have you had to beat him lately, Mr Heron?" When this was vehemently denied he asked, "Anything happened out of the ordinary?"

Dee wished Frank and Lily did not so obviously exchange glances.

He pounced on that. "Something, eh? Something upset him?"

Dee spoke in her most casual tone. "His aunt and cousins left for a visit to Spain. That didn't affect him, except he was pleased to have the swing to himself. His uncle has since been ill, which made him sad, but no reason to disappear." She changed her tone. "Our fear is that he was seen waiting outside our gates and someone has abducted him. For God's sake find those gypsies."

Constable Naughton got up. "Ay, they went Carlisle way, we think. Word's been sent down the line. They'll be found." He looked hard at Frank and Lily. "If you think of anything that might give us a clue, you'll let me know?" He caught sight of the church sexton thrashing the brambles at the edge of the wood. "Keeps folk busy. Nothing exciting happens in their lives." He took his leave.

Jack went out too. "I'll keep 'em off the stables. They'll frighten the horses."

Dee had been watching Lily, who had suddenly drawn breath as if an idea had struck her. She waited till they were out of hearing and then leapt to her feet. Dee had never seen such passion in her mild eyes.

"It's him. I know it." She was pointing upwards. "He's got him prisoner there. Or he's killed him and hiding the body."

Dee rose in horror. "No, oh no. Lily!"

Lily pushed past her and ran to the stairs. Frank leapt after her but she slipped from his grasp, ran up, dashed through the dismantled partition and pounded on Mateo's door.

"What have you done with John? You lost your son so you took ours. Where is he? You evil beast, give him back to me!"

She kept hitting the door with her clenched fists till Frank clasped her waist and drew her off. At the same moment the door opened slowly, and a haggard figure in a grey bedgown with grey in his beard stood there like a ghost of himself. His eyes moved from Lily, struggling and shouting in Frank's arms, to Dee's face, and rested there with a look so piteous that Dee thought her heart would break.

"Lily's hysterical with worry," she said. "Oh Ralph, come out of there now. Come and join us. Help us to think where John can be."

Lily beat her feet on the ground. "Get in there, Frank. Search. He must have drugged him. He's a killer. You know he's a killer."

Ralph moved from the door and gestured her in. Lily tore out of Frank's arms and dashed in, hurling Mateo's possessions and the bedsheets and pillows aside. Dee saw Ralph take a step towards her and then stop and hide his eyes with his hands.

Lily came out. "Search the attics," she ordered Frank, and turned to Dee. "I am not hysterical. I want my boy, and it came to me just now where he could be. That man nearly murdered my husband, and I am not going to let him take my son."

Ralph was leaning against the wall within touching distance of Lily. He put a hand out now, and she shrank bank.

"Oh Lily," he muttered. "You couldn't hate me more than I hate myself – but I wouldn't harm your boy."

She looked round the large front bedroom, which was Spartan in its orderliness, and when she had opened and shut every chest and cupboard and peered under the bed she turned with doubtful eyes. Frank came down from the attics at the same moment and looked in the twins' room, and Nurse's.

"I had to convince her," he murmured to Ralph. "We are torn apart with worry. Come on downstairs now."

Dee said, "Go outside for some fresh air. Wind and sun will do you good."

"No, no, there are people about. I must put things to rights." He stepped back into Mateo's room.

Dee pleaded, "Don't lock the door. Don't shut yourself away."

Lily looked up into his face. "*Your* son is *not* dead."

Ralph shook his head. Pain distorted his face. "Better if he were. She will corrupt him. She is corrupting him at this very moment." He made a dismissive gesture. "Leave me. I cannot help you with John. I cannot help what you think of me. Wish me dead. It's what I wish myself."

He began to close the door, and now it was Lily who flung herself against it.

"No, please." She was in floods of tears. "You are ill. I was cruel. I am so sorry." She put her hands up to clasp his. "You have been here grieving all the time. I think I was mad, but I saw all this space up here where we hadn't looked and you—"

"The evil spirit of the place."

"No, no. Forgive me."

Her streaming eyes yearned, Dee could see, for a redemptive word. Instead, he bowed his head, took her in his arms and wept on her shoulder.

"Oh Lily, if I had had you beside me all these years..." This was too much for Frank. He strode forward with clenched fists raised. Ralph released her. "Yes, come on, brother. Knock me down. Kill me. Put the record straight."

Lily flapped her hands at them both. "Stop it, stop it. We are all mad."

Dee heard a knock and a shout below. "Hey, Missus."

They all froze like statues, listening, and the shout came again.

"News," Dee breathed, and called, "Coming."

Frank and Lily overtook her on the stairs. She heard Ralph murmuring, "People!" as he disappeared into Mateo's room, and then she was down in the hallway and there was the sexton, with a triumphant grin on his face, hovering in the kitchen doorway. He passed a torn piece of paper into Lily's outstretched hand.

She gave a small shriek when she looked at it. "John's written this. It's his big printed letters. Oh look, Frank. There's his name, but it's all smudged with wet."

"Ay, it rained in the night," said the sexton. He was obviously delighted to have found a clue. Dee, eager to look, trembled with excitement.

"But where did you find this, Mawson?" Frank asked him.

The sexton had a wide mouth with several teeth missing. Now he gave them the benefit of a big grin. "Stuck in a holly bush by the gates."

Lily showed it to Dee. "What's that word? I can't read it."

Dee was thinking, Where could John get paper and pencil? They use slates and chalk at school. She said aloud, "This smeared word could be 'GON'. He's left the 'E' off. 'JOHN GONE TO', and then the paper's torn."

"It *is* the gypsies!" Lily's face was puckered with fright. "They have seized him, and they tell him to write 'Gone to school' so no one will follow them. That pencil mark – it's a curve, like the top of an 'S'. Oh my baby. We'll never see him again." She sobbed against Frank's chest.

The sexton said, "It's a clue, sir. It is *something*. But I have to be getting back to work. Vicar's got a funeral tomorrow and there's a grave to be dug."

"Why did he say that?" Lily cried when he'd gone. "John's dead and we'll never find his body."

It was not till next morning that Constable Naughton came back. They showed him the paper.

"Well, it ain't gypsies," he said. "They never came this way. After Hexham market they headed further west, like I thought. They was found near Brampton, with only their own bairns. Never would take a child, they said. This paper? John could have dropped it anytime. He practises his letters at home, I suppose."

They all looked at each other. There was a huge emptiness where their one clue had been. Naughton told them men were dragging the river.

They were glad when he went away.

Dee wandered into her office, where she hadn't been for three days. Her notebook lay on her desk next to the pot containing her drawing pencils. She frowned. The book was askew and one of the pencils lay beside it. That wasn't how she left things. She sat down on the chair, put the pencil back and picked up the book. She flipped through the pages and found that a blank one had been torn out. From her apron pocket she drew John's paper and laid the ragged remnant in the space. Next second she was running to the kitchen calling Lily.

"John *was* sending a message."

"What? Oh Mother Dee!" She followed her back to the office and stared at the book and the paper. "Yes, I see he used paper torn from your book—"

"He took this page that morning *before* he went up to the gates. I wondered how he could write up there with nothing to rest on. He wrote here at this desk while you were putting his dinner bag ready. He didn't intend to go to school." Dee's mind was galloping along with John's. "He had something planned. He would have to hide till the cart had come and gone. Then he sticks the message in the holly bush and sets off—"

"Where?" Lily's excitement faded. "We're no further forward."

"We've learned he's not in someone else's hands. He is in charge of himself."

Dee took off her apron. "I shall go to the school. Speak to the children. A friend might be hiding him in an outhouse or barn and it's their great secret."

"Oh, if I could believe that! But if it was a secret, why would he leave a note?"

"We don't know what he said. 'John gone to stay with friend'? He was astute enough to guess we might be worried."

"Worried? I've been out of my mind. Frank and I will go to the school. I'll ride behind him. I'm not frightened holding on to him."

Dee was delighted to find Lily eager to be doing. "Very well. I'll tell Jack to saddle Prince."

When they'd gone, Dee sat down at her desk with a great sigh. Had she built too much on what she'd discovered? Was her imagination running wild? She couldn't discuss it with Jack. There was only Ralph in the house, apart from Rosie, who was engaged in a major scouring of the east kitchen. She looked up when Dee appeared.

"I'm making it nice for when they come back, ma'am. I should have guessed my lady's plan. She dismissed cook the morning they went off – said she couldn't stomach another of her leek puddings. Said I'd have to find another in the village. I'm sorry Sir Ralph has took it so bad, but he'll pay me when he's well, and now wee John has got you all worried."

Dee promised to see she was paid, and went upstairs. Ralph had left his empty breakfast tray outside the door. Thank God, he's eating, she thought.

She tapped at the door. "There has been a development."

He opened it after a few minutes. "I was asleep. I don't sleep much at night. What's happened?"

She asked him to come into the big front bedroom and sit down at the window. Then she told him about the note. "I haven't it with me. They took it to the school. Can you remember anything John said or did before this happened?"

"I saw little of him. I was in town too much. I...I saw Mateo on the swing reading a book." He gulped and breathed hard before he could go on. "John came running and asked what he was reading. I was on the bench studying some papers."

"Yes?" Dee saw it was agony for him to recall a day of Mateo's presence.

"Mateo told him the story and John asked intelligent questions. I was only half-aware of them, but I remember it now."

"Has he taken the book with him?"

"No."

"Can I see it?"

Ralph fetched it. We are having rational talk, Dee thought. Surely he will come among us now. But when he handed it over he was choking with tears, and he disappeared back into Mateo's room without a word more.

She took it to the bench under the parlour window and flipped through till the word '*stowaway*' caught her eye. Was that it? 'John gone to sea'? She skipped to the end. The hero had stowed away on a naval vessel and improbably risen to become an admiral.

When Frank and Lily came back gloomily, with little to report, she said, "Newcastle quayside. It's starting to rain. We'll go in the carriage. I'll tell Jack."

She explained her new idea.

Frank said, "That's little to go on. It's noon and here comes Da. He always knows when it's dinnertime."

"I'm not hungry," Lily said, "I'd rather be doing something."

Jack went back to the stable to harness Rusty to the carriage, while Dee cut and buttered hunks of bread and put them in a basket with cheese and apples.

Frank was shaking his head. "One of us must stay in case there's news."

So it was Jack, Dee and Lily who set off on the fifteen-mile journey, with Dee biting her lip after half a mile, wondering if she had been wildly impetuous.

In Newcastle, Jack halted the carriage near the Custom House because he could see a stone water trough by the roadway. He stared along the quayside at the giant cranes. "My, look at them!"

Dee thought, He's forgotten what we came for. But her own doubts about the trip sharpened as she looked about.

The Custom House loomed with rows of pedimented windows above arched doorways. There were warehouses and shipping offices and people scurrying, intent on their own business. A merchant sailing vessel was loading.

Passengers waited to board – a family with a boy like Mateo. Is this where *he* stood? she wondered. Is this where John stood, hoping to stow away? The river was crowded with keelboats, barges and steam tugs, the crews endlessly yelling at each other. Seagulls screeched. She covered her ears. What would it be like for a four-year-old?

"Shall we ask at each of the company offices?" Lily suggested.

Dee realised Lily was used to North Shields fishing quay when the fishing boats came in, so she let her take her arm and lead her to the nearest office.

There the name *JOHN HERON* leapt out at them from a poster under the heading *Missing Boy*. They clung to each other in shock and dismay.

"We've come on a fool's errand." Dee was near to tears.

Lily said, "Now we're here we must make inquiries. That man behind the desk has a kindly face." She walked up to him, and he leaned forward to hear her above the noise. Dee marvelled at her boldness.

"Pray tell me, if a child wanted to stow away on any of these vessels, how would he go about it?"

The man's eyes opened wide. Then he cocked his head towards the poster on the open door.

Lily nodded. "I am the boy's mother, and this is his grandmother."

"And you think he tried to get on a ship?"

"We clutch at anything," Dee said. "Is it possible to stow away?"

He chuckled, and quickly composed his face. "It's not easy. Grown men can do it. Boys are smaller but they can't help shuffling and getting hungry."

"If they are found," Lily asked, "is the ship turned back to take them home?"

He shook his head. "A ship's captain has to answer to the owner for delays."

"And no one here reported seeing a child?"

He pointed outside. Crowds, including many children, thronged the quayside.

"He'd tag on to a family. Truly, ladies, we've all been racking our brains."

People were lining up behind them. They thanked the man and returned to Jack, patient as ever, holding Rusty's reins as he drank from the water trough.

He said, "Rusty must rest and be fed before we go back. I've asked about and there's stables not far – up the hill and head west, the man said. Up the hill and head west." Dee was thrilled to see Jack taking so much initiative.

134

They found the place, and Dee realised it was not far from Heron Mansions.

"While Rusty recovers I'll look there. You two eat the food."

Heron Mansions had the same gaunt look that she remembered: tall and grey. John wouldn't be there. He'd heard of it but had never been. But maybe I can do some good, she thought. That poor widow who owed rent – Ralph gave her a week. That was the last time he was here. I wonder if I can find her.

She looked at the front doors of numbers two, three and four with the names of the tenants, and picked out *Mr and Mrs Jacob Stone* in the basement of number four because *Mr* had been scratched out recently. It was the only house with area steps down to a front door. She went down and knocked.

She could hear a chair scrape, so she waited, and at last the door was opened and a crinkled face under a mob-cap peered round.

"Mrs Stone?" She nodded. "I want to help you. Are you behind with your rent?" She nodded again and a gleam of hope lit her eyes. She'll think I come from some charity, Dee thought. "I am Sir Ralph Barnet's mother. I thought I'd let you know he is ill and will not be troubling you for the rent for a while longer." The woman held her hand to her ear. She had winced at his name, but when Dee repeated the rest more loudly a look of pure relief came into her eyes. She held open the door.

"Come in, milady." Her voice was a faint croak.

Dee went in out of curiosity. It was on such as these that old Sarah's wealth had been built, and Ralph had inherited it, spending much of it on Sheradon Grange. She looked round the room with a spasm of guilt. There was a rocking chair with the horsehair bursting out of it, a three-legged table and a stool. Dee suspected other furniture had been chopped up for a fire, but there was none in the grate now.

"I should make you a cup o' tea," Mrs Stone squeaked out, "but the coalman won't come till he's paid." She pointed to the rocking chair. "Sit ye down, milady."

Dee declined, but put her hand into her purse and laid two half crowns on the table. "You must have a fire. Autumn is setting in." The woman's eyes widened at the sight of such wealth.

"I am sorry Sir Ralph's ill," she said, "but he's a hard man. If he puts me out it'll be the workhouse for me."

"I am waited for," Dee told the woman, "but I will see that you get help."

"God bless you, milady." She held open the door and then put her hand to her mouth with a hoarse chuckle. "Funny, you coming like this. The bairn that was here the other day pretended to be Sir Ralph's nephew. Canny lad."

Dee felt her jaw drop. A great burst of light exploded in her head. John! John had been here!

She turned and grasped the woman's hand. "Oh tell me. When was this? He is missing. He's my grandson, my other son's boy, John Heron."

"What? I thought he was boasting, the way children do. If he'd said he was *John Heron* I'd ha' known he was family. I was here when Mr Joseph and Mrs Sarah Heron was in charge. Sit ye down. I can tell ye all about them old days." She has found some voice now, Dee thought, and will be hard to stop.

"No, no, please tell me about John, the little boy." She almost shouted at her ear. "He is missing! Please, where did you see him? When?"

The old woman shook her head. "I don't know one day from another. I was scrubbing me steps. Even Sir Ralph says no one's place is as clean as mine."

Dee made her sit down in her rocking chair and pulled the stool up close.

"You were scrubbing the steps and you saw a boy in the street above?"

"Nay, he called out, 'Hey, missus, where's the sea?' He come up from the river, so I laughs and says, 'Gan away back to the river and follow it till it finds the sea for you, but it's a mighty long way for a wee boy like you.' He says, 'I'm not a wee boy, I'm six,' though I didn't quite think he talked like a six-year-old."

"Only four," Dee murmured, but Mrs Stone was fairly launched.

"I asked him why he was on his own and he said his da and ma was waiting for him where the ships were. Oh, says I, you don't need to go as far as the sea to find ships. The ships is in the river. I asked him, 'How did you get lost?' So he tells me they'd all come on the train and he'd stopped to look at the engine and then his ma and da were out of sight. So he'd walked on by the river and looked up this street and saw our big sign, 'Heron Mansions'." She gave a chuckle. "Eh, ma'am, I laughed when he telt me his uncle owned this place. 'Go on with you,' I said."

"What did he say?"

Mrs Stone seemed exhausted. "Eh, I don't know. I seen nobody to talk to since then till you came. And that's strange, you being his grandmother."

"It's not strange. We've been looking for him today at the quayside."

Mrs Stone sat up. "Quayside. That was it. I says to him, 'There's ships at the quayside. Keep to the road by the river. It's not far.' He just thanked me and ran off. Eh, I'm right sorry he's not been seen since." Her eyes peered fearfully at Dee. "I'd ha' kept him here if I'd known. It was over in a minute and I thought no more of it." She was eyeing the coins on the table as if she feared they might be withdrawn.

Dee patted her bony arm. "I am so thankful to you. This is the first news we have had. There have been posters out all over the place."

"Eh, I haven't passed the door, with not a penny to spend."

Dee opened her purse and added a few shillings to the half crowns.

Mrs Stone began to cry. Dee bent and kissed her and restrained her as she struggled to get up. Then she went out with a smile and a wave, and was running up the street like a young thing until she found herself bent double and panting at the top. I was right, I was right with 'John gone to sea'. I knew it.

Then the awful truth struck her. She had to tell Frank and Lily that their boy could be stowed away on a vessel anywhere on the sea; and how they were to get him back she had no idea.

Chapter 14

Sheradon Grange, October
(one month later)

Ralph

Ralph sat on the window seat in the front bedroom and saw that the trees were turning inexorably to yellows and reds. It was good that nothing halted nature's progress even though life in the house was at a standstill.

He no longer locked himself in Mateo's room, but could not endure to go downstairs among the truncated family. John was dead, or living an unknown life on a ship travelling God knew where.

His mother had told him about Mrs Stone, and how they had gone straight back to the quayside to urge messages to be sent to every port where a vessel from the Tyne might dock. They were advised to have the offer of a reward added to the posters. Lily had no notion as to what Frank could afford. Dee thought they could raise fifty pounds, which would tempt any ship's captain. Ralph told them to make it a hundred and that he would pay.

"But what is the state of your business?" his mother urged. "You answer no letters, even when they come from your bank. Is your lawyer collecting your rents? No, we will leave the reward at fifty pounds."

She was right, of course. Rents, houses, investments, stocks and shares had no significance if he had lost Mateo to inherit them. He had no energy anyway to read letters, let alone answer them. His mother had pestered him to write to Mateo. She laid writing materials before him. "Tell him you love him. You are missing him." He told her he had no address.

"You know the place is called Castillo de Villena and is not far from Santiago de Compostela. It will find him."

"And she will not let Mateo have it." The very thought of her power over his son had reduced him to a weeping hysteria. His mother's arms about him could do nothing to stop it, and she hadn't mentioned it again.

He spent days at the window and nights in Mateo's bed. Today an autumn gale set the treetops swaying in a crazy dance. Leaves flew horizontally. White clouds shredded as they chased across the sky. And a man on foot trotted round the curve of the drive, and Ralph jerked back from the window. He didn't know him, but strangers had a way of looking up at the house, and he mustn't be seen.

He could hear the bell jangling and then Jack's voice calling, "He wants to come in and speak to Frank."

Lily called back, "I'll run to the cottage to fetch him."

He got to his feet and shuffled along the landing to the head of the west stairs, and heard his mother take the man into the kitchen. "A mug of ale this blustery day."

He heard the front door open as Lily came back with Frank, and he could see the tops of their heads pass down the passage to the kitchen. They shut the door.

Exhausted from the effort, he went back to the bedroom, sank into the easy chair and closed his eyes.

He woke to his mother shaking him. "Oh Ralph, Ralph! It's John. He's alive! We can get him back, but the man wants a hundred pounds, not fifty. We've had the fifty in the house in banknotes since we advertised the reward, but fifty more...!"

It was her bright face suffused with tears and laughter that roused his sluggish brain. Her words filtered through more slowly, but when he'd grasped them he sat up. "Who is this man? It could be a fraud. Don't pay him."

She laughed and held out a paper. "No, no, look. Look at this!"

He saw big sprawled letters. 'HE IS A GOOD MAN. PAY HIM. JOHN.'

He said, "Anyone could imitate a child's scrawl."

"No, truly. John often curled the 'J' the wrong way. He's done that and then corrected it." She pointed to the bottom of the 'J'. "Ralph, he's alive! He wrote this recently. The paper is clean."

139

"But where is this man holding him? There must be a gang of them. He could take the money and go."

"Oh Ralph." The joy had died out of her face. "I came up. I thought you could help."

He pushed her aside and struggled to his feet. "I can write a banker's draft this minute, but I will see the man I give it to first. Frank has no business head."

"Frank has money in the bank, but not enough. Will you really? Shall I send the man up to you?"

"No, I will come down." He said the words without reflecting what an enormous step that was. "Give me a few minutes."

She looked at him with hope and excitement in her eyes, brows raised and mouth open. Then she scurried away downstairs. What had he done? He had no mirror up here, but Rosie had refilled his water jug this morning. He washed his face and combed his hair and beard, and took from the tallboy a Turkish morning robe he'd never worn, because Sophia had bought it for him. He inserted his pocketbook into its tasselled pocket and, trying to feel like someone else, he made his way again to the head of the stairs. Take one step at a time, he told himself, and hang on to the banister. When he reached the bottom and turned into the passage to the kitchen, he saw the door was wide open and a galaxy of faces was turned towards him: Jack, his mother, Frank, Lily and a man of middle age, rugged from sea and wind.

They had heard him coming and were all standing up. It was too late to flee. His mother greeted him with her most radiant smile and closed the door behind him. Then she gathered them onto chairs and stools round the table and pointed him to the seat with arms at the head. He hesitated. It was like a board meeting. He wanted the man on his own, but there seemed no help for it. Perhaps he was dreaming. He sat down, aware of the red satin over his knees. He was acting in a play.

"This is Sam," she began. "Sam is asking for one hundred pounds and then he will tell us where John is." She looked the man in the eye. "My elder son has a few questions he would like to put to you."

Before Ralph could say a word, the man blustered out, "Look here, sir, fifty pounds is the reward money and has to be divided among the crew, but the boy's had bed and board for nigh on a month, and the master had to hire a trap to bring us out here. What's a hundred pounds to the likes of you, sir, living in a great mansion?"

He laid both fists on the table, and his blue eyes stared out like a challenge.

Ralph knew he must speak, but the process of framing words was all clogged up. On the stairs one possible question had come into his mind.

"The name of your ship?" he managed in a husky voice.

Frank came to the rescue. "He's told us it's the *Tyne Belle*, a collier. Coals to London. They had fair winds both ways. But he won't tell us where John is."

Ralph took out his pocketbook and put it on the table. He tried to focus on the man's face. "When I buy, I want to see the goods." He noticed Frank's hand was clutching a roll of something. That must be the fifty pounds in bank notes. Lily had an ink pot and pen in front of her and was watching him, one finger poised ready to push them towards him. Her small bosom was heaving up and down.

They believed they were going to get their son back. Of course they did. They had to; but Ralph felt his brain beginning to churn like a steam paddle. Nothing had been said so far that could not have been planted in the mind of a ship's master by the sight of a poster on the quayside. The childish writing could be a fake. He was not convinced by the appearance of the letter 'J'. Sam must be the mate. He spoke too confidently for a common sailor. He had been sent by the master to try this out.

He took a deep breath and fixed the man with his eye. "How and where did you encounter this boy in the first place?"

Sam answered readily. "You think we abducted him? I'll tell ye how it was. We was anchored in the river while the keelboats from Lemington Staiths loaded us up."

Ralph saw Jack sit up and beam with delight. That was his world on the waggonway from Wylam Colliery to Lemington Staiths leading Sandy the horse. Ralph's mind leapt back to his early childhood, when his 'Dada' passing their window with the coal wagon was the great excitement of the day. He pulled himself back to the present.

The man was saying, "There's a landing stage and steps, and a new hand was to join us there. He was going down to board a hired rowing boat when this boy calls from the top. 'Where are you going in that boat?' 'To yon collier,' says he, 'and then out to sea.' 'Take me with you,' says the boy. 'Why would we do that?' our man says. So he says, 'Don't you know I'm the captain's boy?' Well, the hand's new so he lets him on, and he gets on deck and the boat's gone back afore anyone else notices. It's the busiest time casting off from the keelboats and getting underway. The boy had the sense to crouch down in the fo'c's'le while all the activity was aft and the trimmers were at work on the coal. We was miles downstream before the master found him. If we'd turned back we'd ha' missed the tide."

"What?" cried Lily. "We have been suffering all these weeks for that?"

"Nay, Missus. Your boy is the coolest liar I ever seen. He tells the master his family died from smallpox and he's always wanted to go to sea and he'll work and get strong and not be any trouble."

Lily gave a small moan and hid her face in her hands.

Sam appeared gratified by this, so Ralph asked him sharply, "So you believed all that till you saw the poster on Newcastle Quay with the name 'John Heron'?"

The man had no time to answer. The door flew open. "That's me! I'm home."

John stood in the doorway.

The cacophony of sound that followed was too much for Ralph. He covered his eyes and ears, but sensed another presence in the room. A big man had followed John and was protesting loudly about knots undone and how fast the boy could run. Inside Ralph's head a terrible ache reminded him that Mateo had *not* come home.

The clamour of voices subsided. He found his mother was bending over him and murmuring, "There were just two men and a pony trap actually at the gates. John broke free of cords but he is unhurt, and they are desperate to get away now and report to their captain. They say he'll expect a hundred pounds. We do thank God that they brought him safe home." He saw that the pen and ink were by his pocketbook. "The draft should be paid to Herbert Gray, master of the *Tyne Belle*."

His fingers shook as he dipped the pen in the ink, but he controlled them by thinking of each letter as he wrote it. When the thing was done and blotted, he heard Frank mutter, "God bless you, brother. I'll pay you back."

Sam's voice said, "Much obliged, sir," so he looked up to see Sam's big grin as he pocketed the banker's draft and roll of notes. A red-faced, stout man looked over Sam's shoulder and touched his cap. Sam, as they sidled out, wagged a finger at John, now standing in the middle of the kitchen with Lily's arms tight round him.

He said, "Now, Johnboy, don't you ever do that caper again, mind."

They had gone, and Ralph sat back in his chair, utterly spent. He felt the atmosphere of joy and relief, and rested his own eyes on the boy to convince himself this had truly happened. He looked inches taller, and his hair had grown to an untidy bunch of straw. Aware of Ralph's gaze, he wriggled away from Lily and stepped up to him. His lips were trembling.

"I'm really sorry, Uncle Ralph, that I didn't bring Matty back."

The words jerked Ralph upright. "Bring Matty back—"

"That's what I went for. That's what I put on the note. 'Gone to Spain.'"

There was a general exclamation from the others. "Gone to *Spain*!"

John looked round at them. "Yes, I knew you had to cross the sea to get there. I'd have told him to come back. His Papa was ill. You *look* ill, Uncle Ralph."

Ralph put out a hand and took hold of the boy's arm and drew him close.

"Let me understand this. You thought you could get to Spain by getting on a ship and sailing across the sea and there would be Spain and Mateo and you could bring him back with you."

John nodded. "I knew I might have to ask where he lived. I didn't think it would take long. I was very cross with the captain when he said they were going back to Newcastle."

Lily cried, "Didn't you *want* to come home?"

"Not without Matty."

Then he turned away from Ralph and was in her arms again, sobbing his heart out. Ralph sat, oblivious of the others, and found his own tears flowing like an unstoppable fountain, soaking his scarlet robe in great dark patches.

Dee

Dee could scarcely believe her eyes next morning when Ralph appeared in the kitchen at eleven o'clock, clean-shaven, dark hair neatly combed back, and wearing suit and waistcoat and white cravat. The clothes hung on his emaciated frame, but he looked years younger.

"Good morning, Mother. I have set Rosie to scour Mateo's room. May I join you at your dinner hour? Is John up?"

She couldn't help taking a joyful step towards him, but he held up a hand.

"No comment, please. A one-word explanation: shame. As soon as I am fit I will set my affairs in order, then I go to Spain."

Her eyes applauded him; her heart sang. Then she answered his questions. "We will have a feast today. Jack went early to the village for provisions. Of course you must be with us. As for John, he was scrubbed down yesterday and put to bed in a clean nightgown and slept at once, but in the night he kept coming to me or Frank and Lily saying his bed was too soft, but of course it was to be sure he was truly home. Now they are talking seriously to him about his conduct, especially the lies."

"How could he have thought of them – at four years old?"

"The hero in Mateo's book used similar ones." Ralph drew in his breath, but she pressed on. "You and I have learned to our sorrow that truth is not to be sacrificed to expediency." She gave him a wan smile. "But you're right. John is too clever for his age. He knew he'd be recognised at Prudhoe station, so he walked to Stocksfield and attached himself to a family with children and slipped through. He says he taught the alphabet and simple words to the men who couldn't write. Sam was his best friend, though, because he showed him the workings of the ship. But the captain was suspicious and locked him up when they docked in London. Truly, Ralph, he has so much to tell I think he will never stop talking."

"Will he go back to the village school after this great adventure?"

"He wants to tell them all about it – but can he ever be a normal boy again? Ah, here he is!"

He came running in and stopped in his tracks when he saw Ralph.

"Who's that?"

"I'm better now you are home."

He swore. "Oh, it's Uncle Ralph!"

"John!" Dee cried.

Ralph smiled. "He will drop that talk soon enough. Come, John, I want to show you on Mateo's globe where Spain is."

"Oh, I know now there are lots of countries over the sea as well as Spain." But he took Ralph's proffered hand and trotted off with him.

From that moment Dee saw a new pattern of life evolving at Sheradon Grange. They tried John at the school but Mr Bunson said he was too disruptive, so Ralph unobtrusively became his tutor while he built up his own strength. He never called the time with John 'lessons' because, as he told Frank and Lily, "All I do is answer his questions. Even if I tell him I have letters to write, he wants to know who to and what about. Then he wants pencil and paper to write one himself."

Sitting still, however, never lasted long. He had to be out of doors. Frank was busy in the cottage trying to earn enough to pay Ralph back the fifty pounds, so Jack took him for walks but couldn't keep up with him, or he stood patiently to catch him when he climbed impossible trees.

Dee invited a few children to tea after school but John could outrun them all, and was cross when they didn't grasp the rules of his games. Dee sensed that Ralph disliked hearing other children about, so she didn't repeat the experiment. Lily tried playing hide and seek with him in all the new space, for they had dismantled the partitions, but that meant echoing footsteps, which tried everyone's nerves.

In November they heard that Mr Bunson was retiring at the end of term and a young man was taking over.

"I'd better go to school now," John said. "I don't want to be put down a class. I can be good if I try."

So peace and quiet filled Sheradon Grange; and Ralph felt well enough, by late November, to take the train to Newcastle to look into his affairs. He came back with heavy brows.

"I have been neglectful, and must mortgage Heron Mansions."

Dee was appalled. "Oh Ralph, are you heading for bankruptcy?"

He laughed uneasily. "You have memories of your father. No, I have some sound investments growing, and I've told Frank he doesn't owe me fifty pounds. His boy saved my life. I have enough in the bank for this trip to Spain."

She inquired warily after Mrs Stone. He shook his head.

"I am sorry, but news of her death was in a letter from my lawyer which lay unread. The money you gave her was found in her room and saved her from a pauper's funeral." He paused and studied her face. "Mother, I know not what happened to me all those weeks. All I want now is to be on a ship for Spain."

But this could not be soon. The winter of 1840–41 was appalling all over Britain and much of the continent. Ice and gales closed shipping lanes, and roads and railway lines were blocked by snowdrifts.

At Sheradon Grange they had, sadly, to eat their own chickens, but Dee had laid in good stocks of flour and salted butter. There was also a cured ham, a side of beef, sacks of potatoes, onions and turnips and jars of pickled beetroots. The loft was full of apples, the pantry shelves lined with jars of blackberry jam and crab-apple jelly, all produce of their own woods. Dee and Lily had been busy in that sad autumn when they had no news of John.

All of them, including John with great enthusiasm and a small spade, worked at clearing ways though drifts to some of the cottages beyond their gates so they could take provisions to the old and poor. Ralph grew stronger with the exercise, but he admitted to Dee that if he could have had Mateo wielding a shovel beside him he would have been happy. Lily couldn't dig, but she could use a stiff brush to sweep away the new snow as it filled up the stable yard and the path to the shed.

At last the sun shone, and early April produced a warm sun, melting the last tired banks of snow by the driveway. Ralph said he hoped to travel to Spain by the end of the month. The new Penny Post service resumed, and letters held up for weeks began to arrive.

One afternoon John came back from school with a letter in his hand.

"Bunny-Hop told the school we're not supposed to have letters delivered to us at school and then he gave me this. It says 'John Heron' and 'Ovingham School' and it's from *Spain*. But why would anyone write to *me*? Open it with your pocketknife, Uncle Ralph."

"Spain!" It was a concerted cry of delighted amazement.

They were all gathered in the kitchen, which as usual was the warmest place.

Ralph's hands shook as he fumbled for his pocketknife and broke the seal.

"It's *my* letter." John tried to grab it but Ralph lifted it high.

"You'll tear it."

John danced with impatience as it was carefully unfolded. "Now me." He peered at it. "Oh, it's writing, not printed, but that word's 'John'."

"It's from your cousin Maria. Written in English. Your mother shall read it aloud." They all sat down at the table, John squeezing next to Lily so he could look.

Dee saw Ralph's colour coming and going. He was breathing hard.

"She has let the child write," he muttered. "What can that mean?"

Lily was nervous and her first words were too soft. "It's dated October."

"When? Speak up."

"October. They must only just have reached Spain."

"Read it, Ma," John demanded.

146

"'*Dear Cousin John, I hope you are happy at school and are working hard.*'"

"I always work hard."

Ralph reached across and closed John's lips with his fingers. "Don't interrupt." John giggled and closed them himself.

"'*We have been in Spain two weeks. The house is big and I can see mountains from my window. There are many servants. Mamma has told them all the rules we must obey. Today Guido has brought Lucia and me into town with a maid called Brigitta. We are to buy new dresses but first she is visiting her mother who is ill. That's where I am now so I can't write much. Guido has gone for provisions and will come back. Lucia is playing with Brigitta's little girl. John, do you remember my big toy bear? I have the smaller one here but the big one was sadly left behind.*'"

John released his lips to shout, "She never had a toy bear. They both had china dolls. I used to go in their nursery but there were no bears."

"Silence," Ralph roared. "This could be important." Dee shot him a look with a flash of understanding.

Lily went on, "'*Please tell the Big Bear that Smaller Bear is missing him very much and was very sad to come away without him. He even wrote to Big Bear on the ship but perhaps it never arrived. I wish Big Bear could come across the sea and join us. I must stop now. We all send our love. Brigitta says if I send it to your school she will post it. Your loving cousin, Maria de Villena.*'"

John said, "What a funny letter! How can I give a message to a bear when there isn't one?"

Ralph had risen and was walking about the room. He kept his face turned away as he said in a strange voice, "Mother, come to your office for a few minutes and we'll work it all out. You'll get the letter back, John, I promise."

Dee, feeling his stifled emotion, followed him, and the moment he shut the door behind her he took her in his arms and wept tears of joy on her shoulder.

"You grasped it too," he said when he could speak. "I knew the girls had no bears. I don't know how we'll explain it to John."

"I shall tell him it was her joke and he was to guess the bears are you and Mateo. But come, sit down and let us study the letter. It tells us so much."

They read it through together. "Yes," said Ralph, "she has forbidden any of them to write to me and told the servants not to post letters to this address. Brigitta would see no harm in Maria writing to her little cousin at school. But we see Maria doesn't trust Guido or Lucia, and Mateo is always supervised."

"So, when Maria was allowed into town, he told her what to write if she had an opportunity. Oh Ralph! He wrote to you on the journey. It should have come before the winter closed in, but Sophia made sure it wasn't sent."

"She is a monster. I know not how I will deal with her when I get to Spain. She has imprisoned Mateo. Pray God I can keep myself from strangling her."

"No, Ralph, you are the victor and must be magnanimous. He loves *you.*"

A shadow crossed his face. "Six months ago. Much may have changed."

"But you still hope to bring him home? And the girls?"

"Oh God, Mother, I know not what to hope. How can I know anything till I find them and see how they are living? She will never let any of them go without a fight, and she will have her family and friends in high places and she…"

Dee laid her hand on his arm. "Be calm, my dear. Suggest that you have Mateo for a visit to England. Be forgiving, even loving. Surprise her. Let the children see only good in you and they will want to be with you more than with her. You do not want to involve the law – ours or theirs."

He inclined his head. "If I can master myself – if…"

John burst back into the room. "I want my letter. I need to reply to Maria. Then you can take it with you, Uncle Ralph."

Lily said from the doorway. "I'm so sorry. He escaped from me."

Dee looked to see Ralph rebuke the boy severely. He smiled up at Lily and put an arm round John. "Your son has right notions. Impulsive, perhaps, but good at heart." He gave him the letter. "Keep it always in a safe place, John, and keep a copy of your reply. Ask your father or mother how to spell words you don't know. I will see Maria gets it."

John peered into his face. "Are the bears really you and Mateo? That's what Da says. Shall I call you that in my letter?"

Ralph nodded. "Yes, I think I will feel very comfortable to travel there as a bear."

Dee beamed and patted his arm. "Ay, a big, handsome friendly bear."

Chapter 15

Santiago de Compostela, early May 1841

Ralph

Ralph lost the purpose of his visit for five whole minutes as he stood before the cathedral of Santiago de Compostela in childlike wonder. It was enhanced by the evening light and the glowing sky into which its pinnacles soared. A man in rough clothing drew near and stood beside him. As soon as Ralph became aware of his presence, the man asked him something. Ralph guessed the language was Galego, the peasant tongue of Galicia province. He asked him in Castilian what he had said.

"You want bed for tonight, sir?"

Ralph started to explain that he'd rather find his own accommodation but the man, showing a wide grin of broken teeth, picked up his bag and, hoisting it onto his shoulders, took Ralph's arm in a firm grip and hurried him towards the corner of the piazza, where a side street led away to a lowlier part of the town.

Ralph could have pulled away easily, but he had been seasick on the French coastal craft in which he had travelled from Biarritz to Corunna, and the hired carriage in which he had ridden to Santiago had been almost without springs, and the jolting had left him exhausted. The thought of a bed – any bed – was alluring. His purse was strapped to his body in a money belt, but he sensed that the man's grin was triumphant rather than sinister.

He was shown a ground-floor room at the back of a tall house that seemed to house many families, judging by the number of children playing on the stairs and women in shawls sitting on benches outside in the fading light. The noise of their chatter penetrated to the back room, but he flung himself down on the bed and the man grinned and went out, shutting the door and not demanding any money.

Ralph was drifting into sleep ten minutes later when a woman tapped at the door and came in with a plate of what looked and smelt like chopped spicy vegetables and a glass of some pale liquid Ralph couldn't guess at.

She set them on the bedside stool and, grinning at him just like her husband, went out again. A wooden spoon was the only implement. He tried a mouthful, feeling he must take some nourishment, but the spice was too hot for his taste. He was very thirsty but he knew it was dangerous to ask for water, so he sipped at the drink. It was sweet and slightly alcoholic with a faint taste of lemons, so he drank it and lay back on the bed, too weak and weary to unpack his bag.

The woman came back after a quarter of an hour and threw up her hands when she saw he had eaten nothing. He mimed waves going up and down and vomiting. She nodded and laughed.

He sat up then and beckoned her closer, and began slowly in Castilian to ask if she knew of the land owned by the de Villena family. She shook her head, still chuckling, and, taking out the plate, she fetched her husband.

Ralph repeated his query. The man grinned – when was he not grinning? – and gestured in a direction which Ralph suspected was south.

"How far?" he asked. The man shrugged. Perhaps distances in Spain had not yet adopted the French kilometres. "An hour's ride?" That was a safer unit of measurement.

"Ay," the man said, "or two."

"Depending on your mount?"

He nodded vigorously with a hearty laugh.

"Where could I hire a mount tomorrow morning?"

"Ah! Fandoro's! Only Fandoro's. Good horses. Cheap. I fetch at sunrise?"

Sunrise in May! Ralph shook his head. "Three hours after sunrise."

"You listen for cathedral chime – boing, boing, boing – nine times?"

Ralph smiled. "That will do very well."

He asked for water to wash, and candles. The small window looked onto a yard with a high wall and he suspected little sunshine ever got into the room, which was bare except for the bed and stool and some hooks on the door for hanging clothes. At least the empty corners showed him that it had been swept not too long ago, and the bed, though thinly covered, did not stink of urine. He decided he had done well to accept the hospitality of this cheerful couple.

Before he got into the bed, he took from his pocketbook the folded paper which John had given him for Maria and, smiling to himself, he read it through.

'Dear Cousin Maria, Thank you for your letter but I'm not allowed to get it at school. I laughed about the bears. I gave Big Bear your message. It made him happy. Please write to me again. I never had a letter before. I wanted to go to Spain to bring Small Bear home. I got to London but had to come back. I hope you will come soon. Your cousin John Heron.'

He thought, I must be wary how I give this to Maria or she and Mateo may be in trouble. It had taken several laborious hours for John to complete this and write a copy to keep. The letters were big and uneven, but Ralph didn't think many not-yet-five-year-olds would have had the persistence to finish it. With his enterprise and determination, he was a remarkable boy. How had Frank and Lily produced him? He thought tenderly of his own Mateo but found himself struggling with a pang of jealousy. Mateo had a nervous and reclusive nature. Dear God, he thought, I may actually set eyes on them all tomorrow!

On the voyage, pictures of the outcome of his mission had filled his head, but now that he was here in Galicia, practicalities engaged his mind. Dare he entrust his bag to the keeping of this man, and ride with nothing but his pistol and money belt to the de Villena mansion? Once there, how would he proceed? Would there be gates and a gatekeeper? Would Guido deny him entry? Should he produce pistol or money as persuaders? Putting John's letter back in his pocketbook, he found his hands were shaking with the uncertainty of it all.

He shivered. The sun had gone down and the room was chilly. No fire had been offered in the narrow hearth. He must try to sleep to be fit for the morning so, keeping most of his clothes on, he blew out his one candle, slid under the bedcovers and closed his eyes.

After a restless, flea-bitten night, he sank into an early morning sleep of exhaustion, and was wakened by the cathedral bells, not the chiming of the clock but a joyful peal. It was full daylight. There was a tap at the door and the man looked round at him with his cheerful grin. Behind him came the wife with a breakfast tray.

"I forget," the man began. "She remind me." He indicated his wife as she set the tray on the stool, all smiles. Ralph realised he was hungry.

"I forget it is a big feast day – Saint Philip and Saint James. You not need a horse. The widow Condesa de Villena will bring her family to church. You eat breakfast and go to church. She you want to see will be there. Save journey." He beamed with delight.

'*Widow* Condesa'. The word turned Ralph cold. It is as she said. I am a dead man. Do I expose her in the cathedral before her friends?

The woman was babbling some long tale to her husband. Ralph took the tray onto his lap. Could he eat now? He must try. She had made what he remembered as a typical Spanish omelette.

As they showed no sign of leaving him, he began to eat, which delighted the woman. She nodded at him several times and never left off smiling.

The man said, "She knows gossip of all our noble families. You are acquainted with the condesa?"

Ralph shrugged to indicate a slight acquaintance. This set the man off. "Very sad story, but women say romantic, of course. She married an English nobleman. He commanded a privateer to rid the seas of pirates – your young English nobles, if you'll pardon me sir – wild and reckless." He was chuckling. "But she – the daughter of a great diplomat returning home from somewhere – their ship was set upon by pirates. Every soul killed but her, so they flung her into the sea. And who is there to save her but your English nobleman? What a story! The old king made much of them at court. We never saw them here. Our nobles buzz round Madrid like flies round a honeypot. But they had children and took them to see England. Very sad – he died and now they are back and live on the estate."

The woman interrupted to babble something else, in which the name 'Juan de Villena' struck Ralph's ear.

"Oh," her husband said, "gossip has it the condesa will marry a distant cousin when the mourning period is passed."

Ralph nearly choked on the mouthful he had just taken. The man patted him on the back.

When he could speak Ralph asked, "The service for the feast day – when does it start and end?"

The man spread his hands. "Something going on all day. Processions, singing, carrying crosses and effigies through the town and back to the cathedral, decorated carts, flowers. The hatters and apothecaries parade, for it is their saints' day, you understand, sir. It resumes again after siesta and all finish in the cathedral in the evening."

"When do people coming in from the country start arriving?"

He shrugged. "Any time from now. From the de Villena estate, maybe ten o'clock. The footmen have to take the carriages outside the town when the passengers have been set down in the piazza."

Ralph looked at his pocket watch. It was barely nine. He foresaw a long day, so he asked, "Can I leave things here and stay tonight?" Much nodding and smiling from them both. "And will you tell me your names and what this street is called?" More delight. He wrote down 'Tomaso and Alicia Lopez' and 'Calle del Pantano'. They left him then to get ready, and he extracted some coins from his money belt to have handy in his coat pocket. After some hesitation he left his pistol at the bottom of his bag. There will be big happy crowds, he told himself. I am better without it. But he still had no notion of what would happen if he actually encountered his family.

When he left the room and walked down the passage to the rectangle of sunlight in the open doorway, he found Alicia already sitting out among her neighbours. He handed her a piece of paper on which he had written his name and home address, and asked her if she wanted any payment now.

She shouted for Tomaso and he came from an inner room. He looked at the paper and grinned at Ralph. "Ah, Sir Barton, I trust you. Stay long – long as you like."

Ralph clapped him on the back and made his way to the piazza, to be engulfed in heat and crowds. Was it possible he would pick out anyone he knew in this thronging mass? There were also several entrances to the cathedral, and carriages were arriving and departing all the time, as more and more well-dressed people were set down and made their way inside.

He began to force his way across the piazza. He was focusing on people stepping out of carriages when something on the door of a carriage leaving the square caught his eye. He drew in his breath sharply. He had seen it on an embroidered purse Sophia carried about, and on some of the linen she had brought with her: the de Villena family crest. He reached the cathedral steps and stumbled up in his haste. Be calm, he admonished himself. If it was indeed their carriage, they couldn't have gone far inside. But the great wide aisle was thronging with people. To his right, a group of schoolboys scrabbled for the holy water in an unseemly mob, with a master trying to control them.

One of them, at the back – his heart stood still – was Mateo.

His first instinct was to shrink behind a pillar and take in his face, like a thirsty man gulping water. My boy. My own son. So still, so patient, so shocked! Of course he wasn't with the boys. He had hung back, pushed aside by their rush, reverently waiting his turn. So he had been separated from his mother and sisters. Ralph turned his head to the crowd proceeding down the aisle. Sophia was tall and she would be wearing an extravagant hat, but he couldn't see her. There were flags hanging from poles at the ends of pews, and great festoons of flowers. But he mustn't lose Mateo. He turned his eyes back and there he was, solemnly crossing himself.

There could be no thought of consequences, no hanging back. He had come for his son and he was barely ten yards away from him. He stepped forward as Mateo was narrowing his eyes to search for the others, his head going from side to side. Ralph stood in front of him.

"Mateo!"

His arms were outstretched ready to embrace him. The effect was horrific.

Mateo's mouth fell open. He put his hands up before his face. He gasped. "No, oh no. No."

Ralph's hopes fell about him. "Mateo!" He was indeed poisoned. He had been taught hatred. There was only horror at the sight of him.

"Mateo," he said again, and gripped the hands that covered his son's eyes so he could look into the terror behind them. "I love you. I have come for you. I am still your father, whatever she says."

Mateo had gone as white as death. His breath was coming in short bursts.

He pulled his hands away. "Keep away from me. You are dead. You are frightening me."

A light flashed in Ralph's brain. The boy was seeing a ghost. The terror was real.

"Oh Mateo, look at me, touch me. I was ill but I never died. I am here in person. Maria's Big Bear that was left behind."

Mateo stared, mouth still open, breaths slower, colour creeping back. He put his hands on Ralph's coat sleeves. Then he lifted them to Ralph's face and felt its warmth. Next second his arms were round him and his face was alight with joy and disbelief.

"Oh Papa, Papa, is it really you? How came you here? We thought you were dead. Mamma is in mourning for you. Have you seen her?"

Ralph was on the alert at once. He looked round. God, he spotted her! She was looking the other way. "Outside, Matty, quick." He pulled him round a phalanx of soldiers in flamboyant uniforms and made for the entrance.

There were huge columns ornamented with sculptures and the great semicircle of steps reached round them to their left. He galloped down them and dragged Mateo along by the wall of the cathedral and into a recess. In front, a stall selling sweetmeats concealed them.

They were both panting. Mateo looked up into his eyes. "Why? You don't want to see her? She'll worry. She'll wonder where I've gone."

"Let her." No, that was spat out. Ralph struggled for calm. His mother's words flew into his mind, and his own reply: 'If I can master myself.' He drew a long slow breath and smiled. "Just for now, Matty, just for now. Time with you first. Please. You cannot begin to know how I pined for you. You wrote to me from the ship. Oh, if I had received that, I would not have been ill."

"You got Maria's letter – Big Bear and Small Bear. Thank God you got it. But you didn't reply?"

"The winter – the shipping lanes closed. I got it in April. I have John's reply – here in my pocket." He produced it and handed it over.

Mateo put it carefully in his own pocket. "She will be delighted – but I must not let Mamma see it."

"She told you I was dead?" He made his voice as neutral as he could.

"She had a letter from a friend. It came before winter set in, and Mamma said she would go into mourning. Oh, we must go inside and find her." As he said it, he took a step out of the recess and stopped. "No, I see. She will be shocked. We were not to make contact. But oh, Papa, this is so wonderful. I can't believe it. You shaved your beard! Oh, how did you know where we would be? It's a miracle."

"I was told the local nobility would come for the festival. It *is* a miracle that I saw you and that I am here with you after all this time. I was brokenhearted when she took you away. Tell me, you didn't want to go, did you?"

He shook his head. "I didn't mind so much about school, but I hated leaving home, you and Grandmamma."

"Do you still think of Sheradon Grange as home?"

155

"Oh yes. Every day I long for my life there."

Ralph felt a huge lump in his throat. He couldn't hold back. He took Mateo in his arms and sobbed. Mateo sobbed too.

When he could speak Ralph said, "I have come to take you home."

Mateo looked stunned. "Take me? Just me? I couldn't leave the twins."

"All of you."

"Mamma? She wouldn't go – she wouldn't let us – I don't see how…"

He seemed distraught.

Ralph adopted a voice of sweet reason. "You see, she took you away without my consent. She deserted me and took my children. The church would rule against her. But I don't want it to come to that. If possible, we will talk peaceably together. We will go and find her presently. But tell me first what your life is like here."

Mateo shook his head, and Ralph wondered if it was too soon to ask such a question; but then the truth came tumbling out. "Oh Papa, it is tedious beyond words. I am not to go anywhere without Mamma or Guido. I have a tutor in Greek and Latin, which I could enjoy, but he is so dreary a teacher! I want to learn about our estate and how the land should be farmed to make life better for poor tenants, but that is not the way of Spanish noblemen. I am not to speak English or read English books. I am to learn the de Villena family history. But Mamma tells me what to think about the present day. Maria Christina is always right whatever she does. She is the regent to her daughter, the little Queen Isabella."

"Has she not been deposed? I see reports in *The Times*. Has not General Espartero taken over the presidency?"

Mateo looked impressed. "Yes, they say the Cortes will make him regent. Mamma says Spain will suffer military rule as a punishment, but *I* don't know. I am not allowed to have ideas of my own. I try to read about England in the newspapers, and you seem so united under a new queen and a strong rule of law. Oh Papa, you and Grandmamma encouraged me to read widely and think, and I see now that Mr Hurst was a good schoolmaster who would never suppress his pupils. But we were practically on board ship before I knew what was happening. I'm so sorry, Papa."

Ralph had been keeping his eyes on the cathedral steps, and now he stiffened and shrank against the wall. Mateo looked at him anxiously.

"Your mother has just come out with Lucia and Maria."

Mateo peeped round too. "I should go to them. They will be frantic.

And the opening service must have started. See, even the crowd on the piazza has gone quiet, and people are standing still in their places."

"We will cause a rumpus if I come with you. Go and join them till the service is over. Then tell your mother I am alive, here, and wish to speak with her. I will wait at that café there with the yellow awning. If she will come to me, well and good, but if she will not, I will ride over and see her tomorrow, and she will have to speak with me." He pressed into Mateo's hand the paper on which he had written Tomaso's address. "It's where I am lodging. In the oldest part of town, leading off the piazza at that corner. Don't show this to anyone else."

Mateo put it in his coat pocket, where he had put John's letter. "I don't want to leave you, Papa, now I have found you, but I suppose I must. There will be more crowds coming to see the processions. We intend to stay till evening, but if Mamma tires of the noise we will go home."

"I'll stay near that café, but if you can't come, I will understand – but I pray God I'll see you tomorrow."

Mateo's lips trembled. "She may bar the gates. I don't know how she will take this. I'm afraid."

"Nay, have courage. She may rant and rave, but she will not hurt you. Look – they are still on the steps, peering about. Go now."

He watched as Mateo crept close to the wall. When he reached the steps, Maria saw him and leapt with glee. Sophia turned and clasped him in her arms, and they went into the cathedral together. The sight of a family happily reunited smote Ralph's heart.

Mateo

Mateo heard nothing of the service, and when the procession of the cross passed down the aisle he barely noticed the gold, purple and scarlet of the bishops' copes, the jewelled mitres, the elaborate canopies carried by six altar boys in snowy white, the waving censers. His whole mind was filled with dread. He had to tell his mother that the husband she believed dead was alive and demanding to see her.

Lucia and Maria kept looking at him, sensing his nervousness. People were beginning to follow the procession. His mother picked up her parasol and began to move out. He must speak now. He pulled at her sleeve.

"Mamma, I've just seen Papa. He's outside at the café with the yellow awning, waiting to speak to you."

She stared at him. Was that shock or disbelief in her eyes? Or both?

"What nonsense is this? Your papa is dead." Her voice was a harsh whisper. "You've seen someone at a distance who reminded you of him. What were you doing outside anyway?"

"He took me out. He was here in the cathedral."

Maria was on tiptoe to catch their words. "Did you say Papa is here? He's alive! Oh where, where?"

Mateo pulled his mother's sleeve again. "Please, I'll take you to him."

Now his mother began to shake. She sat down abruptly. Her face, under its heavy powdering, looked suddenly old. "He cannot be here. That woman wrote that he wasn't likely to live."

"Mamma! Are you saying you never had any official word he was dead?"

"She didn't write again. The posts stopped."

"You wanted him dead. You've always wanted him dead."

His mother drew her fan from her bodice and made a great flapping with it.

Lucia took note of what was going on. "Is Mamma feeling faint? Let's get out in the air. I can't breathe in here. The incense!"

Mateo said, "The café with the yellow awning is not fifty yards away. She can get a drink. Come on. We'll all go. Don't you want to see Papa – after all this time?"

"Papa!" Lucia squeaked. "He's dead, you stupid boy. You've seen a ghost."

"I am *not* stupid. We were told a wicked lie that he was dead. He's out there. He has shaved his beard. He looks younger. He looks well."

Maria pushed out into the aisle, dodged dawdling bodies like a little sprite and was gone in a moment.

Their mother sat up with a screech. "No, Maria!"

"Good," Mateo said. "She's gone to find him. Now, come along, Mamma." He tried to pull her up. "You'll have to go after her."

She struck him on the arm with the fan. "I won't. I can't. You go and bring her back. Lucia, stay with me. I will not meet him."

Mateo stamped his foot. "He said if you don't he'll ride over tomorrow to see you. He has come all this way to speak with you, with all of us. We're his *family*."

"No, he cheated on me. He is dead to me. Get Maria. We will go home. We must find Guido and the carriage. Where is Nurse?"

"She sat at the back the other side. I'll get her and tell her about Papa."

158

"Just bring her here. She will know where Guido has taken the carriage."

He found Nurse and hissed, "My father is here but Mamma won't see him."

Nurse looked him in the eye. "Is this true? She will be in great shock."

"Of course it's true. She'll tell you herself." Mateo was no longer in awe of Nurse. She had shrunk in old age and he had grown. He pitied her as a servant of long standing who was still ordered about like a young woman.

Nurse produced smelling salts from the vast linen bag she carried about. "There, milady." She settled down beside her.

His mother had already stiffened into her pose of proud dignity, her back straight. She glared at him. "Get Maria at once and we will go home."

Lucia pouted. "We'll miss the fun." They could hear the cheering from the streets as the clergy procession was being joined by the decorated carts and performing dancers and acrobats.

Mateo slipped easily out of the emptying cathedral and, keeping to the sides of the square, spotted the yellow awning. As he grew closer, he was thrilled to see his father sitting underneath it, with Maria on his lap and her arms round his neck, gazing into his face. They looked round as he approached.

He put on a rueful face. "She won't come. We are to go home."

"Oh no," Maria cried. "We haven't seen anything yet. I will stay with Papa. He says you've got my letter from John, Matty."

He produced it. "I haven't read it."

She took it and opened it up. "Oh, I can read this. It's big English writing."

Mateo said, "Papa, I told Mother you would come to us tomorrow."

"I'd rather intercept your mother as she comes out." He stood up, setting Maria down and kissing her.

"They might go a different way out. The carriages are some distance away. I must take Maria to her. Nurse and Lucia are with her."

"Well, I'll not be foiled so easily. Set off and I'll keep you in sight."

Maria stood still till she had read her letter. "You two are still Big Bear and Smaller Bear. I shall be Baby Bear." She put it into the hanging pocket under her dress. "I shall write to John at home and bribe the stable boy to post it. John is clever to write all that."

"Maybe you will see him. I want to take you all home."

She looked up with wide eyes. "That big nursery and the woods we can play in and the swing?"

He nodded. Mateo, seeing fearful battles ahead, took her hand. "We must go, Baby Bear. Follow us, Papa. I don't know what will happen."

Ralph

Ralph could see at once what would happen when he followed Mateo and Maria into the cathedral. There were many servants about, preparing for the later ceremonies to take place, but standing in the central aisle stood Sophia, facing him, rigid with defiance and flanked by two huge men in the uniform of the cathedral guards. She had guessed he would try to force a meeting here, and she was ready. Mateo and Maria hesitated to approach her, but she waved them behind her like a hen gathering her brood out of danger and, pointing an imperious arm at him, she declared, "That is the man. He is hounding me. Pray remove him from the cathedral."

The guards stepped forward. Ralph thought of the pistol he had left at the Lopez house, but he couldn't have threatened them with it here. Bribery wouldn't work either. He said, loudly and clearly, "This is a sacred place. I will hire a mount and follow her home so that we can have polite speech, not a public brawl."

One of the men laughed. "There's not a horse to be had in Santiago today, and if you harass this lady or her children the authorities will protect her and them."

Mateo stepped out from behind his mother. "He is our—" Her hand clapped across his mouth. The men took two paces towards Ralph, who held up one hand, not in surrender but to halt their advance.

"Gentlemen," he said, "this is unseemly. I am leaving the cathedral." He addressed Sophia for the first and last time. "I will visit *peaceably* tomorrow."

He turned on his heel and walked out, noticing that the workmen had all stopped to witness the scene.

Outside, the heat and noise added to the fury boiling inside him. He must seek somewhere quiet, if that was possible. Seeing her had roused all the hatred and bitterness he had meant to lay aside. He had hoped she might consent to come back to England for a visit if she saw the children were eager for it.

Blindly he stumbled through the piazza and into the side streets. Heading anywhere to get out of the town, he came to an opening in the walls where he could shed Santiago and its festival and see dried-up fields around him. Looking up at the sky, he realised he had headed north-west. If they did decide to go home, they would not come this way. The road, anyway, was becoming a sandy track, parched dry like everything else. Groups of people were passing, heading into the town, so he turned aside and followed a footpath by a gully with a trickle of a stream at the bottom. Far from the road, he sat down on the bank and struggled to calm his mind.

He must hold fast to the beautiful moment when he and Mateo had sobbed in each other's arms, and then the joyful sight of Maria running towards him with her arms outstretched. He had scarcely seen Lucia peeping round her mother's skirt, but at least he knew that two of his children loved him still. He took several deep breaths, savouring that happiness.

But that woman... He got to his feet and began walking fast to escape the image of her standing there defying him. She held all the cards. If he rode out tomorrow and found their mansion, she could bar it against him. She could punish his children and he could not prevent it. Nevertheless, he would go, and if that was a failure, he could start the laborious process of trying to get them back through the offices of the church, or even the state. His heart sank at the thought of it.

His walking had brought him to a place where the stream opened up into a pool. He was desperately thirsty, but lean, stunted cattle were crowded round, drinking from the shallow water. He must go back. He was not weary in body but worn out with conflicting emotions and the impossibility of his mission.

Santiago was waking up, after the hour of siesta, to the sound of music from massed bands and choirs. Ralph listened for a while, to keep his mind from thought. He ate and drank at one of the many cafés and watched some of the grand carriages collecting their occupants, but saw no sign of his family. He was again cut off from them. He had seen with delight that Mateo was less diffident, more spontaneous and open with him than he had been before their one-to-one talk. But now would he ever see him again? The music penetrated his consciousness. It had become solemn and moving. He put his head in his hands, and tears flowed.

The sun was low when he made his way to the Calle del Pantano. Tomaso and Alicia were delighted to see him, gave him supper and would have talked till dusk, but he asked for a mount from Fandoro's for eight chimes of the cathedral clock in the morning, and begged to retire to bed. The noise of revelry went on long into the night, but in a strange way it eventually lulled him to sleep.

Chapter 16

Mateo

The carriage drive home was tense and silent. Mateo looked up with distaste when the sprawling family home came into view. It had battlements to justify the name of Castillo, but he longed for the solid symmetrical shape of Sheradon Grange against its wooded hillside.

Cousin Juan appeared on the front steps. A portly man in his mid-fifties who wore a neat wig to conceal his baldness, he always dressed in the latest Madrid fashion, and despised the country. Mateo had never liked him, but his declared ambition to become his stepfather had produced real loathing.

Now he came tripping down the steps to help his mother out of the carriage.

"My dear Sophia, what brings you home so soon? Are you unwell?"

"Upset. Not unwell. Who do you think was there in Santiago? Ralph Barnet!"

"What? He is alive?"

Mateo crowed with delight at the shock in his cousin's eyes. He heard no more of what was said between them as they went straight to his mother's small parlour on the first floor. Guido, who left the horse and carriage to the attentions of the grooms, said to Mateo, "You are for Hellhole, young man. She gave orders."

'Hellhole' was the name the children had given to the punishment room in the basement where they could be locked in and left in darkness if they had been exceptionally naughty.

Nurse, who was the last to climb out of the carriage because of her rheumatism, looked up sharply. "Milady said nothing to me about that."

"Young master is under *my* charge, not yours, you stupid old woman."

Maria and Lucia looked aghast. Guido had been rough with Nurse of late because of her increasing disability, but verbal abuse was new.

Mateo said, "I'm not going unless Mamma says."

Guido shrugged. "She *will* say. You displeased her greatly. You are still a child and owe her a duty of obedience."

Mateo walked straight past him and up the steps. His anxiety was all about the outcome of the morrow. After the confrontation in the cathedral, he couldn't imagine what might happen. He went up to the room that had been the nursery and was now the children's sitting room. Maria and Lucia joined him, chattering about Guido and Nurse.

"Nurse never liked him," Lucia said.

Maria nodded. "When her rheumatism got bad, he said Mamma should get rid of her. He doesn't like seeing her hobbling about. I used to think everyone had a good side, but I can't see Guido's. I suppose I'm growing up. Do you think I'm growing up, Matty?"

Mateo flopped onto the old ottoman that had been put up here. "We all are. We'll have to now if we have to choose between Papa and Mamma."

Lucia, her face solemn, stood by his legs stretched out on the cushions. "They can't make us do that. It's not fair. I'd have to choose Mamma."

Maria laughed. "That's because she's never sent you to Hellhole. Will you let them put you there, Matty?"

"Yes. I shan't let Guido and one of the grooms manhandle me. But when I'm grown they won't dare try it."

Lucia said, "Papa is tall but he didn't want to fight those guards today."

"He went with dignity. That's what I shall do."

Brigitta tapped at the door and looked in. "Her ladyship is too upset to have you come down for your dinners after siesta. Will it suit you to have me bring you something on a tray in an hour or so?"

"I'll come down and help you," Mateo said.

Brigitta looked shocked. "That wouldn't be fitting." Then she gave a little giggle. "You've learned funny English ways."

"They were Grandmamma Heron's ways. I've seen her carry two coal buckets. 'If a task is there,' she would say, 'do it.'" Brigitta raised her dark arcs of eyebrows and went out, still giggling.

She's pretty when she laughs, Mateo thought. I've started to notice girls. Nurse said it would happen soon. I could talk to Grandmamma about it – but will I ever get the chance again?

Maria jumped onto the ottoman and patted his legs. "You look ever so sad, Matty. Is it about Papa? I'd choose *him* if I had the chance."

Mateo gave her one of his rare smiles and a quick hug. "Me too, Baby Bear."

After their dinner Mateo went to his room to learn Greek verbs. He was interrupted by a knock. Brigitta called out, "Master Mateo, you are summoned to her ladyship's parlour."

It is the Hellhole then, he thought, and put on his coat, because it would be cold down there. On the landing before the parlour door, which was slightly ajar, the girls were waiting for him. Maria grabbed his hand.

"I have to speak to you, Matty," she whispered. "Something happened while you were in your room but if she sends you—"

Their mother's voice barked, "If you're all out there, come in at once."

She sat stiff and straight, and the moment they lined up in front of her the words snapped out as if rehearsed.

"Tomorrow that man will come. He did not die, but he is dead to us. Lucia, you behaved well this morning. Stay in your sitting room upstairs till he goes. You may go to bed now." Lucia scurried out.

She pointed her fan at Maria. "*You* were wild and wicked."

"I'm sorry, Mamma," came a small, meek voice.

Mateo looked at Maria in astonishment. Their mother fluttered her fan.

"Oh! Well, I am glad to hear it. Make no attempt to see that man tomorrow or it will be the punishment room. You may also go to bed."

Maria gave a demure curtsy and murmured, "Goodnight, Mamma." But as she passed Mateo she gave a despairing look and mouthed 'Oh Matty'. She must be desperate to speak to him.

What could he do? He was left facing his mother. I will not be quelled, he determined, and fixed his gaze on her. For a second he saw fear, and her eyes shifted about the room till they caught her reflection in the mirror, her dress black against the rose-embroidered hangings, her colour high, her glossy ebony hair intricately piled up, requiring a poised neck. She lifted her head and turned on him. Anger had come back.

"Mateo, traitor! You took his side. He has no rights in this family. I have friends in high places. He will leave and never come here again."

"And will cousin Juan be your companion then?"

Her eyes dilated with shock. "Companion! What are you saying?"

"He wanted to marry you." Mateo couldn't believe his own boldness.

She blustered, "Always his family's notion. Never mine."

"But always *his* notion."

She poked her face towards him. "What has that man said to you? Juan has never been more than a second cousin to me." She drew back, and Mateo thought he saw a tear shine. "I was free to love your father. I once thought the world of him."

"Welcome him tomorrow, then."

She shook her head violently. Mateo, embarrassed, could only bite his lip while she fought to control herself and, glancing at the mirror, reared up again, straight-backed.

"Tomorrow I will discard these widow's weeds, and when we have seen him off the premises I will devote my life to you and the girls." She held up a warning finger. "But you will spend tonight in the punishment room, and then" – she took a deep breath, and now her gaze became tender – "you will prepare for the life of a Galician noble. We will attend the little queen's court in Madrid when the brave Maria Christina is brought back from Paris. Reflect on these things tonight. See your life ahead clearly, my son, and pray for your country, that right will prevail."

On this high patriotic note she flourished her hands before his face and gestured to the door.

I don't understand her, he thought. She changes every moment. I used to love that tenderness; but was it ever real?

Guido and two grooms were waiting for him. He waved them aside and began the walk round to the back premises, where steps next to the coal chute led down to storerooms, the wine cellar and the small punishment room. They followed him but, seeing he was going quietly, only Guido came down the steps behind him. He grinned as he closed the door, and Mateo heard the bolt shoot outside. Darkness enfolded him, but not before he had seen a covered dish and flask of water on the shelf. He was to be imprisoned till after his father had been banished tomorrow. Maria would not be allowed to come to him. Despair gripped him.

There was a rustling in the corner next to the door. He knew there were rats, but this one suddenly gripped his leg. A strangled scream broke from him.

"Shush, Matty, shush. It's me." A head rose up and a hand pulled on his coat.

"Maria! Mother of God! What are you doing here?"

She clasped his waist. "Keep hold of me. I hate the dark."

He put his arms round her. "She never said *you* were to be sent here."

"I'm not, I'm not. Just listen. I had to see you. I've come to get you out."

"But we're *both* locked in now. Are you mad?"

"No, listen. There's a hole in the wall low down, hidden by a leather flap. It opens to the coal cellar. I discovered it last time she locked me in here. It's too small for you, but I can squeeze through, climb the chute and come down the steps and pull the bolt back. Then you can walk out. I don't think anybody knows it's there."

"But I'll be discovered if I go back to bed."

"You're not going back. Didn't you realise I *had* to speak to you? Oh Matty, this is urgent. You are to warn Papa. Nurse thinks there's a plot against his life if he rides here tomorrow."

"What? *Nurse* thinks!"

"Listen, Matty, just listen. She took me into her room earlier and told me she had seen from her window Guido talking with two men outside. She swears money was passed. She knows those men by sight. Guido does business with them. They're smugglers. Guido is making a fortune, she said, and will go to hell anyway. But this is different. This would be murder."

"Murder! Murder Papa! That's wild talk. Smuggling, maybe."

"Listen! Let me finish. Wasn't Guido outside the parlour when you came out?"

He muttered, "Yes."

"Well, Nurse caught me on the stairs and said she had seen him tap at cousin Juan's door just before. She leaned right over the banister but out of sight behind the pillar. When he opened the door, cousin Juan asked Guido, 'Is it arranged?' and he said, 'Yes, sir. You'll not be troubled with him tomorrow.' That was it. The two men are hired killers. It will look like a highway robbery, and Papa will be dead."

Mateo stood, his arms slackening round her, his mind absorbing this. If Papa was dead, cousin Juan could marry Mamma! Was it believable? He shivered as a worse suspicion stabbed his brain. Had the order come from her? That tear? A regret for love gone? A vision of a new life ahead?

"Matty?" He could feel her little face peering up at him.

"Mamma? Is she behind this?"

Maria jerked back. "No – oh no. It's *Mamma* Nurse wants to protect. She is frightened that if it happens Mamma will be – what's the word…?"

"Implicated?"

"Yes. It's not Papa Nurse cares about. She never wanted to go to England. She was glad Mamma left him." He felt her arms cling round him more urgently. "You *know*, Matty. Mamma is everything to her. Hasn't she always told us, from a *baby*? She *delivered* her. She was her nurse, and then of course she was ours. She's passionate about Mamma. And about nothing else at all."

"Why did she tell *you* her suspicions?"

"Well, silly, she can't get down the basement steps. There's no handrail. She said I was to let you out. She watched when the back stairs were empty and told me to run down, but when I got here the door was ajar and no one was about. I didn't dare wait around for them to bring you, so I went in and crouched in the dark corner. I knew I could go through the hatch thing when all was quiet."

Mateo still stood, clasping her, his little sister, caught up in this momentous situation, loving the excitement but ignoring the consequences.

"You must go back, Maria, but you'll get all black climbing up the chute."

"It doesn't matter. Nurse will be looking out for me."

"But what does she expect me to *do*?"

"Go and warn Papa to go back to England. He'll never be safe in Spain."

"What? Go to Santiago? How? I can't get at my horse. The stables are locked up against thieves and Mamma has two guards patrolling the grounds."

"Nurse said they go to sleep under the portico. She said fifteen miles should be nothing to a sturdy lad like you. But how will you find Papa?"

"I know where he's staying." He felt in his pocket. The paper was still there. He had money too which he had not spent in the city. He tried to think what walking fifteen miles would be like. But if he could get there and find the place, what then? Would his father agree to go back to England, achieving nothing? Would he take Nurse's story seriously? And what, he asked himself, do *I* do? Walk back tomorrow morning? How do I account for my escape? I mustn't get Maria into trouble.

"What are you thinking, Matty? Don't worry about tomorrow, Nurse won't tell. But I'd better go back to her. It isn't quite dark outside yet, but the candles will be lit indoors. I know Brigitta is on late duties and won't squeal if she sees me running up the back stairs. So I'll go now. Are you ready?"

Mateo was struggling with an idea so immense that it could not possibly be looked at from all angles. There was only one clear beam of light coming from it. He swallowed hard. He squeezed Maria's shoulders in a fierce embrace.

"If I *do* act on this crazy suspicion – *if* – there's only one thing that can happen, Baby Bear. I'll have to go with him – to England."

"Oh Matty! Nurse didn't mean that. You can't."

"If he stays and this *is* a real plot, they'll get him one way or another. But he won't give up his mission. If *I* go, he'll go."

"Then I'll come too."

"You can't. You're too little. I'll come back sometime. No one will try to kill *me*. Of course, I'll come back to see you all. I can live in two countries, share my time. You and Lucia have a lot of growing up to do. Keep in touch with John."

"But I would write to *you*."

"Mamma will be angry with me. She wouldn't let you."

"Matty, you *can't* go."

"You must tell me through John what happens. Watch Guido and cousin Juan. When Papa doesn't appear, they will think they have succeeded. Keep your eyes out for those two men. They'll report they never found him." He thought to himself, What if we are imagining it all? But I'm going, I'm going in what I stand up in now. I have possessions in England. I'm going to escape this place. I'm going to escape to Sheradon Grange.

Tingles of excitement raced up and down his spine.

"Right, Maria, I must set out. Where is this hole? Let me feel you get through it."

"I'll have to lie on the floor and squirm. I never tried it when I saw it before. I thought I'd keep it a secret. She only put me here for an hour that time. But I can do it. Only you mustn't go away from me. I can't bear it."

She was down on her knees as she spoke, and flattened herself in her frilly festival dress to the dirty floor. He bent down and got his hands on her slender hips and eased her through. He could hear her scrambling up the chute. It would be slippery, but she would grip the sides. He picked up the covered dish and the flask. These were awkward but essential. He didn't hear her on the steps, but next thing he heard the bolt pulled back, and the door swung open. He could see her shape now. The moon had risen. She was untying her petticoat.

"What are you doing?"

"Make a bag. Put the food in. Tie it so. Carry it over your shoulder."

"Good. You're a clever darling."

"Matty, you'll come back tomorrow."

"No. I am set for England now."

"But Papa wanted to take me too. The woods, the swing. Grandmamma, all of them. I didn't know how much I loved it all." She was crying now. He didn't want that.

"Go to Nurse, quick. Don't tell *anyone* I'm really gone or they'll come after me. It'll be a mystery how I got out. Go, Baby Bear, or I'll be discovered and shot as a thief."

She clung round him sobbing, then tore herself away and ran back through the storeroom to the back stairs up to the servants' quarters.

He stood for a moment, listening. All was quiet. He mounted the steps to the door at the top. It was bolted on the inside, as the men would have gone back to their own rooms the way Maria had gone. He let himself out and stood peering round.

The excitement drained out at his toes. What if he was seen from a window? How could he just start walking and hope to find Papa? The covered dish – it was wooden – banged against his back. I'll eat the food and bury the dish, he thought, but I must get some distance away.

He tried to think clearly. In the months since they had come here, he had ridden and walked over large tracts of the estate. He knew the direction of Santiago. He could find his way through de Villena land. After that – I will trust in God, he told himself, and my instincts.

Straight ahead of him was the vegetable garden. In the early days in October he had come out to weed the beds – which looked uncared for by Sheradon Grange standards – but his mother had forbidden it. Now he plunged at speed straight across, not minding where he walked, desperate only to be out of sight of the house. A running figure in the moonlight would certainly rouse pursuit. At last he passed a belt of trees and could draw breath and slow to a brisk, striding pace.

Then the enormity of what he was planning broke upon him. Had he made a wild decision on the basis of Nurse's speculation and Maria's childlike credulity? Nurse hated Guido and was jealous of Juan. But the thought of his father, and a journey to England and a welcome from Grandmamma and Jack, kept his legs moving. The uncertainty about finding his father and how he would react must await his arrival in Santiago. Getting there was what mattered now.

Chapter 17

Ralph

Ralph woke to the sound of fireworks going off. He couldn't have been sleeping long if the revelry was still continuing. Then he realised that it was a knock on the door that had wakened him. It was repeated urgently. Was there a fire?

He called "Come in!" in English, not thinking where he was.

The door opened slowly and a hand with a candle appeared.

"Come in, Tomaso. What is it?" Now he spoke Castilian.

"It's me, Papa." Mateo slipped in and stood by the bed.

Now he knew it was a dream. He turned over to settle again. For a moment it had seemed so real. That was uncanny.

The voice came again, and a hand touched the bed. "Papa. I'm here."

Tomaso's voice came from outside the door. "All right, Sir Barton? He *is* your son?"

Now he started up and Mateo jerked back to save the candle. "Papa!"

"God in heaven, am I dreaming? Is it you, Matty?"

Tomaso's head appeared. "I wake Alicia. Refreshments for the boy. He said he has long walk."

"Oh, yes please," Mateo said. "But I'm sorry if you have to wake your wife."

"She not sleep deep. Fireworks. Will they never stop?" He went out chuckling.

Ralph, still half-thinking this was a dream, shifted his legs.

Mateo set the candle on the stool, sat on the bed and gazed into his eyes. "I can't believe I've found you. It feels like a miracle."

"You can't be here. I *must* be dreaming."

"I've walked from home, Papa, and as soon as you can be ready we should set off for home. I mean real home, Sheradon Grange."

Ralph shook his head to get rid of sleep. Had Mateo got up in the middle of the night and longed so much to go home to England that he had set off walking – what, fifteen, or was it twenty miles? Brave, impulsive? Mateo? It was hard to believe; but his heart was singing. He clasped the boy's hand resting on the bedcover and looked up, wondering, into his face. "But I was coming to you tomorrow, and would have brought you back if I could."

"Papa, that's why I've come. It's not safe for you to go there. You were going to be attacked on the way like a victim of a highway robbery. We must escape before they discover I'm missing. Let's eat what the woman brings and go. I have nothing to pack. You are dressed." He got up. "I can feel your boots here by the bed."

Ralph swung his legs to the ground and pulled them on. "What hour is it?" He took his money belt from under the pillow, put some coins in his pocket and more on the bed, strapped on the belt and buttoned his coat over it.

"Just after three," Mateo said. "I heard the chimes. The walk took five hours. I thought I'd missed Santiago altogether but then I saw the light in the sky from all the braziers. Stars flew up, and I realised it was fireworks."

"You must be exhausted. How do you know about a plot for my life? No, I hear the urgency in your voice. Save your breath." As he spoke, now very wide awake, his brain was telling him over and over again, My mission is accomplished. I have my son.

Alicia brought a tray. Mateo took it from her. The inevitable omelettes sizzled on the plates. She was wearing a shawl over her bedgown, and one of her best grins. Ralph thanked her and asked if she could fetch Tomaso. She yelled his name, and he came so quickly he must have been in the passage.

Ralph said, "My son has brought news and we need to return to England. Can we get any sort of shipping nearer than Corunna?"

"Surely, surely. At Padron they will arrange something. You want horses.

Fandoro not go to bed tonight. People bring all their mounts back. They rest and eat hay now. You eat and they will be ready for you. I tell Fandoro. Two good horses."

"How will we get them back to him if we are boarding a ship?" Mateo asked, with a mouthful of omelette.

"Ah, young sir, there are idle men at the inn will ride them back for you if you leave money with Fandoro for them." He was looking at the coins on the bed.

"And what do I owe *you*, Tomaso?" Ralph asked.

He grinned broadly and named the exact sum he could see on the bed. Ralph suspected it was inflated for the festival time, but the man could not have been more helpful. Ralph swept up the coins and placed them in his hand.

"Good. Eat up. I bring horses."

"That was cheap lodging," Mateo said when Tomaso and Alicia had gone.

Ralph passed his hand across his forehead. "Nay, I know not what is cheap here. Are you too weary to ride?"

He laughed. "Too weary to walk."

"Who is behind this? Is it your mother?"

"Oh Papa, no. It did cross my mind, but no. Let me explain when we are getting away. I feel nervous till then. They may find I've escaped." He gobbled up the omelette, and Ralph ate his last mouthful and picked up his bag.

Outside, two horses had just been led up. One was equipped with saddlebags, so Ralph distributed some of his belongings between them and tied his empty bag to the saddle. Mateo danced with impatience.

When they were mounted, Alicia wished them a safe journey in Galego, and Tomaso led them round into the next street, where Fandoro's stables occupied one side. Ralph paid a withered old man, who was apparently Fandoro himself.

"Sir Barnet and young Barnet," cried Tomaso, "may the blessed saints Philip and James go with you." The last they saw of him was his wide gap-toothed grin.

In the town there was still light from the many braziers, but once outside on the road to Padron, their eyes had to get accustomed to the dim moonlight. As soon as they could distinguish the pale, sandy road ahead, Mateo wanted to gallop, but such an activity was not in the competence of either of their mounts.

They reached Padron in half an hour. It was not asleep, as many pilgrims to Santiago came on here to see where Saint James's body was brought ashore. They found one inn still bustling with customers, so they tethered the horses, Ralph repacked his own bag, and they went inside.

They asked the innkeeper where they could go to get a boat to a French port.

He chortled, his belly wobbling. "You could be in luck, sir. There's no regular service, but a French lugger beached here this afternoon. The crew are asleep now in my back room. I don't know their plans, for I don't speak their lingo."

"I can speak a little French." Ralph said. "Have they rested long?"

"Four or five hours. They drank heavily. Do you want me to wake them?"

"Oh yes," Mateo said. "Can you give us a lantern to light us to the beach?"

Ralph had misgivings about a French lugger. They were coastal vessels doing a little fishing, a little trading, even smuggling. They might take passengers at a price, but how long they would take to get to Biarritz he couldn't imagine.

The landlord, however, could be heard waking them up in the back room. He came to the door and beckoned Ralph and Mateo to come in.

Ralph had picked up his French in his buccaneer days, but he was not prepared for the rush of language that came from the older-looking man in a sailor's cap. A few questions, and a plea to speak slowly, drew from him the information that they had been innocently fishing but were chased away by a steam vessel and beached here to escape from it not knowing where they were.

When Ralph offered him money to get them to a French port as quickly as possible, his manner changed. He seemed disconcerted and tongue-tied. The two younger men were eager, but he shook his head at them. An argument seemed about to break out, but the landlord stepped in to ask about the horses tethered outside.

"I'll pay for their stabling tonight," Ralph said, "and if we don't need them again can you have them sent back to Fandoro's in Santiago in the morning? He has money to pay for them." The landlord seemed satisfied and wanted to know if they were going with the Frenchmen or would like a mattress in there, the inn being full. Ralph noticed that the last customers had begun to drift home or to other lodgings.

Mateo whispered, "Papa, I think they've persuaded their father to take us."

Ralph looked at the three men more closely in the candlelight, and decided Mateo was right to assume it was the lugger's captain and his two sons. The father seemed satisfied now, and shook his hand. "Call me Captain Jacques. We agree. You pay how many days it takes. We need more provisions for you."

Ralph negotiated with the landlord for two loaves of bread and a cheese and two bottles of ale. While this was being fetched, the two sons lit their own lantern and slipped outside.

"They go ahead to make ready," the captain said. "Good boys."

Maybe, thought Ralph, but when we are out at sea what is to stop them robbing us and throwing us overboard? We may run from a doubtful danger into a certain one.

"How far is it to the beach?" Mateo asked the landlord.

"Less than two kilometres." He fetched a lantern and lit it. "Maybe I get to my own bed soon. There are still two hours till sunrise."

"I am sorry if we've kept you up," Mateo said.

He shrugged. "Ah, Galicians can make a festival last for days. You English, it is all work. That is why you rule the world." He laughed and his belly shook.

Mateo shifted his feet, and Ralph noticed him wince. His feet must be sore.

The French captain was slowly gathering up his possessions into a big sack. He seemed to want to take as long as possible. Mateo bit his fingernails.

At last the man was ready, and he made for the outside door. The innkeeper put his huge bulk between him and it. "You owe for half a night's lodging."

"What he say?" the captain appealed to Ralph.

Ralph told him what he owed.

"We didn't have beds," he complained, and looked hopefully at Ralph.

"Oh, pay him, Father, and let's be going," Mateo said.

Ralph offered the landlord a few coins. "And can we keep the lantern?"

He shrugged again with a grimace, dropped the coins into his vast apron pocket and hustled them out; they could hear him bar the door behind them and close the window shutters. The horses had gone, so an ostler must have been given orders to stable them. One episode was closed and a new one opened. They were now in the dubious hands of a French lugger crew.

When the way was pointed out, Mateo strode ahead despite his painful feet.

The captain grumbled, "Young legs."

At last there was the sea ahead of them, and a beach, white in the moonlight. The two young men were gathering up the sails, which had been spread out to dry, anchored with large stones. Mateo was watching them. Ralph asked the captain if they needed any help. He shook his head and hurried forward to speak to his sons. One pointed to something in the stern of the ship and he nodded.

Mateo came, limping, to join Ralph on some boulders by the shore and watch their progress with the sails. He kept turning his head and looking up the way they had come.

Ralph smiled. "Surely you do not fear pursuit here."

"I think how friendly Tomaso was, and how eager he would be to help if someone claiming to be our friend asked where we had gone."

"So now tell me what happened."

"Yes, but listen, I suspect these men are smugglers. Are we safe with them?"

"I have had my doubts. Why do you think that?"

"I could see the two sons ahead of me, and they turned aside at a cottage. I kept watch in the shade of some trees, and when they came out they were carrying between them a box with handles. They hurried ahead, looking back to see if we were coming. You weren't, and I kept out of sight till they reached the boat and stowed the box away. I didn't show myself till they were lifting the stones off the sails and you and their father were approaching."

"It doesn't surprise me. I think he took me for an official at first, so he spun the yarn of being chased by a steamboat. Then he was puzzled how to answer my request, but his boys must have said they could get the goods aboard and passengers would be a good reason for their voyage. I believe we are safe while we know nothing." Mateo nodded. "Now please, Matty, tell me about yesterday."

Ralph listened with increasing concern as Mateo unfolded the tale.

"What? She locks you up sometimes – even little Maria?"

"Wait till you hear what Maria did." He described finding her in Hellhole and why she was so anxious to save her Papa. "Can you believe cousin Juan plotted murder?" he finished. "He hates you, I know. You stand in his way."

Ralph sat, mulling it all over, deeply troubled that Mateo and a child as young as Maria should have been forced to make such drastic decisions. Mateo peered at his face in the half-light.

The men were calling them to come. Ralph got up and pulled Mateo to his feet and put his arm round his shoulders. "Whatever was being planned, I have a son and a daughter to be proud of. You did what you felt to be right, with considerable hardship to yourself. Above all I am thankful that I have you with me now."

Mateo gave one more look toward the land. No horsemen came galloping.

He looked up at Ralph. "I'm thankful to be going home with you, Papa," was all he said.

Ralph gripped his hand for a moment and then offered his muscle, along with a few men beachcombing who came up to help to launch the lugger. The sails were roped to the two masts and lay folded on the deck ready to haul up. The three men might be smugglers, but he saw them as angels. The Atlantic rolled in gently. A pale light was growing over the land behind them. The coast stretched northward and then east along the Bay of Biscay to France and thence to England. For perhaps the first time in his life, he gave thanks to God.

The voyage progressed well with a steady south-west wind. At first Ralph and Mateo could sit in the stern and converse quietly. They spoke mainly of England, and Ralph told him of John's great adventure, touching lightly on his own physical and mental state. Mateo declared he was longing to see them all and would thank John for his efforts and grow to love him as a brother.

"Maria wants him to keep writing to her. She had no chance to write a reply to his, but she has decided to join us in the family of bears and be Baby Bear. I do love her and will miss her greatly. I had to promise her that I would come back."

Ralph shivered at that. If he let Mateo go, would he ever see him again? He said nothing.

Mateo added, "For a visit, of course. I see my future in England rather than Spain."

Ralph thought that could change when he inherited the title of Conde de Villena. He said, "I wish all my children's futures to be in England, but time will tell."

After the first day's sailing, Mateo took an interest in the working of the lugger, and also in learning the French language. His curiosity about new things had never been satisfied, Ralph understood. He was an eager learner, and the crew were happy to encourage him. Ralph had acquired his seamanship on larger vessels but he was impressed with the handling of the lugger and, the weather being fair, neither of them was seasick.

All was going well until they were off the coast of France and a steam launch flying the French flag approached them and signalled them to heave to. The captain became very nervous, but Ralph said he would speak to the official who demanded to come aboard.

He shook his hand and acted the part of an innocent Englishman abroad.

"These good people are giving us a passage to Biarritz, where we take ship for England. This is my son. Travelling like this is an adventure for him. But we do not want delays. We achieved the pilgrimage at Santiago de Compostela and are now anxious to be home. His school expects him back soon."

"It's a strange way for you to travel – but I don't blame you for wanting to leave Galicia when highway robbery is still rife there."

Ralph tensed. There must be a reason for that remark. He raised his eyebrows as in a question, but nodded too as if he understood.

"Ay, that was an unlucky Englishman, Monsieur Richard Bell. He did the Pilgrim Way, too. His poor widow said he was so moved that he rode out from Santiago alone to commune with the good Lord, only to be set upon and robbed and killed. They won't find the killers. They retreat to the hills or flee the country."

He turned to the captain. "Next time I search your lugger. Good day to you all."

He was rowed back to his boat, and the captain drew a long breath and grinned at his sons. They got underway again, taking course for the harbour at Biarritz. Ralph and Mateo were left looking at each other in horror.

"Oh Papa! 'R.B.' Your initials," Mateo whispered. Ralph, cold and shaken, could only nod. "'R.B.' on his saddle bags perhaps? We must find out if it happened the day we left. Oh Papa, was I not right to get you away quickly?"

What fear or hatred, Ralph was thinking, could have prompted such a plot? Is she behind it? Is she so desperate to be free of me? Can I believe it was I who escaped such a fate? He imagined being dragged from a horse and beaten to death. He was sick with guilt for poor 'R.B.'

Their successful arrival in Biarritz was clouded with this news and, seeking it in the French papers, Ralph found the crime had been committed the same morning that he and Mateo had left Santiago. The journalist had written that the victim seeking his God would undoubtedly go straight to heaven. Ralph found no comfort in that.

Practicalities, however, had to occupy his mind before they could take ship for England. They both needed a bath, and Mateo needed new clothing. They found a small hotel with a vacant room, and a tin bath was sent up with a jug of warm water. Ralph went out himself when he was refreshed, and found a gentlemen's outfitter where the prices were not too outrageous.

On the way back he passed through a marketplace and spotted a stall selling silver images of saints, crosses and other charms. Two men were shouting that their wares would bring good fortune from the blessed Saint James of Compostela. Despite their false whiskers he recognised the sons of Captain Jacques. He would not betray them, but murmured to a lady heading for their stall, "Madame, I fear you will find the silver rubs off after a few days."

It was something for him to smile about with Mateo when he returned to the hotel. Next day, when they reserved a cabin on a steam packet sailing for the port of Newcastle, Mateo's eyes shone. "Oh Papa, Sheradon Grange!"

Chapter 18

Sheradon Grange

Ralph

It was the lovely time of late May when, leaving their bags to be sent up, Ralph and Mateo chose to walk the three miles from the station after the confines of the journey. Ralph could scarcely believe he had his son beside him on this familiar road. The joy was too intense.

The evening was still, and the woods in their brilliant new green were like a painting. Mateo kept giving little sighs of happiness. They scarcely spoke. As they turned into the familiar gateway and started down the curving drive, they looked into each other's eyes and saw the excitement shining there. Who would see them first?

John was at the parlour window when they turned the corner. He leapt in the air and next moment was rushing out of the front door.

"I guessed it would be today, but you've *walked* from the station!"

What? There was a second of disappointment. They were *expecting* us, Ralph thought.

The others emerged, all smiles. It was a wonder to see his mother's passion as she hugged Mateo. This moment might never have happened, he reminded himself. I might have been a bloody corpse. He swallowed. There was an unreality about it all, confusing the delight of homecoming.

John was shouting to everyone, "See, I guessed right."

His mother and Mateo were in tears of joy, which spread to Lily. Jack and Frank clasped Ralph's hand by turns, and Lily held up her wet cheek to be kissed.

"But how did you know we were coming?" Ralph asked.

"I got Maria's letter," John cried, "so we knew you were on the way, but the post was quicker than you."

Mateo grabbed him. "Maria has written! When? What? Tell us – stop leaping about, you elf."

Ralph said, "Oh Mother, is Maria all right?"

"Come and read the letter. It puzzled and alarmed us, but it did suggest you had got safely away. It's wonderful that you are here, looking so bronzed and well." Ralph saw how her eyes turned from himself to Mateo as if she felt they might disappear again. "We have prayed for this moment."

They went inside, drawn naturally to the kitchen, where Jack made up the fire and put the kettle to boil. Then his mother took the letter from the mantelshelf and handed it to him. Mateo leaned over his shoulder to look. Ralph read it aloud.

"*Dear John, I am writing this to you but the letter is for all of you. I don't know what the two bears will have told you already. They should be with you before you get this.*" Ralph broke off. "No wonder you were puzzled. We will fill in the gaps presently. '*There was a great fuss when they found Smaller Bear had escaped. Lucia said I was a long time coming to bed so I spoke up and said it was my idea to run down and pull the bolt back. I didn't want Nurse blamed. Mamma was furious with me of course and wanted to know where you'd gone, Matty. I was starting to say you wanted a long walk and would come home soon when the post-boy came with news from the town about a horrid murder. The bears might not know of this so tell them, John. An Englishman called Richard Bell was robbed and killed only two miles from Santiago early this morning. I thought Mamma was going to faint away and Cousin Juan went white.*'"

Ralph had to stop for a moment as the words struck him cold. Sophia knew. Or did she know? Women did faint at such news, but Sophia was surely of tougher metal. Mateo was pressing closer to see what came next.

"*Mamma dismissed everyone except Cousin Juan. They went into her parlour and are still there. So I am writing this quickly for Brigitta to give the post-boy. He's downstairs. The servants are feeding him and asking more questions. So I must stop. I wanted so much to go with Smaller Bear and come and see you*

181

all but he said I was too small. I'm Baby Bear to him but you are still smaller, John. I hope you can read all this. I love you all. Maria.' The last bit is a scrawl, evidently in haste," Ralph added.

"Come on," John said. "Explain. Big Bear is you, Uncle Ralph, and Smaller Bear is you, Matty, so I guess you were locked up somewhere and Maria let you out. Tell us everything that happened."

Ralph pressed his hands over his eyes. Everything? No, not a plot to murder him. Not to John anyway. Better not to any of them. He exchanged a glance with Mateo, who was standing behind him and perhaps guessing what he was thinking.

"Well, John," he said, "you know I went to fetch Mateo home. When I got to Santiago there was a festival going on and your Aunt Sophia and Mateo and the twins came to it, so I saw them in the cathedral. Your Aunt Sophia didn't want me to take any of them home and Mateo upset her by saying he wanted to come, so when they went home she locked him up in their basement. Maria sneaked down and let him out. So he decided then and there to go home with me. He walked all the way, fifteen miles, to the town, and we started our journey that night."

John pranced round the room. "*I* went all the way to London. Da says that's about *three hundred* miles."

"Sit down and don't boast," Frank told him. Then he asked Ralph. "Why did the journey take you so long?"

Ralph gave a short laugh. "There was a French lugger beached nearby so we asked them to take us to Biarritz. It took longer than we expected but it was an adventure. Mateo learned some French."

"Good, but I'm also wondering why Maria thought it important for you to know about this murder."

Ralph spread his hands in a dismissive gesture. "I might have ridden that way to ask Sophia to let Mateo come for a visit. Since *he* came to *me* I didn't need to, but I didn't know there were still highwaymen about."

His mother broke in to ask what he and Mateo would like to eat.

Frank and Lily got up and took John's hands. "Bedtime for you."

"I'll go if Matty comes and reads me a story. I liked the one about the boy who ran away to sea."

"We don't strike bargains about bedtime." Frank said. "Come now, and when Matty's had his supper—"

"I'll come," Mateo said, "but that book gave you too many ideas."

"*Everything* gives me ideas, but I won't do that again, because Da and Ma went all thin and pale while I was away."

Later in the evening Ralph, sensing his mother's eagerness to speak with him alone, said, "Tell me how your great novel is progressing," and she jumped up at once and ushered him to her little office. The fire was low, but he made it up from the coal scuttle and sat her in the armchair, drawing her desk chair close.

"Save the novel for now, Mother. You want to know more of my story?"

She nodded. "I pray I'm wrong, son, but fearful imaginings have come into my head. Juan and Sophia hired killers to be rid of you. Maria found out and freed Matty to go and warn you. You had your boy, so you took the nearest transport and got out of the country. Tragically, a man – perhaps like you in build and dress *and* with your initials – died the next day. Mistaken for you?"

He shook his head several times, not in denial but at her perceptiveness.

"Mother, I fear you are near the truth, and I feel sickening guilt for the man – but oh, let it not be *Sophia's* plan. Juan and Guido I can just believe. But my own wife! You cannot guess, Mother, how I have weighed doubt and certainty against each other since we heard of the murder."

"So it was not just now in Maria's letter? I thought not. And has Maria's account added weight one way or the other?"

"It hardens my suspicion of Juan. He hoped to marry Sophia. Mateo saw how shocked he was when she told him she had seen me in the cathedral. It was from gossipy Mrs Hammond that she'd learned I was ill and not likely to recover. When the posts resumed after the winter she heard no more. She *wanted* to believe I had died. She told the children – Mateo thought I was a ghost. But to plot my death – no! I have had to leave the girls with her. If she sends Juan away I will feel easier."

"Mrs Hammond couldn't write again. The winter carried *her* off. But oh, Ralph, this Juan? You must have known him for years. Can you see him as a murderer?"

"I first met him when we arrived in Madrid and he clasped Sophia in his arms and told him his home was hers from that moment on. I saw his expression change when she introduced me as her hero, her saviour. Privately she laughed with me about his disappointment. But she accepted the use of his apartment in Madrid when we were married. He was often there. Maybe his devotion flattered her."

Dee shook her head sadly. "I want to understand her *and* Juan. Was he angry when Mateo was born? The heir to the de Villena land?"

A rush of warmth flooded Ralph's whole being as it came home to him that he had his son back at last, and to keep. He looked his mother in the eye.

"Oh yes, I could feel Juan's jealousy, hatred. And she changed too. She resented my love for my son. A man was not to be interested in a baby."

"And you hated her to pet him like a baby when he became a little boy. So you began to love her less?"

He stroked his chin. He must be honest. "Mother, I *never* loved her as you and Jack love each other. It was a wild passion, a part of my wild life at that time. To my shame I admit I loved her *body*, but the meeting in the cathedral killed that too. She stood there, cold as a post, defying me."

His mother leaned forward and took his hands in hers. "I'm sure Sophia loved you when you first came and you wanted us to accept her. And she went on needing your love till you were too engrossed in business. Oh Ralph, I know too well that rejected love turns to hate…"

He stared at her. "But she only loved me to make money. Are you saying I brought this on myself?"

She shook her head, but he could feel that the thought was there. Was it possible that there was a tiny speck of truth in it? He brushed it away.

"No, no. My mistake was to think I could blend my two lives when I decided to come to England. She never tried to fit in here."

"*I* could have been more loving." Her eyes were full of regret.

"No, her mind is clouded by her narrow vision of life. She had her mad passion in her youth, but now? Could she desire that slimy snake, Juan, enough to seek my death? I never wish to see her again, but what will she do to my girls? Maria longs to be here. How can I rescue her?"

"She won't hurt *them*, but I think she is a poor creature torn between love and hate. Maybe she suspected Juan the moment she heard of the murder. When Maria was writing her letter, Sophia was questioning him. From what you say he had a strong motive. He wanted her."

Ralph inclined his head. "I have been blind. I needed to keep making money for her extravagances. I put Juan from my mind when we came here. I knew they corresponded, but I dismissed it as business. He was overseeing the castle and land, which he pretended was not fit for our habitation. He never wanted me to see it, and I wanted to come back to England. I thought I was giving her enough here." He drew a deep sigh. "She has my girls now.

I never got close to Lucia, but Maria…! She flew into my arms that day. And that very night she freed Matty to warn me. She saved my life." Tears came to his eyes as he saw her little figure darting through the crowds in the square, intent on the café with the yellow awning.

His mother must have sensed his emotion. "Please tell me it all – your three days in Spain. I need to picture it."

"For your novel?"

"Oh, that is a poor thing. To be close to you, Ralph. To live it with you."

She gave him her paradise smile, and he relived it all for her.

She put her arms round him then. "I thank God you escaped."

"Will Frank and Lily guess as much as you have?"

"Perhaps not. They weren't watching your face or Mateo's as I was."

He stood up, weary of talk. "Well, I doubt if we'll hear more of the dreadful murder if the Spanish authorities believe it was highwaymen. But now I want only to enjoy my son, to see him grow, to cultivate and develop his mind." He yawned and she rose too.

"He'll go to Mr Hurst's, I suppose."

He stiffened. "Oh! Not yet. I have no such plan." He was not ready for such a thought. "He will be asleep now. I shall go and gaze at him in that room where I was sick at heart. Goodnight, Mother."

He wished he could blot out Spain, but two days later another letter came from Maria to John. John gave it to Mateo to read to everyone at dinner time.

"*Dear John, I am forbidden to write to Smaller Bear because Mamma knows he ran home with Big Bear so please share this with everyone. She is also cross with Cousin Juan and Guido and has told them to leave.*" Mateo lifted his eyes and Ralph flashed him a delighted smile, turning it on his mother too. She nodded. Mateo resumed. "*She cries a lot and Nurse tries to comfort her. I asked her if she was crying for the Bears – only I didn't call them that – and she said no, it was because the country is now under military rule and the Cortes has made General Espartero president so he's in charge of the young queen. I know she was upset when we heard that, but I don't believe that's what's making her sad. I wish I could be with you all especially for your birthdays soon. We can write through Brigitta who has agreed to use Sheradon Grange not the school on the letter and the Bears can tell you things to say if they want to. Give everyone big hugs from Baby Bear.*"

"Is that all?" John demanded. "What's a Cortes?"

"It's the Spanish Parliament," said Mateo. "Well, you can write back a longer letter."

"I shall." But with cricket and summer weather all he wrote was '*Granda Jack is building a tree house for my fifth birthday and Matty's thirteenth and I'm playing cricket. Old Bunson's gone and the new head's terrific. Uncle Ralph is keeping Matty at home and teaching him himself.*'

Mateo added a paragraph, which Ralph saw because John showed him the letter to check spellings before it was sealed up. Mateo had written: '*You and Lu must be very loving to Mamma. She is suddenly bereft of a man's support. Papa doesn't want to talk about the murder – or anything Spanish, in fact – but he loves to hear news of you, of course. He hasn't mentioned my going to Mr Hurst's, so I've said nothing. For the moment I just love being here. Grandmamma thinks I will want to spread my wings soon. If I could fly to Spain and bring you and Lu here I would, and Mamma if she could be happy with Papa, Your loving Smaller Bear.*'

Ralph sat with this in his hands, contemplating the truth that his son was growing up and would indeed spread wings. He thrust the thought away, wrote that Big Bear also sent his love to his dear daughters, and the letter was sent.

Chapter 19

Tynemouth, May 1846
(four years later)

Dee

"Dee Heron, you must be past fifty. I know I am. What is *possessing* you?"

Jenny Batey lay back among the rocks, laughing and digging Jack in the ribs. "What's got into the woman? Can you not keep her in order, man?"

"Nay, I love to see her as happy as this. Dancing on the sand. She's beautiful."

Dee heard them and twirled faster. She was exulting in the sunshine and yellow sand and a wild wind rolling in the waves, white foam and azure blue, an uproarious change from the everlasting green of home. But it was other things that had conspired to lift her spirits to these ridiculous heights. Her publisher, little Septimus Brandling, had told the *Newcastle Courant* that he was publishing her hundredth *Moral Tale*, and the paper wanted a story. To combine the interview with a visit to Jenny and the seaside was a great excitement.

Other spurts of delight had happened lately. Mateo had won a scholarship to Cambridge when he was not quite seventeen, Mr Hurst would take John at only nine after the summer with his eleven-year-olds, Frank's latest bridge design had brought him a big contract, and Ralph's shares in a new mine were soaring.

She knew she cut a strange figure – a short, well-bosomed woman past her middle years, with grey hair under her bonnet, her shawl flung from her shoulders and wafted as accessory in the dance, her worn boots twinkling beneath her woollen skirt, too warm for the day – but she didn't care. Jenny, her co-grandparent, might laugh, but here was Jack, rising up to come and join her in the dance, clumsy as he was but exulting in seeing her so carefree.

He soon tripped himself up and sat down on the sand. "Nay, I'm spoiling it for you, angel. You go on dancing while I go up to the prawn seller and get something more to eat, for we've eaten the pies Jenny brought."

"Do that, darling, but I'm out of breath now, and will sit by Jenny till you come back."

She watched his bumbling figure climb the cliff path. Although he had put on weight, he was still a fit man and she loved his steadfastness as much as ever.

Jenny said, "Well, now he's away for a while, tell me the spicier news. Is Matty after the girls now? I was astonished last time I saw him how fast he's growing. He's a young man, and you say he will be off to Cambridge come the autumn."

"He's terrified of girls and still shy with boys. It's been a struggle for him these last two years at Mr Hurst's. Ralph finally realised that he must let him go among people. Cambridge life will be very strange – so far away from home – but at least there are no young women there."

"I wager there are plenty in the town, though. I bet there's not a student comes away after three or four years and still a virgin."

"Jenny! I hope that's not true. Are they not watched over at all?"

"Nay, I don't know, but the young are getting ideas younger and younger these days. John told me he is going to marry Maria when he's older, and he's only nine now!"

Dee laughed. "Maria has humoured him with writing from time to time – childish things, but her letters told Ralph all he wanted to know about how Sophia was surviving. He dreaded her suddenly fleeing to England, with all the turmoil in Spain. But now the general in power has been overthrown, so loyal Sophia is happy. Parliament has declared the little queen is of age at thirteen."

"Thirteen! My Ally's Jess is thirteen and she cannot rule herself, never mind a country. But I thought my lady Sophia was too tough to be upset by a few riots."

"No, she was nervous when her cousin Juan left, but Maria says she's raised one of her footmen to steward status. Apparently he's clever at figures and can manage the estate. So now he sits at meals with them, Maria writes."

Jenny chuckled. "I wager he does more than sit at meals. No wonder she doesn't need Ralph if she has a younger man in her bed."

Dee was shocked. "Jenny, she wouldn't – she's a proud woman."

"If a woman's desperate, pride goes out of the window."

Dee sat silent. Was she an innocent fool never to have thought of this? Maria wrote so guilelessly of Eduardo driving their mother about the estate in the small trap. Those girls are eleven now, approaching womanhood. Ralph should bring them away from her.

Jenny gave her a poke in the ribs. "Come on, Dee. Don't go solemn on me. You were dancing on the sand a minute ago."

"I am suddenly seeing a dark side of everything that made me happy. Miners are on strike with starving families, but Ralph has kept the mine open with men from Cornwall, Wales and Ireland."

Jenny put her hand over Dee's mouth. "Don't start preaching politics on a day like this. You'll work yourself into a frenzy like those waves out there. Thank the Lord, here's Jack coming back!"

Dee drew a great sigh. Life for Jenny was tough but fun. Human beings were a rum lot, but their evil doings were mostly laughable.

Dee looked up as Jack approached, cradling his bag of prawns. Dear Jack! He wanted to love everyone until wickedness stared him in the face. Then he would seek excuses for the perpetrator, and was grieved if he found none.

Later that day they walked back to the pie shop, and Tom scolded Jenny for being so long. She only laughed.

"Nay, you old grumbler, you missed a treat. Dee dancing like a fairy on Tynemouth sands."

"Some fairy," Dee heard Tom mutter.

"And she is going to be in the newspaper, so next time she comes we'll have to bow and curtsy like she was the queen herself. Are you off now, Lord and Lady Heron?"

"Eh," Jack chuckled as they hurried to the station to catch the little train to Newcastle, "will they really bow and curtsy? I'd like to see that."

But when they reached the *Courant* office, Dee was as nervous as a girl. Wanting an independent income, she had resumed *Moral Tales* when she was struggling with her big novel, but she had not expected press publicity. She gave her name to the boy at the desk.

"Ah," the youth said, "It's the *editor* wants to see *you*, Mrs Heron," and he actually bowed, which tickled Jack.

He led them up a dark narrow stair and knocked on a door marked *Mr J. P. Roy: Editor*. Mr J. P. Roy rose from behind his deck and shook their hands. There was a jaunty air about him that reminded Dee of someone from the past, and his first words were, "You'll not remember me, Mrs Heron, from the Wylam murder?"

Dee shivered. The young pushy reporter. No, she did not want to be reminded of that. She looked him in the eye. "You were on the *Chronicle* then."

"Well remembered, madam! I have risen, you may say, to higher things."

"The older man," Dee said, "from the *Courant*? He was very courteous."

"Josiah Peterson. In happy retirement. He plodded on writing up garden fetes and charity balls. He was not comfortable with murders."

"Well, we can forget about that one," Dee said stoutly. "You want to know about my hundredth story, I believe."

"That is the trigger, one might say, but a piece about Dione Sharon is nothing without Dee Heron." And he proceeded to rattle off events in her life which had reached the newspapers: her parents' suicide, her marriage to Jack, the drowning of Joseph Heron – always referred to as the Wylam murder, although it was no such thing – and her famous outburst at her younger son's trial. "You have had tragedy and drama in your life, but, I hope, much happiness since then."

As Dee sat, devastated by all these memories, Jack broke in with a merry grin, "Oh ay, sir. Happy times. Frank and Billy – I should call him Ralph – get along famously, and we've got grandchildren." He counted on his fingers. "Two boys and two girls – but we don't see much of the wee girls now, for they're in a place called Spain." He looked at Dee. "I've got that right, haven't I, angel?"

Mr Roy clapped his hands. "Ah, the Spanish connection. I've been finding out about that. Billy Heron became Sir Ralph Barnet and was quite a buccaneer for a time. So you're not all happily living together at Sheradon Grange at present?"

Dee said through stiff lips, "My daughter-in-law is showing her daughters their estate in Galicia. None of this is relevant, and it won't be in your article about the *Moral Tales*. I'm not sure that I want an article at all, and I think, Jack, we'll go home now." She stood up.

Jack had to get up too. "But, angel, the gentleman was being very pleasant. He knows all about us."

"Precisely," she said. "I believe there is an earlier train we could catch." She looked at the editor who had risen with a grin on his face. "If you wish, Mr Roy, you can print that I have enjoyed writing the *Moral Tales* and will continue as long as Mr Brandling has a market for them. Good afternoon."

Not in the least disconcerted, Mr Roy made a small bow and opened his door for them. Casually he remarked, "How fortunate we are in this country to have the freedom of the press! Good day, Mrs Heron, Mr Heron." His smile, she decided, was definitely sinister, and they were hardly out of the building before she realised her impulsive departure might have unpleasant consequences.

A week later she received a short letter from Mr Roy telling her an article would appear in the *Newcastle Courant* to herald the publication of the hundredth *Moral Tale* by the North Country grandmother Dione Sharon. She would be sent a complimentary copy of the paper.

"It will do very well for lighting the fire," she told Frank and Lily.

"Now, Ma, you know you are secretly excited," Frank said, and Lily added, "Father Jack liked the editor and doesn't know why you hurried away."

"I just want to live quietly here, not talked about."

Frank ruffled up his fair curls. "*I'd* be glad to be in the papers. I hope they report on my bridge."

When the paper came, Dee took it into her little writing room to read alone.

One glance showed that her fears were justified. Telltale names jumped out at her after the first paragraph, next to a reproduction of the cover of *Oswald the Owl*. She read that with some satisfaction. The story was praised not only for its moral sentiments but for the charming line drawings by the author. The next paragraph declared that if Dione Sharon's writing was gentle and sedate, the life of Dee Heron was not. Her eyes darted on. Everything was here: the wealth of the Sheradon family '*in lovely Sheradon Grange near the charming village of Ovingham*', followed by the collapse of the business, the desertion of her betrothed, the '*dashing army officer, Sir Ralph Barnet*', her parents' joint suicide, her swift marriage to '*lowly Jack Heron, a waggonway driver for Wylam pit, who became the unlikely love of her life*' and the birth of two sons. '*Was this the happy ending?*' the article inquired. '*Alas, no.*'

Dee could hardly bear to read the rest. Mr J. P. Roy had evidently read up his own notes on *'the trial of Francis Heron for the murder of his uncle, instigated by his jealous brother Billy.'* He had summarised it expertly to bring out the drama of her own intervention when the jury seemed about to pass a guilty verdict. *'The writer of* Moral Tales *confessed to the court that her husband was not the father of Billy and she had treated her two sons so differently that enmity had grown between them.'* She skipped the flamboyant description of the transformed Billy's life and how he had romantically married a Spanish condesa and bought back Sheradon Grange for his mother. She glimpsed *Moral Tales* again in the last paragraph. Yes, Roy was suggesting that the brothers' families, with four children between them, had made a harmonious home there and *'should now provide – as the* Moral Tales *always did – a happy ending.'* And then there was a final sentence in which he had added, *'The* Courant *understands, however, that the Condesa de Villena has resided in Spain for the past four years with two of her children. We trust this does not represent another family split to haunt our dear author, Dione Sharon. May she bring forth many more of her charming* Moral Tales for Children.*'*

Jack, Frank and Lily must have been hovering in the hallway. When she flung the paper down with a burst of angry tears, they rushed in.

Jack had his arms round her in a moment.

"Angel, what has he written to upset you so?"

Oh, she had Jack, who thankfully couldn't read. She could rest in his love and recover her sense of humour. She changed her sobs into laughter and beamed into his eyes. "Yes, I was moved, but they are happy tears. Look, there is your name, see – *'Jack Heron'* – and he describes you as the love of my life. Nothing else he's written is important, but he grasped that."

Jack goggled at the page, red-faced. "Ay, that's my name all right – and isn't that a 'W'? Is that 'Wylam'?"

"Yes. He got your job correct too, driving the pit wagon."

"I never told him that!"

"These newspaper men are very clever."

"Ay, they are that." And, seeing Frank and Lily pick up the paper to read it, Jack plodded out to the stables to check on the horses.

Frank said, "Phew! If Ralph buys the *Courant* while he's in town today he'll be furious."

Dee put her hand to her mouth. "It's Friday. He meets up with Matty from school and they come on the train together. Matty will be appalled!

What? His dear father almost got his brother hung for murder!" She gulped as the horror of it shook her.

Frank squeezed her shoulder. "It says we were reconciled."

"And I treated my sons differently, which is a crime in a mother." Sobs rose up as she remembered something. "Matty said lately, 'This home is a sanctuary of love and harmony.' Oh Lily, we can't stop him seeing the paper."

Lily said, "Don't fret, Mother Dee. You'll talk him through it as honestly and as gently as only you can. You recall John was once teased at school that his da had been in prison. I told him about his great-uncle Joseph falling in the river and a silly fisherman telling the constable he'd seen Frank push him. Uncle Ralph was asked in court if *he'd* seen a push and he said 'no', so the charge was dropped. I made little of it, but what I said was true."

Dee slapped the paper. "But the *whole* story is here in black and white."

Frank said, "I'm sure *I'll* hear comments. I will simply say there's some truth in it but it's a long time ago and we've put it out of our minds now."

Dee shook her head. They were trying to be helpful, but for the rest of the day she was dreading Ralph's fury and grieving for Matty, who would surely feel hurt and dismay at this revelation.

They were late that evening, and Dee hurriedly put the stewpot back on the fire when they walked into the kitchen. Ralph laid the *Courant* on the table. Dee peered at his face. His eyes met hers, and the dark depths of them were not ablaze with anger but seemed to be appraising her.

Puzzled, she still felt the need to defend herself. "Pray don't think *I* told Mr J. P. Roy all that. It was all there in back numbers of the newspaper."

He nodded. Then the corners of his eyes smiled as he looked at his son.

Mateo was ready with a flow of words. "Oh Grandmamma, we had such talk on the train and walking from the station. Papa says I'm nearly a man now and it's good for a man to know his forebears had great ups and downs in their lives and grew wiser and kinder because of them. It makes me love you all more deeply and, Grandmamma, I understand now why you strive so hard after truth and love."

Dee felt her throat swell. "Oh Matty!"

His long, lanky body leaned over her. "But I hope it hasn't upset you – it all coming out again. There should be laws to stop the press printing so much about living people."

She laughed through tears of relief. "Laws of libel if they print lies – but everything he wrote was true, even his speculation in the last paragraph."

Mateo looked at that again. "But it is *not* a family split. I love my sisters and miss them, and Mother too." He looked tentatively at his father. "It's occurred to me, Papa, that I ought to visit Spain before Cambridge. It's a while since Maria wrote."

Dee saw the colour drain from Ralph's face. I don't want him upset again, she thought. He has managed the boy so well.

He said nothing for a few seconds then burst out, "She would keep you there. She would never let you go to Cambridge. If you ever visit Spain I would have to go too, and that's impossible at present. I have too much in hand."

Dee said, "And, Matty, your father's life might be in danger. We know not where Juan and Guido are – or, indeed, if Sophia is innocent."

Mateo looked shocked. "Oh, she is. I'm certain. I could go alone."

From shy, nervous Matty, that was astonishing. What had these new revelations stirred up in him – a yearning for action, something dramatic in his own life after his years of uneventful study?

Ralph sat heavily down at the table. "Let us eat and put away such thoughts. You have told me you have much work to do before Cambridge. Write to Maria if you wish, through Brigitta as usual, and inquire after them all. We need to know the latest news."

Frank came in. "Lily is trying to settle John. These light nights he thinks he should be out playing cricket."

He noticed the *Courant* on the table and Ralph's solemn face. "*I'm* going to shrug it all away if people question me."

Ralph looked up at him with a snort of a laugh, tapping the paper. "Oh, that! Yes, shrug it away. *You* can. You are the innocent."

Dee was ladling beef stew onto plates for him and Mateo when Jack came in, drawn from the stables by the aroma.

"Is it that time, angel?"

"It's Ralph and Matty's late supper, but there's plenty. You can all sit and partake. You too, Lily," as she came in, swiftly followed by John in his nightshirt saying, "Hey, *I'm* hungry."

Frank pointed him to the door. "Bed!"

"I promised him one mouthful," Lily pleaded, "if he promised never to come down again after goodnight is spoken."

"It was a vow on my cricket bat, so I can never break it."

Laughter lifted everyone's spirits, and when they had all parted to their beds, Dee put the *Courant* on the embers of the fire.

Chapter 20

(next day)

Dee

Dee woke with the early light and crept to her writing room to rekindle excitement over her unfinished novel. Presently a tap at the door revealed Ralph, fully dressed for the office.

"I'm sorry, Mother, I couldn't sleep. I heard you get up. I need your advice." He drew up a chair close to her desk. "Mateo is serious about going to Spain. That wretched article, that final paragraph."

She let him talk of their great conversation on the way home and the effect on Matty. "He was pleased with my confidence and believed in my repentance. But now he is asserting himself. Have I lost my authority? He never had initiatives before."

She was about to reply when a gentle knock sounded.

"Jack, wondering if I'm coming to breakfast."

But it was Mateo who looked in, his face crinkled with anxiety. "It's from Maria to me direct, not John, though Mamma forbade her." He was holding a letter.

Ralph stood up. "Post time already! I'm catching the early train."

"No, Papa, please don't go. Something very worrying has happened. You and Grandmamma ought to read this."

His tone was urgent. Ralph sat down again and Mateo put the letter on the desk. Dee, a tight cramp in her stomach, saw a hasty scrawl. The date was May 3rd.

Darling Matty, it's festival day, four years since Papa came. We were going to Santiago when a gentleman and servant came and asked for Don Juan de Villena. Luiz said he'd gone away so he asked for Guido Martinez. He was told the same thing. Luiz came to Mamma and said he wanted to speak to the condesa. Mamma was very agitated and refused absolutely. She told Luiz to fetch Manuel, our big groom, to turn them away. They did go but the gentleman said we would hear from him again. He left a calling card. The name was Richard Bell! He must be the murdered man's son. Luiz said he was young, tall, broad and dark-haired. The address was Carlisle, England. I couldn't see any more. Mamma is very upset. Eduardo can't sooth her, only Nurse. Nurse told me, "I'd have betrayed the villains if I'd known where they are." If the son is after his father's killers how did he come to us? Four years to the day, well, tomorrow, since it happened! What if he suspects Mamma! Tell me what you and Big Bear think. My love to everyone, Baby Bear.

Dee looked at Ralph. He was shaking his head. "This is bad. I trusted that was all buried in the past. There was a brief report at the time – a Carlisle man murdered and robbed by bandits in Spain, but nothing more."

Dee was shivering. "Who could have sent the son to Sophia?"

Mateo cried, "But Mamma is innocent. She sent Cousin Juan and Guido away. We *should* go to her. She has only Nurse, who is old and frail."

"She has Eduardo." Ralph spoke it in a neutral voice. Dee had pondered Jenny's view of that relationship since their talk at Tynemouth. Did Ralph suspect that? Now he rose and paced round the small room, knocking over books and papers without noticing.

He came back to Mateo. "If she is in trouble, *she* must write to *me*. We'll give her time. Maria's letter is dated two weeks ago. Write a secret letter back to Maria. Tell her not to worry. Juan and Guido must have fled the country. This man will find the trail cold."

Mateo said, "He has chosen the anniversary, when people's memories are sharpest. Oh Papa, this thing is unlikely to die away."

Ralph was staring up at the ceiling, his jaw set, his fists clenched. He snapped out of the pose and looked at his pocket watch.

"I must catch that train."

"You've had no breakfast."

"And I have no appetite for any. Mateo, write what I suggest to Maria. Tell her to keep us informed. I'll be back tonight, Mother."

He was gone.

Mateo stood, looking at Dee, with a rueful face.

Mateo

A week later Mateo was in the house with only Rosie. From long habit he had obeyed his father and written to Maria as instructed, but he was unhappy with it. Papa, he reflected, called me a man. If he became a new man I can too. *I* can decide where my duty lies. Is it to Mamma, who is frightened and needs my protection? I *will* go to Spain – but how? Papa would have to give me the money.

He was sitting at his desk in the corner of the drawing room with a Latin prose. John was at school and the others had gone to visit a farm near Hexham, his father riding Zephyr, Uncle Frank riding Prince, and Rusty drawing the carriage for his mother and Aunt Lily. No one had suggested he should abandon his studies and go too, so here he was, conscious only that Rosie had promised to bring him a mug of coffee at eleven.

If I was a man, he thought, I would dare to ask her if she would let me kiss her, just to see what it was like. He mimed accepting the coffee and then standing up, holding out his arms and framing the words with his lips. Of course I won't, he told himself, sitting down again and looking at the Latin sentence he had just written. He could use an ablative absolute to avoid a clumsy clause.

He had just crossed it out when he heard the clip-clop of a horse. The thought of a visitor was terrifying in his lone state. He peered at the bend in the drive, which he could see from his desk. What he saw was a stranger, trotting on a smart roan and looking directly at his window. He shrank back. It was a dull morning, and perhaps he was invisible. The man disappeared from view while he dismounted and hitched his horse to the tethering post beyond the front porch. Mateo swallowed and waited. The knock came. He should go, but Rosie would hear in the kitchen. Perhaps the man would just deliver a message.

He heard their voices, and then her footsteps in the hall and her tap on the drawing room door. He gulped, "Come in."

"A gentleman wanted your father," she began, holding out a calling card. Mateo jumped up in alarm as the man appeared behind her.

"I am happy to speak to the son," he said. His voice was friendly.

Rosie started and looked over her shoulder. "Oh well." She put the card into Mateo's hand. "Will that be two mugs of coffee?"

"Yes please, Rosie." He indicated an armchair to his visitor and Rosie scurried out. The man didn't sit down. Of course – he was waiting for them to be properly introduced to each other. Mateo looked at the card. *Richard Bell Esquire* – and an address in Carlisle. Richard Bell! He couldn't help a sharp intake of breath and a wide-eyed stare at the man. He was everything Maria had described. And he was watching Mateo intently.

"The name means something to you?"

"Well, yes, sir." He was floundering. "But I thought you were in Spain."

"Oh, really? Why would you think that?" The friendly manner had gone.

"I – I heard something." Mateo saw he was on dangerous ground.

"From your mother, perhaps?"

"No, no, truly. Please, sir, you had better come back when my father's here."

"I'm sure I will – but there is no reason why I should not have a pleasant talk with you and a welcome cup of coffee." He held out his hand and the smile was there again. "In Spain you are Mateo de Villena – and Matthew Barton here, perhaps? I am Richard Bell at your service. Pray let us be acquainted."

Mateo put out a limp hand, which was firmly gripped. He was aware that his palms were sweating. "I am called Mateo here, or Matty," he murmured.

The man sat down and invited Mateo to sit opposite him in the chair facing the window. Mateo sat, not lifting his eyes from the man's expensive riding boots.

"You don't ask me the purpose of my visit?"

"I'm sure you'll tell me, sir."

"You have heard of my father's murder?"

"Yes, sir. I was very sorry to hear of it. Four years ago. It was reported."

"Many murders are reported but you remember that one?"

"It happened the day I was last in Spain. That's all."

"You and your father, whose initials are the same as my father's?"

Mateo tried a little shrug of his shoulders and a half-smile. "A coincidence."

"You and your father left very suddenly, did you not?"

"We'd finished our business."

I mustn't answer his questions, he was telling himself. Papa would be interrogating *him*. Papa will be angry with me.

"How did you travel home?"

Mateo looked up and blurted out, "Why does that matter now, sir? Why have you come to us? It was four years ago. Why?"

Richard Bell held up his hands in a calming gesture. "Why now? I understand your curiosity, young man, and you are entitled to an explanation. I think we will allow the coffee to come first. This is a charming house. Your grandmother was born here, I believe. She has had an interesting life."

As he spoke, he put his hand into the inner pocket of his riding coat. Mateo thought, he's going to shoot me to avenge his father; but what he drew out was a copy of the *Newcastle Courant*. That cursed paper!

"A neighbour brought it to me on my return from Spain. He believed it would interest me, and it did. Of course, I was coming to visit Sheradon Grange anyway, but the article quickened my interest in you all. Ah, here is the coffee, and it smells very good." He actually leapt up and drew the coffee table between them so Rosie could set the tray down.

"Eh, thank you, sir. I hope it's the way you like it." She gave a little bob and cast approving glances at Mr Bell. "Will you manage it, master Matty? I have a smoothing iron heating." He nodded and she went out.

He is more her age, Mateo thought, with a pang of jealousy. She thinks of me as a mere boy. 'Master Matty'! She's put out the best cups for him. I'll make a mess doing this.

Under Mr Bell's amused looks, he managed it with only a few splashes on the tray. Thankfully he sat down again and took a gulp, which was too hot, so he spluttered.

"Pray be at ease, young man," Mr Bell said, which only made his cheeks hot too. "I interrupted your studies. I'm sorry. Where do you go to school?"

"In Newcastle, but I'm going to Cambridge University in the autumn."

"So young. You must be very clever."

"I'll be seventeen next month."

"When do you expect your father home?"

The change of subject flustered him more. "I don't know. They didn't say."

I must start asking the questions, he reminded himself. "You were going to tell me, sir, why you waited so long before you began to inquire about your father's death." Oh, that was so clumsily put! His hand shook as he picked up his cup again.

There was a pause. Mr Bell drained off his cup and poured himself another. Then he replied in a sharp tone as if he *had* taken offence. "Let me tell you, young sir, I have longed for the chance to investigate my father's murder for four bitter years." Mateo mumbled some sort of apology, but he went on. "My widowed mother returned from Spain a broken woman, her faith shattered, her mind deranged. But on one thing she was clear. I was not to go to Spain. 'It's happened,' she said. 'You cannot bring him back. Spain is an evil country. I will not lose you too. Put your energy into his business as he wished, and make that his memorial.'" He flashed a glance at Mateo which was hard to read. "I wanted to go to university, but I did what she demanded, and very well too. Now I am a wealthy man. Last year, unknown to her, I employed a Spanish-speaking detective to go to Spain and accumulate all the information he could about Santiago and events at the time of my father's death: movements of people, processes of law. In March my mother died."

"Oh sir, I'm sorry to hear it." Mateo was growing in confidence now Richard Bell was revealing so much about himself.

"*I* was *not* sorry," he said. "Life was hell for her. I can only pray she is with my father now." The passion faded from his voice, and he drank his second cup and smiled at Mateo. "You can see how my visit to you has come about."

Mateo paused in the act of pouring another cup for himself. "Well, no, sir, unless you mean that newspaper article. But there is no connection—"

"Is there not? It tells me that your mother and sisters have stayed in Spain, living near Santiago. I know you were with them before that and then your father came, but not to stay. After only one whole day in the town, he left in the middle of the night because you came to him with some news that made you both hurry off together back to England. Early that morning my father was murdered. Strange goings-on, would you not think?"

"We had nothing to do with it. We never met your father. Bandits attacked and robbed him."

"I know that. But I have strong reason to believe that a murder plot was behind the bandits. They were to do what bandits do, but this time they were not working for themselves. They were hired men."

Mateo, in a panic now, recalled Maria's letter. This very man sitting before him had been quite lately at their door asking for Juan de Villena and

Guido Martinez. Frustrated there, something had made him leave Spain and come to England to find Sir Ralph Barnet.

"You are puzzled," Richard Bell said. Mateo realised how cleverly he had placed him with the light on his face so he could watch his every expression. "You see, my helpful detective had already interviewed many people in Santiago about the festival of St Philip and St James. Some members of the Cathedral Guard recalled a woman with three children being harassed by an Englishman whom they chased from the cathedral. They found out she was the Condesa de Villena, whose husband had died some months before, or so it was reported. Local gossip said that a cousin, Juan de Villena, was hoping to marry her."

Mateo had to break in. "My mother had been told a lie."

"Allow me to proceed. My detective also learned that this cousin Juan had left the area with a manservant, Guido Martinez, shortly after my father's murder."

"That proves nothing!" The words would come out. I mustn't speak, he thought. I'll make things worse. He clasped his hands together in front of his mouth.

Richard Bell went on as if he hadn't interrupted. "What my detective had *not* done was interview every place in the city that took in lodgers. An impossible task. But there I was fortunate. It was my first visit to Santiago, and I was standing with my bags in the piazza, marvelling at the cathedral, when a little man came up to me and asked in English if I needed a bed for the night. The hotels were all full."

Tomaso! So friendly, so chatty. Richard Bell, he was certain, would have used an alias in Spain so that everyone would talk freely to him. Nothing delighted a community more than gossip about their local nobility. Tomaso would happily have revealed to his new English guest that a Sir Ralph Barton wanting to contact the Condesa de Villena had stayed there at the same festival time, four years before, and that his son had arrived and they had hastened away in the night. The murder the very next day was bound to have been mentioned too. Dear God, he could see how easy it was to suspect that his mother had planned to be rid of the husband she didn't want and marry another. And when she found her husband had escaped back to England, of course, for her own safety she would send Juan away.

Fearfully anxious now, he looked away out of the window, longing for the others to return. They could be hours yet.

Richard Bell was smiling at him. "I believe you are seeing why I have come here, especially since I read this article. I was despairing of further progress in Spain. My detective had not been able to discover any serious efforts by the Spanish authorities at the time to find the culprits." He leaned forward confidentially. "Did you know, being Spanish yourself, that the old system – if you can call it that – of the Holy Brotherhood was closed down in 1835?"

"Oh yes – the *Santa Hermandad*." Mateo was on sure ground there.

"Indeed – but the replacement, the Garda Civil, was not properly established till two years ago. If I can interest them in a murder that fell in the time between, they may take it up, if only to show that law and order is now rigorously enforced."

"But are you…are you going back to Spain, sir?"

Richard Bell sat back in the chair and stroked his chin. "Oh, I will, but not till I am utterly convinced of the perpetrator's identity. The real perpetrator. The actual villains had no grudge against my father – or yours, for that matter. But somebody most certainly wanted *your* father out of the way."

Mateo sat tight, his elbows pressed into his ribs, his thumbs against his closed lips. How long could he stay like this, he wondered, and would Mr Bell interpret silence as an admission that he knew the answer? He was in an agony of indecision.

Richard Bell watched him with that hateful little smile. Then he suddenly said, "You were a man of action that night, weren't you? I measured the distance to the town. Fifteen miles. You must have been on horseback."

"I *walked*!" The indignant words popped out.

"Impelled by the warning you had received? From a sister, perhaps? The one who wrote to you about my visit. Little girls like listening at doors, don't they?"

Mateo jumped to his feet. "No! I shan't stand for this. You want to trick me. I don't *know* about your father's death. He was robbed and killed by bandits. It's very sad, but you should leave it and not try to upset innocent people's lives."

Richard Bell rose too, his eyes blazing. "And you, who loved your father so much that you walked fifteen miles through the night – a mere boy of twelve – to save his life, would you not move heaven and earth to find his killer if you had failed in that mission – if he had been hacked to death next day, his body flung to the ground and left for strangers to find? Would you not? If you loved him as I loved my father?" His voice cracked.

Mateo's lips trembled. A lump came up in his throat. He was ashamed. This man had been so in control and suddenly he wasn't. He was a human soul driven by grief. All Mateo's natural compassion welled up. Whose side should he be on? He sank back into his chair.

"Oh sir, I'm so sorry. I should be helping you if I could." He looked up piteously and the words poured out. "I love my mother as well as my father – though they are living apart, which troubles me. But you seem to be pointing the finger at *her*, and I know she couldn't have – I cannot bear to think it." Life was all awry. He bowed his head and sobbed. Papa had once plotted Uncle Frank's death, but held back at the last moment. Mamma was agitated, he recalled, when she sent me to the Hellhole. Had she just hired killers to remove Papa from her life? No! But can anyone truly know another person?

Richard Bell came round the coffee table and laid a hand on his shoulder.

"Nay, weep not, young man. I am sorry too. I had one thing in my mind – to get at the truth. I never thought I might be trampling on anyone's feelings."

Mateo peered up into his eyes and saw genuine sorrow. They could be open with each other now. That was a huge relief. He said, "But you did, sir. Your visit to our home in Spain upset my mother and sisters."

"Only because they feared for someone they knew." He went back to his chair and sat down. "If you *do* want to help me, tell me about Juan de Villena."

Mateo brushed a hand across his eyes and breathed deeply several times. If that was where the man's finger was pointing, he *would* help him. Juan was expendable.

"I remember him from when I was small. He was always about. We stayed in an apartment in Madrid which I think he owned. I never liked him. I knew he hated Papa. When Papa said we would go to England I remember high words. Mamma kept saying, 'It's only for a visit, Juan.' And we went back to Spain and the twins were born there. I knew his family had meant him to marry Mamma, though he was older by a decade, I think. They are really second cousins. The family is scattered, but it was my grandfather who owned the big estate."

"And when your sisters were still small, your father prevailed in the argument between Spain and England? You made your home in Sheradon Grange with the rest of his family. Did he want to get you away from Juan?"

Mateo shook his head. "If you think my Mother let Juan make advances to her, you are wrong. She loved Papa. She told Juan to oversee the estate in our absence. It had been neglected."

"He would like to have inherited it himself?"

"That had been the family's plan. But I am certain Mother never wanted him. To her he was old and bald."

"Not at all the romantic hero like your father?" Richard Bell smiled brightly.

"Not at all. She was passionate about *him*. She always said so."

"I don't doubt it. But you use the past tense. How did the split come about?"

Mateo squirmed. "I don't think that concerns your investigation, sir."

"It's painful for you. I'm sorry, but it *is* pertinent. Maybe I can guess. This house is a country mansion, but on the outskirts of the coalfields of Northumberland. A Spanish grandee like your mother would increasingly feel out of place. Your father's family included people she would call peasants. So she took you and your sisters away, but not – you would say – to be reunited with her cousin Juan?"

"Certainly not. She wanted us to live on the family estate in Galicia which we had never even seen. I am the heir."

"But Juan continued to live in the castle?"

"He was family. He acted like a sort of steward."

"And how was it she believed your father had died?"

"He was ill. A lady she knew wrote that he was like to die and then nothing more was heard. It was the bad winter of '40 to '41, and the posts were stopped."

"So Juan had no confirmation of your father's death?"

"I wonder now if he pretended he *had* had official word. She told us children our father was dead, and we mourned him. When he appeared in the cathedral that festival day, I thought I was seeing a ghost. I told Mamma he was alive, and she didn't believe me till she saw him with her own eyes."

"You have to admit, she didn't *want* him to be alive." Richard Bell said it gently, but Mateo saw at once how crucial that scene in the cathedral had been. The guards' account was in the detective's report. When Tomaso's gossip was added, and Richard Bell had been turned away at the de Villena home, it was inevitable that he would scurry back to England to find the man he believed to be the intended victim.

He was shaken. There was only one thing more he must say. "Mamma sent cousin Juan away when the news of your father's death was brought to her."

"So you believe she suspected him and the manservant Guido Martinez?"

"Yes. She must have."

"And someone had already overheard their plot, which made you rush to save your father?"

They had come round to that again, but this time it was asked tenderly. He must admit it now. "It was our old nurse. She had been mother's nurse too. She is devoted to her. She heard them. She even saw from the window the men being paid down in the rear courtyard. She said Guido had dealt with them often. He was building a fortune. That's why he and cousin Juan could disappear and take up new identities somewhere when they found their plot had gone wrong."

"You are clear in your mind now that this is how it all happened?"

"It's the first time I've ever laid it out like this. You've made me see it from the outside. I mean like a jury."

"You would testify?"

"Oh, but it won't come to that. They'll never be caught. The Garda Civil will never trace the actual murderers after all this time."

Richard Bell smiled, rose and held out his hand. "I have kept you too long. I expect to come back and see your father, if only to look on the man in whose place my father died."

Mateo scrambled to his feet. "You wouldn't harm him?"

"Indeed no. There is enough violence in this world." He opened the door to the hall and Rosie scurried to the front porch and fetched his hat and riding crop.

"Oh sir, I was just giving your fine beast a drink and a carrot." She held up the bucket in her hand as evidence.

Mateo, startled by the sudden ending, saw the man to the door and unhitched the rein for him.

"Thank you," said Richard Bell. "We are friends now, but be sure of one thing – I will not leave it to the Garda. *I* will catch them. All four. Be sure of that."

He sprang into the saddle and was gone with a cheery wave.

Mateo stared after him. Until those last words he had felt exhilarated that their meeting had reached a pleasant ending. But there was to be no ending. Richard Bell would persist till he succeeded. And what might that mean? He broke into a new sweat. I might have to testify in a Spanish court of law. What have I done?

Rosie appeared beside him. "Eh, master Matty, whatever did he want? You were going at it hammer and tongs."

He shook his head. "Not at all. It was a very civilised conversation."

She grinned and headed back into the porch. "Well, I heard loud voices once – from the kitchen, of course. Will he come back? He was a fine-looking man."

Mateo followed her into the drawing room, where she collected the coffee tray. "Will he still want to see Sir Ralph?" she asked.

"It's quite likely. You may admit him." She was lingering, looking at him curiously. He said, "I'll get on with my work till the others come home." She had to go, and he closed the door firmly behind her.

He sat down at his desk, but had no heart for the Latin prose. He dreaded their coming. What would his father say? He got up and went out to the swing and rocked himself, but that seemed childish and frivolous. He walked up into the wood and smelt spring in the air and underfoot. Bluebells were sprouting. Life was reasserting itself; but his own was dominated by a dead man. If he went to Spain now, Richard Bell would be sure it was to warn his mother she was not safe from more questions. Would she even want to see me? he wondered. Does she hate me now for choosing to live with Papa?

At last he heard carriage wheels and hurried round the house to see his father leading another horse, a big grey, nearly as big as Zephyr.

"Your birthday present, Matty."

Mateo didn't know what to say. The mare was a beauty and looked docile, but all he wanted to do was unburden himself about his visitor.

He went forward and stroked her neck. "She's tall!"

"You're still growing." His father dismounted and put an arm round him. "Do you like her? She answers to the name of Venus, but if you don't like it I'm sure she'd get used to something else."

"No, she's lovely as Venus was." Then he whispered, "Oh Papa, Richard Bell has been here, while you were out."

His father's face changed. "What? I hope you didn't let him in?"

"He came in. We had a long talk. He's a good man. He only wants to find his father's killer. As *I* would if *you* had been the victim."

Grandfather Jack had led Rusty to the carriage house. Uncle Frank, holding Prince's rein, offered to take Venus too to see her new stable, since Matty seemed reluctant to get hold of her rein.

"Oh, yes please, Uncle. I'll try her out soon. She's beautiful." Aunt Lily had gone into the house, but Grandmother came over to them. "What's happened, Ralph?"

She misses nothing, Mateo thought. She'll be my ally.

His father said, "Only a visitation from Richard Bell. God knows what this innocent has said to him."

"But Grandmamma, he knew almost everything. He's had a detective finding things out. He'd worked out that cousin Juan wanted Father out of the way and that I'd warned Father. So the killers mistook his father next day and Cousin Juan and Guido ran away. There was almost nothing I had to add."

His father struck his temple with the flat of his hand in a too-familiar show of anger. "But you added it. He has confirmation. My God, what will come of this?"

Grandmamma laid a hand on his arm. "Now, Ralph, don't blame the boy. If he has been honest and open it shows we have nothing to hide."

"I am thinking of *her*." And that was all that was said for the moment.

Mateo followed Uncle Frank to the stables and saw Venus installed. Looking into her liquid dark eyes he found solace in telling her softly all that had happened.

"Ay, that's the way, Matty, get her used to the sound o' your voice."

Grandfather was rubbing down the other horses.

How comfortable, Mateo thought, to be Grandfather Jack! I will be wrung out later like a squeezed cloth till Papa knows everything that passed between Richard Bell and me. And that was exactly what happened at bedtime.

"You actually shed tears in his presence? He will attribute that to a deep-seated fear that your mother truly did plan my death."

Mateo denied it, but he convinced neither his father nor himself. He lay long awake and at last slept with ghastly dreams that his mother, because she was an aristocrat, was awaiting execution, not hanging.

A month passed quietly, and Mateo and John shared their birthday in the treehouse. The treehouse had had to be enlarged as they were so much bigger, but this was now a family custom. Jenny and Tom came from North

Shields. Maria wrote a formal letter with birthday greetings from their mother and Lucia.

Separately, in a 'Brigitta' letter to Mateo which he shared with his father and grandmother, she wrote:

I know I'm disobeying Mamma, but I must tell you she has cheered up because nothing more has happened. So she has written to a friend in the royal household about her desire to pay homage to the young queen by presenting her daughters at court. That's us if we can believe it! She joked that we could play with Queen Isabella at girlish games because the poor soul must be weary of affairs of state. We are to stay at Cousin Juan's old apartment in Madrid but he won't be there. She says he and Guido are abroad. Eduardo is managing the journey but Mamma expects Nurse to come despite her poor stiff joints. I pine for you all and long to see Sheradon Grange. It's dull here but Madrid will be exciting. Give the family my love, especially Papa. Your loving Baby Bear.

Mateo looked at their faces to see what they thought of that.

His father sighed. "Going to court, indeed! They'll want new clothes. That woman is filling her head with trivia."

"Oh, come now," Grandmamma said, "I liked pretty dresses at her age."

They were discussing the letter again in the evening sitting outside on the bench when Richard Bell walked round the corner of the drive. Mateo gasped and they both looked at him and back at their visitor.

He doffed his hat with a smile, and Mateo whispered, "Papa! It's Mr Bell."

"And he is not unlike you, Ralph," Grandmamma murmured, "only you rarely smile like that."

Mateo got to his feet and held out his hand. "Mr Bell, let me introduce my father and grandmother." This was how confident people behaved. He hoped it would compel normal courtesy from his father.

Mr Bell bowed to Grandmother. "The redoubtable Dione Sharon."

Grandmother giggled and blushed like a schoolgirl. Papa frowned. He thinks that's an impertinence, Mateo feared. But he shook the man's hand and invited him to join them on the bench.

"How charming to enjoy a summer evening so pleasantly," Mr Bell said. Grandmamma got up. "Even pleasanter with something to drink."

"No, no, pray do not disturb yourself. My time is short." He looked at Father. "Sir Ralph, we have unspoken thoughts between us. Perhaps you have a painful but unwarranted sense of guilt, and I an equally unwarranted feeling of resentment that my father died in your place. Let us put any such feelings to rest, and be friends."

Mateo watched his father struggle with this. "The sentiment does you much credit, sir," he managed to bring out, and Mateo marvelled that his pitman father had learned the language of gentlemen.

They clasped each other's hands again and Richard Bell said, "And I must apologise if I cause any of your family distress while I continue to pursue the hunt for my father's killers."

The reply came quickly. "It is inevitable that you will, sir, but it is your right to do so. However, after this time and with the chaotic state of Spanish law four years ago, I think you have little chance of success."

Mateo saw what might be a flicker of triumph in Richard Bell's smile. "You are right, but I wanted to tell you one thing I have learned from the man working for me in Spain. An unofficial amnesty has been granted to the many villains engaged in smuggling and banditry if they will emerge from their mountain hideouts and accept work in the city or countryside for the benefit of the community. I understand several of the older men have been seen in the bars of Santiago already, weary of their precarious livelihoods. My man is unobtrusively listening to their tales of exploits when their tongues are loosened by drink."

What his father would have said to this Mateo would never know, because Uncle Frank, Aunt Lily, John and Grandfather Jack appeared along the path from the old gamekeeper's cottage, where they had been to look at Uncle Frank's model of his bridge. John, always running rather than walking, arrived first and stopped abruptly when he saw the stranger.

"My other grandson, John Heron," Grandmamma said. "John, this is Mr Bell from Carlisle."

John stepped up to him. "Did you come on the train? We always go to Newcastle and I've wondered what the other way is like. It's longer, isn't it?"

Mr Bell smiled. "Much longer." He stood up. "And I must be catching the one I came on as it returns. I've achieved the purpose of my visit, and will enjoy the walk to the station on this lovely evening."

First he had to be introduced to Grandfather and Uncle Frank and Aunt Lily, and John was despatched to the kitchen for a mug of ale, which Mr Bell drank standing up, and then he strode off up the drive.

"Pleasant fellow," Uncle Frank said. "Business acquaintance, Ralph?"

Mateo saw his father shrug. "More or less," and he remembered that the other half of the family were unaware of the drama behind Maria's original letter or the threat hanging over the de Villena family.

When he was alone at bedtime with his father Mateo asked, "Do you think Mr Bell came all that way just to tell us of possibilities?"

His father nodded. "And to look on me. You said he wanted to do that. He has a bland manner but sharp eyes. I felt like an exhibit under his scrutiny."

"I'm sure he is a good man."

"You are like Jack. You want to believe everyone has fine instincts." He gripped his shoulders and studied him at arm's length, then abruptly took him in his arms and held him tight. "Oh my boy, how am I to part with you to Cambridge? You are so young and innocent. I felt at once the implacable character of that man under all the genial smiles. You will meet many people in your new life. Trust no one till you have proved their worth over time."

Mateo gently extricated himself and tried to lighten the moment with a little laugh. "Oh Papa, I'm the opposite of John. I'll always hold myself back. I did with Mr Bell till he revealed his deep love for his father, and then I felt on sure ground with him."

"Well, well, I'll say no more of him now. Indeed, I hope we will hear nothing more from him. Goodnight, son. Sleep sound."

Mateo watched as he left the room and saw his father's hand brush tears from his eyes. Father, Cambridge, Spain, Mother, not kissing Rosie. He should feel overwhelmed, but all of a sudden he didn't. It was a lightning-flash moment. He would really be a man soon.

Chapter 21

June–Autumn 1846

Mateo

No rain fell in June, and Grandfather Jack cut their meadow with John's help. Mateo was ashamed of his own attempts with a scythe and scurried back to his books. Cambridge was growing nearer. It was impossible for him to imagine how it would be. Mr Hurst had been to Oxford but had told him only that the life there was what you made of it yourself. There were those who frittered their time away and those who steeped themselves in it. "You will steep," he said.

His mind was jolted back to Spain when a Baby Bear letter came to John with a drawing of a bear in a frilly dress curtsying to the young queen.

"So they are now in Madrid," he said when John showed it to them all at suppertime. "Mamma will feel happier there. I think, Papa, I will not visit. She has what she loves – balls and parties. She knows I hate such things, and I know *she* has no interest in books and study."

His father slapped him on the back. "Wise boy."

John said, "Maria says she wants me to write about Mr Hurst's school when I start there. She wishes *she* could go to a school where you sleep in a big room with other children. But *you* don't do that, Matty?"

"No, I board on my own with Mr and Mrs Hurst till I leave at the end of July. You will be with the younger boarders in the new wing at the back."

"I bet we'll get up to some fun there."

"I hope you'll not disgrace yourself. He doesn't stand any nonsense and you're going to be the youngest there, so you'll have to work hard."

John gave him a playful punch. "Well, *you'll* be one of the youngest at Cambridge, won't you?" He cocked his head to one side. "Of course, you'll be a Scholar and have your own horse. That'll make you very grand."

Mateo shook his head. "I don't want to be grand." Shivers ran up and down his spine. His excitement was tinged with dread.

Aunt Lily said, "Would *you* like to go to university, John?"

He screwed up his face. "What? Sit still for three years with my head in a book? I want to be *doing* long before that. I want to make a difference in the world as soon as possible. I won't stay at old Hurst's longer than I have to."

"Mr Hurst is not old," Grandmamma said.

Uncle Frank laughed "Well, he was *my* schoolmaster. He must be in his sixties."

"And that's not old. Is it, Jack?"

"Is it what, angel?"

"Sixty, old?"

"Nay, you're as lovely as the day we married."

Listening to them all, Mateo had a new pang of fear about leaving them in the autumn. There was an easiness and jollity in the atmosphere here despite the past history – or because of it?

He had seen it help his father to be less intense, and he knew it helped him too. He had found the same thing at the Hursts'. Mrs Hurst was busy with good works, but she had been happy to chat and laugh with him about her day's doings as one adult to another. Yet she found time to mother the younger boys in her brisk, loving way. But there would be no Mrs Hursts at Cambridge.

September came, and he watched John blithely set off for school, annoyed only that his parents went with him the first day. On the Saturday morning he came back alone by train, not having written a word to them during the week.

"You didn't expect *letters* in such a short time?"

"I wrote you three," Aunt Lily protested. "I wanted to picture what you were doing all the time."

"We had fun in the dorm. We tied Fatty Fred up in his sheets one night."

"But that's cruel!"

"They knotted my shoelaces together and I was late for class. It's what you expect. Hurst doesn't like whiners or telltales. His missus pats you on the head and says, 'I know what happened. Forget it.' She never fusses." He looked pointedly at his mother.

"Did you *learn* anything?" Uncle Frank asked.

"I learned that Waters knows more than I do, so I must pass him before the end of term."

Mateo listened to this with a mixture of envy and disgust. John was a braggart, and Mateo believed a gentleman should never boast. I know he's very sharp, he was thinking. He picks up and remembers everything he reads or hears but swiftly dismisses what fails to impress him. Mr Hurst will not hire an expert Classics teacher for him as he did for me. He said to me when I left, "If ever there was a lad set for the academic life, it is Mateo de Villena Barton." I never boasted about *that* to anyone.

His father had decreed that they were to ride to Cambridge, taking a leisurely trip to see the country and for a time of close understanding before the parting. Mateo's box would be sent by carrier and they would travel light, arriving in good time for the start of the Michaelmas Term.

Inevitably the day arrived. It was a misty autumn morning, and when Mateo said goodbye to Grandmother his eyes were as misty as hers.

"It will make me very proud to write letters addressed to Queens' College, Cambridge," she said with her arms tight round him. She held him for so long that his father had to tell her the horses would be feeling the chilly air.

They were about to mount when the post-boy arrived. "Letter for you, Sir Ralph!"

His father frowned. "I've settled all my business for a short holiday." He looked at the writing and groaned. "It has come from Carlisle. I know not that I want to look at it." But he took out his pocketknife and broke the seal. Mateo watched his face, and saw his attention grabbed and his frown darkening. Then he stuffed the letter into the inner pocket of his riding coat and, using the mounting block, climbed into the saddle. "Come, Mateo, we have more important matters in hand. Thank you, Jack," he said as Grandfather released the leading rein.

Mateo, from Venus's back, waved to Grandmother in the porch. Her stocky figure, bonnet awry from hugging him, stayed imprinted on his mind. Christmas vacation was an age away.

When they had trotted a mile or two in their own thoughts, Mateo said, "Papa, you *are* going to tell me what Richard Bell said?"

His father turned with a bright smile. "Oh, I think not. It was addressed to me, but he sent you his good wishes for your studies at Cambridge."

"But if it concerns his investigations, you know how anxious I am."

"And that is just what I don't want you to be. You are entering a new life, new friends, new surroundings."

"I sent Maria my college address so she could write to me. If she has heard anything, she'll tell me. I said she could let Mother know where I am as well."

"Did you indeed?"

"And I sent Mother my duty and begged her to pray for me in my new life."

"Really? You value her prayers?"

Mateo thought, He wants to divert me from the letter. "Yes, I believe her prayers are heartfelt, whatever she may do or say, and if there is news that may touch her in any way I ought to know it."

His father fell silent and they trotted on, the mist clearing with the promise of a glorious day. When they next spoke, it was of the sunshine and the autumn reds and yellows in the wooded hillsides.

They had spent two days on the journey, and were lying awake on the second night listening to a noisy argument in the inn parlour below. It was only nine o'clock, so they had not blown out their candle, but their bodies were weary and they were glad to lie prone on a not uncomfortable bed. Unexpectedly his father turned over towards him and looked into his eyes.

"You deserve to know the contents of that man's letter. You have had several opportunities to take it from my coat, but you are too honourable to do it. Here, take the candle to your side of the bed." He fished the letter from his coat, which was hanging on a chair by the bed, and handed it to him.

Mateo sat up and read with rising alarm:

My dear Sir Ralph, I trust you will rejoice with me that the two brutes who killed my father are now almost certainly known to my detective and also to the Garda Civil. Their names are Lucas and Gerardo Sanchez, brothers. As I mentioned when I saw you, my detective has been listening to the talk of some of the "reformed" villains, especially in their cups. One evening in a Santiago hostelry an argument broke out over whether "gentry" were more honest than peasants. The general feeling was that they were only honest because they could afford to be. Gerardo, who was by this time well drunk, maintained that they were not *honest. He knew a rich man who hired a poor man to do his dirty work for him but failed to pay him when the job was done. At that Lucas intervened to say the job hadn't been done right, which made Gerardo aggressively angry. He swore that a man was to be killed and a man was killed. So they should have been paid. Others began to laugh and tease him. "That old moan of yours." "It must be four or five years gone at festival time." "That poor old Englishman cut down in the middle of his prayers, his lady said. Who was the rich man who never paid up?" Gerardo seemed about to give a name but Lucas leapt on him and knocked him off his stool, then peered about to see who might have been listening. My detective looked round his newspaper and remarked in Castilian, "I beg you to keep your quarrels quiet so a gentleman can read in peace." He never uses the local language of Galego, so people assume he doesn't understand it. The place quietened.*

Next morning he went to the local law officer and reported what he had heard. The Sanchez brothers, he was told, had taken work as night soilmen, so far without transgressing the law, but the matter would be looked into as there was no amnesty for murderers. My detective will persist if nothing is done and when they are taken into custody I feel sure that Gerardo at least will implicate his paymasters. If he believes he will hang he will certainly not let them escape.

There was a formal signing-off, with an assurance that he would keep Sir Ralph informed, and finally the pleasant message to '*your excellent son*'.

Mateo drew in his breath and looked at his father. "I go cold thinking that you might so easily have ridden into the path of those men that May morning."

"If *you* had not walked all night to warn me. Mateo, I never forget for a moment that I owe you my life."

"I was thinking of Nurse and Maria warning *me*."

"They too, indeed. But I have been pondering what may follow now – what, indeed, may already have happened in the intervening time while letters travelled. Maria will tell you if the law goes looking for cousin Juan at his old address in Madrid. Do you know how long your mother and sisters planned to stay there?"

"No, that wasn't mentioned in her letter. Oh Father, this puts Cambridge quite from my mind, yet we are on the way there."

"That was why I didn't want you to see this." He laid his hand on the letter. "You must put it out of your mind and close the door on it."

"That's impossible."

"No, I shall try to do it myself. But for you it should be easier. You will have new scenes and new friends to distract you."

"I'll think of it every night and pray that the one these brothers may name is not..." He hesitated. "...my mother."

"Do you still fear that?"

"I cannot forget the scene in the cathedral. The guards and other witnesses learned who she was, and very quickly who you were. What is fixed in their minds is that the Condesa de Villena didn't want her husband there. Will they not think she might plot to be rid of him – of you? Oh Father, how can I go to the university with this hanging over her head? What? She may be under arrest now. She may be in prison! She will go mad there. Should we not go to her?"

"You are not going to give up the university for *her*."

They talked well into the night. The argument from below died down, but their voices murmured in the silent inn till they lay back exhausted after Mateo had consented to ride on in the morning. His father had insisted that he register his presence at college if he ever wished to accomplish a degree there. Besides, nothing more might happen in Spain for months, he said, and how foolish he would feel then... At that point Mateo felt sleep drifting over him.

The rest of their journey passed in a maze of scenes. Each impressed him momentarily but floated out of his consciousness as another took its place. All the time, worry about what might be happening in Spain hung about his thoughts.

It was very different when they arrived in Cambridge. The shock was palpable. Passing one stately building after another, he drank in great draughts of ancient learning. They stabled their horses at an inn, where his father planned to stay two nights to see him settled, and then followed directions to Queens' College. When they came to the vast gate with its twin towers, he was even more overwhelmed.

"Why, it's the grandest of them all! Oh Father, am I truly allowed to be here for three years?" His father nodded, smiling.

There were swarms of students, the old hands easily distinguished by their familiarity with the place and their fellows. Raucous greetings were exchanged, while the new ones like himself crept rather than pranced. I can keep myself to myself, he thought. I only want to learn. I want knowledge to open up to me. The ancients, their wisdom, philosophy. He drew great sighs of delight.

At the porter's lodge, a student was called to show them to his room. They mounted a staircase heavy with polished wood.

"Freshmen share," the begowned young man said at the first landing, "so you must be one of those lofty creatures – a Scholar. Here's your room." He opened the door. "And there is your box – found its way to the right place. How fortunate!"

He bowed them in with a flourish and bounded back down the stairs.

"A condescending manner," muttered his father, but Mateo could only stare at the desk and empty shelves portending hours of study. He was astonished to find himself impatient to be alone. This is my territory, he crowed silently, pulling the cords off his box and beginning the thrilling business of unpacking and standing his few books on the middle shelf and hanging his clothes in the closet.

His father, looking at the small hearth, where a fire was laid but not lit, said, "Now, you must order coals when you need them. Never sit shivering at your desk. I will set up a bank account here for you." He paced over to the small window. "You overlook a courtyard, and on the opposite side the chapel. No doubt there will be prayers every morning according to the Anglican Prayer Book. Will you attend?"

Mateo looked round from arranging his notebooks and pens in the desk. Fleetingly he thought, Mother would not approve, but she is far away. My life now is nothing to her. And what happens to her is nothing to do with me. We are separate human beings. To think of leaving this for Spain is preposterous.

"I'm sure I will," he said. Day-to-day decisions are mine now, he reminded himself. Papa will be departing very soon.

During the next two days before term was to start, his father discussed every aspect of what he imagined his life would be, and was profuse with his advice. Does he envy me? Mateo wondered. He knows nothing of higher education.

On the day they said goodbye at the foot of the stair, which Mateo now thought of as his own, his father's too passionate embrace with tears in his eyes left Mateo with the guilty thought: Life has stifled me so far. Now I am truly free. It was an extraordinarily heady feeling.

He ran back up to his room. He was enfolded in his new gown and in the embrace of Queens' College with its vaulted ceilings, its stained glass, its lawns on which you absolutely must not walk – magnificence such as he had never imagined.

So far he was scarcely aware of his fellow students. The presence of his father had kept them at bay. Now those on his staircase asked his name. He rashly ventured, "Mateo de Villena Barton," and instantly regretted it. They said, "What? Are you Spanish?" He shrugged and replied, "Half." "We'll stick to Barton," they said; and having learned he was a Scholar and from remote Northumberland, it was his remoteness that seemed his most impressive characteristic, and from then on he was largely left alone, which was just how he wanted it.

Of his tutor, though, he had great expectations, but after their first meeting he decided he must withhold judgement. The man showed no sign of genuine interest in one among many new students he would be obliged to supervise. He is an elderly man, Mateo thought. Wave upon wave of young men have come and gone under his tuition. I will astonish him by working harder than any of them.

After the first three days he wrote a general letter to all at home, giving a pen picture of his room, the awe-inspiring chapel, the dining hall and his first lecture. Then he was surprised to find in the letter rack at the foot of his stair a letter from his father actually written the day he arrived home.

The news was both tragic and reassuring. His father had received a sad, bitter letter from Richard Bell. His detective in Spain had died – poisoned, he feared. The Sanchez brothers had vanished before any arrests were made. He could not himself return to Spain, so the Garda Civil would lose interest. His father added, 'I think he has exhausted his savings, poor man. But now I trust that this news, my dear son, will free your mind from any distracting worries.'

Mateo had a pang of guilt that he had already dismissed his mother's danger from his thoughts. Now he could do so with a clear conscience and think of her and his sisters enjoying the excitements of Madrid – if he thought of them at all, for he was already packing his brain with the pages of the first book on his reading list.

In a few weeks he was known as the most dedicated freshman at Queens' – a badge he carried about with him as he scurried from his room to the lecture theatre or the library, dodging the cold winds that swept across the Fens from the east. When his head ached with too much reading, he went to the stables and rode out on Venus and explored the countryside.

Letters from Grandmother chatted about daily life at Sheradon Grange. His father wrote more sparingly, but was full of advice on exercise and how to spot fraudsters when purchasing the necessaries of life, and was there still sufficient in the bank? He wrote back that he was in rude health and had plenty of money.

As November drew on, he realised the Christmas vacation was not far away. It would be strange to leave his sanctuary and the intensity of study which had carried him forward on a magical wave week after week. Then one day he returned from the library and was surprised to find a letter from Maria in the rack. She had only recently sent one to say Mamma was happy and in no hurry to leave Madrid.

The short day was closing in, so he lit a candle when he reached his room and climbed into bed for warmth.

Maria wrote: '*I don't want to worry you, dear Matty, but the Garda Civil have been here inquiring after Cousin Juan.*' Oh no, he thought, not that. He wanted to put it on the fire and pretend it had never come. He was compelled to read on.

Mamma became quite hysterical with them which was a pity. She kept saying we knew nothing of Juan which made them wonder since we are living in an apartment still in his name. They also asked when we had last employed Guido Martinez. In her flurry she gave a wrong date.

There were two of them and one was writing everything down. They were stiffly polite but said they might come back as they were making inquiries about an incident in forty-one. Then they asked us quite casually, Lucia and me, where our father is. I said he has business in England. Lucia just nodded and Mamma said "Yes, yes, very important for him to be in England." "How sad for you to be separated!" the chief interrogator commented as he took his hat and walked out. I thought his tone very sarcastic and Mamma kept asking us, "What did he mean by that?" She doesn't know what to do now. She misses Eduardo who went back a month ago to see all was well on the estate. She would like to be gone if they come back but is reluctant to be near Santiago where it all happened. Nothing may come of this but I had to tell you. I still send Baby Bear letters to Cousin John but he may be growing too old for them now as he doesn't always reply. I wouldn't tell him about this of course and I leave it to you whether to tell Papa.

Mateo leapt from the bed to pace his room. On his desk was a Latin oration he was writing for a Roman Senate trial of a fictional case. He ground his teeth in fury that a real-life one should intrude upon work that was giving him so much joy. Then came dismay that his mother had handled her inquirers so badly, and finally a resurgence of his deep-seated fear that she might indeed be the most guilty of all.

I will not tell Father, he thought. Putting it into words will make it more real. I will answer Maria tardily and hope she is right that "nothing may come of this".

Of course, his reason told him that the matter was unlikely to end there, since, for the first time, the Garda Civil seemed to be taking an old murder seriously. But the place for logic – in his life at present – was in ancient Rome. He put the letter away with his other letters in a wallet at the bottom of his clothes cupboard. Then he sat down at his desk and read his oration as far as he had gone. Inspiration came at once, and he picked up his pen and began the next sentence.

Chapter 22

Sheradon Grange, early December 1846

Jack

At Sheradon Grange, Jack had already pinpointed in his memory where the best berried holly would be found in the woods at Christmas time. Sometimes when he wanted to remember things, Dee wrote them down and pinned the paper up in the kitchen. Though he couldn't read it himself, he asked anyone, even John, what it said. But things out of doors, in the stables, the garden or the woods were his territory, and their location stayed clear in his mind.

It was the third week of December and a day when dusk began to fall very early. There had been a biting wind all day and it had now piled a dark mass of cloud above the house. As he walked down from the sloping wood a few snowflakes began to drift among the black branches. He blew on his fingers. Dee will scold me, he thought, for not wearing those woolly gloves she knitted for me. The flurry of whiteness thickened around him. You should be saving this for Christmas, he admonished the dark cloud, but then all such thoughts flew out of his head as the sound of carriage wheels came to his ears.

He quickened his pace to a run. Visitors made him nervous, but he must be on hand to hold reins or help them down; and who on earth would be coming at this time? As far as he knew, all the family were snug at home, including Mateo, safely returned from Cambridge a few days earlier. They would certainly all be in the kitchen, which was the only really warm place in the house. The shutters were already closed to keep out the cold.

Trotting round the side of the house, he saw carriage lamps approaching at the corner of the drive, the snow settling on the driver's hat and shoulders. It was a small, closed carriage with one horse – a hired vehicle from the town, he guessed. As the carriage drew up at the porch, the horse shook its head to be rid of the snow.

The driver shouted out, "Sheradon Grange?"

"Ay, that's us." Jack bustled forward.

As he did so, the door opened and, without waiting for the step to be lowered, a girl jumped out and flew into his arms, propelling him backwards.

"Oh Granda Jack, I'm so happy to be home!"

He gasped. "What? What? Who is it?" She was muffled to the eyes in a hooded cloak with a fur collar.

"Maria!" she cried. "And here are Lucia and Mamma."

The names sounded a little gong in Jack's bewildered brain. He saw that the carriage driver had alighted and was lowering the step. He should have done that. He felt the young body warm in his arms and tried to look into the face.

"Eh, but wasn't they little girls, Lucia and Maria? When they used to live in t'other part of the house?"

"Oh darling Granda Jack, we've grown."

A second girl descended, similarly wrapped, and turned to give a hand to the tall lady following. Jack couldn't disengage himself quickly enough to help, but she was down and pressing something into the hand of the driver.

"You'll be wanting stabling," Jack called to him.

"Nay, I'll put up at the inn at Ovingham. This is going to be a right storm o' snow. I'll not get to Newcastle this night." He was getting baggage down as he spoke. Jack grabbed the two largest pieces and bore them into the porch. This was something he could do. The lady had not spoken, and he couldn't make out her face. She seemed to be looking down, with one gloved hand hiding her eyes.

The words "my lady" came into his head.

"Get in under the porch, my lady," seemed to be the obvious thing to say, so he said it.

The carriage driver dumped the last bags at his feet. "That's the lot." He ran back and climbed up to his seat. "Goodnight, ladies!" He turned the carriage and was away up the drive, the wheels making lines in the newly fallen snow.

They were all now under the porch, but the wind was driving the snow in.

Jack fumbled with the door handle. Maria squealed, "I want to see them all. I can't believe we're really here."

Jack pushed the door. "Eh, I don't know. Was we expecting you all?"

Now he could see down the passage. The kitchen door opened. They had heard voices. Frank's face appeared.

"Hello! Who's there?"

Maria shouted, "Uncle Frank!" Other faces appeared. Jack saw Ralph stagger backwards with his hands up to his open mouth, then John burst from the crush in the doorway, ran forward and stopped, suddenly shy.

"Maria?"

"No," she giggled, flinging her arms round him. "Baby Bear! But my! *You've* grown."

Dee had come into the passage. Everything will be all right now, Jack thought. She'll know what to do.

She said, "Sophia, my dear, are you frozen?"

The tall lady, muffled as she was with shawls, bowed herself forward over Dee's sturdy shape and burst into sobs.

Mateo

In the kitchen Mateo, thrilled and devastated, was held back by his father's grip on his arm. Desperate to greet his sisters and fearful of his mother, he met his father's eye. The expression in it was stern, the face white.

"Did you know of this?"

"No, Father. I never thought they would come here. I did know they'd had a fright. Maria wrote. Two men from the Garda Civil asked questions. I'm sorry. I should have told you."

He saw Aunt Lily putting the kettle on the hob. There were noises and voices in the passage. He longed to see them all, but at that second all he could feel was the torrent of emotions – horror, anger, excitement – coursing through his father's body.

Grandmamma helped the drooping figure of his mother into the room. His father took a step back and his eyes probed her.

Grandmamma helped her to the one armchair. As she sank down Mateo heard her say in a choking voice, "Where is he?"

"Mamma, I'm here." He stepped up and knelt at her feet. She put out a hand and touched his hair. Her eyes flew open.

"Mateo! I thought you were at Cambridge! Oh, my boy is a man." Her arms went round his neck and great gulping sobs broke out afresh. Mateo was sobbing too now. She *did* love him. She *had* longed for him. But he couldn't forget his father standing somewhere behind him. It was he she had meant, and the note in her voice was terror.

"Where is your father?" she managed to say at last.

"I am here." The deep-spoken words sounded close. Mateo moved away and his Mother lifted her eyes. They were very red, and her cheeks were grey with fatigue. She was not his poised beautiful mother. She was gaunt and frightened.

"Ralph," she gasped. "Forgive me. I come back to you. We always together now. Always."

He looked at his father. The jaw was set hard, but the eyes wavered. Mateo knew him so well now. The public exposure of his shock, his dismay at her presence in his home – he would loathe it.

Mateo realised his sisters and John were in the doorway, holding their breath. Maria was signalling to him her delight at seeing him, her lips mouthing 'Matty, Matty,' but everyone had fallen silent. His father must say something. But he didn't. His mouth was slightly open and his forehead had creased into a heavy frown.

Maria couldn't hold back. She darted to his side and clasped him round the waist. "Oh Papa, Papa. I've longed for this moment. I've missed you so." She had pushed back her furry hood, and her bright eyes and rosy face peered up at him.

"Maria!" His voice was a husky breath. Then he did break down, utterly and shamelessly. He drew her towards the table and sank onto one of the kitchen chairs and clasped her in a passionate embrace.

The kettle boiled over. Grandfather Jack rescued it. His face too was running with tears. Aunt Lily was crying. Lucia, who had not spoken a word, was crying. Mateo gave a long sniff and managed to dry his eyes with his handkerchief.

Grandmother Dee said loudly and clearly, "Wet clothes on the rack and we'll have a nice pot of tea." Then she added, "It's all right, Jack, these are happy tears."

Grandfather lifted his big shoulders, and a beam of delight spread across his face. "That's good, my angel. Happy tears."

It was easy for Grandfather Jack to be reassured, but Mateo, embracing his sisters with real joy, couldn't escape the stabs of fear that pricked the back of his mind. As they all began to move about, following Grandmamma's orders, he saw his father compose himself, gently release Maria, stand up and walk away to avoid his mother. She had risen, and Aunt Lily had helped her out of her cloak, murmuring about the bad weather giving them a cold welcome. His father wouldn't look at her. He is willing her away, Mateo thought, trying to believe it hasn't happened, just as I did when Maria's letter arrived and I wanted to write my Latin oration.

Here came Maria, pulling at his coat, and hissing softly to him. "I'm sorry it's happened like this, Matty. It was so sudden. We packed up in a day. I was singing and dancing with joy but I did scrawl a letter to Papa, only she tore it up. 'We must surprise them,' she said, 'for that will show me if we are welcome there.' All the way she has become more and more anxious. And now look at Papa!"

He had stopped in front of the larder door, staring across the room, apparently at a half-eaten apple John had left on the mantelshelf. Grandmamma had to push him out of the way to find something to feed everyone.

Mateo looked down at Maria. She came up to his shoulder now and had almost a woman's figure. Where was the little girl who had briefly shared his prison?

"He'll come round. I pray God he'll come round. But to have you all here, for me – that's wonderful."

Lucia edged her way to them. Her face was pale and pinched. "I don't really know you as our Matty. You're a man. I'm tired. Will we sleep in our old rooms? We've come into their part of the house, haven't we? Can we get through to ours or will all the doors be locked?"

These words must have penetrated his father's brain, because his head jerked up and he turned his eyes on their little group.

"Who said that? Is that you, Lucia? Come here. You haven't greeted your father yet."

She hesitated. "You don't love me like you do Maria."

"No, no, why do you say that?"

"I didn't come out of the cathedral to find you like she did."

He stared at her. "What? That scene still fresh for you? It is for me, God knows."

"It's the last time we saw you – till now." Her lips were trembling. "I don't know why we left home in such a rush – and I'm so tired."

He looked about, his eyes again avoiding their mother, now back in the armchair, with Aunt Lily coaxing her to drink some tea.

Grandmamma was giving orders to Grandfather about fires. With an arm about Lucia, their father led her over to them. Mateo, hopeful for relief in practical matters, followed with Maria and offered to help lay fires.

His father said, in his normal voice, "Jack, the fire in my room upstairs can be revived. The bed is aired. The girls can have it tonight till we open up other rooms. I don't know if this is a short or long visit, but this child is tired."

Lucia murmured, "Mamma said we'd come for ever."

Grandmamma said quickly, "Let's deal with the present moment. Supper, then bed. The broth pan is on the fire and bread and butter are on the table."

Maria said, "I'll have some. We had horrid tripe and onions at a tripe shop on the quayside while a porter found us a carriage to hire. Mamma has never travelled without servants and was quite bewildered."

"What about poor old Nurse?" Mateo asked.

Maria put on a sad face, her head on one side. "Of course – you don't know. She died three weeks ago. Worn out, I think."

Mateo, quite shocked, crossed himself.

His father said, "May she rest in peace. She never liked me, but she was a loyal soul to – the family."

Uncle Frank appeared from the stairs. "I've taken the bags up and put them all in the big front – your room, Ralph. The unused rooms are devilish cold, till we get some fires going. Yours was low but there were enough coals in the scuttle to get up a blaze."

"Where are all the servants?" Lucia asked in a small voice.

"Goose!" said Maria. "There was only Rosie when we left, and she lived out. I'll carry those newspapers and the basket of kindling. Come on, Lu, it's much more fun here." She was running up as she spoke. "And see! We can get straight into all our rooms. No doors! That's lovely."

In the next quarter of an hour three fires were lit and hot coals were placed in warming pans. Cleaning up at the washstand in their father's room revived Lucia a little, and when she saw her nightgown unpacked on a warmed bed she consented to come down and have a few mouthfuls of bread and broth. They sat at the table as they arrived, and Grandmamma and Aunt Lily ministered to each. John, who had had his Friday tea late when he came back from Newcastle, sat down next to Maria and helped himself from her plate. "Baby Bear's got too much," he giggled.

Mateo heard his father say, as he left the room, that he would move his things to Nurse's old room so the girls could go to bed as soon as they were ready. His mother's eyes followed him.

"He shun me, Dee. He not speak to me." She seized Grandmamma's hand as she put down a plate with slices from their salted beef.

"Be patient and loving and he will come round."

"Where I sleep? He not want me in our old room. I am his wife."

"We are warming up the girls' old room. Jack and Frank have moved one of the beds nearer the fire. You should be quite snug there."

"Are we to be one family? You've done away with the partitions."

"Ralph did that the day you left. You can't imagine how wretched he was."

Mateo, across the table from them, was intent on his mother's changing expressions. He caught the words, though they were softly spoken, and Maria and John were having a noisy exchange at the other end of the table about sea travel.

"Yes, but a collier was much more exciting!"

Grandmamma said, "Sophia, we will be one family, but you must make him fall in love with you all over again."

His mother's eyes flashed, her colour was high. She looked like her old self for a moment.

"Oh Dee, I never love anyone else."

Mateo left the table. He had finished eating and he wanted to hear no more. This was what he would take to bed with him, his heart wanting desperately to believe it, his mind telling him it couldn't possibly be true.

Ralph

Ralph hung a clean shirt in Nurse's tallboy. No one had used this room since the day she left, and now she would never come back. The poor old soul had gone thankfully to her maker. Death was the biggest change of all. This is a lesser change, he mused. Three more people come to live in our house. There's space for them. Am I not man enough to face that?

He fetched his shaving equipment and arranged it on the marble washstand. A newly lit fire was struggling in the narrow grate. Everything about this room was on a small scale. Already he was irritated by that. He kept bumping the walls. He sat down on the bed, wrestling with his reluctance to return to the kitchen. If I don't reappear tonight, he thought, Mother will be anxious and suppose I have fallen sick again. Why should I? I have Mateo back who is my joy, for Cambridge has not affected his sweet nature and love of home life. And I have my two girls whom I will love deeply as they grow into womanhood. But her...!

"Ralph?" Her voice sounded outside his door. He shuddered. She repeated his name and added, "Please speak to me."

Get up, he ordered his numbed limbs. I am no coward. Get up. She's afraid of me. She's nothing now but a woman, overwrought and weary with travelling.

He stood up quickly and snatched open the door.

There she was, drooping like a spent flower. He drew her in and sat her on the bed and stood looming over her.

"Well, you've come back, then."

He saw it was hard for her to lift her eyes to his, but he wouldn't sit on the chair opposite the bed. He met her gaze as he had in the cathedral when she had utterly rejected him. That was a humiliation in front of their children which had scarred his soul. Now he put all the power he could into his stare, and she broke down. Sobs choked the words, "Oh Ralph, please, have large heart. Forgive me." It was a good act, he thought, but he could see through it.

He smiled then and put his hands on his hips, deliberately projecting sarcasm at her. "But I know why you have come. Fear. You were afraid to stay away. The law cannot pursue you if you act the loving wife – a wife who could never have plotted to have her husband murdered."

She gasped and clapped her hand to her mouth. Was that true shock? Oh, if it was! It might be a tiny ray of light, a hope that he might endure her presence.

"Ralph! Is that what you believe all these years?" Her breast heaved once and then again. He could see her thinking how to go on. "Oh, yes, I fear those men. *They* believe I am murderer. They from Garda Civil. You know that?"

"Yes, I know it, so you packed up and came."

"Not at once. Oh, for long time I yearn – that is the word? – for you, my husband. At last I must come."

"You would have married Juan. Then you had Eduardo."

Again she showed shock. "Juan want me and I repulse him. Eduardo! What you know of him? A mere boy. I could almost be his mother. You are man, strong, brave, bold. My man for life."

Her eyes were caressing him up and down, like snakes, he thought. She can be all lies. Will I ever know the truth?

He said, "Why did Juan and Guido disappear so suddenly?"

She straightened up and laid her hands on her breast. "*I* dismiss them. I see guilt in their faces when unknown man die. I know Juan want me and all our land. He make it like work of bandits. But he find you are escaped. I tell him I know he is murderer but I not hand flesh and blood to justice. He must leave my house. So he go, he and that evil Guido. I discover he linked with big underworld of smuggling. They vanish away, maybe France." She paused for breath, then burst out: "And you linked *me* with *them*? Your wife! The mother of your children! Oh Ralph, my beloved. Unthink the thought!"

She rose from the bed and put up her arms as if she would embrace him.

"No!" He took a step back and almost sat down on the chair behind him. He steadied himself, holding up both hands to ward her off. "For all these years your actions have belied your words. You left me. You took my children away from me. You heard I was ill and told them I was dead. You dallied with your cousin so that local gossip gave out that you would marry him. When I turned up you would have had me thrown out of the cathedral if I had not walked out. You took as a threat my promise to return next day and you let your cousin know you would be glad to be rid of me. Maybe you did not directly order my killing. I would like to believe that. But now, because you need me as protection, you have come to tell me you've always loved me! Do you take me for a fool?"

She backed to the bed and sank onto it with a great sigh, not of defeat but of protest. "That is such a – how you say – catalogue of half-truth. Why you think I leave you? You neglect me for your businesses. You want our son go to poor little school in horrid coal town when he heir to great Spanish family. You link our noble name to vulgar pie shop people. So I escape to home. But we women cling to first love. There you stand now, feeling so strong and powerful, and I love you with a passion. You can't believe how much." Her voice cracked and she hid her face in her hands.

For the first time he knew she was not acting. What she said was true in this moment. But that was Sophia. Love, anger, delight could last seconds. She had seen before her a man, tall, broad-shouldered, strong-featured, who belonged to her and must be hers again. But daily living with her, as he knew too well, was a roller coaster of petty likes and dislikes, moods, sudden decisions, sudden changes of mind. She is the same woman she was six years ago.

He stepped forward and lifted her up. "You are to sleep in the girls' old room, and they in my bed." She twined her arms about him.

He pulled open the door. He would not let her body rouse him, starved as he was. "You are shivering. This fire has done nothing. It's too early for sleep. We'll return to the kitchen. See," he said, pointing to the small landing window that faced east, "you are to be marooned here." The snow was building up against the glass.

"If I can be marooned with you…" she murmured.

He hurried her down to the kitchen, where they were all gathered round the uncleared table, asking and answering thousands of questions. For once the buzz of voices was a relief, and the glow in his mother's face when she saw them come in together warmed him through.

Chapter 23

December 1846–March 1847

Dee

Dee was pleased that the cold spell did not last and neither did Ralph's endurance of Nurse's cramped room. Sophia behaved herself impeccably. The first morning she praised Rosie for struggling up from the village through the snowdrifts and accepting the work of extra rooms without grumbling.

"Well, you're back, milady," was all she said.

"And no going away, dear Rosie. We get you some help, of course, but it remain one house. Sir Ralph has spoken."

"My sister, Peggy, is looking to enter service," Rosie said.

"Bring her tomorrow – but of course I consult Sir Ralph."

And she did, in the humblest fashion.

"And when are you going to learn to speak correct English?"

"Yes please. Our girls tell me it is not so good. I try harder."

"I *will* try harder."

"I will try harder. Thank you, Ralph."

And she returned meekly to Rosie.

"How long can she keep this up?" he asked Dee.

"She wants to be back in your bed."

"Never!"

Dee bided her time. Peggy came next day, and Sophia asked Dee whether she wanted one girl each or whether they should work together round the house.

"Together," Dee said. "Rosie will show Peggy what to do and then they will settle it themselves."

"And we not need a man? Your Jack is so good."

"And John loves to fetch wood and make fires when he is at home. Give him any tasks. He cannot be still for a moment."

"You are so wonderful family. I teach my girls work, work, work."

A warm wind came up and the snow melted away. Ralph was able to ride into Newcastle and attend to his business interests. He deliberately stayed away for one or two nights, saying the room he kept for himself in Heron Mansions was more comfortable than Nurse's room.

When he came back, Sophia and both girls ministered to his needs with warmed slippers and a tray of supper before the drawing room fire.

Dee saw little of him in their kitchen, but she was well aware of what was going on. Sophia had brought their own kitchen back into use and was asking Rosie to show Maria and Lucia simple English cooking. Maria took to it with delight. John's noisy presence vanished back to school for one more week before the Christmas holiday. The house remained quiet and orderly, apart from the bedroom arrangements, where the girls had begun to hang garments in Ralph's closet and he had to search for a new razor blade among their petticoats.

In the second week, Sophia tapped at the door of Dee's writing room.

"He has gone to town, Mother Dee. What more I do to make him love me?"

Dee, pleased that she used Lily's name for her, corrected her question gently. "'What more *can* I do?'"

"Yes, yes. Ralph, he correct me but I know not what he *think*."

"Have you a scent he liked when you were courting?"

"I have wee bottle, tiny, tiny bit. But it not go with apron."

"Leave off the apron and put on something charming to go with your new character." Dee looked into the black eyes that gazed back at her so hopefully.

"I will, dear Mother Dee. But my *love* is not new. I always love him."

"Love, joy, peace, truth. If we practise them always, they become habitual."

232

Sophia nodded. "I take your advice. You understand your boy."

That evening Dee, Jack, Frank and Lily were at supper when Ralph put his head round the door. Seeing they were all there, he hesitated.

Dee got up. "Come in, Ralph."

He shook his head. "Just to say the girls are settled in their old room. Maria says they loved to make up tales of elves in the woods they see from that window. Well, goodnight, all." He disappeared before anyone could make a comment.

Ralph

Ralph knew he was seeing Sophia at last as a desirable woman – no more, no less. And she was his. He alone was entitled to her. He was still wary of her, but not of her body. He could enjoy her, and he intended to.

Much later, when the grandfather clock chimed midnight, she sighed in his arms. "Oh Ralph, I am young again. You are young. We are restored."

He heard her but couldn't answer. No words would come. He was falling asleep, and he had the best night he had had for many years.

Next day he could see in the faces of Mateo and the girls that the reunion of the family gave them a deep, abiding joy.

He transformed Nurse's old room into an office where he could retreat from Sophia if she forgot to be her new self. Without the bed there was room for a desk and an armchair, where he was dozing one afternoon when Maria peeped in. He had had no time with her on her own, and beckoned her in.

She perched on the desk chair, turning it round to look at him, eager-eyed.

"Papa, I can't believe how happy we are."

"Good, but I want to understand about your sudden coming. There is more I should know. What happened after you wrote your letter to Matty in Cambridge?"

She cocked her head to one side. She was rosy from a turn on the swing, and the breeze had blown her black curls round her cheeks. She was a pretty girl with high cheekbones, like Sophia, but more appealing because her nose and chin were smaller, her figure slight but rounding. She would not grow tall and imposing, but she would captivate the men very soon. In two years she would be fifteen.

I don't ever want to lose her, Ralph thought. I have her and must hold onto her. That means I must keep Sophia here at all costs. And I must get to know Lucia, who seems to be hiding herself away like someone with a dark secret.

Maria pursed up her lips. "Mamma was very upset by the Garda Civil's visit, and one day she looked out and screamed that the second officer was across the street watching our window. I wasn't sure it was he, but suddenly she made up her mind. 'We must go to your father,' she said. 'I need to be at his side.' So she sought an audience with Maria Christina and told her she had heard you were very ill and she must go to England at once. So the queen put some of her own guardsmen at our disposal as far as the port, and we were never stopped or questioned."

"You didn't go back to Santiago?"

She shook her head. "Mamma had taken against the place. We had most of our things in Madrid, so we packed what we had. She wrote to Eduardo, of course, but there was no time for him to send anything from home."

"You still call Castilla Villena home? I might have visited it on that May morning but for your quick thinking and courage."

She jumped from the chair and into his arms. "Oh Papa. You would never have reached it. That poor man died in your place. I felt so guilty about him, and yet so thankful it wasn't you. It was a horrid time without Mateo to comfort me. Lu was no good. She didn't want to talk about it at all."

He held her close on his lap. "What was *she* like? Your mother?"

"Quite hysterical for hours on end."

"Because I survived?"

She sat up and peered into his face. "You don't believe she ordered it!"

He sighed. "I wish I knew for sure. What did she say to Juan and Guido?"

"Nothing in *our* presence."

"But how did they seem when their plot had failed?"

"Oh, they faked horror. 'A shocking thing to happen! We must keep within doors.' That sort of talk. When they'd gone, I told Lu what Nurse had seen and that I'd sent Matty to warn you. She listened, but went quieter than ever. I so wanted to share our feelings about it, but she wouldn't. She was better when we went to Madrid, and Mamma was too. We went to parties and people asked about you. Mamma said you had to be in England but she expected a visit soon. Papa, I have to believe she really loved you deep down all the time."

"My darling one, she tells lies. You say she lied to the queen herself?"

Maria squirmed in his arms. "Just a necessary one."

234

"Your grandmother has taught me from bitter experience that lying can become a very bad habit. The consequences are never good."

"They were that time."

"If you lied to me I could never trust your word again."

"I promise I won't."

"And would you be sad if you never went back to Spain?"

Again she cocked her head to one side, and this time bit her thumb too. "Never's a long time. Maybe one day. I love the people here – Uncle Frank and Aunt Lily and John, though he's a mischief, and especially Grandmamma and Grandpapa. Grandpapa's like a child. He wants things simple and right, and Grandmamma – well, she's so clever she *makes* things come right."

"You sum them up well. Now my legs are going to sleep." He eased her off them. "I think we will hear no more of the murder, and maybe we will visit Spain sometime, or Eduardo will think he's managing the de Villena land for himself."

She stood up and stretched. "I think he's loyal to Mamma, but he didn't like being in Madrid. Without the land he felt like nobody."

Ralph digested that with interest. He wanted to know so much about Sophia and Eduardo, but it was not a topic he could discuss with Maria.

She looked at his desk. "You were adding up rents from Heron Mansions."

He laughed. "I was, till I grew sleepy."

"Are you able to afford us being here?"

He chuckled again. "That's what I was finding out."

"Seriously, Papa. Mamma says we mustn't expect more servants so Lu and I must be our own chambermaids, and when Rosie's busy Grandmamma will teach us everything about housekeeping. John's bursting to leave school and do big things. *I* want to be more than a stay-at-home lady without a purpose in life."

"I'm sure you will."

After that early snowfall, Christmas was mild and wet, and Mateo went back to Cambridge by train. He had confessed to Ralph that Venus was an unnecessary expense at college because he seldom rode anywhere. John was now as tall as the girls and begged to have Venus to teach them to ride. Maria was thrilled, but Lucia, after a brief trial, said she couldn't bear to be so high above the ground.

It was a Saturday early in March when John told Maria he would take her towards the village and she could try trotting back.

"I'll run beside her and hold a lead rein," he told Ralph, who had come out to watch them. "Baby Bear's more than ready. She sat well from the first day."

"I saw her." Ralph sniffed the air. The day was alluring with the freshness of spring, and he had been at his desk for an hour, assessing all his business interests and the dividends that were likely to come in. He sat down on the bench under the drawing room window and watched as they went up the drive. In a few minutes they were back, John excited and Maria alarmed.

"What's up? Have you had a tumble?"

John snorted. "Baby Bear tumble! Not likely. No, we met that Carlisle man on his way here, walking from the station, so I said we'd come and tell you."

Ralph, deeply shocked, met Maria's anxious gaze.

"He says he has news for us, Papa."

"Damnation. Well, get down, but for God's sake don't tell your mother. Keep her indoors if you can. I'll speak to him out here."

John helped Maria down, but he was bristling with curiosity.

"Why the excitement? I thought he was a businessman, Uncle Ralph."

"Business can be exciting," was all Ralph could answer. He wondered how long the other half of the family could be kept in the dark.

As he spoke, Richard Bell walked quickly round the corner, waving his hat at them. His manner spoke of jaunty confidence, which trebled Ralph's fears.

"Go in, both of you, and tell no one who's here."

Maria looked shocked. "But I—"

"Come on," John said. "I'll teach you chess instead of riding today. Mr Hurst runs a chess club for the clever boys, and I beat Watson the last day of term. We'll take Venus to the stables first. Come on." Ralph was amazed to see the ease with which John managed horse and girl, both equally disgruntled.

They disappeared as Richard Bell came up. "Lively children!" He held out his hand and Ralph had to shake it, though his stomach froze at the touch.

"Mr Bell. Mild day." He indicated the bench. "You have some news?"

The man was in no hurry. "Your daughter. Pretty girl. The family visiting from Spain?"

"I'd prefer to hear what you have to say."

"Your clever son will be back at Cambridge. Doing well, I'm sure."

"Thank you. He is. Now to your business."

"I would have been pleased to meet your wife."

"She is occupied." He hadn't meant to confirm her presence here, but Richard Bell was infuriating him.

"Ah, well." Bell sighed. "I thought you might all be interested to learn that the Garda Civil have become very concerned because they now have *four* murders to investigate in Santiago de Compostela."

"Four?" Ralph couldn't hold back the exclamation.

"The body of my detective friend has been exhumed. I was right. A post-mortem revealed arsenic."

Ralph was gripped now. "What made the authorities exhume him?"

"It happened that the landlady where he last slept was doing a clean sweep of her rooms ready for spring visitors when she discovered a wallet of papers under his mattress. My name and address were on the first letter inside. She took the wallet to the Garda's office for them to send it to me. Garda officers read that top letter and were excited by it. It was the last letter my friend wrote, which was never sent. In it he wrote that he was being followed about the town by a woman. Then, in a more wavering hand, that he felt ill. He had eaten and drunk in different places, but she was always there. At the bottom of the page he scrawled that he had learned she was the mother of the Sanchez brothers. He wrote: '*in her grief at losing them again she is taking vengeance on me. She has slowly poisoned me. I still hope to send this letter...*' But he never did."

Ralph shook his head. "Poor man! What else was in the wallet?"

"Copies of all the letters he had written to me – every detail of his investigations into the murder of my father in May 1841. Their own records would confirm that he had reported his suspicions of the Sanchez brothers, but the villains had vanished before arrests could be made."

"So you are calling that the second murder? What about the others?"

"The third and fourth were uncovered when the bodies of both brothers were found by hunters in a ravine in the mountains. They had dagger wounds, as well as internal injuries from their fall. They were brought down for burial and their mother made a public scene of her grief. She was heard to boast that the one who had driven them away had died by her hand, which confirmed the suspicions that my friend had expressed in his last letter. Hence the exhumation and the charging of her with the murder of my friend."

Ralph had been drawing deep breaths of relief as the story unfolded. The murderers of this man's father were both dead. His revenge was complete, for they had evidently died violently, perhaps quarrelling between themselves.

He stood up and held out his hand. "Thank you for telling me all this. Your father and your friend are avenged, though I have pity for the Sanchez mother."

"I too, for her mind was deranged by grief, as my own mother's was." He sighed. "We don't know what women are capable of when their passions are aroused." He turned his head and waved a hand. "Ah! I see your lady wife has spotted us from the window." He grabbed Ralph's arm. "Man! She knows who I am, and seems to have fainted away."

"God in heaven!" Ralph made for the front porch and met John coming out.

"Hey, Uncle Ralph, I said it was only Mr Bell but Aunt Sophie collapsed onto the sofa. The girls are fetching Gran."

Ralph cursed himself for standing up so abruptly. On the bench they were not visible against the wall.

Sophia had not fainted, but was in hysterics. When she saw Ralph she cried out, "We are haunted. That man is here!" Then she saw him in the doorway. She shrieked. "Why you let him in?"

Richard Bell dodged round Ralph and approached Sophia with hands spread, palms uppermost, in a gesture of peace.

"Your ladyship, condesa, dear madam, I mean you no harm." He turned the gesture into a courtier's humble bow.

Ralph saw that his mother and the girls had crowded into the room. His mother had brought smelling salts.

"I thought she'd fainted. Good morning, Mr Bell. You seem to have found us at an awkward moment."

"Oh Dee, make him go away." Sophia struggled to regain her composure.

"I believe you had completed your business," Ralph said to him. "Perhaps you should take your leave now."

"With all the family assembled—" he began.

John broke in. "Granda isn't, and my da is out building bridges and Ma is too shy to come in and Matty's at Cambridge."

Maria giggled, but Lucia crept to her mother's side and peered into her face.

Richard Bell smiled at Ralph. "I thought madam condesa might be pleased to receive news of the cousin she has not seen for four years."

"Cousin!" shrieked Sophia as Ralph felt a sickening lurch of his stomach. "What cousin?"

"Why, Juan de Villena, who calls himself Conde, I believe."

"No, no. I not know him any more." Sophia snatched out her fan and made violent shooing motions with it. Lucia tried to stop her.

Maria moved to her other side. "Cousin Juan won't come here to bother us."

"Indeed he will not," Richard Bell said, "since he is in custody at present."

"Custody!" Sophia screamed the word. Ralph swallowed. This was getting too close to her.

John clapped his hands. "Auntie has family in prison! That's exciting!"

Ralph thought, I ought to banish him, but he'll only listen at the door. All will know soon. This is a boil that must be lanced, and I believe the moment has come.

"Sit down and be quiet," he ordered him. "Let us all sit and hear without interruption what Mr Bell has to say."

Richard Bell gave him a small bow. "That is what I hoped to be invited to do from the beginning."

He took the armchair, from which he could observe Sophia's face. Ralph saw his mother move across to sit with Sophia and the girls on the sofa. He himself drew forward one of the two Queen Anne chairs, where he could observe her profile, and John pulled the other close, perching eagerly on the edge. They all looked at Richard Bell. Ralph thought, Under those theatrical smiles there is hard steel, but I do believe he speaks the truth. The truth must break forth.

Bell began quietly, "All the information I have received came in a letter from an officer of the Garda Civil – the one who called on you at your Madrid apartment, my lady, in late October." Sophia shuddered. He turned to Ralph. "Two suspicious-looking pedlars had crossed the border from France and were wandering about the market in Santiago picking up gossip. They certainly learned that the Condesa de Villena was no longer in residence. A maid of the de Villena household, who was in town for her mother's funeral, overheard them speaking of this as they left a public house. As you know, it is easy to disguise a face, but this servant knew their voices and had quite a shock."

"Brigitta!" squealed Maria. "Oh Mamma, she couldn't come with us because her mother was so ill. She must have died."

Richard Bell gave her an indulgent smile. "Brigitta, then. She reported to the Garda office that the men they had sought – Juan de Villena and Guido Martinez – were in Santiago. She could describe them, so they were quickly arrested."

Sophia gasped and then covered her mouth.

"So what is the charge?" Ralph asked.

"Plotting to murder Sir Ralph Barnet."

Sophia gave a sharp cry, and there was a general gasp. Lucia went white and gripped her mother's arm.

Richard Bell let the reaction subside and then went calmly on. "Of course, Guido says Juan ordered it while Juan says..." He paused and beamed at Sophia. "...it was you, my lady."

Lucia leapt to her feet. "Never, never, never."

Sophia was shaking violently. "Of course not, my darling."

Lucia rushed on, pointing her finger at Richard Bell. "It was not an order at all. It was a joke. I heard her – Spanish, of course – Mamma, I'm sorry. I was hiding in your boudoir. You came in with cousin Juan. All you said was, 'Ralph might fall off a strange horse and break his neck.' You were laughing."

Ralph met his mother's eye. She showed the same horror and alarm that had struck him. Sophia turned her head from side to side, her mouth hanging open.

Maria glared at Lucia. John bounced up and down with excitement.

Richard Bell smiled. "Do I detect a situation that reminds us of Henry the Second and Thomas à Becket?"

"Hey!" cried John. "I know about that. Mr Hurst told us stories of the kings and queens of England. The Archbishop was murdered in Canterbury Cathedral and Henry crawled there on his hands and knees in penance. But what does it mean? No one's murdered Uncle Ralph. He's still here."

"Young man," said Richard Bell, "my father was murdered in his place. The killers got the wrong man."

"Whooh! *That's* why you're here! You want vengeance on Aunt Sophia! I bet she never meant it. As Lu says, it was a joke."

Sophia rose from her seat and took one step towards Ralph. He got up quickly, fearing she might faint, but she flung her arms round his neck and sobbed against his chest.

"Kill this man! How could I ever...?"

He had to put his arms round her and brace his legs to support her weight. He could see, over her shoulder, Richard Bell still seated, watching her, his face inscrutable. *Was he seeing his father's true murderer at last? I let her into my life again – and now this!* He wanted to thrust her away, but she was still holding him tight. Then, in a second, he sensed a change in her. Passion, prompted by terror, was giving way to an idea.

She let her sobs subside and, still embracing him, she looked round at Richard Bell. "You see how I love my husband. See too, you silly man, how it was between Juan and me. Always I scoff at his wanting me. Lucia tell you what I say to him. I sure she is right. It was how we talk. We come upstairs, I tease him, I laugh at him. We reach my boudoir door. 'Oh, you want never see him again?' I say. Then I say what naughty Lucia heard. I know what he would like. My own Ralph fall off horse. And I widow and he marry me. I laugh at him and his silly hopes."

Ralph could feel her panting as invention gripped her and the lies poured out. She was clever and quick-thinking – qualities he admired in his mother. In Sophia they were cunning. She had seen an abyss yawning before her.

Richard Bell fixed her with his eye, and there was no smile in it. "The Garda officer you saw, my lady, is a man of cold logic. He would answer that outburst of yours by producing the two men you summoned to throw your husband from Santiago cathedral only hours before your merry banter with cousin Juan at home."

Ralph could feel Sophia shrink against him as if struck by a blow. But even then she rallied. "What? A loving couple's tiff! Have you never had such a thing?"

"I am not married."

Sophia threw back her head and laughed. She peered round at Ralph. "How he understand then our wonderful marriage? Ups and downs. Yes. Comings and goings. Yes. But always that deep deep attraction from the day he plunge into ocean to save my life. I tell you that many times, my girls, you know it well."

Ralph was distressed to see that they were both sobbing.

He heard John say, "Hey, stop that, Baby Bear. You never cry."

Into the tension came the clear voice of his mother.

"This has gone far enough. Say no more, Sophia, and Mr Bell, if you have a heart, think of the children. This is our drawing room, not a law court.

We are a family. If any family member does wrong to another member, pray leave it to us to deal with it."

"Well said, Mother," came a new voice, and Ralph saw his brother standing in the doorway. Their eyes met, and Frank's look became full of meaning. It said, I did my forgiving years ago. You and I are brothers now.

Ralph sank back onto his chair. Sophia slithered to the floor and clung to his knees. I am no better than she, he was telling himself. In another world I plotted my brother's death. This is my punishment – to have this creature as my wife.

Frank was now looking round at them all and asking, "What's going on here? Lily was too frightened to come in, and Father said there were strangers here so he mustn't intrude. I see you, sir," to Richard Bell, "though I'm afraid your name escapes me, and the nature of your business."

John ran across the room to him. "Hey, Da, I'm glad you've come. It's been very exciting, but the females have gone all weepy. There's been a murder in Spain and it mattered who said what, but *I* knew about King Henry and the Archbishop."

Frank laughed. "Well, that makes everything clear."

The tension should have eased. Ralph saw a giggle trying to chase away Maria's tears, and his mother smiled. Sophia wriggled up and draped herself on him, murmuring, "My saviour, my protector."

Richard Bell stood up, and his eyes swept the company.

"I may return when I have been to Spain to see two of my father's murderers receive just punishment. Two are already dead and buried, awaiting Judgement Day. Only God and the fifth person know the whole truth. Certainly, if that person set foot on Spanish soil, arrest and interrogation would follow."

Sophia peered up into Ralph's face. Her black eyes spoke terror. Richard Bell turned his gaze to the window and the clouds galloping across a bright sky.

"One day," he said as if concluding a public address, "justice may leap national boundaries. A world body chasing every malefactor would be a fine thing. Pray God we can bring it about. Sir Ralph, I left my hat on the bench outside. Let no one disturb themselves. I will pick it up on the way out. I am sorry to have caused trouble, but I trust the pieces of this family will shake down and fit together like a jigsaw puzzle that ends up as a beautiful picture. In due course, my lady" – he focused on Sophia, and Ralph felt her shrink as if under an evil eye – "I hope to marry and have a family of my own, if I can find such love as yours. My only family – my parents – were cruelly taken from me, and until I see justice for them, I am unable to make my own family." He bowed. "Good day to you all."

To Frank, clutching John in front of him, he gave a nod. "I predict that this boy will do great things in life with good guidance." He passed into the hall.

Ralph heard his mother say, "Some refreshment, sir?" He shook his head.

"My only regret, Mistress Heron, is not seeing your other grandson, the charming Mateo. You must be proud of two such fine young men."

With swift steps through the porch he passed the first bay window, snatched his hat from the bench and disappeared up the drive, almost at a run.

Into the general sighs of relief, John asked his grandmother as she returned to the room, "Why did he say that about *parents*? Was his mother murdered too?"

She looked all round for an answer, then shrugged her shoulders. "Perhaps she died of grief. None of us knows the whole story."

"I don't – but Baby Bear will tell me what she knows."

Maria called across the room, "Only if you promise not to tell a living soul."

"Yes, but it sounds an exciting story – good enough for a book by Grandma."

Ralph, with Sophia draped against him, heard echoes of his own words when he left the family home after Frank's acquittal. He had suggested she could make a story out of that tale as long as she changed the names. But life is no fiction, he thought bitterly. It has to be lived through and somehow endured.

Lily appeared, hesitating at the door. "Has the visitor gone? The kettle's boiling. Would anyone like tea?"

Sophia reared up. "A glass of good Spanish wine." She moved towards her with wavering steps. "Dear Lily, our one visitor has gone, never to return, we hope."

"There's a bottle unopened from Christmas, my lady." Jack looked over Lily's head. "I'll fetch it."

Ralph thought to stop him, but it might be a fine thing if she were to drink herself insensible.

"Come along," his mother said. "All to the kitchen. There will be a good blaze there. This fire has sunk right down. We were too engrossed to notice."

John pulled Maria up from the sofa. "So tell me everything."

She looked round at her sister, sitting stolidly staring into space, the tears still wet on her cheeks.

"Come on, Lu," Maria said. "You know things I don't. What were you doing in Mamma's boudoir?"

"I wanted to try her scent." She gave a great sniff. "What did I say wrong? I wanted to *help* Mamma. That beast was accusing her." She got up and suddenly pointed at John. "And what did *he* understand that we didn't?"

"Oh, that." John laughed. "King Henry said, 'Who will rid me of this turbulent priest?' But he didn't expect his knights to rush off and slay the Archbishop rather messily in his own cathedral. He was just cross with him for the moment, like I suppose your ma was with your da. Unfortunately this cousin of yours and his helper got the wrong man – this fellow's father. Well, fortunately for Uncle Ralph. Have I got a notion of what happened?"

Maria put her arm through his and squeezed it. "A very good notion, John. Baby Bear thinks you're very clever." She pecked his cheek and they went out, with Lucia trailing after them.

Ralph looked all about the empty room. The boil had been pricked, but the poison of lies was still there. He dragged his feet slowly to the door and followed them to the kitchen. Frank was there, marshalling them all to seats round the table. Frank was innocent, unburdened, the husband of Lily. For a moment he could hate him again as he had in their youth.

Chapter 24

Easter

Dee

Dee couldn't help feeling warm towards Richard Bell for his praise of her beloved grandsons. When Mateo came home for the Easter vacation she delighted in their different natures: John boisterous, guilelessly boastful, utterly open; Mateo quiet, more reserved than ever, but, at the news of Richard Bell's visit, how tender to his mother!

"Oh Grandmamma," he confided to Dee, "she is bruised like a crushed flower. I'd forgotten how lovely she can look, but she is very sore that she was condemned out of hand, and I am sure she is innocent."

Dee had seen how Sophia had painted and powdered tastefully for his return and put on a gown of delphinium blue, shrouded with a black lacy shawl which she clutched continually as she murmured of her ordeal at the hands of 'that man'. "I needed my fine son to speak for me." She caressed his arm.

He still preferred to come to Dee's kitchen and watch her at work. One day she was baking a pie for dinner when he came and draped himself against the wall.

Dee said, "Spend more time with your mother. Tell her about your life at Cambridge. You have said little since you came back this time."

"Nothing new to tell." He scooped up a knob of dough and ate it.

She playfully smacked his hand.

"Nay, tell me. I long to enter into that strange world. If I had been born a man I would have gone to university and obtained a degree in – let me see – philosophy, perhaps." She laid the pastry on the baking dish and trimmed the edges.

"Of course you would, Grandmamma."

"Well then, tell me about it."

"I'm reading Classics – Greek and Latin."

"I know *that*. Tell me about your days."

He was silent; then came a little choking sound, and he turned away from her. She laid down the knife and dried her hands and clasped him from behind.

"Matty, pet. You're crying. What is it?"

He gulped. "It's lonely. *I'm* lonely."

"But you're surrounded with a crowd of fellow students."

"That's what makes it lonely." He sniffed.

She left her pie and drew him to the settle. "Come, tell me before anyone else comes in. We are speaking of freshmen who were all as new as you at first."

He nodded, taking gasping breaths. "Everyone on my staircase found friends in the first week. By the end of term they were in tight knots of twos or threes or fours. When I went back after Christmas I thought, I must break into one of these groups, but it was too late, of course. I'm the outsider, the one who works all the time. They teased me at first, but now they just ignore me. I'm a shadow walking about. If they hear me coming they look up, but it's only Barton, so they get on with their talk or their game or whatever."

"And what do you do then?"

"Go to my desk and hear them laughing next door or running up and down, and they go out and come back tipsy."

"You don't want to do that?"

"No, but I wouldn't mind being in the town, just to see life. At first I would get Venus and ride into the country for the fresh air and exercise, and I loved that, but I was always alone and I wanted company. I really wanted female company. There was the daughter of a bakery..." He paused and looked anxiously at Dee.

"You got friendly with her?"

"Heavens, no. I just looked at her. She was pretty, but she went away and

I didn't see her again. So I brought Venus home, and John and Maria ride her."

"Oh, but you must have her back for the holidays."

"And ride off on my own? You see, even John and Maria make a pair. Lucia's such a funny little thing I don't seem to get near her."

Dee got up. "I must get this pie in the oven."

"Of course. I'm sorry."

"No, something must be done about this. Going away from home should mean a circle of new friends."

Jack had built up a good fire and the bread oven was hot enough for the pie. She slipped it in and faced Mateo. He was wiping his eyes and trying to smile.

"It's my fault," he said. "They're all decent fellows. Well, some of them go with the ladies of the town. I hear them laugh about it."

Dee remembered what Jenny had said: 'Not one leaves college as a virgin.'

"Save yourself for a future wife, dear boy. When the time comes you'll be glad you did." He smiled wanly and nodded.

His mother came into the room. "My boy closeted with his grandmother as usual. Why you not closet with me, Mateo? What were you talking about? Tell me."

"We were talking about life at Cambridge, Mamma."

"Time you leave that place. You'll soon be a man. We should be planning for a noble Spanish young lady for you." Dee thought, She's listened at the door.

"But Mamma, I'm not even nineteen till June."

"I'll write to Eduardo, make enquiries."

Dee heard Ralph's footsteps in the hall, and the door was thrust open in his vigorous way.

"Ah, here you are, and Mother as usual being useful."

"I too. It is useful to speak of Mateo's future. He need a wife soon."

"He *will* need a wife soon – except he won't. He will keep his head down and graduate with a first-class degree."

"In Spanish nobility we arrange marriages in good time."

"Spanish nobility won't be eager to mate with a de Villena. Not now."

"Oh, cruel, cruel to say such a thing."

"No, it must be an English girl. Otherwise you wouldn't see the wedding."

"More cruel."

To cheer her and shame Ralph, Dee asked their family to eat with them and share the pie. Mateo looked at his father.

Ralph stroked his chin and looked at Dee. "No, you and Jack come and eat with us. Rosie and Peggy brought some mutton chops and are showing the twins how to cook them. You join us and bring your pie."

Sophia rose. "I *will* give fresh orders." She bowed herself out.

Dee said, "Frank and Lily will be back with John as it's Friday."

Ralph shook his head. "They told me they had several houses to look at and will eat in Newcastle."

"Houses? What do you mean? They said they were shopping."

He clapped his hand to his mouth. "Damn it. You didn't know. Yes, they were shopping, but you know it's easier for Frank's work if he lives in Newcastle."

Dee sensed a sick, hurt feeling rising which she must crush quickly. Frank had been keeping something from her.

She shrugged. "Oh, I know he hopes Mr Trace will make him a partner."

Ralph looked relieved. "So it makes sense for them to rent a small property in the town. John would be a day pupil at Hurst's. Look, I'm sorry I said anything. They wouldn't want to upset you needlessly if they didn't find anything today."

Dee bent down and with a cloth opened the oven door and peeped in. Then she drew herself up and fixed him with a straight look.

"I am not *upset*, but I don't like to be kept in the dark. I've always expected Frank and Lily to have their own home one day." She sighed. "But Jack won't like it. Changes! Well, you may host supper in the dining room, and I will bring the pie."

So, she thought, I am to lose Lily's help, and my sweet Frank and lively John. Instead I have an unpredictable woman to keep happy and a shy grandson to turn into a mature man, and two girls pulled this way and that between their father and mother. And the son left to me is by no means the solid, confident man of business he would like to appear. He is a tangled mass of emotions.

When they were at dinner, she looked at Ralph across the table. Is he pleased Frank is leaving? she wondered. His brother is a daily reminder of his plot against him. Now he believes his own wife planned *his* murder. Can *he* condemn *her*? Frank forgave him because I failed to love Ralph from his birth. But has Ralph failed to love Sophia?

Her lightning mind flew over the years since they had settled in Sheradon Grange. The hints Sophia had dropped, Ralph's impatience with her, his admission that she was never his considered choice, his single-minded devotion to his son. The picture was there of a jealous, unloved wife. Her first revenge was to remove his boy from him. But her love? The early passion for her hero, her saviour – had it wilted under neglect? Did this cousin Juan's devotion tempt her to – what? But since she came back, Dee thought, impelled by fear, I have seen longing looks following Ralph about. Of course she made a show of it to Richard Bell, but it is there, simmering, eager to be blown into a flame.

Frank, Lily and John returned on the late train. Dee stayed up, unable to settle to sleep till she heard their news.

"Mother Dee," Lily burst out as soon as they were in the kitchen, "we are so sorry but it has happened much sooner than we thought. We are to move to the town in less than a fortnight." She clasped Dee round the neck and wept.

Dee put her gently at arm's length. "I see nothing to cry about."

John said, "We'll keep coming back 'cos I'll miss Baby Bear. And Matty and I must have our birthday in the tree house."

Frank said, "Look, Ma, I was going to tell you—"

"Never mind that now. Ralph let it out by mistake, and my mind has got used to it." She squeezed John's shoulders as he bounced up close to look into her face. "Of course I'll miss you about the place, but if it's a good move for you all then it's right. What is the house like?"

"It's in a newly built terrace, and we will be the first occupants. It has water and drainage and gaslight all built into it. Imagine that!"

"The rent must be expensive."

"It's what we can afford, but I regret that the bit of rent I give you will have to cease. If I earn more in Trace and Heron Engineers I'll help you out, of course."

"Go on with you. We'll manage. Ralph pays me rent, you know, and we grow more of our own produce every year. My *Moral Tales* still sell, too."

"Ma, you're taking this very well." Frank gave her a hug, Lily stopped crying and Dee made a drink of chocolate for them all before John was sent to bed.

The day after they moved was also the day of Mateo's return to Cambridge. He left early, as there would be three train journeys. Ralph went with him as far as Newcastle and gave him extra money to invite 'his staircase' to a supper. It was Dee's idea, but she was afraid he anticipated it only with dread. Sorrowful for him, and all too aware of the emptiness of the house without Frank's family, she began, with Peggy, a big scrubbing of their bedrooms. John had left some books, saying, "We'll stay overnight when I come for my birthday in the tree house with Matty – and at Christmas, of course."

She and Peggy had been working for an hour when Maria came running up the stairs calling "Grandmamma!"

"In here – John's room." Was Sophia hysterical? She had been weepy when she said goodbye to Mateo. Dee put her scrubbing brush on the window ledge and went out onto the landing so that Peggy would not hear what was amiss.

"Oh Grandmamma!" Maria was panting. "A letter has come from Spain addressed to Papa, but Mamma has opened it and read it and now she is all upset again. Lu is trying to comfort her."

"I'll come down." No peace, she thought as she descended the stair behind Maria. She could hear loud sounds coming from the drawing room.

It was in Spanish, but Dee distinguished the name of Juan several times. Sophia looked up as she came in with Maria.

"Oh Dee, my poor cousin – they find him guilty!"

"Did you not expect such a verdict? You told us he was guilty."

She slapped the letter on her lap. "This man – Señor Bell – go to the trial. He wrote what they say and sent it to me."

Maria stamped her foot. "To *Papa*."

"Juan is not Papa's cousin. He my flesh and blood. Only Guido is guilty."

Maria's mouth fell open. Her eyes were wide as she compelled Dee to meet her gaze. She said softly, "Nurse heard Guido telling cousin Juan, 'You won't be troubled with him tomorrow.' He meant Papa. He hated him."

Dee sat down by Sophia. "You dismissed both Juan and Guido."

She waved her arms about. "No, no. He went with Guido to protect *me*. He want to draw suspicion to himself. He stayed away. He so noble."

Maria stamped her foot again. "Mamma, you are lying!"

Lucia reared up. "She's not. Listen what else is in the letter. Tell them, Mamma."

Sophia tapped the letter again. "Yes, yes. See what a monster Guido is. He return from France the mountain way. And who does he meet? Those very men, the Sanchez brothers, the hired men. They demand the money for the job. From Guido, you see, not Juan. They know who plan it. So what Guido do? Pretend draw out money but draw knife. Stab them both. Throw bodies in ravine. Juan tell the court. He solve their other murder. Plead – how you say – clemency."

Maria plunged her hands in her hair as if she would tear out clutches of curls. "Lies, lies, all of it lies. How would cousin Juan know this if he was not there himself? The men demanded money from *him*, the boss. Oh, Guido would kill them. Cousin Juan wouldn't soil his hands. I always hated him. He was…slimy. And we know he and Guido arrived in Santiago together. Brigitta saw them, heard them saying that the family had left the estate. Why did they come back? Did cousin Juan hope to grab our land? He thought that old murder was forgotten. He knew nothing of a son wanting vengeance. Mamma, you can't say it was only Guido." She poked her furious face at her mother.

Sophia slapped it. "Because Juan love me, you silly girl."

Maria turned away, sobbing. Dee grabbed the guilty hand and held it tight.

"Smack me too if you like, but you must face this, Sophia. Juan may have loved you once, but from what I gather it is the de Villena estate he coveted. Now he is terrified for his life and making up stories in desperation. Richard Bell said that when Juan was arrested, he blamed you."

She pulled her hand away. "That man! I not believe a word *he* say."

Maria turned round and shouted at her, the tears still flowing. "I can't believe a word *you* say. Papa said if you tell lies people won't ever trust you again. I'll never trust you, and that's horrid 'cos you're my mother. I hate you." She flung herself against the window curtain and buried her face in it and sobbed.

Dee saw that Lucia was silently crying onto her mother's shoulder, and Sophia was sitting staring ahead, her face very flushed. Dee wanted to comfort Maria, but she must make Sophia see reason first.

"Come, my dear," she began.

Sophia flashed round at her. "Your son lecture me on lies! He told me the biggest lies on earth so I marry him. Why I not marry Juan and keep family happy?"

Dee said quietly, "Ralph has learned the virtue of truth. So have I. When you know the truth, you can face it. How can you face a network of lies? Your daughters are hurt by yours because they love you."

Maria looked round. "I don't. I hate her. She wanted to have Papa killed."

Lucia shrieked, "She didn't. I heard what she said."

Maria marched back and stood over her sister. "You heard *one* thing she said. What about all the other things? She talked and talked to cousin Juan in her boudoir. Would he have sent Guido to find two ruffians to kill Papa if he didn't know she'd be pleased?"

Lucia shouted back, "She sent them away afterwards. We heard her. She was angry."

"Of course she was angry, you goose. They'd failed. Papa was still alive, so she couldn't marry cousin Juan. I didn't believe it then, but I do now. She's a murderer."

Sophia uttered a long piercing shriek. She rose to her full height and staggered across the room. Horrible animal noises came from her, which brought Rosie running from the kitchen and Peggy from upstairs. Dee tried to intercept her, but she thrust her aside so hard that she fell to the floor. Jack appeared in the doorway, horror on his face, and rushed to Dee.

She scrambled up. "I'm all right. See if you can catch her and hold her. It's hysteria. Girls! Don't get in her way. She might hurt you."

Dee saw Jack approach her, muttering soothing words as if she was an excited horse. "Now then, my lady. Quiet now." But this was a flesh and blood woman thrusting her curves at him, and he hesitated to touch her. Dee could tell from her wild eyes that she wasn't seeing him. Her arms were waving about. Any moment now she would lose balance and fall over.

"Grab her, Jack," she commanded in the voice he had to obey instantly, and he did. "Bring her to the sofa." That was not so easy, but between them they manoeuvred the mad creature till they could deposit her on the cushions, and she sank back, quivering in every limb and still making noises like short barks.

Lucia bent over her, crying, "Don't, Mamma. I can't bear it."

Maria stood, eyes hard, lips compressed.

"Should I run to the village for the doctor, ma'am?" asked Peggy.

Rosie said, "You'll get used to her, Peg. She'll be round in a minute."

Dee thought, She's never been as bad as this. Tantrums, yes, but this is worse. Ralph won't want the doctor to see this.

"We'll try her smelling salts. I keep them on the kitchen mantelshelf."

Peggy, who was as quick on her feet as a bird, was there and back in a few seconds, but she didn't hear Lucia spit at Maria, "It's *your* fault."

252

Rosie missed that too as she was opening a window to let in the fresh spring breeze.

Maria hissed, "I spoke the truth," and looked at Dee for approval.

Dee nodded and took the little bottle from Peggy's hand.

Sophia's noises had already subsided, and when she sniffed the salts her eyes opened. They fell on Maria, and she shuddered.

Dee dismissed the maids, not knowing what might come next.

Sophia was looking about her. Dee realised she was checking who was still in the room. She passed the back of her hand across her forehead in a theatrical gesture. "What happened?"

"It's all right, my dear. You had a bit of a turn. Stay there quietly."

Lucia clung to her. "It was horrid. Are you really better now?" She glared up at Maria, who was watching, stroking her chin just as her father and brother often did. What is she thinking? Dee wondered.

Jack was hovering from one foot to the other. "Can I do anything, angel?"

"Stir up the kitchen fire and put the kettle on the trivet. I shall come and make us all some coffee."

He went out, grinning with relief.

Dee offered the smelling salts to Sophia, but she waved them aside. "I not need those things." She pressed her hands to her head. "I remember nothing. I heard nothing what was said. A sudden pain. Tight across here. But it's gone. Mercifully gone. Did I frighten you, my darling girl?" She squeezed Lucia.

Maria sprang into action. "Show me how to make coffee, Grandmamma."

They went out to the kitchen, and Dee told Jack he could go back to the stables. The moment he was out of the door, Maria said, "She acted that, didn't she? The whole thing. I hate her." She pressed her face into Dee's pinafore and sobbed.

Dee was shocked. So bright a child, and so hurt by all this horror!

She eased her gently back. "Is that what you really think?"

"Well, wasn't it an act? She was better so quickly."

Dee knew that was true. The cessation of the sounds, the opening of the eyes, the assessing of the people was a performance. Yes, she thought, this woman can flash from terror to an astonishing control of herself. It is a gift. But she shook her head. "She couldn't help that scream she let fly, and rearing up to thrust away your word – 'murderer'."

Maria screwed up her face. "Well, maybe *that*. But she lied when she said she had a sudden pain and hadn't heard anything. And when Rosie and Peggy and Grandpapa ran in, you said it was hysteria, so she played it out. Oh Grandmamma, has she a devil in her? I'm afraid for Lu and me. She hit me. My cheek's stinging."

The kettle hissed, and Dee hastened to make the coffee. There were beans in the grinder, so she let Maria wind the handle while she set cups on a tray.

"Dear child, she was hitting out at the word you spoke. She is wrestling with her own conscience. We must be gentle with her."

"I want her to go away. We could be happy without her." She watched Dee pour the water over the grains. "Lu would be better too."

Dee sighed. "That's not going to happen." She added a strainer and spoon to the tray. "We are on trial to see if we can love her into a right frame of mind."

Maria stared. "Love?" She shook her head, but followed Dee as she carried the tray to the drawing room.

They found Lucia curled up, weeping, her mother's arms round her. But Sophia looked straight ahead – as if she is probing an unfathomable future.

When Ralph heard about his opened letter he was ready to storm up to their bedroom, where Lucia told him Mamma was resting and shouldn't be disturbed.

Dee laid a hand on his arm. "Nothing will be gained by anger. Only love and forgiveness will heal this family. The girls won't speak to each other. Sophia is trying to blot out Maria's existence. Lucia is frightened and unhappy. You alone can bring something new to this scene. Matty must not come back to see this. Now I do believe she was complicit in seeking your death. Maybe Juan cajoled her into picturing a new life in Spain, married to him, and the family all settled there. She is a wayward impulsive creature. Are you able to show love and forgiveness?"

He looked at her in amazement. "No. Never."

"Not if she confesses?"

"She can't do that, because she is all lies."

"Evil people have been transformed before by love."

There was a flash of startled guilt in his eyes, but he shook it away.

"You love her if you can. I'm too tired to try. I've come from unrest on the streets of Newcastle. There may still be miners' strikes. All this affects business, which pays the bills. I just want to come home to peace and food and sleep."

"And I want peace too," Dee snapped back before she could check herself. "Did I ever ask to have a hysterical woman to care for? If you are too busy and she is unfit, I also have three young people to nurture, which is a great responsibility. How was Mateo when you said goodbye to him at Newcastle?"

He sat down on the settle and rubbed his face. "God! Was that only this morning? It's been a long day. He was gloomy. Look, I'm sorry I brought all this into your life, Mother. I should take them away, as Frank has done."

She shook her head. "Nonsense. Jack and I rattling around in this place? I love your young brood, and want them to grow up as good citizens, but I need your help." She looked at his slumped shoulders. "I see you are tired. The stew pan has been ready awhile. It only needs to go back on the fire for a minute. Call your girls in a cheerful tone, and if Sophia is able to come down, speak to her kindly and she will fall on your neck with gratitude. That alone could transform the girls too."

He dragged himself to his feet with a half-smile on his face. "You are a genius at demanding the impossible."

He was back in ten minutes with Maria and Lucia clinging to his coat tails.

Lucia was wearing a most unusual smile. "Mamma is coming down. Papa only held out his arms to her and said, 'Come on, wife, it's supper time,' and she leapt into his arms and clung to him. She's putting on her best dress."

Maria said, "Lu thinks she's forgotten what I called her this morning but I know she hasn't, because she looked daggers at me."

Lucia flashed back, "She can't forget what she never heard. She said so. Didn't she, Grandmamma?"

"Whatever was said this morning has become the past. We are living in now, and now is the time for love, as your father has so rightly shown you. Lay the table, girls."

Sophia appeared in a low-necked evening gown of primrose yellow with a flounced skirt and lacy cape, just as Jack tramped in from the woods. She recoiled a step at his muddy boots. He retreated into the back kitchen and pulled them off. Dee took him his slippers from the hearth.

He whispered, "That's never her what was bad this morning."

She nodded. "Say nothing, unless you tell her she looks lovely."

Lucia was saying, "Mamma, you are beautiful."

So, as he came hesitantly to the table, Jack managed to mumble, "Ay, you are that, my lady."

"I thought we were in the dining room," she said with a small laugh.

Maria sat as far from her as she could. Ralph was left with a place beside her, where Dee saw his eyes stray toward her partly exposed bosom. She flirted with him like a girl and joined in the conversation, which Dee steered towards the departure of Mateo and Frank's family. All the time Dee was remembering the morning's scene and struggling to reconcile the two Sophias. Much as she longed to believe her own counsel, she knew this family of four were still a long way from healing, and the drama in Spain still had to reach a conclusion.

Chapter 25

Newcastle and Sheradon Grange, June 1847

Ralph
Ralph let his eyes drift over the white rectangles of paper on the highly polished mahogany surface. Desultory talk flowed over him as more members arrived. He felt detached from it all, because of his secret impatience to be on the train home for the birthday party this afternoon. Mateo was eighteen and John ten. Frank and Lily had brought John the day before, and Tom and Jenny would already be on a train from North Shields. He wasn't pleased that he had to attend this board meeting today. He had spent last night in his room at Heron Mansions, and his disjunction from the family had come home to him forcibly.

How Sophia would behave, no one knew from one day to the next. The Bateys' coming could be disastrous. That she should be linked to such people in any way was an affront to her susceptibilities.

A cheerful Mateo had arrived only two days before at the end of his first year at Cambridge, and Sophia had greeted him with tearful hugs. "You have made friends at last, but your poor Mamma still has few of any standing in this barren county. Your Papa has been too occupied to take me visiting your so-called gentry."

He began to be aware that the board members were now settling into their places, and the chairman was saying, "Well, gentlemen, shall we start without him?"

For a second, Ralph wondered if they all realised that his mind was far away, but he noticed one chair was still unoccupied.

Somebody said, "He returned from Spain only yesterday."

Ralph remembered with a start that one of their number, whom he had not yet met, had gone in an advisory capacity to a Spanish railway company. England was so far ahead of the continent in setting up a network of train lines that help was often sought by companies abroad.

There was a tap at the door and a well-tanned gentleman, perspiring from haste, came in, murmuring apologies, and took his place. He was introduced as 'Mr Horsley' to those he had not met before, and when he came to Ralph he started and stared at hearing the name 'Sir Ralph Barnet'.

"Well, well, there can't be two Sir Ralph Barnets from Newcastle. Have you by any chance a Spanish wife, sir?"

Ralph agreed, very guardedly, that he had.

Mr Horsley nodded a few times with a buttoned-up expression and, seeing that the chairman had already lifted his sheaf of papers to open the proceedings, he said to Ralph, "Pray allow me a few private words, sir, after the meeting."

Ralph could take in very little from that point. He felt sick at the stomach. Though he was asked his opinion several times, he gave replies completely at variance with his usual decisiveness. The clock on the wall, a heavy, menacing object, showed him the morning ticking away.

At last they were all standing up and shaking hands as they dispersed, and Mr Horsley made his way round the table towards him.

"Sir Ralph, I know not what news you may have had from Spain lately."

Dear God, he thought, it must be the executions. He said, "My wife hears from the steward of her estate – routine matters."

Mr Horsley dismissed 'routine matters' with a wave of the hand. He was so brimming with his news that Ralph shrank in on himself.

"Ah, well, this is only two weeks old, for I witnessed it myself. Gruesome business, but there's a cruel streak in the Spaniards – bullfighting, you know."

"Can you come to the point, sir?"

The man fished in his greatcoat pocket. "Do you read Spanish?"

"Tolerably."

"Ah, then I will let you have this Madrid paper to confirm what I say."

Ralph almost snatched it from his hand. "If it saves talk, good. I will read it on the train. I can catch mine if I go now. I'm much obliged to you, sir."

He left the man standing, mouth agape, and hurried to the station. It was a relief to be away, but the paper felt like a bomb in his pocket. If it spoke of Juan's execution, as he feared, he must hide it from Sophia at least till after the birthday party. And what then?

As soon as the train had shrieked and puffed its way from the station, he unfolded the paper and found the report of the execution of Count Juan de Villena and his accomplice, Guido Martinez. Ralph's eyes lighted on his own name linked with the victim, Richard Bell, '*believed to have been mistaken for Sir Ralph Barnet, husband of Condesa Sophia de Villena, who resides with him in England near the town of Newcastle.*' The next paragraph stated that Count Juan's defence had been that the plot to kill Sir Ralph was entirely the condesa's work. This was not believed, but with his last breath he was heard to curse her. There was more about the murder of the Sanchez brothers, but Ralph stuffed the article back into his pocket.

It was impossible to sit still. He got up and walked up and down the train. The thought of Mr Horsley knowing this and telling his friends and acquaintances was unbearable. Somehow he had lived down that other article in the *Newcastle Courant*, but this was ten times worse. He had now re-established himself solidly in the business world, and though he felt that the eccentricity of his wife was already known, the suspicion of a plot to murder him was another matter altogether. If Horsley talked about it, or if it got to J. P. Roy's ears at the *Courant*…! He struck his hand on the side of his head, almost knocking his hat off. Then he realised people were staring, and he walked quickly back to his seat and gazed out of the train window till he reached his station.

The walk to Sheradon Grange cooled his head, though the day itself was brightening and foretelling a hot afternoon for the picnic in the treehouse. He had to face that with this paper in his pocket. He took longer steps, breathing hard. She is not to see it, he vowed. When she took the children away, was it for the arms of Juan? Surely not. He must have been fifty then, short, stout and bald if he left off his wig. God, it's horrible to think of them garrotting him. But I am only forty-four, tall and strong with not a grey hair. She cannot grieve for him.

He walked faster. Juan has met his maker, and if I am to crush local gossip it must be with her. Can I ever bring myself to love and forgive, as Mother requires? Thank God my dear boy is home for the long vacation. I will ride out with him, enjoy his company. He tells me that the party he gave 'his staircase' has transformed his life. He is still a curiosity, but they call him 'a good fellow after all'.

Cheered by thoughts of Mateo, he found himself turning in at the gates of Sheradon Grange and hearing voices, John's as usual the loudest. They must be at the treehouse, which he would see the moment he turned the corner. There it was. John, Mateo and the girls were all on the platform looking over the railing. John saw him first, leaned over, grasped a branch below and somersaulted onto the ground.

"Hey, Uncle Ralph! A fellow came asking for Aunt Sophia – well, the Condesa de Whatsit, he said – so I sent him into the drawing room."

"What? Mr Bell?"

"No, not the Carlisle man. He talked funny so I suppose he was Spanish. I warned him she could be a bit excitable, and he said he knew. Did I do wrong?"

Ralph's heart was pounding. "Very likely." He hastened inside, passing Jack and Frank carrying out the trestle table for the picnic.

There was no one in the drawing room except Tom, asleep in the armchair, his belly protuberant. From the kitchen he could hear Jenny's laughter with his mother and Lily. It flashed through his head that an officer of the Garda Civil had already taken Sophia away. Was that a relief, or would she jump overboard as she once did in the face of danger? No, he could hear movement above in the bedroom.

He rushed upstairs. The door at least was unlocked. He flung it wide and there was Sophia, struggling in the arms of a young, handsome dark-haired stranger.

She shrieked, "Ralph!"

The young man pushed her away, and Ralph realised that that was what he had been trying to do. The impulse to knock him down vanished as she ran into his arms, crying, "Oh, brutal! They have garrotted them both. Eduardo came to tell me."

"Eduardo!" Ralph looked hard at the young man. He could imagine a starved Sophia promoting him to more than the office of steward. He breathed sensuality in every limb.

He was bowing now, his face moist, his eyes obsequious. "Eduardo Casares, your honour. Milady upset and like to faint. I try prepare her for bad news but it too much. I so sorry come when you have party. The young vizconde not see me. He up tree. I go away. I not trouble you."

Sophia, wrenched with sobs and clinging to Ralph, managed to gulp out, "No, no, he stay, come so far. Spare rooms now."

"My brother and his family occupied them last night." He looked at Eduardo. "There are three good rooms in the attic, the floor above this."

"Attic, you call them. Good. Eduardo happy in attic."

"Both Mateo and I will be glad to discuss several matters with you, Señor Casares. I am sorry to hear your news, but it was not unexpected." He was thinking, I will lock our bedroom door and hide the key tonight or I will never sleep. She will be burning to climb those attic stairs. "Sophia, pray compose yourself. You knew this must happen when Juan lost his appeal. Can you bear to come down and join in our boy's celebration?"

She tore herself away and, breathing in gasps, planted herself in front of the mirror. She passed both hands across her face. Her breaths slowed. She drew up her head. "Few minutes, then I come. Send Rosie to help me."

Ralph sensed Eduardo's admiration. He even felt a flicker of it himself.

"Very well." He turned to the door. "Señor Casares, come and meet Mateo. He will be…interested to see you." He refrained from saying 'pleased', having little inkling of Mateo's view of the man's elevation to steward.

"He grow very much tall," Eduardo ventured as they went down the stairs. He pointed to the drawing room door. "The young boy, he tell me go in there, but a person there. I…not go bedroom, but she see me from up there and so excited and I such news – she tell me come up – not good. I very sorry, milord."

"Just call me Sir Ralph."

"And I Eduardo, please."

"Very well."

They had reached the front porch when Jenny Batey came running along from the kitchen with a tray of cutlery.

"More visitors, eh?" she exclaimed. Eduardo looked round. "My! You can come any time, young man. Keep a place for me next to you." She giggled. "I'll pop these on the table and tell them 'another chair'."

"I not intrude on picnic."

"You can intrude all you like, eh, Ralph?" She tapped his arm. "Business acquaintance, eh?"

"Eduardo is from Spain, Mrs Batey. He is steward to the de Villena family."

"Oh my." She ran on to set down her tray and returned to eye him up and down with a very knowing look. "Pleased to meet you, I'm sure, Eduardo."

He bowed over her hand. Ralph thought, He'll think her a servant, but her use of my Christian name has puzzled him.

"Please will you tell my mother he is here and that my wife is coming down, but I beg no one to inquire into the news he has brought – to spare her feelings."

She scuttled to the kitchen, no doubt to say a great deal more than that.

Rosie and Peggy now brought out plates and napkins. Their starched aprons and little caps would reassure Eduardo of *their* status. Ralph asked Rosie to go up to "my lady".

Now Mateo spotted Eduardo from the treehouse, slithered down the little ladder and came running over.

He clasped Eduardo's hand and addressed him in Spanish. The girls followed and they soon formed a chattering group moving away from the others.

John came up. "Hey, Uncle Ralph, Maria says he's their steward and he'll have come all the way from Spain to tell about the execution. This is going to spoil the party, isn't it?"

Ralph considered him. "Tell me, John, why do you start every remark with 'hey'?"

"Oh, do I?" He looked momentarily surprised. "But hey, it's exciting having someone in the family actually executed for a murder – a murder he didn't do himself but sort of contrived it to happen."

His words struck Ralph like a knife. He backed towards the house wall and sat down on the bench. Here was this child – so like Frank, with his unruly fair hair and round face, but pugnacious, which Frank never was – speaking of an execution in the family. Has he forgotten the tale of his father's near-hanging? Lily skated over it, she said, but will I ever escape while my own wife is plagued with a like guilt?

He drew John towards him, and his eyes searched his face. If Frank had died, this boy would not be here.

"Hey, what's up, Uncle Ralph?"

He had to smile. "Nothing. Just remember that what has happened is a very serious thing and will not be mentioned during the party."

"No – I mean, yes, it must be awful for Aunt that she made a joke to a fellow and he did something which means he's dead now. If she comes to the party I'll think she's a real brick, and I'll tell her so."

It was a fresh way to see it, but Ralph said, "Do. She'd like that."

It was a while before she came down. The plates of food were already laid out – slices of ham, hard-boiled eggs, stotty cakes oozing butter, little fancy cakes and pastries, and two baskets piled with fruit.

Mateo said to John, "We can't eat in the treehouse. That would be rude to our guest."

"Just the sweet things. He won't mind that. And I've already said Lu and Baby Bear are to come up, but we'll wait to see if your ma comes."

She made her entrance at that moment. Paint and powder had covered signs of weeping, but she had put on a black silk gown with buttoned bodice and full skirt that accentuated her stately figure.

"She's gone into mourning for that cousin," John muttered. "Not very festive." But he went to meet her. "Hey, Aunt Sophie, you look mighty grand. I'm sorry about the news you've had, but I think you're a brick for coming to the party."

She raised her eyebrows. "A brick? What you mean, 'brick'?"

"Brave. Very brave."

She let her gaze fall on his upturned face with a sort of wonder, Ralph saw. She laid a hand on his shoulder, lifted her head, arched her back and moved with him to the table. "Good afternoon to you all."

After that, though her dignified presence dominated the gathering, the party proceeded according to tradition: conversation over the savoury course, followed by the sweetmeats taken into the treehouse by the young people. Lily managed to keep her father quiet while Jenny tried to flirt with Eduardo, but Frank drew him into talk about the progress of the railways in Spain. This reminded Ralph of the paper in his pocket. He had feared Sophia would utterly collapse when he broke the news but, hearing it from Eduardo and cheered by John's word, she was giving one of her best performances. Was it possible, then, that he could survive if Horsley spread rumours that his wife had once tried to have him murdered so she could marry another? If he dared to take her about and she could act both the grand lady and the devoted wife, would people say, "That can't be true. The old lover might have plotted such a thing, but not Lady Barton"?

It was June, so the daylight stayed long after Frank, Lily, John and the Bateys had departed for the train to Newcastle. Ralph had seen Sophia take

John aside when goodbyes were being said. She pinned a piece of ribbon on his coat.

"You are my knight errant. I give you my favour. You defend me anywhere and everywhere." She kissed his cheek.

He skipped about singing, to the tune of D'ye Ken John Peel?, "I'll buy me a sword with a blade so true and fight for this lady no matter who…" the rest of the tune being to *la la la* as his inventiveness ran out.

Maria ran after him calling, "You're Baby Bear's knight too. Don't you forget that!" He waved a hand to her and called back, "I'll write a song for you too."

The evening was so lovely they decided to stay outside. There was beer for the men and lemonade for the ladies, but Sophia soon rose, saying, "What a day! I keep up spirits for your birthday, dear boy, but now I seek my bed. Are you not weary from travelling, Eduardo?"

He looked startled and shook his head. "It pleasant here, my lady. I tell young vizconde about estate. He ask me questions, and Sir Ralph."

She inclined her head and went into the house.

On an impulse Ralph said, "I'll show you around our premises, Eduardo, if you would like a little exercise."

He jumped up eagerly and they walked round to the stables. There Ralph suddenly turned and faced him. "I want you to be totally honest with me. Have you ever been my wife's lover?"

"Oh Sir Ralph!" The man's complexion was too brown to show blushes, but he broke into a sweat.

"If you are honest, I will not be angry."

He gulped a few times, thought for a moment, then shook his head. "Not lover, no. Different thinking in Spain. I servant, she give order. I obey." He looked round at the horses as if they might help him out. "She say I have good hands but then – you see – more. After Don Juan left house – little time – then she need."

"She was Juan's lover?"

"Oh sir, we speak of the condesa."

"Very well. You needn't answer that. Were you questioned about the murder of Richard Bell when the Garda Civil recently took up the case?"

"Oh yes, Sir Ralph." This was a safe subject. "I tell them. May '41. I footman then. I see Guido and two men in courtyard – back part – like here. Sanchez brothers. When I young boy in town they older – little bit – always in trouble."

"You saw Guido give them money?"

"Yes, something – perhaps."

"And Conde Juan – as he liked to call himself?"

"Not see there, but he and Guido…" He locked his thumbs together.

"Did you see them executed?"

He shuddered. "No, Sir Ralph."

"You were quickly elevated to steward after they escaped to France?"

He looked uncomfortable. "My lady test many servants." He tapped the side of his head. "Good school. Me top scholar. She show me – how you say – ropes? I understand quick." He shook his head. "Not boast – hard in English."

Ralph smiled and clapped him on the shoulder. "You are doing well. I like your honesty and your modesty. We will return to the others. I'd like Mateo to spend some time with you about the finances of the estate. He is a very good classical scholar, but I have lately explained to him the workings of a modern business, and now he wants to understand the finances of owning land, the state of the tenants, the produce – everything, in fact. Can you stay a few days?"

He held up three fingers. "I hope this too. I bring – accounts, books?"

"Ledgers?"

He grinned. "Ledgers, good word – two, three years' ledgers."

"Good man. Explain them in Spanish to Mateo. My Spanish is tolerable but I am more comfortable in English."

Eduardo nodded and tapped his own chest in agreement.

They rounded the corner of the house and saw Mateo in talk with his grandmother while Jack nodded on the bench.

She got up. "It's cool now. Rosie and Peggy have gone home. They cleared everything up and prepared Eduardo's room. Wake up, Jack. We're going in."

Ralph was thinking, There is more I could ask this young man. Tomorrow I will gain deeper insight into their lives in Madrid and Galicia. That woman is soiled goods. I am condemned for my sins to live with her, but the more I can understand, the better I shall tolerate her. He took the newspaper from his pocket and put it on the kitchen fire. When he went up, he found Sophia asleep with wet cheeks.

In the three days of Eduardo's stay she was quietly dignified, but Ralph knew she dreaded what he might learn from Eduardo as he and Mateo walked with him about the grounds. She had no need to be fearful. Eduardo admired her too much to believe her guilty of anything but too great a desire for male company. He blamed Juan in everything. Juan had neglected the estate but had made money with Guido's smuggling racket, and could offer the condesa security – *if* she could marry him. So he secretly plotted the murder. When it went wrong, of course, she guessed what he had *tried* to do and dismissed him. Skating over her elevation of himself, he admitted she sought high society. "She bloomed at court, but I come from the countryside," he said, talking more freely in Spanish. "My grandfather was a tenant to the de Villena family and I found work as a footman, but my heart was in the land, how it was being worked." He shook his head sadly. "Spanish noblemen do not interest themselves in agriculture. It is our shame. I want to encourage good work on the land so it can show a profit and reduce rent for the tenants. I have fertilised the soil this year and we will do better. I have shown the young vizconde the ledgers."

On the third morning, when Eduardo was packing his bags, Mateo said to Ralph, "Papa, I am so happy. Now I can trust him to run the estate till I can take charge of it."

"You…" Ralph heard the words like an icy blast. "You would wish to live in Spain when you have taken your degree?"

Mateo looked a little dashed. "Mostly I feel more English than Spanish, but I have a duty there to manage the land, for the sake of those that live upon it and depend on it."

"Of course. I feel the same about the mines I own and my shares in railways." Do I? he wondered. Is that truly honest? He hurried on, "But deputies can do the work. My solicitor can be trusted in my absence. Owning land is more romantic. Sheradon Grange is precious to me, but I put it in your grandmother's name. I own only Heron Mansions and a few other properties in Newcastle." He finished a little bitterly, "I must secure these to your sisters for their marriage portions if you are to be a Spanish count with vast acres."

Mateo looked at him earnestly. "Oh Papa, you have taught me so much, and it will never be wasted. Of course I will spend time in England. Travel is going to be so much easier and quicker as engineers like Uncle Frank make improvements to trains and steamships. Yes, please leave the girls your property in Newcastle."

"And there is your mother. She will wish to live as the dowager in your great mansion. She is still young in years—"

"But she says she can never leave here. She is afraid to go to Spain."

"The fear may pass."

"I would be afraid for her to come. But I trust *you* would come, Papa."

Ralph had hoped for that, though it was hard to imagine burdening his mother with Sophia for a matter of weeks or months. "I would be delighted to see the place and visit Santiago again. I could look upon that magnificent cathedral under happier circumstances."

"Yes indeed." Mateo looked radiant, but Ralph felt only a wistful longing for a freedom which might never be his while *she* lived.

As they were talking outside, Jack brought round the carriage to take Eduardo to the station, and Sophia appeared in the porch, dressed for a journey.

"I see Eduardo as far as Newcastle." She stated it as a settled fact.

"What? You will do nothing of the kind." Would she ever come back? What had she in mind? Elope to France with him as his wife?

"Oh yes. He so good to come so far."

"We could all go," Mateo broke in. "I like the train ride."

Ralph knew he had work he could do there. "Very well. I'll get my coat." He was thinking, I will visit some tenants and show Mateo how I care for them.

Mateo ran to tell his grandmother in the kitchen. Jack went up to the attic to carry Eduardo's bags. They came down together, and Ralph wondered briefly if Eduardo had ever understood who Jack was.

Mateo came back with his grandmother, and Eduardo bowed to her many times to thank her for her hospitality.

Sophia muttered to Ralph as she climbed first into the carriage, "I want only little time with him. He *my* steward."

The train journey was uncomfortable because she was cross. She couldn't embrace or kiss Eduardo at the quayside as she would have liked, Ralph thought. But the first person he saw, disembarking from the very vessel Eduardo was to sail in, was Richard Bell.

Mateo had seen him too. "Don't let Mamma see him," he whispered.

Then Eduardo exclaimed, "Why, there is Señor Bell, who was at the trial!" He hurried over to him and shook his hand.

Sophia, of course, looked round. "Oh no! Keep him away from me." But Richard Bell, a porter struggling behind with his luggage, came over, all smiles.

"Well, Lady Barton, how delightful to see you and Sir Ralph and my old friend Mateo, grown taller in the air of Cambridge. I see Señor Casares has preceded me in bringing the news from Spain. I lingered many days longer to visit my father's grave and pass some time with the Garda officer who first took an interest in the death of my friend. He has restored to me copies of all his letters, and so my great crusade for justice is all but at an end." He smiled at Sophia with his eyebrows raised. "You are, perhaps, returning on the train I hope to catch."

Ralph had gripped her arm as she drooped against him. The man's words had taken the strength from her legs. He said quickly, "No we have business in the town. My brother lives here now, and we will lunch with him. Good day, Mr Bell."

He was not disconcerted. He bowed and withdrew, giving some orders to the porter about his luggage. The crowds gathering on the quayside hid him from view, and Sophia straightened her back and spoke as if no such encounter had taken place.

"We are early for your embarking, Eduardo. Let us find an eating place and take some refreshment."

Mateo held Ralph back so she and Eduardo could walk ahead. "Did you note what Mr Bell said, Father? His crusade is *all but* at an end. And his look at her was so full of meaning. What could he have said to the Garda officer? That he has one more culprit to catch? I fear we have not heard the last from that man."

Ralph shrugged. "He can do nothing. Your mother has said her last word on the matter, and Eduardo is positive that the plot was solely Juan's. I pray God that this whole nightmare is over with his death and Guido's, and very soon Eduardo's departure – if only she will not mourn *his* absence. I know I must be very tender with her and give her more of my time."

Mateo nodded vigorously and they followed Sophia and Eduardo into a coffee shop, where no mention was made of meeting Richard Bell. Sophia held up when the time for parting from Eduardo came. He bowed over her hand, which his lips momentarily touched, and Ralph saw her whole body quiver, but she said coolly in Spanish that she was grateful for his visit but he need not come in person again to make his reports. That would be a needless expense.

Ralph drew a long breath of relief. Could she truly be content with an end to her Spanish life for all time? I must expect jealousy if I ever go with Mateo to see his land. But now I must make England happy for her.

Chapter 26

Ralph

A new life begins now, Ralph thought, as they walked away from the quayside, and Sophia remarked, "You say we lunch at your brother's. Are they expecting us?"

He had thought of heading for Heron Mansions, but this might be better.

He said, "No, my dear, but I wager they'd be pleased to see us as we are in town. You have not visited their new place, I believe?"

"Will Frank not be at work and John at school?"

"Not on Saturday mornings, as many schools do, and Frank likes to spend time with him then. We can call, and if we are invited to stay, well and good."

There were cab stands on the quayside but no cabs about for the moment, so they watched the activity on the river like any normal family. A cab arrived and they made their way out of the town, remarking on the valley of the Ouseburn river as they crossed it to pass through Byker and into Heaton, where they entered a pleasant street of terraced brick houses with ornamental stonework over the windows which gave it an air of gentility. There were small trees and shrubs too in the tiny gardens in front, and many had window boxes planted with geraniums. Lily was out watering hers, and looked astonished as the cab drew up.

When Ralph descended and helped Sophia out, she was backed against the house wall in a state of nervous shock. Mateo followed and greeted her with a cheery "Surprise visit, Aunt Lily!" which put her more at ease.

"Dear child," said Sophia, stepping up and kissing her cheek, "we were in the town and have come to see your pretty little house."

"Oh yes, how lovely." She dropped the watering can on the ground and pushed the front door wide. "Please come in. Frank and John will be back for lunch shortly. They are playing cricket up on the park. You must join us. I'll just see – I made a salad." She directed them into the front sitting room and ran back along the passage.

Ralph followed her. "Don't bother yourself, Lily."

A modest bowl of lettuce and watercress with chopped celery and radishes sat on the kitchen table. Three hard-boiled eggs lay in a dish, and a rough-shaped loaf stood on the breadboard with a crock of butter beside it. The back door was open to the sunny yard, where three chairs had been set out. John's school blazer and Frank's jacket were draped on two of the chairs, and the back door to a lane was slightly ajar. All spoke of a hot June day and a spontaneous urge to play cricket.

"I can add enough for us all," Lily said, putting three more eggs into a pan as she spoke. "It's so nice to see you."

Ralph felt a longing to pick her up and hug her. She was small, demure and predictable, all opposites of Sophia; and an era ago he had believed this sweet thing was his for the asking. These were distracting thoughts. He shook them off.

"Actually," she said, "I was looking out for the pie man. I can get six, not three, and we'll be all right." She looked at the loaf and giggled. "I can't make bread like your mother's. Would Sophia like some lemonade? I have a bottle keeping cool in a crock behind the shed where it's shady."

"Have you enough for us all? It's a thirsty day."

"Oh yes, it's a big bottle. I can hardly lift it." She set some glasses on a tray while he went out for the bottle.

They were just carrying it through to the sitting room when they heard a tinkling bell in the street. "It's the pieman," she said.

Ralph set the bottle on a little table in the hall and fished in his pocket.

"Here, Matty, run and get six pies." He gave him a sixpence.

Matty ran. Lily took the tray of glasses and laid them on a side table in front of Sophia. "Pray refresh yourself, Lady Barton. It's only lemonade."

"Delicious – but 'Lady Barton' from you to me? Are we not sisters?"

"Oh yes, I'm sorry. You see, I was in service once, and bringing in the tray it just slipped out."

Sophia gave a merry little laugh. "Not the tray from those dear little hands, I glad to see."

Ralph wondered how far this cloying sweetness would go as Matty came back with the pies and they heard the voices of Frank and John in the kitchen.

"Hey, Ma, why have you put three more eggs to boil?"

John came bounding in as he said it, and stopped with mouth agape. Taking them all in, he took a step towards Sophia and made a flourishing bow.

"My lady, I have returned from jousting with this warrior" – pointing at Frank – "and soundly beaten him."

She held out two fingers. "My knight, you shall be rewarded. Pray drink a health with me to your next bout."

"There won't be another one," Frank said. "He's lost our two cricket balls hitting sixes into the bushes. We've spent the last half-hour looking for them. Good morning, Sophia, good morning, Ralph, Matty. This is an unexpected pleasure. Do I see lemonade? I'm mighty thirsty."

They all drank till the bottle was empty. Ralph, wearing suit and waistcoat, looked enviously at Frank's rolled-up shirt sleeves and bronzed arms. Lily scuttled out to see to the eggs.

With a little rearrangement of furniture and finding plates and cutlery, they were all able to sit round the table in the kitchen.

"Charming!" Sophia said, looking out at the yard. Lily had brightened it with pots of flowers, and beyond the high back wall were trees. A big shed occupied the right-hand wall, leaving the small shady space before the larder window.

"Frank's workshop," Lily said. "He built it himself. It keeps the sun off the larder."

They chatted about their move and all they had done since. A little talk strayed back to the birthday party and Eduardo's visit.

It was Sophia who closed it off by explaining their presence in Newcastle.

"We thought we would see him aboard his steamship for London. How he go after that no matter. Here we are and so good company."

The word 'Spain', Ralph noted, was not even mentioned.

They were considering whether the afternoon was too hot for a walk up the lane where it was almost countryside when there came a knock at the front door.

Lily jumped. "Oh Frank, can it be the coalman come for his money?"

John sprang up. "I'll go."

He was back in a moment. "It's the Carlisle man, Uncle Ralph, asking for you. Shall I let him in?"

"God in heaven!" Ralph got to his feet. "How did he find me here?"

"You told him we were lunching with your brother," Mateo said.

"And how did he know the place? Well, I will get rid of him."

His heart was sinking to his boots as he went into the hall. That whole episode was *not* dead and buried. He clicked the kitchen door firmly behind him after a quick glance at Sophia's face showed him the horror in her eyes.

Richard Bell was waiting patiently on the doorstep, not wearing his smile.

Without a word, Ralph drew him into the sitting room and sat him in a chair. He looked up sadly.

"You are not pleased to see me?" Ralph shook his head. "You will be less pleased when I tell you what I've done."

Ralph took a chair opposite him. At least this was a different opening, but not auspicious. "Well?"

"You may have a visit shortly from the *Newcastle Courant*."

That was like ice down his back. "How is that?"

Richard Bell wriggled uncomfortably. It was the first time Ralph had seen him not in command. "Do you recall, Sir Ralph, that a previous article in that paper was helpful to me in my earlier investigations?"

"Perfectly."

"I have since been in contact with Mr Roy, the editor, about doing a piece on the need for international cooperation on crime. He wanted a local connection, but I was reluctant to use the real case of my father. Now today, when I saw you at the quayside, I thought it would save me a journey if I could catch up with you in Newcastle for a final visit to round off my great campaign."

Ralph snapped, "There was no need for such a thing." He remembered how Mateo had commented on the words 'all but at an end'.

"I do see such a need. So I resolved to visit you at your brother's, where you said you would be lunching. No cab came quickly enough for me to follow you, so I bethought me of my acquaintance Mr Roy. I went to his office and inquired if he knew the whereabouts of Mr Frank Heron, engineer. He said there had been an advertisement placed for an apprentice for Trace and Heron Engineers, and he gave me this address."

"Very fortuitous for you. So what is the regretful thing you have done?"

"Mr Roy is no fool. He said he had helped me out twice now so I owed him a favour, and he was short for next week's paper. I was in haste to find you and your wife here, so I pulled from my pocket a Spanish paper I had purchased, with a report of the trial of Don Juan de Villena."

"Hell's flames!"

"Nay, it was the mention of Juan and Guido living in France out of the reach of Spanish justice that I thought I could use to illustrate my original idea."

"With yourself as the local connection?"

"Only if he insisted – but Roy looked at the paper and said he wanted to know what it said, so I translated it for him. I didn't know that a clerk behind a screen in his office was taking it down in shorthand. The man came round the screen saying, 'I got it all, Mr Roy.' Then Roy smirked at me. 'I smell a strong local connection. Don't trouble yourself with a worldwide system of law. I'll follow this up myself.' So I fear a reporter will soon be here. I apologise most humbly."

"We must get away at once." Ralph moved towards the door.

"He'll follow you home. Roy is a hunter on the trail of a story."

"And you are no better. You have come here to stir things up again."

"I only wish to see your wife to close off the case."

"It is closed. I never want to see you again."

Richard Bell stood up. "Be glad you have eyes in your head to see anything, Sir Ralph. You are lucky not to be lying in a Spanish grave."

Ralph gulped. The wretched man can never see me without seeing his dead father. My anger is an affront to his memory. But he must not see Sophia. I will fend off reporters. She must not be knocked out of her new direction.

The kitchen door clicked. and John came at a run. "Ma says would Mr Bell like a drink of tea? We haven't any beer."

"I thank her, but I only wish for a word with her ladyship."

"Well, you can't. She doesn't want to see you. She nearly ran out of the back gate but I said I'd protect her. I'm her knight errant, you see."

"Very noble of you." Mr Bell said. "Give her that, then."

Ralph was distracted by the sight of a young man in the street looking at the house number. John had vanished again as he stepped back from the window.

"He's coming here. He must be the reporter."

Mr Bell looked round. "He is. I saw him at the *Courant* office."

"Damnation. He's seen us. But I shan't answer the door. He'll hardly dare to break in."

"The door's on the latch. The boy left it like that."

The young man tapped smiling at the window. He mouthed 'Sir Ralph Barnet?', raising his eyebrows, and then simply walked in.

At the same moment there was an eruption from the kitchen. Sophia's voice howling, Frank's and Mateo's voices soothing her and then John bursting out, yelling, "That was a mean trick. That paper's upset her." Then he saw there was a stranger in the hall. "What? Who are *you*?"

Ralph grasped that Richard Bell had handed John the Spanish newspaper. The scars on her soul would be inflamed tenfold. Ignoring the reporter, he muttered to Bell, "Are you proud of your handiwork?"

"The surgeon's knife hurts but can root out the poison."

The reporter was grinning at John and holding out his hand, "Bob Hobday of the *Courant*."

John tentatively took it. "John Heron." Then he withdrew it quickly. "Hey, you've not come to hound my poor aunt too, have you?"

"The *Courant* never *hounds* anybody."

Ralph took charge. "My wife is unwell. I must insist that you both leave this house immediately."

"I only want to ask the condesa a question – and you too, Sir Ralph."

Sophia herself emerged from the kitchen, with both Frank and Mateo trying to restrain her.

"Where are you, husband? You seen this paper? Send these men away. What they bring is all lies."

Ralph took her in his arms and held her tightly. They were now crowded in the small hallway. Over her shoulder, he glared at the two men and pointed them to the front door with a jerk of his head.

Bob Hobday said, "I have an account of the trial of Juan de Villena. Can your lady confirm he lied about her guilt? That's all I want to know."

"Of course he did," Ralph snapped at him. "Juan was the villain and is rightly punished. Print that if you print anything. Who will care in Newcastle about a Spanish criminal? Now get out. You too, Mr Bell. What more can you seek?"

"The truth. That's all I have ever sought."

Bob Hobday did go out, and waved his hand to someone up the street. A cab pulled up outside but, motioning the driver to stay there, he came back in.

Ralph had helped Sophia to an armchair in the sitting room and was tenderly caressing her hands.

"Say nothing to them, my darling. They will be gone in a moment." *Love*, his mother had said. *Only love.* Sophia looked into his eyes in wonder.

Lily came in with a cup of tea and knelt beside her. "Sophia, dear, drink this and you'll feel better."

Frank addressed the two men still hanging about by the open front door. "This is my house. I ask you to leave immediately."

John had disappeared for a moment, and now he came back brandishing a wooden sword. "Yes, off you go."

Mateo shook his head at him, but John was fired up.

"One more question," Bob Hobday called into the room. "That Juan said he was your wife's lover, Sir Ralph. Can you confirm that?"

Sophia screamed again and half-rose from the chair.

"Never," shouted Ralph. "This lady is my loyal wife. Get out and print that."

John ran at Bob Hobday and drove him back outside across the tiny garden. The sword caught him right in the groin. He doubled up with pain and grabbed John by his mop of hair.

"You little villain!" He whirled him to the ground and his head struck the edge of the pavement. The startled cab horse reared and its hoof caught John on the forehead. Hobday, scarcely glancing at him, scrambled into the cab, and it rattled away down the street.

It was over in seconds.

Sophia sprang from her chair and pressed her face to the window.

"John not moving."

Frank, Mateo and Richard Bell struggled in the doorway to get to him. Ralph helped Lily up. She had been knocked sideways, upsetting the tea over her dress.

"John!" she gasped when she could look from the window, as the others gathered round him. Mateo, aghast, was shaking his head over the still body.

Sophia screamed, "He dead, my little hero! There is a great wound on his head. No, oh no. It is Juan's curse. John die! For *me?* No. Never." She was panting, with huge sobs tearing at her. "Dear God, make him live. I confess. I am dirt. I confess my wickedness. I am dirt. Why they all be good to me? Oh God, kill me and spare the child. Kill *me*. I am all lies. Ralph, Ralph, tell the world."

He had been moving to follow Lily who, white-faced and dripping tea down her bodice, had rushed to join the others. Sophia's stream of words arrested him.

"I not live if the boy dead." She turned and grabbed at him. "Ralph, kill me. I try to kill you. I lie always. I not loyal wife." She peered up into his eyes. He had to look at her, not at what was going on outside. The dread that the boy might die was, for one moment, pushed away. He could see her soul bare, laid open. In that second he knew he yearned to love her. "Kill me," she cried. "Strangle me. I rotten. You love me! No. Not fit to love. I murderer. I say it. Murderer. Deserve death." She slithered down and finished in a heap on the floor.

Frank and Richard Bell were heaving John into the room, with Lily trying to hold a handkerchief to his bleeding forehead. Mateo followed, saying, "Thank God, he was only knocked out, I think."

John's eyes opened and were darting about the room.

"Hey," he mumbled, "what happened? What's up with Aunt Sophie?"

She raised her head. "Is that his voice?"

Ralph lifted her up and draped her back into her chair as John was lowered onto the sofa opposite her.

She stared at him and then crossed herself over and over again.

"Your aunt thought you were dead." Ralph, sick with relief for John and for her words buzzing in his brain, sank down on the upright chair next to her and clasped her hands in his. She had confessed. From deep inside him he felt tears welling up, and he turned his head to hide them from the others. He was aware of Lily sending Mateo for a bowl of water and John trying to explain that he had lain still because if he opened his eyes the world went round and round.

Then he became aware of Richard Bell standing before Sophia's chair and looking down at her. Astonished, he saw tears pouring down the man's face as he gulped for words.

"Lady Barton, Condesa de Villena." She looked up at him, her eyes wide. She scrabbled at Ralph's hands and held them tight. Bell heaved a deep breath and struggled on. "It's over, my lady. Finished. Thank you. It is enough. I heard your words. I saw you in a heap at my feet. Why should I seek more? The others are dead." He turned his eyes to Ralph. "Forgive me, good sir, please forgive me, as I forgive you for living. I have brought you much trouble, but in the end we have the truth. My father can rest in peace. *I* can rest. You never wanted to see me again. You never will now. I see you have tears too."

Ralph had risen and faced him. On a sudden mutual impulse, they embraced. Ralph knew a moment of incredible happiness.

As they drew apart, Richard Bell turned again to Sophia, who was weeping now as if she could never stop.

"My lady, I must say one thing more. When I was speaking with the officer of the Garda Civil before I left Spain, I said to him, 'My mission is not finished till the condesa admits her share of guilt'" – Sophia, her eyes riveted on him, nodded her head in a desperate gesture – "'but if she does, I beg you to close the case. I will forgive her, and I would be grateful if Spanish justice could do the same. Juan and Guido never repented. The condesa was a troubled, confused woman at that time, and I believe Juan told her of his plot and she consented. If I write to you that she is shriven, will you, as a good Catholic, lift from her any more fear of punishment in her native country?' The officer agreed, and we shook hands on it."

Ralph saw that Sophia couldn't speak but understood him. She could only nod a few times more.

Bell turned towards the sofa, composed now, and looked at John, sitting up as Lily bandaged his head and Frank gazed at him with heartfelt thankfulness.

"John Heron," said Bell, "you were never wounded in a better cause. As her knight errant, you have served your aunt well." He looked about at all the faces and stopped at Mateo. "I suggest you do not take your mother to Spain for a long while. Why not Cambridge when you achieve your First in Classics?"

Mateo reddened and didn't answer. Ralph could see he was overwhelmed by all that had happened.

Richard Bell made a bow encompassing them all. "I take my leave."

Lily said, "I hardly know – but will you not have some refreshment, sir?"

"No, I thank you. I shall walk with a light heart the few miles to my train to Carlisle. God bless you all." He found his hat on a peg in the hall and strode out with springing steps, passing the window with a smile and a wave.

Mateo went at once to his mother's side and knelt by her.

"I heard you, Mother. You were in a panic for John?"

She shook her head in slow exaggerated motion. "Too many lies."

"Did you hope – if you said it – John would recover?"

"God and the blessed Virgin would be kind to him." Ralph thought the words were being dragged out of her. "Juan cursed me." Her eyes were huge as she looked into her son's face.

"But is it *true*? We all heard you. You called yourself a—"

"Murderer. Yes." She burst into a flow of Spanish. "Your mother tried to have your father murdered. You have to believe that. You will never want to see me again. I will have to go away. Your sisters will be told, and they will hate me. I can see how it will be. I will have to go into a nunnery." She turned her head to Ralph and relinquished his hands, pushing them away. "Don't pretend to be kind to me. You hate me. How can you not hate me?"

Frank and Lily were helping John up. "You must rest in your bed."

"Must I? This is exciting, but they are talking Spanish now. Did someone bring my sword in? I'd like to fight for Baby Bear too one day."

Mateo said, "It's in the hall, John, but you know you really hurt that man."

"He deserved it." As he passed Sophia's chair he said, "Aunt Sophie, I still think you were joking with that Juan fellow all those years ago. You're feeling bad because he took you at your word, and then he pretended to be innocent and blamed you because he didn't want to be executed. You will let me be your knight errant still?"

Frank and Lily got him out of the room while he was still talking.

Sophia broke into fresh sobs. "So sweet boy, but see Mateo, see Ralph, he muddled with the lies. It is truth, truth with me now. I shout it to the world and then silence, silence in a nunnery. I never forget my sin."

"No, Mamma. Don't talk so. You heard what Richard Bell said. He forgives you, and the law in Spain will forgive you. He used the word 'shriven'. You know what you must do now. You must speak the words of repentance and hear God's word of forgiveness."

He stood up and faced Ralph. "Father, on the way back to the train we must take Mother to the new great Catholic Church in Newcastle – St Mary's."

She sat up straight and crossed herself. "Yes, yes. Mateo, you are right. The priest there not know me at all. I speak all truth to him. Only truth."

Ralph nodded slowly. He had always struggled to reconcile her behaviour with her faith. It might be no more than superstition, but what had just happened was real. "If John is recovering, we will go."

Sophia sat quite still now. He pressed her hand and ran upstairs to find Frank. John's was the small front bedroom over the hallway. He could hear Frank telling him to try and sleep. "You're getting a bump the size of a cricket ball on the back of your head."

Lily came out of the larger back bedroom, fastening the buttons on a fresh dress. "Yes, that blow was worse than the horse's kick. Oh Ralph!" She flushed up. "I didn't see you. Come to see the patient?"

"Yes, and take our leave. But a thought has just struck me. You should complain to the *Courant* about that reporter. He used excessive force on a ten-year-old boy and drove off without so much as a glance to see what harm he had done."

"He *was* provoked," Lily murmured.

"No, you're right. I will complain," Frank said. "His whole behaviour was rude and pushy. I really thought for a ghastly moment he'd killed John. He was out cold for a few seconds."

"Will you come with me to the *Courant* office then? I think we can get that story stopped."

"Yes, if it helps. I certainly don't want *my* name dragged in."

Ralph put his head round John's door. "We're leaving. Take care for a few days, and mind what you do with that sword."

"Yes, Uncle Ralph. There's a deal more I want to know about you and Aunt Sophie, but I'll have to wait, I suppose."

"Yes, a long time."

They went downstairs and found Mateo had run to the public house on the corner of the road to Newcastle to inquire the whereabouts of a cab stand. "There's none out here," he was told, "but we can hire you a carriage and driver."

"It's coming as soon as it's hitched up," he said, "but it'll be horribly expensive, I'm afraid."

"No matter. You've done well. How is your mother?"

"She's tidied herself up and put on her hat. She's very calm."

"Good." For the moment, that was all Ralph wanted from her.

Frank buttoned his shirtsleeves and put on his coat and hat. The carriage, a small open one big enough for the four of them, drew up. Lily came out to wave them off.

"I'm sorry it's been an upsetting day for you, Sophia. John gets too enthusiastic, but he will be all right now." Sophia gave her a slow wave.

Lily picked up the watering can from the tiny garden as they drove off. It was an age, Ralph thought, since they had arrived to see her tending her geraniums.

In the town, he asked the driver to stop one street away from the *Courant* office. He didn't want Sophia to see the sign, or J. P. Roy to see her from his window.

In the event, his task and Frank's was easier than they expected. Mr Roy was not surprised to see them.

"Ah, Mr Heron, father of the injured boy. How is he? Hobday was mighty worried."

Frank didn't make light of it, Ralph was pleased to see, but Roy quickly interrupted to say, "I'm dismissing Hobday. He has a 'bull in a china shop' approach. He also produced nothing useful. No story in a happy marriage. Luckily a rejected lover has thrown himself off the Tyne Bridge, so we have something much more exciting for next week's issue than a couple of villains getting their comeuppance in Spain – even if *you* were the target, Sir Ralph. Too much muddle in that tale, and too long ago."

As they walked back to the carriage Frank repeated, "'*Luckily* a man has killed himself'! Does the profession of journalism coarsen the holder?"

Ralph, solely absorbed with relief at the outcome of the meeting, shrugged his shoulders.

They found the carriage, where Mateo was absorbed in watching his mother. She was tense but quiet, her hands clasped before her face, the fingers interlocked.

When they reached the church, she looked up and her eyes were drawn from its grand façade to the top of the tall tower. She rose and put her hands in Ralph's as he helped her down and led her to the main doorway. There she checked him.

"Stay here. I go in alone and find priest."

He was surprised, but released her, and she slipped inside. He looked at Frank and Mateo, now standing on the pavement. "I can't tell how long she will be."

"I'll travel back to Heaton with the carriage then," Frank said. "Nay, I can pay his fare." Ralph was pressing money into his hand.

"I insist. All this – disrupting your day – even John's hurt – is my wife's doing, and therefore my responsibility. I can only pray that she is making a new beginning." He grasped Frank's hand and he climbed in. The driver turned the carriage in the street, incurring angry abuse from impeded traffic. They could see his responding gesture and hear his laughter.

Mateo said, "Can we go inside and look? We're in the sun here and I'd like to see the place."

Ralph agreed readily. The afternoon was as hot as ever, and as soon as they entered the coolness of stone walls he slipped into the back pew and sat down, emotionally and physically spent. He saw Mateo go to the holy water, cross himself on the forehead and genuflect towards the high altar. Then his eyes closed and he fell asleep.

When he woke, Sophia and Mateo were standing in the aisle next to the pew, not speaking. He brushed his face with his fingertips and shook himself. Sophia immediately turned to him.

"I see you so tired, my husband, and I think what you endure in our marriage. I think I never love you so much as now asleep."

He got to his feet and looked into her brimming eyes. The moisture and the light from many candles made them glow like dark pools.

He knew he could break down into a flood of weeping, so he said with a sniff, "Perhaps I should stay asleep then, eh?" And managed a smile.

"If we go now," Mateo said, "we can catch the early evening train. Do you think you can walk there, Mother?"

"Of course." She put her hand on Ralph's arm and guided his reluctant feet outside.

Passing round the side of the church, they could see the work in progress on the new station building.

Mateo said brightly, "Uncle Frank told me it's to be in the classical style and could be the finest station in England. And the new bridge over the river will carry the railway, with a road suspended below. That's never been done before."

Ralph wondered if Mateo was talking to hide his embarrassment. He must sense the intensity of emotion between his father and mother. It was there in her hand on his arm, and in their eyes meeting and not observing the masons and scaffolders at work.

Can this last? was the question going through Ralph's head. I long to take home to Mother a truly new woman.

On the train Mateo made comments on the scenes passing the window but, rousing no interest, he soon lapsed into silence.

At last, as they set off to walk to Sheradon Grange, Sophia said, "The priest say I not to be nun. He say, 'Good wife and mother. God give you duties. Do them.'"

"No penance?" Mateo said. Ralph saw puzzlement in his still-young features. What a deal of life the boy still had to live through!

"That is penance," Sophia said. "Live with all who know my sin. That is penance."

Ralph understood. For him to come back and live among his family on home ground had been a daring act, which he had approached with brazen confidence. His Spanish adventure, marriage and fatherhood and the acquisition of wealth had all taken place since he had left home under a cloud. Still, he had not anticipated his own vulnerability. It was his task now to help Sophia, whose case was worse. Three men were dead, and the one she had wished dead was the one constantly by her side.

Mateo said nothing more, but Ralph saw him take his mother's hand and squeeze it as they walked on. It was pleasant walking. The evening was cooling, with a gentle westerly breeze on their hot faces. When they walked down the drive of Sheradon Grange, they saw all four left at home sitting on the bench waiting for them.

Jack said, "Eh, your mother and the girls has been worritting about you being so long. I wanted to meet each train with the carriage, but my angel wouldn't let me."

Ralph saw his mother was laughing. "*He* was worritted most. I guessed you'd be having a good day enjoying the delights of town for a change."

She was assessing Sophia's face after her farewell to Eduardo. Something about her look seemed to puzzle her. "All right, my dear?"

Maria was watching her too, with a wary expression. Lucia was skipping round her. "*I* was anxious, Mamma."

Sophia waved her hands to calm her. "I tell you all about today – soon. I cannot now." She looked at all their faces. "Not now. But soon. I have vowed it will be soon."

Then she ran into the house and up the stairs. Ralph heard an explosion of weeping. He looked at Mateo and murmured, "You see – penance." Then he turned to his mother and said, "No tears for Eduardo, Mother. I believe I have brought you a new woman, and my girls" – looking at them – "a new mother. Be very gentle with her."

They all nodded solemnly and went into the house to prepare supper.

Epilogue

Dee's grandchildren

Chapter 27

Santiago de Compostela, July 1855 (eight years later)

Mateo

Mateo looked up from the ledger's worrisome figures and gazed out over his stables to his fields stretching to humpy hills, baked brown under an unrelenting sun. He thought of Sheradon Grange with its green lawns and woods and its beloved people. For the second time, he had not been there on his birthday. 1854 had been a tumultuous year, with an insurrection in Spain and a disastrous fire on Tyneside in which his father lost several properties by the river. The Spanish government was still unsettled, and Mateo's last letter home had revealed his low spirits.

The evenings were sad and lonely. With a houseful of servants, he lacked companionship. He thought often about two young ladies he saw at Mass every Sunday, the daughter and niece of the Conde de Mereno, whose land abutted his, but the conde spurned friendship with the de Villena family. Scandals were not easily forgotten. His daughter was beautiful, like her stately mother, but it was the smile of the niece that he treasured as they passed by. I will never know the lovely soul behind it, he mourned constantly.

He heard footsteps on the stairs and a tap on the door – the maid bringing him his evening glass of wine. There were two glasses on the tray.

"Please, sir, you have a visitor."

His heart sank. It could be another neighbouring landowner coming to complain that his ideas of educating the peasantry were revolutionary.

"Surprise!" cried a strong youthful voice, and a face with a huge grin looked round the door.

"John!" Mateo leapt up. "John, what on earth...? How wonderful!"

The maid put the tray down and scurried out.

Mateo flung his arms round his cousin and wept with joy at seeing a familiar face. Then he held him at arm's length and gazed at him. They were the same height now. He hadn't seen him for nearly two years. At nineteen, John was a man. His fair hair was still unruly, but his features were stronger.

"Are you alone?" Mateo looked through the open door.

John pushed it shut. "Quite alone, Matty. Spur of the moment." He laughed. "Here you are in sunny Spain with your head in dusty old account books. No wonder you sounded miserable in your last letter."

"That was to my family and Grandmamma."

"Maria showed it me. You don't mind?"

"Not a bit. Sit down and tell me about everybody. I can't believe you're here. You've taken my breath away. Have a glass of wine."

"Beer's more my drink, but since it's here..."

He gulped it down and smacked his lips.

"Heady stuff. Well, everyone's flourishing, mostly due to old Hurst's venture for slum children – what I've been working on the last two years. You know your ma was very fragile for a long time, keeping quiet at home, missing you at Cambridge, and even more when you came here and she daren't come with you." Mateo nodded. "Well, she's busy as a bee now, and your Pa is looking at her with new eyes. I'd say he's fallen in love with her all over again. Differently. Deep."

Mateo flushed with happiness. "What is she busy with?"

"This slum school. She's going about and getting people to subscribe to it, and I've seen her when I visit Grandmamma. They're all sewing, even Lucia, making clothes for the children. Maria brings a bundle to Newcastle and helps with the little ones. They play numbers and letters games while her knitting needles go like lighting. When summer's over she'll have woolly clothes for them all."

"You don't call her Baby Bear any more."

John laughed. "She's a fellow worker."

"She always wanted to be useful, but what you say about my father and mother makes me very happy. Tell me about this slum school. How many people work there? How do you pay them?"

John was surprised. "Why d'you ask that?"

"When I saw what you were planning in Newcastle at my last visit, I longed to do the same here. We have so much ignorance and poverty."

"Well, it was an old warehouse, you know, and I built the classroom walls under a craftsman's tuition. Now it's finished, Hurst said I could come here, and paid my expenses. Four teachers, like Maria, are volunteers."

"Are *you* going to teach?"

John laughed. "Hurst tested me on Class One when I was fifteen to see if I could ever take over his main school. He's in his seventies now. His verdict on my teaching was 'Too impatient. Too boisterous. Startles them.' So I'm still a general handyman, but mainly I go round the heads of industry who are prospering – like your da, now he's got his insurance after the fire – and I browbeat them into joining a trust to finance the school."

"I hope Father has helped with funds."

"Nobly. Oh, I was forgetting." John took off his coat and pulled up his shirt to reveal a money belt. "I have a banker's draft for you from him."

"Well, thank God for that!"

Mateo's fingers shook as he unfolded a draft for one hundred pounds.

"Praise be!" He crossed himself. "Funds are *my* problem. When I first came in '49 Eduardo showed me the accounts, neatly balanced. But he'd married Brigitta, and they have a growing family and now rent a house in town. He still stewards, but goes home at night, and then I mess up the books trying to find funds for the school. It's for the poor cottagers, the *camameiras*. There's a cottage and empty barn but it's taken more than our income to get them ready. Eduardo's not pleased."

"Ay, well, I'm here now. Maria said, 'Matty needs you.' So I told the parents and caught the next train."

"What are you saying, John? Do you mean you can stay a few weeks?"

"As long as you want me. My portmanteau's in the hall, waiting to know what room I'm to have in this castle."

Mateo broke down in tears again.

"Hey." John patted him on the shoulder. "I should have come sooner. You've had it rough. Wasn't it your first year when the vines were diseased?"

"The whole wine harvest was lost, right across Galicia."

"And then didn't you have a grain harvest ruined with rain day after day?"

"That was in '52. We were on the verge of famine."

"And after that there was a cholera outbreak, and you wouldn't let anyone come over till it died down."

Mateo gulped back his tears and tried to smile. "Oh John, I was not ready for this. I was only fit for a fellowship in Classics at Cambridge."

"Which you declined for this." John's shoulders shook with laughter. "Come on, Matty, I want a room and a whole goat for my supper, and tomorrow you shall show me this barn and cottage and tell me all your plans."

Mateo went to bed that night with prayers of thankfulness, and slept till the sun was high and John was standing over him saying, "Where's this barn then? Do we ride or walk?"

They rode. From that moment, John took over the project. He suggested riding round all the cottages and chatting to the families, showing them that literacy could lift them out of poverty. The shrine of Saint James was attracting more pilgrims, which meant more hotels in Santiago. "Work for those who can read, write and add up," he told them through Mateo, who translated his English into the peasant language of Galego. "We will have your school set up in a week."

He cajoled a married couple in the de Villena household to move to the cottage, with the promise of higher pay. Miguel, who had worked in the castle gardens, could start a vegetable plot with the boys, and Sara, a good seamstress, could teach the girls sewing skills. Both could read and write. He told Mateo to pick a few children at a time for serious lessons. "And I must work on the language. Maria taught me a little Castilian, but I'll soon make headway now I'm living here."

John living here, thought Mateo. What a wonderful sound that has!

His presence was indeed a joy, and Mateo grew daily more in awe of his young cousin. He had a way with people of all ages that engaged them, even when he mangled their language. He soon won Eduardo round. "I'm here to get Mateo's project going with funds from England. Please just carry on stewarding."

Confidence sat easily on John, but he was ready to admit failure.

After two weeks intensively mastering Castilian he rode over to the Castillo de Mereno to ask the conde to send his own cottagers' children and contribute to the venture. Mateo sweated at his daring.

John spread out empty hands on his return. "The old man says you are mad. 'Educate the *camameiras*! We'll have a revolution like France.' I told him the people were crushed there. Kindness breeds respect, I said. 'False!' says he. 'Kindness is weakness. Away, English fool, and take such ideas with you.'"

"Oh John, I'm sorry."

"Never mind, Matt. I had a quick word with two friendly young ladies outside – his daughters, I suppose. *They* seemed interested."

Mateo felt the hot blood rush up his face.

John laughed. "Ah! You are courting one of them?"

"No, no, I see them at Mass on Sundays, that's all." He managed to add, "One is a daughter, the other a niece."

"Is she the one with a deformed shoulder?"

"Yes, she had a riding accident, I believe."

"Well, we should cultivate them. I'll go to Mass with you on Sunday."

"To see *them*?"

"No, truly, Matty, I like church on Sundays."

Mateo was ashamed that John had already made their acquaintance when he had mumbled no more than 'good morning' for years.

They didn't have to wait till Sunday. The young ladies came to see *them*. He and John were behind the barn with Miguel and the boys when they heard hooves, and hurried round to find the young ladies dismounting and the children clamouring to hold their horses.

Mateo was overwhelmed. He stood tongue-tied.

"We had to see what was going on here," the beautiful one declared. She had all the self-assurance that her looks gave her. She held out her hand.

"Julia de Mereno. I know you are Mateo de Villena and you Señor Heron."

"John. Plain John." He showed his filthy hands and bowed without touching her. How could he be so easy? Mateo marvelled.

The other girl gave a little bob and murmured, "Emilia Garcia. Oh sirs, I hope you don't mind this intrusion." She lifted her eyes to John. "I am sorry my uncle was so abrupt with you."

That smile lit her face. Mateo saw that her features were not unlike her cousin's, but her upper lip was longer and her nose slightly upturned, so she missed the classic profile of Julia, but she emanated a genuine concern and kindliness. As she faced them, the deformity of her shoulder was not pronounced.

John said, "Come and see. The lads are learning horticulture and the girls are inside with their teacher."

Sara, with the girls sitting round her on old pieces of carpet, was telling them her life story. Sewing materials were laid aside. She jumped up and curtsied, and the girls followed her example.

Emilia said in Galego, "We don't mean to interrupt. Pray carry on," while Julia looked round the barn walls and turned to John.

"You must brighten it up with pictures."

"We will when we get any suitable. Mateo only has portraits of long-gone de Villenas. Perhaps you have some jolly ones hidden away in cupboards."

She raised her black eyebrows. "And you'd relieve us of them?"

"Anything. If we can't use it we'll make it into something else."

"But, you see, my father doesn't approve of your school, and I doubt if he would give it so much as an ink pot."

"Surely he'd let you bring your own childhood books."

His boldness alarmed Mateo, yet he could see Julia found it amusing. Emilia gave Mateo a tentative smile.

"*I* can bring a few books tomorrow."

Mateo struggled for words to thank her. I am falling in love, he thought, already. She has a wonderful character ready to burst forth, given freedom from that uncle. But she is shy like me. Pray God she *does* come tomorrow.

John was telling Julia how they had visited every child's home to urge them to come.

Julia laughed. "My father would drop dead before he'd do such a thing. Come, Emmy, we'll leave them in peace."

John's verdict as they rode away was, "Julia, pretty but shallow. Emilia, plain but deep. I'll flirt with Julia and you can have Emilia."

Mateo shook his head at 'plain' but said nothing.

When they got back, they found letters from home, with another banker's draft from his father and a letter from his mother.

Your sisters and I are making clothes for your camameiras *now that the Hurst Street School has enough.*

'You should have a wife to help you with this work but do not follow a fleeting passion. Have total trust together as your father and I have found at last. I long to guide your choice but I still have flutters of dread about Spain. This lovely family has been so kind that I have scarce done penance but the

Lord is merciful. Keep to Him, my son. Neglect not Mass now John is there.

'We all hope to be with you next June for your birthday and John's. Lily can scarcely wait so long and Mother Dee tells dear Jack he will see you in your ancestral castle, which excites him. Your letters are a delight and I show them to Frank and Lily on their regular visits. She complains of the brevity of John's.

Mateo shared this with John, who laughed.

"Ma has written a whole page about a robbery up their street and ends with a warning for me to take care in *'that lawless country'*."

Mateo smiled, but his thoughts were of his mother's words. He must learn to *know* Emilia.

To his delight, the young ladies came next day with saddlebags of books. Julia and John resumed their teasing banter while unpacking them. Mateo indicated by smile and gesture that Emilia could see how the vegetable patch was progressing. They watched the boys digging, and then Miguel approached with a wheelbarrow of manure.

Emilia put her hand over her nose.

"Oh, I'm sorry." Mateo was ashamed and took her arm to lead her back.

"I'm sure it will grow excellent vegetables." She was smiling that paradise smile like Grandmamma's.

He realised he was still holding her arm, and relinquished it at once. She turned as they walked back, and tucked her arm in his.

Looking into his face she said, "It helps where the ground is rough. There are bricks scattered – from the internal wall you built?"

Her closeness was overpowering him, but he managed to answer, "John is going to make a path here. He works with the boys and they love it."

"Can I see their schoolroom?"

He took her inside. Julia and John were at the girls' side by the bookshelves.

Julia glanced at them and called out, "We mustn't be long, Emmy. Mamma has arranged a final fitting for my new dress at noon."

Emilia smiled at Mateo. "There is to be a ball for her birthday." She sat on one of the benches and looked at the desk for the teacher. "Will that be you?"

"I think I can manage a few at a time, but I've never done such a thing before."

Her interest had raised his confidence. He pointed to a big slate against the wall. "I found that in a store cupboard with a box of chalks. I can write letters for them to copy."

She gazed at him then and lifted her brows. "What you are doing is noble."

Julia popped her head round the partition. "Time to go." With a regretful smile Emilia joined her and they rode away. 'Noble'! Mateo burned with hope.

At the end of Mass the following Sunday, a footman handed to Mateo and John invitations to a ball at the Castillo de Mereno in two weeks' time.

The condesa approached Mateo and spoke behind her fan. "The conde is not so pleased, but it is our daughter's birthday and he has allowed her some choice of guests. I am afraid the de Villena name was tarnished by the dreadful crime of Don Juan, so the invitation is made out to you with your father's name, Lord Barton, and to your cousin, Señor Heron."

Mateo, utterly flummoxed, mumbled that his father was not an English lord, but John broke in to say, "Madame, we will be honoured to accept your kind invitation."

"Then pray reply formally and leave early and my husband will not be upset." With a flourish of her fan, she mounted into their carriage.

Julia laughed as she followed. "You'll find our balls are tedious things."

John winked at Mateo as they drove away. "Maybe, but a chance for you with Emilia."

John, Mateo thought, has read my heart.

Julia was right. The conde's baleful eye subdued everyone, and even the dancing lacked exuberance.

Julia, in a low dress of ivory white, striking against her jet-black hair and high colour, cornered Mateo in the chattering time before the supper when her parents were passing among the guests, dampening rather than promoting conversation.

"A few swift words, *Lord* Barton." She giggled, but her bosom was heaving with haste and excitement. Mateo hardly knew how to look at her.

She began, "I must be quick. I've done my greeting duties and my parents are not looking this way. The fact is, I have seen what goes on between you and Emilia—"

Mateo couldn't help exclaiming, "Goes on! I assure you—"

"Don't," she said. "It's plain to see, and believe me, I heartily approve.

But listen, let no fears of my father hold you back. She is yours for the asking, and he will be glad for anyone to take her off his hands."

Mateo opened his mouth to protest at such an expression, but she silenced him with a raised finger. "Just listen. Her mother was my father's youngest sister and she fell in love with Frederico Garcia, a spice merchant. Of course, a noble lady could not marry a man in trade, but she did. She was of age and they eloped. The family disowned her, but cutting her off without a penny had no effect, for Señor Garcia was a rich man. Sadly, he caught cholera from some shipment that came into port, and passed it to his wife. My parents took in Emilia, their three-year-old orphan. My father said, 'We cannot allow the Garcia grandparents to have her.'" Julia imitated his tone of voice and giggled again. Then she rushed on, "She was to be my companion. I have only brothers. She was so sweet. I ordered her about all our childhood, but she has forgiven me that. She understands now I was jealous of her."

"*You* jealous of *her*?"

"Yes, O foolish man. She is cleverer than I. She studied, she read, she taught herself English. My father thought it excessive for a woman, and after she had her fall and didn't please his fastidious eye, he tired of her about the place. He began to grumble about having to support her, though she is a wealthy woman."

"*She* is!"

"Are your eyes gleaming? No, you are not that sort. Yes, she comes with money neither she nor anyone can touch till she is married. At her birth, her father put a large part of the fortune he had then in a trust for her dowry. So my family has fed and clothed her, and are beginning to resent it. Mamma has tried to arrange a marriage, but none of our acquaintances of the nobility will look at a daughter of trade. So the field is clear, Mateo de Villena Barton. That's what I wanted you to know. Now I must circulate the room, as the ball is in my honour. You and John could slip away after the supper – such as it is. But act fast with Emilia. You are just what she needs, and she deserves to be happy."

She darted away, a flitting white fairy among the flowery dresses of the ladies and flamboyant waistcoats of the men. Mateo was left dumbfounded, his brain absorbing everything his ears had greedily seized upon, and his heart throbbing with excitement. Marriage, which had never seemed more than a golden glow on the horizon, had leapt into the present. But, recalling his mother's letter, he warned himself, I hardly know her. No, that's wrong. I know much more of her than she does of me. What can *I* offer *her*?

John appeared, edging his way towards him through the crowd.

"There you are, lurking in a corner as usual. Emilia asked me where you were. She's in pale blue with cunning flounces round her shoulders so that you wouldn't know there's anything wrong with her."

"There *is* nothing wrong with her, John. I am going to marry her."

John's eyebrows shot up. "What, man? That's quick work. She didn't know that three minutes ago."

"Hush. I haven't asked her yet. But I've made up my mind."

John exaggeratedly wiped his brow. "That's still quick work for our Matty!" Then he looked solemn. "But hey, you'll have to see her uncle and set out your prospects and ask permission to court her and all that."

Mateo nodded several times. He had already glimpsed the hurdles to cross before he could stand in the cathedral with her, but for once in his life he, on his own, was going to make something happen.

John must have seen the determination in his eye and the set of his jaw. He slapped him on the back. "Well done, Matt. Go after her and get her. See, there she is, talking with that old lady in the far window."

Mateo looked, and felt the scene perfectly revealed Emilia's character. She was smiling and nodding as the old lady's lips moved fast. Of course she would sit by someone that others would avoid. He could not break in upon them, but he tore a page from his pocketbook and wrote, '*I will call upon your uncle tomorrow and request his permission to pay court to you. M.*' He folded it up and, going over to the window, made as if to pass by, but held out the note to her at the last minute. She glanced up, surprised, and took it, her eyes inviting him to join them.

He heard the old lady say, "Your beau, Emmy? Very handsome. As I was saying, my husband in his last illness..."

The first step was taken. He walked on, quivering with excitement. 'Very handsome', indeed! That was a surprise. A long, gilded mirror between the two windows showed a tall, slender, black-suited man with dark hair waved above his forehead and expressive deep brown eyes. The man had a new identity, shoulders back, sure of himself.

Nevertheless, the old nervousness was uppermost when he sent in his card to the conde next day and was ushered into his smoking room, where the stout gentleman did not rise to greet him but looked up with a deeply creased frown and bloodshot eyes. Unhappy timing, Mateo thought. He was drinking late. But with a straight back and head up he explained his business.

"I request permission, sir, to pay court to your niece, Emilia Garcia."

The conde's thick eyebrows made one line across his face, but he didn't look displeased. "That's a new way of coming for money for your crack-brained ideas."

"Coming for money!" Mateo's shock must have been obvious, as the conde made a placatory gesture with his hands.

"Maybe you are unaware. She has a handsome dowry – some compensation for her deformity."

"Deformity! I see nothing, sir, beyond her beautiful nature and wonderful smile. My acquaintance is small, I know, but I wish her to be my wife." Mateo kept his legs braced, arms by his side, eyes fixed on the conde's face.

"What can you offer her?"

"Myself, my home, my estate – which is beginning to prosper, since my vines are producing well and I am improving soil conditions for my crops."

The count waved this aside. "Money in the bank?"

"Not much."

The count actually laughed. "As it happens, 'tis no matter." Then he frowned again. "But I am not aware of your meeting my niece except at Mass and last night's ball. On your occasional visits here, I made sure you were in and out double quick. So what do you know of her feelings?"

"Very little, sir." If the conde didn't know where the girls' morning rides had taken them, he had better not reveal it. "This is why I come for permission to pay court to her."

"Well, man, you'd better get on with it." He rang the bell that stood on his desk. A footman appeared. "Ask Señorita Garcia to come."

"Oh sir…" Mateo had not expected this.

"No time like the present."

She was speedily there in the room in a morning dress of forest green buttoned to the neck. She flushed to her neat hairline on seeing Mateo.

"Well, girl, what do you say? This young man has come a-wooing. Does that please you?"

She drew a sharp breath. A wide-eyed, split-second glance was all she gave Mateo, but he tried to convey regret for her embarrassment in a hopeful but sympathetic smile.

Much to his admiration she recovered her composure, faced her uncle and spoke out clearly in a bell-like tone he hadn't heard before.

"Honoured uncle, what little I know of this gentleman has pleased me, but I would like to walk with him about the garden and learn his mind from his own lips."

The count gave a little grunt and waved them away. "Off you go, then, and don't come back till you've settled the matter."

Mateo, in a daze at the speed of events, followed her as she walked fast to a side door which led through an orangery to a walled garden with an arbour that reminded him of his mother's 'bower' at Sheradon Grange. *She* would be pleased with a Spanish Catholic daughter-in-law, but would his father? Grandmamma, of course, would immediately picture Matty and Emmy starting a family and providing her with great-grandchildren.

Emilia was gently nudging his arm. "Will you sit here or walk, sir?"

She was more poised now, not the shy flower like Aunt Lily that she had seemed at their first meeting.

"What *you* will," he said.

"We will walk, then," and she headed for a gate in the wall.

Seeing lawns and flowerbeds he said, unsure how to begin, "You have a gardener who can create something lovely."

She gave him a quick smile. "We have a man who can follow orders. I tell him what to do."

"Then you shall create a garden for *my* home," he said, not thinking of the implication of his words.

She compressed her lips. "Are you not running ahead of yourself, sir? All you know of me is that I was interested in your school. Uncle asks me if I wish you to woo me when all I know of you is that your land adjoins ours and you care more for your cottagers than my uncle does for his. Of your family – I remember you with your mother and sisters at Mass in the cathedral when I was still a child, but you went away. They stayed, but later went to Madrid. I did hear of a murder and, years later, of a de Villena cousin who had employed some killers to do it and was executed. Julia thought it very exciting, since we had met him when he lived at your place, but I wanted no details. I never met your English father, who I understand is a titled gentleman, though perhaps not a lord." She flashed another smile. "I now know your lively cousin John, but no one else in your English family."

She stopped speaking and looked at him with the full radiant smile he already loved. "Is that enough to help me to the most important decision of my life?"

Ruefully, he shook his head. "I meant to start gently with your uncle's permission. A request to go riding with you, our cousins being our chaperones. But, indeed, I know not how two young men can properly become friends with two young ladies without families arranging it for them."

"I trust John is not hoping to woo Julia. She would never…" She checked herself. Suddenly she looked shy and uncomfortable.

"Marry anyone untitled," he finished for her. "I am sure John has no such thought. They are both outspoken and already have a jolly sort of friendship. I – and I believe you – would move more slowly."

She arched her eyebrows. "You acted on a very brief acquaintance."

He felt a hot blush rising. "We have been neighbours a long time and I…" He wanted to say 'have yearned to know you better', but that would expose his pathetic diffidence. "I love your interest in my poor little school."

"I felt an interest…" She looked down at the grass beneath their feet. He hoped she was going to say 'long before that'. But she just added, "Let us walk back to the seats and start to know each other."

Sitting on the sun-warmed cushions in the arbour, they were physically close, yet she was still virtually a stranger. But she began to speak low and swiftly about herself: the loss of her parents, which she remembered in tiny, vivid scenes, her father on a bed seen through an open door, her nurse lifting her from her mother's feeble arms, a carriage ride, strange rooms and faces, and finally a big girl with jet-black curls holding out her arms to her and saying 'I am Julia'. "She was five. I was three. Now she is twenty-three. So my life has been here. Some travelling, which my aunt wished, my uncle not. But I have never been to England. I have read English history and literature, including all your Jane Austen, so I know what is proper in England." She laughed. "There is a start."

Mateo hesitated. She had not said she was a tradesman's daughter. Living so long in the house of a Spanish nobleman, she would be shocked if he said his father had once hacked coal. But his mother's letter had spoken of trust from the outset.

"I will tell you everything," he said, "even if my hopes lie in ruins."

"Please," was all she said.

When it was done, he thought what a tale it was – of profligacy, seduction, deception, jealousy, attempted murder, revelation, repentance, recklessness, bravery, passion, betrayal, a bungled murder, confession, redemption, and through it all love, struggling but always triumphing.

She sat very still for some minutes. Then she murmured, "It cost you much to tell all that." After another silence, "I would love to meet your grandmother."

Mateo bit his lip. A lump was rising in his throat. "You shall, next June. I trust they will all come. I miss them so much. We had a tradition that John and I celebrated our birthdays together with all the family. It could be here. He will be twenty and I twenty-eight."

She looked surprised. "I thought you were younger. You wear no whiskers like our men."

"I will grow some wherever you like."

She gave a spontaneous laugh, lifting her shoulders. Then she burst out, "You would take me despite my deformity?"

"Oh, that is nothing. You are loveliness itself. But tell me, would *you* take *me* after that family story?"

She sat with hands folded in her lap while he waited on tenterhooks. Then she said, "I heard nothing to your discredit. That you are a master of Classics from Cambridge tells me we both love study. That you want to be a good landowner tells me we share a sense of duty. That you have a heart of love for your family warms mine. I lost parental love, which I know I had as a tiny child and have yearned for ever since. Julia is fond of me, but…"

She broke off because a footman creaked the garden gate and put his head round. "Ah, señorita, you are here! I looked before but no. The conde wishes to know if you are ready to return to him. I beg your pardon, but he grows impatient."

She rose at once and Mateo looked up at her in wonder. He had to stand too.

She waved the footman to go ahead. "Pray tell the conde we are coming."

Their eyes met. Hers were brimming with tears, and her hand trembled as he took her arm. He felt the lump rising again in his throat. She is going to refuse me. My connections are just too lowly and my story too tempestuous. She knows her duty to her ancestors.

They walked back to the conde's smoking room, which was now a positive fug of smoke. He had a glass of wine at his side and a half-empty bottle beside it.

"Well?" was all he said.

Mateo coughed, and she answered while he was still unable to speak. "With your permission, uncle, I will accept this gentleman."

Mateo gasped and couldn't control the cough that followed.

"And a wedding date? I must have a date."

She turned towards Mateo with her loveliest smile. "We were speaking of next June, were we not?"

Oh true, he thought, she is so clever. They will all be here. I can't believe this. He nodded, not daring to breathe.

"Very well. I will alert the condesa, who will need every moment to decide what she and Julia will wear. Off you go."

Mateo grabbed her hand and stumbled out with her into the clearer passage. Somehow they found their way outside through the main front door. There he took deep breaths of the fresh air and looked at her. Tears were wetting her cheeks.

"Oh, dear lady," he cried, not knowing what to call this being at his side, "you have been bounced into this and it goes not with your will. I am desolate, I…"

She faced him on the wide steps and took hold of both his hands.

"Mateo Barton, these are happy tears." Her bosom heaved and she began to sob with passion. She gasped out, "I never believed anyone would want me. I would live out my life here – oh, I must tell you – I have loved the sight of you ever since you came back. It was a secret joy if I had a glimpse of you, but to have you – as my own – for life – I dare scarce believe it."

Now he had his arms about her. *She* had yearned for *him*! That was indeed a miracle. His own tears of wonder that this could be happening to him soaked the shoulder of her dress. He laid his head against it and felt the protruding bone. She was special. She was his.

A voice called, "I salute the happy pair."

Julia, on horseback, came trotting round from the stables. She flung herself to the ground, ignoring the arm of the groom who followed her.

"I have been looking for you. Papa says it is all settled, and I claim the first kisses from you both."

Somehow – Mateo didn't know how, except they were holding hands – they removed themselves from the top to the bottom step and were embraced by Julia.

It was all more unreal than a play and yet the most intensely real thing that had overtaken both of them with the speed of light. Now, Mateo thought, I am free to have time with someone I may call Emilia to her face, who is to be the most important person in my life; and the other important people know nothing of her yet.

It felt as if he had just run a fast sprint in a few seconds and could scarcely breathe.

"We must tell John," he said aloud.

Chapter 28

Castilla de Villena, June 1856
(9 months later)

John

It was a week after the wedding, and carriages were waiting to take the English family to the port of Bilbao to embark for home. The newly-weds were to go too, so it was John in his working clothes, sleeves rolled up, bronzed arms embracing them in turn, who was to oversee the school for the next six months till their return.

He was beginning to regret his offer as his mother clasped him, sobbing. "When you come back, you are never to leave us again. I can't bear it."

His father said, "Now, Lily, our boy is a man. He will do great things, but we will always be there for him." He clutched him briefly and released him.

Grandmother Jenny said, "Don't spoil goodbyes with tears, our Lily. Johnny lad, your Granda Tom would have enjoyed these few weeks but he'd likely have disgraced hisself at the wedding, so it's well he popped off when he did."

Uncle Ralph took John aside. "You may feel your tasks here are finished when Matty and Emilia come back." John nodded. "But there may be a greater work for you after this. A charitable trust back home is organising a mission to set up a school in the poorest part of Caracas, the capital of Venezuela. I have a mind to put your name forward since you are a Spanish speaker and experienced in such work. Think about it." He clapped him on the shoulder.

John, struggling to remember where Venezuela was, smiled at his uncle. "I will think of it, sir, and thank you for your confidence in me."

Aunt Sophia, who looked delighted to be returning to the safety of England, joined them. She had spent most of the time in the Castillo de Mereno hiding behind her fan in fear of questions.

"It is a *Catholic* charity, John. Our priest was in Caracas as a young student helping after the terrible earthquake of 1811. Mateo tells me you have attended the cathedral here. You should be admitted, you know."

He wasn't sure that he wanted to be admitted to anything, nor was he ready yet for an adventure to Venezuela, wherever that was. He had only begun to enjoy the family and they were off again.

Lucia looked unusually chirpy as she jumped into the carriage. "Bye, John."

He looked at Maria for an explanation and was astonished to find her with trembling lip.

"Hey," he teased, "Baby Bears don't cry. You're always the happy twin."

"Lu hopes to have a betrothal to announce when we get back. An iron and steel heir at church has noticed her."

"But that's trade."

"Mother has accepted the trade in Emilia's family. She's changed so much with Grandmamma's help."

"Why didn't the fellow at church notice *you?*"

She gave a gulp and turned it into a laugh. "He did, but I squashed him flat. He is right for Lucia. When she finds how supine he is she will enjoy ruling their household. I'm glad for her, and she's delighted to have a lover before me."

"Don't you want one?"

She looked him in the eye. "Yes, but I am very particular."

When he gave her a farewell peck on the cheek, a tear fell on his bare arm.

"I wish I had a portrait of you in your bridesmaid dress," he said to cheer her.

She smiled. "You were a fine bridesman to my brother."

Grandmamma Dee came up and echoed that. "I was so proud of both my handsome grandsons. This visit has been an experience, but your grandfather is eager to be home, and I have to admit that the hours smiling and nodding to the count and countess were a little tiresome."

John laughed and hugged her.

Mateo came next to embrace and thank him, his eyes filling up as usual.

Emilia followed, and it struck John how at ease she was after nine months as Matty's betrothed and a mere three weeks with the whole family, the last week as a bride. There was a quiet radiance about her that showed she had fallen into a place where she could flourish. He clasped her hand and gave a little bow. "Safe journey."

Her face transformed into its lovely smile. "Oh John, God bless you," and she leaned forward and kissed him on the cheek.

They were all aboard when Eduardo appeared to wave them off too. It was a kindly gesture, John thought, to show the family that he was not alone and to quell the sorrow that threatened to overwhelm him.

He turned and slapped him on the back. "Right, man, to work. The day is half-gone already."

True to her Baby Bear tradition, Maria wrote soon after they reached Sheradon Grange.

> *Emilia delights in our loving family. Father, who was shocked at their swift engagement, has taken her to his heart and now he knows Matty has shared with her the full story of his life there's not a shadow between any of them. Mamma wants to act the gracious dowager but Emmy's fluency in English and her wide reading dismay her a little.*
>
> *We hope you are not too lonely. Write back and let me picture your life day to day. Does Julia, my gorgeous fellow bridesmaid, ride over to see you?'*

John wrote back, *'Julia came once but was quickly bored with the children. She is a feast to the eyes but no more.'*

Secretly he longed for a soul to commune with and – he had to admit it – a body to enjoy.

He was to return to England at Christmas, and they would all celebrate it together before Mateo and Emilia went back to start their new life as Conde and Condesa de Villena. Eduardo would be in charge meanwhile.

The six months were soon consumed with improvements to the de Villena School, most of which John did himself with his bare hands to conserve the sum Emilia had left with him. It was a few days before Christmas when he said goodbye to Eduardo, who had become a stalwart friend, and took ship for England.

Homecoming was a joy as he and his parents stayed in their old rooms at Sheradon Grange for the festivities. The subject of Venezuela was not mentioned, and he was so exulting in everyone's company that he asked no questions about it.

When they were all at breakfast on the morning he and his parents were to go home to Newcastle, Maria told him that the Hurst Street School was flourishing under a new headmaster and his wife. "I'm not needed there, and nor will you be."

His mother said, "I'm just longing to have you at home after all this time. Your father has so much work since Mr Trace is ageing that I never see him."

And what will I *do*? John thought, suddenly dismayed.

He turned to Uncle Ralph. "Is the Venezuelan thing to go ahead at Easter?"

It was Aunt Sophia who answered. "Dear boy, a problem has arisen. The committee are providing boarding accommodation and need a matron, so they wish for a married couple in charge of the whole project."

John looked at his uncle. "But I was not to be in *charge*, was I?"

"I wanted to propose you. Mateo has told me of your drive and fearlessness."

John was embarrassed to hear his mother pipe up, "Oh yes, but not overseas any more. Frank, you said you wanted clerical help in the office."

His father laughed aloud. "An eagle in a chicken coop." He stood up. "The right work will come, my boy, but now we must catch that train. *I* have work to do."

They went back to the little house in Heaton, which felt like a chicken coop after the Castillo de Villena. But there *was* work to do. Next door's chimney had collapsed onto his father's shed in a gale. It took him two days to repair it.

On the third morning a letter came from Uncle Ralph. '*Father Andrews of the Venezuelan project has come up with a solution. I do not approve it but have agreed under strong pressure that you should be allowed to consider it. Can you come over here at your convenience, and the scheme will be put before you?*'

Much intrigued, John showed his mother the letter and said he was off to the station to catch a train to Ovingham.

She flung her arms tight round him. "You won't do it, John, whatever it is."

"I may not, but I'm extremely curious to know what *it* is."

"But it's bitter cold today."

"Then I'll run to the station." She had to let him go.

The first things he noticed when he arrived at Sheradon Grange were the half-suppressed excitement of Grandmamma Dee and the grim face of Uncle Ralph. Aunt Sophia, they said, was on her knees praying, though for what outcome they didn't say. The twins waved to him from the upper landing and then disappeared as he was hustled into the kitchen, where he met Father Andrews, whose forcefulness of character exploded out of a small, spare frame. His grip on John's hand was fierce.

Rosie set a mug of ale in front of him and then slipped out, leaving only Grandmamma and Uncle Ralph. Grandfather Jack was in the stables.

Father Andrews sat opposite John and leaned across the table, his wizened face only inches away. His dark eyes glowed.

"Young man," he said, "be not hasty in dismissing the notion. We have found you a wife."

"A wife!" Of many outlandish solutions John had imagined on the train, that had not occurred to him. He leaned away from the probing eyes and gave an uneasy laugh. "I am hardly ready for that, sir."

"She has *volunteered* herself," the priest said, ignoring his reaction. "She would be happy to do such work, and believes it is the call of God for her."

Oh dear, John thought, if God is named it becomes serious.

"She may like the *work*," he said, "but not me. She doesn't know me." He tossed off his mug and made to rise. He looked up at Uncle Ralph, regarding him with pursed lips. "I think you could have told the Father I wouldn't want that and saved me a journey."

"You'd better hear him out," was all his uncle said.

Grandmother, washing some smallclothes in the sink, had her back to them, but John could tell by her tense shoulders that she was listening closely.

Father Andrews went on. "You cannot put God out of the reckoning, John Heron. He has spoken to a faithful woman of courage and determination, a little older than you, perhaps, but that is good, for she will counsel you and, if necessary, curb your youthful exuberance."

A fearsome virago with grey locks, a huge bosom and jutting chin reared up in John's mind's eye. "Did you expect me to agree to this without having met the woman?"

"No, I insisted she be here. That was her wish too."

"Where is she then?"

Grandmother Dee looked round. "I said she could sit at my desk in my study and I warrant she is reading my novel to pass the time, for I left it open."

John had half-risen, but sat down again. Was he expected to go and face this being now and tell her God had made a mistake? He was bold enough in most encounters but this was far outside his experience.

Father Andrews gestured him to rise. "The moment is here. You must lay yourself open to God's plans for you. Be not hasty to reject Him."

This is worse, John thought. If I reject the woman, I am rejecting God? I'm getting angry now with this ridiculous idea. I should have taken Mother's advice and stayed at home. Well, if there's no escape I must get it over with quickly.

He scrambled out from behind the table and made for the door. Uncle Ralph followed, which gave him courage, knowing his disapproval of the plan.

It was barely a dozen paces along the passage to the little door on the right on which Grandmother had hung a cloth embroidered with the words: 'Writing. Do not disturb.' He pushed the door open and saw only an empty chair at the desk.

Hugely relieved, he turned back to Uncle Ralph. Then he heard a movement behind the door and peered round it and laughed. Maria was dusting a bookshelf.

"There's only Baby Bear here." He was just adding, "The woman must have taken fright," when in the same breath Uncle Ralph said, "That's your answer then, Maria, which is exactly what I said it would be."

Maria threw down the duster, pushed past them and headed for the stairs.

"No! What? I…" John's brain did a huge somersault. Maria! Could it be…? He shouted it aloud, rushed after her, grabbed her as she made a tiny pause on the bottom step. "Maria! It isn't *you*?"

"Of course it is, you goose." She sniffed. "Leave go. I wish I hadn't done that. It was madness. I couldn't sit still. I dreaded you coming. It was all wrong."

"It was your idea, pet." Grandmother had come along the passage. "I feared it might turn out ill."

"No," said Uncle Ralph, "it has given us the answer we wanted. John only thinks of Maria as a comical cousin – his Baby Bear, as she calls herself."

"Rubbish," said Grandmother. "Look at him. He's already staring at the idea in a new way. Did they not work together on Hurst's Street School?"

John, holding Maria's arm tightly, realised he was indeed staring at a new prospect. Venezuela with a beloved companion, a workmate whose courage and energy and sparkling nature he had always admired. Was it possible? The monstrous creature in his mind's eye transformed into his adorable Baby Bear?

She tried to pull away from him. "Forget it!"

"But I won't. It would be wonderful – beyond dreams – to have *you* there."

She tried again to wrench her arm away. He held on, turning his head from her to Grandmamma.

Grandmamma said, with emphasis. "I know how your yearning eyes rested on her in her bridesmaid's dress. You two are made for each other."

Uncle Ralph stamped his foot. "Mother, will you stop interfering. He is not to take my girl away from me. From the moment she broached the subject I knew it must not happen."

John now wound his arms round Maria, though she wriggled furiously. "Tell the priest, Grandmamma, we are going for a walk."

"It's January!" Grandmamma grabbed a fur-lined cloak with a hood from the hall peg and tried to envelop Maria in it.

"That's Mamma's," Maria protested, but at least she had stopped pulling away, and John, who had hung up his greatcoat when he came in, was able to tug it back on and grab his hat.

"What are you doing, child?" Uncle Ralph demanded. "You saw how it is with John?"

Maria looked up at him. "Yes, I did, Papa, and I owe him a heartfelt apology for putting him through all that. A walk in the crisp air will get us back onto our old friendly footing, and we can forget that it ever happened."

She linked arms with John and marched to the front door.

John's legs moved, but memories and images were crowding so fast into his mind that he felt breathless.

They were outside now, shocked by the biting air, but he voiced his first thought. "Maria, you said you were very particular about a lover."

"Don't talk." She squeezed his arm sharply. "I need my word in first. That charade in Grandmamma's room was the stupidest thing I have ever done. It was hurtful to you and hurtful to me and I don't want it mentioned ever again."

"No," he said. "That can't be. It's opened my eyes and I can't shut them now." Her body pressing against his was a distraction to his train of thoughts, but he ploughed on. "If you speak of stupidity, nothing beats mine for being blind so long. But I see now there was a change. For me it happened when I went to Spain and was torn at leaving you and the school we'd worked on so happily."

"As friends, of course."

"I didn't realise at the time but it was more. I often asked myself what the girl of my dreams would be like and I always said 'someone like Maria'."

"Yes, 'like', I knew that – but not actually *me*."

"Then I saw your tears when everyone was leaving after the wedding."

"Yes, *my* tears, not yours."

"I yearned for you to stay."

"'Yearned'. You got that word from Grandmamma just now. I looked nice in my pretty frock for a change."

She had unlinked arms and was striding beside him over the frosted grass. He had to break through this sarcasm and reach her real self.

"Maria, honestly, there *was* a difference in my feelings even as long ago as schooldays. When you all turned up that Christmas I was excited to see *you*, not Lucia a bit. When we left to live in Newcastle I missed you so much. When you came to work on the school it brightened the days like the sun coming out. And just now, when that priest talked about some woman offering to be my wife, I pictured a monster – and then – what? My own darling Maria. Was that possible?"

She stopped and faced him. "Don't go on, John. You have never seen me as a wife. Oh, once when you were nine you told your Grandmother Batey you wanted to marry me when you grew up."

"There you are, then!"

"You were *nine*. No such thought as an adult. My silly plan proved that. I got the rejection I deserved."

"But the priest said God spoke to a woman and called her to Venezuela. Did he make that up?"

She turned and walked on quickly. He had to run after her. She paused and looked at him, her eyes solemn. "I *do* pray, John. I have always longed for a work that would make a difference in the world, you know that, and we had it with the Street School. But that seemed like a preparation for something bigger. Then you went off to help Matty. I knew he needed you, but I missed you horribly. When we heard about the Venezuelan project I did wonder if a way would come for me to be part of it. I thought God had opened a door when they said they wanted a married couple." Her lips trembled. Tears shone in her eyes and she turned away again. He pulled her round and embraced her.

"Oh Maria, to have you for the rest of my life would be the most wonderful thing that could happen to me, here or in Venezuela or on the far side of the moon."

"No," she said, "now you're sorry for me." Her breast heaved.

"Maria, have we ever lied to each other? I admit these feelings that I want you as a wife are new—"

"Five minutes old."

And then suddenly she was laughing and crying at once. Laughter was what he had always loved about her. What a life they would have!

He said it aloud. "What a life we can have together! Darling, darling Maria."

She gulped, and then sniffed like a little child. "Do you *really* think so, John? So speedily? You always plunge into things. You'll plunge out of it as quickly."

"Never. I'm in now. The thought of anything but a life with you appals me."

"Yet you would have gone to Venezuela without me till this marriage requirement came up."

"I was not committed to it. My first thought was that it would be hellishly lonely, but then I imagined I'd be a humble part of quite a big expedition. It was a surprise to find I might be in charge. But oh, if anyone had said *you* could come!"

"This wind is deadly. We ought to go in, but I need to believe what you are saying. You never had the feelings for me that I had for you."

He dared to ask, "But when did *your* feelings begin?"

"When I was six and you were four and I heard you had set off for Spain to bring Matty back to our pining father. I thought, This boy is special. I have known it ever since and watched you grow into a fine, beautiful, wonderful man."

"No, no. No, I've behaved abominably. How could I have been so dumb? I wouldn't have hurt you for the world. I always loved you – but now I need you so desperately." He held out his arms.

She flung back her head and her eyes gleamed. "Dare I believe you? Oh John, I *have* to believe you." She came a step closer.

The furry hood of her cloak had fallen back off her face. There she was – the familiar, rosy-cheeked, dimpled Maria, but transformed, shining with joy. He *had* loved her, of course, but now how very easy it was to be *in love* with her. Stirred up, he swallowed hard. He wanted her, all of her, now. He drew her to him, clasped her face and kissed her on the lips.

She allowed it briefly. Then the roguish look came into her eyes. "Haven't you forgotten something?"

"Oh God! Asking your father for your hand!"

"There is that – but how about asking *me*? I might like to remember the words of your proposal in future years."

"Of course! And I your acceptance."

"Don't anticipate. Down you go on one knee."

"Hey, the grass is white. That's not just frost."

"No, it's snowing, hadn't you noticed? Thin stuff, but it's getting thicker." She drew the hood over her head and clutched the cloak tight with her hands inside.

He knelt on one knee and swept off his hat. "Maria, will you be my wife? No, that's a bit short. Maria Barton de Villena, will you do me the honour of becoming my wife?"

"Yes, John, I will. Now get up and we'll run."

For all at once the snow was thick about them. Stiff frozen trees and crisp grass accepted it with delight, and the world was one whiteness before they reached the shelter of Sheradon Grange. All the faces were at the drawing room windows, John saw, including Mateo and Emilia – they had kept out of the little drama before – and Aunt Sophia – he wondered if her prayers had helped – and the old priest, clapping his hands at the sight of them laughing and braving the snow.

The door was opened for them and they shook off the snow into the flagged porch. Their radiant faces told their news.

"Eh, that snow came on sudden," Grandfather Jack said.

Grandmamma Dee chuckled. "Like another wedding in the family."

"No!" It was Uncle Ralph's voice, like a cry of pain.

Maria flew into his arms. "It must be, Papa. I could never have married anyone but John, and I'd have been a dreadful old maid to sour your later years."

"You could never be a dreadful anything." His shoulders shook.

John pictured his gaunt grey face after the abduction of Mateo and was stabbed with guilt, but Aunt Sophia swept to her husband's side with a swirl of her velvet skirt. John was thrilled to see him look at her not with irritation but relief, as if to say, I still have this lovely woman to comfort me. Here was a marriage with love restored. Maria and I could never lose ours, he swore. This was heaven.

"Darling Ralph, we are losing all our children within a year, but we have each other. They will come back and bring us babies. See how your mother and Jack have been enriched in their old age. I have been praying for happiness, nothing more."

Father Andrews held up clasped hands. "And where there is love and where there is duty done, there will be happiness."

Lucia, whom nobody had noticed, emerged from the drawing room. "You mustn't get married before me, Maria. Henry wants an Easter wedding."

Father Andrews said, "The Venezuelan party will leave a week after Easter."

"Then a joint wedding!" Grandmamma Dee cried.

"Angel," said Grandfather Jack, "who is getting married?"

John wasn't sure that he wanted to share his great day with Lucia and some unknown Henry, but all he was thinking of now was telling his father and mother. He must take Maria to Newcastle today and introduce her as his bride. They already loved her. Perhaps in the summer they could have a trip to Venezuela and his father could advise the country about the need for railways – if there were none yet. His ignorance of the place came over him like a great wave. In the next few months he must study every scrap of information Father Andrews could give him.

Somehow they had all found their way back into the drawing room. Mateo clapped him on the shoulder.

"You were a brother to me in Spain. Now it will be in law."

Emilia kissed him, and her eyes twinkled. "Your betrothal happened even more swiftly than ours. I will write to Eduardo that he must care for castle and school together till after Easter now. Dear Grandmother Dee, can you put up with us for so long?"

Grandmother patted her arm wordlessly and their smiles matched each other's. Then she announced that a great big pan of beef and vegetables was slowly stewing on the kitchen fire, and was anyone hungry yet?

"But I want to catch the next train," John said, "and invite Maria home to Newcastle for a few days."

"Really?" said Grandmamma, nodding her head to the window. It was darkened, as if a grey blanket hung against it. "Will there be a next train? I warrant you'll be staying here for a few days. Come, there is enough for us all. Into the kitchen, everyone, and get round the table. Jack, when I take the pan off you must get a great blaze going."

They were all jostling along the passage when she stopped abruptly by her writing room door.

Her face lit up. "Why, it's just come to me! This is how I can close my novel. With a double wedding! I was seeking a happy ending and now I have it. God be praised!"